WARRIOR: COUPÉ

Other BattleTech Novels:

The Warrior Trilogy
  by Michael A. Stackpole
    Warrior: En Garde
    Warrior: Riposte
    Warrior: Coupe

The Gray Death Legion Saga
  by William H. Keith, Jr.
    Decision at Thunder Rift
    Mercenary's Star
    The Price of Glory

Wolves on the Border
  by Robert Charrette

The Sword and the Dagger
  by Ardath Mayhar

About The Author

ComStar ROM Division Alert
ROM Headquarters
Langley, North America, Terra
2 August 3030
Subject: Michael A. Stackpole
Observation:

Subject still believes he was born 27 November 1957 and was raised in Vermont. He claims to have a history degree from the University of Vermont and that he moved to Phoenix, Arizona after his graduation in 1979. He has amassed a list of 20th-century game companies for whom he claims to have done work. They include: Flying Buffalo, Inc., FASA, TSR Inc., Mayfair Games, Hero Games, West End Games, Interplay Productions, and Electronic Arts. Though he is unable to explain his longevity, interviews with the subject's keepers suggest it is because only the good die young.

Situation:

Subject was previously incarcerated in the Reeducation Compound in Phoenix, but managed to elude keepers when he talked them into taking him out for Liao food. He tricked his handlers into stuffing themselves, then simply out-distanced them in a subsequent footrace. A check of his known associates—the Phoenix Skeptics and the Blue Thunder soccer team—has failed to produce him.

Despite efforts to shut down all traffic into and out of the Phoenix spaceport, the possibility of his having left the world cannot be discounted. A *Leopard* Class DropShip identified as the *Manannan MacLir* left Phoenix that night without authorization and linked up with a JumpShip at a pirate point just the other side of Saturn. It has not been located.

Recommendation:

The subject should be considered dangerous. He has written books before and has shown no remorse. ROM leadership has issued a "shoot on sight" order if the subject is located. If he is not destroyed, he probably will write again.

WARRIOR: COUPE

by

Michael A. Stackpole

This book is dedicated to those who have, in one way or another, aided and abetted me through the years. More specifically, these people have provided me with the means, motive and opportunity to do this book and series.

They are:

Means: Michael C. Pearo, Thomas Spinner, James Pacy, Susan Jackson, Marshall True, and Michael Stanton.

Motive: Hugh B. Cave, Liz Danforth, Gladys MacIntyre, John Ruhlman, and Thomas Helmer.

Opportunity: L. Ross Babcock III, Jordan Weisman, Donna Ippolito, and Rick Loomis.

They should all be considered unindicted co-conspirators in this work, and for their help I am very grateful.

The author would like to thank Liz Danforth for her insightful commentary on the rough draft and Ross Babcock and Donna Ippolito for editing me into literacy. The restaurant in Chapter 44 actually does exist—in Phoenix, not on Sian, however—and the dishes mentioned are two-thirds of a perfect meal. (The perfect meal adds Hot and Sour Spicy Soup, Moo Shu Pork with plum sauce, and House Special Chicken.) An evening spent there can make even a writer less anxious about being past his deadline...

Cover Art: David English
Cover Design: Jeff Laubenstein and Jim Nelson

Prologue

ComStar First Circuit Compound
Hilton Head Island, North America, Terra
27 February 3029

"You are all fools, blind fools!" Myndo Waterly exploded. "Hanse Davion will drown you in your own juice while you sit here and stew. I demand action! I demand an Interdiction now!"

Her outburst burned away the silent tension suffocating the oak-walled First Circuit chamber, but it did not crack Primus Julian Tiepolo's composure. "Precentor Dieron," he said calmly. "You will refrain from such childish displays of emotion. You owe your fellow Precentors an apology, for they are neither blind nor foolish. What we decide here will be based on intelligent, open discussion, and not be a knee-jerk response to someone shouting that the sky is falling."

Myndo stared back at her vulture-faced superior. *You are tired, old man, and you're dragging ComStar into the grave along with you. I will not allow this to happen.* She broke off her stare, then bowed her head in supplication. "I do apologize, but you cannot expect me to be

v

dispassionate when I see Jerome Blake's life-dream withering."

She looked around the chamber, taking in each of the red-robed Precentors. "Like you, I have labored long and hard to see our mission is fulfilled. ComStar is the salvation of mankind and the Word of Blake is a guide to that salvation. Hanse Davion's war against the Capellan Confederation unravels our work, yet you will do nothing to stop it. How can that be justified?"

Ulthan Everson, the large, blond man standing across from Myndo in the dimly lit chamber, accepted the challenge in her question. "Your vision of the future is not one we share, Precentor Dieron. You have cried wolf so often that we are no longer panicked by your words. You point at shadows as though they had substance. Hanse Davion's war does not contradict Blake's Word. It *fulfills* it."

Myndo shook her golden hair back from the shoulders of her red silk robe. "Blake said wars would fragment the Successor States. Then, and only then, would ComStar rise up to lead mankind to its true pinnacle. Hanse Davion's war has swallowed half the Capellan Confederation. It does not divide. It unites!"

"Pavel Ridzik has created his own nation from the Tikonov Commonality," rebutted a slight, black-haired man. "Fragmentation, not fusion, Myndo."

"Ha!" Myndo fixed him with a harsh stare. "You refer to that puppet state as a fragment? Please, Precentor Sian, do not waste my time. Hanse Davion allows Ridzik to appear to be independent, but we know the Prince has dispatched his trusted friend, Ardan Sortek, to be Ridzik's watchdog."

Myndo smiled cruelly. "You would be right to cite Maximilian Liao as working toward fragmentation, but all he's doing is carving his own realm into bite-sized chunks so that Hanse Davion can gorge himself."

Huthrin Vandel laughed. "Perhaps he hopes the Prince will choke to death."

The Primus shook his head in silent rebuke. "Myndo is correct. Liao's efforts have been ineffective at stemming the Davion tide. Let us not forget that Hanse Davion has justly earned the nickname of the Fox. None of us anticipated his purchasing the loyalty of Liao's Northwind Highlanders with the world of Northwind. The Highlanders returned to their ancestral home and disrupted the Kurita assault on the Terran Corridor. It was a well-planned move on the Prince's part."

The Primus's intervention on her behalf rattled Myndo slightly. *Is it possible that he has begun to see the threat, or is he merely reining in his underlings?* She studied Tiepolo's face, but the man's dark eyes and blank expression gave her no clue to his thoughts.

Myndo looked away toward the other Precentors. "As I recall from our last debate on this subject, you, Precentor Sian, suggested that the Liao counterstrike in January would destroy Davion supply bases and blunt the advance on the Tikonov/Federated border. But Liao's strike played directly into a massive Davion ambush. Capellan offensive capabilities have been destroyed, and their defensive strength is anemic."

Precentor Sian shook his head. "May I point out, Precentor Dieron, that Hanse Davion's troops have not moved forward since the ambush. We project that their next assault wave will come in May, at the earliest. You will recall that not all the Liao attacks were repulsed. The Fourth Tau Ceti Rangers hit Axton and managed to escape after raiding. This attack behind the lines has certainly soured the taste of victory for the Prince."

Vandel ran his fingers back through his black hair. "As the Precentor on New Avalon, I can confirm that the Court is not pleased that this attack was not anticipated. The Fourth Tau Ceti Rangers managed to hurt an NAIS training cadre."

The Primus looked toward Precentor Sian. "Has your staff on the Liao capital yet figured out the significance of the message the Rangers sent out from Axton to Sian before they left? 'Go Fish' is a strange, though economical, communication to send during a military operation."

In spite of herself, Myndo smiled along with her colleagues.

Villius Tejh let the snickers die before he answered the Primus's question. "The message went to Justin Xiang. From what little we've been able to piece together, Xiang is hunting for a New Avalon Institute of Science facility that he believes could hold the key to a new generation of BattleMechs..."

Precentor New Avalon cut in. "That would probably be the Bethel lab complex. Very small, but staffed with some good people."

Myndo looked to the Primus. "Our ROM agents have not infiltrated it?"

The Primus did not reply. Instead, he nodded almost imperceptibly that Precentor Sian should continue.

"Xiang has organized a strike on Bethel using the Fourth Tau Ceti Rangers," Tejh said. "It is believed that their message from Axton indicates that they did not find the lab there. Xiang himself is supposed to lead the assault on Bethel."

Ulthan Everson glanced at Precentor New Avalon. "What sort of defense will Xiang's mission encounter?"

Vandel shrugged. "Davion is constantly moving troops around. If the attack goes off before the end of April, the Capellans will face a company of Davion Light Guards. If Xiang shows any of his usual inventiveness, his people will certainly win out."

Myndo shook her head. "I cannot believe I'm listening to this chatter about one tiny aspect of this war. The Lyran Commonwealth has reshaped its border with the Draconis Combine, and Wolf's Dragoons are singlehandedly holding the Draconians out of the Federated Suns. House Marik is still at war with the Davion-sponsored separatist movements inside its own borders, and Hanse Davion is eating up the Capellan Confederation. What good can this assault by Justin Xiang do? What difference can it make?"

The Primus smiled coldly. "Precentor Dieron, are you well? How often have you admonished us that Davion is the devil incarnate because of his desire to recover the sciences lost over the last three centuries? I should think you would applaud this strike against an NAIS facility."

"I would applaud Xiang's effort if he were to attack the NAIS itself," Myndo retorted angrily. *Don't try to strangle me with my own words!*

"Anyway, this discussion takes us away from the point of my original statement. I demand that we interdict House Davion now! If we cut off all their communications, not only do we hamper their military attacks, but we cripple the Federated Suns. The people of the Federated Suns will suffer if we allow no messages to go in or out of their worlds. This will lead to discontent, fear, and unrest. It will pull the carpet out from under the Prince. It's the only way to stop him."

Precentor Tharkad shook his head. "My dear Myndo, you demanded Interdiction last year. We all agreed to set a threshold for what we would tolerate. We agreed to interdict communications if Davion forces attacked Sarna."

Myndo fumed. "Need I remind you, Ulthan, that this agreement was made before Davion's ambush and before the Prince's only rival, Duke Michael Hasek-Davion, so conveniently took himself out of the competition? Things are far more grave now than they were then."

"But Davion is no stronger," Precentor Sian said heatedly. "Were we to intervene, it would make us seem partial. Hanse Davion could turn his force against us."

Myndo Waterly raised herself to full height. "You sound as though you are afraid of him. We both know that ComStar has more BattleMechs hidden here than any of the Successor States can claim, and you know also that our machines are in better shape than anything even House Davion has. We have nothing to fear from the Fox."

The Primus's eyes smoldered. "In this you are very wrong, Precentor Dieron. Our impartiality makes us a trusted ally to all in the

Successor States. Because of this, they allow us to transmit their communications. Through these communications, we learn about their strengths and weaknesses. We gain knowledge, and that gives us power."

Myndo met Tiepolo's dark gaze. "Of what use is power that we do not employ?"

The Primus's granite expression did not change. "We have not said that we will not use our power. We will not use it bluntly. I will not give the order for our 'Mechs to be deployed because it would present an unfavorable image. I will, however, allow you to create a holovid of Davion troops razing one of our communications stations. With this as evidence, we have a valid excuse for discontinuing service within the Federated Suns."

Precentor Tharkad narrowed his eyebrows. "Will the Interdiction include cutting off information from Davion agents inside the Capellan Confederation?"

The Primus nodded. "In an effort to slow the Davion advance, I have already begun delaying messages containing intelligence on troop strengths and deployments going out from Davion spies."

Myndo looked puzzled. "Why not betray the spies to the Maskirovka? I'm sure Maximilian Liao would be grateful for any enemy agents turned over to his secret police."

Precentor Sian spoke up next. "I would not recommend that approach. Maximilian is under much pressure. He could thank us, or he could accuse us of collaborating with House Davion for not betraying the spies early enough to stop the Davion assault."

The Primus nodded in agreement. "I do not mind delaying reports that will kill warriors, but I refuse to expose spies. That would be akin to killing the goose that lays the golden eggs. We will continue to accept their reports as though we are transmitting them, but the information will come here for analysis."

Precentor New Avalon cleared his throat. "If any Davion spies were exposed, I am certain Quintus Allard would be able to recruit new ones and keep their identities safe from us—at least in the short term. Better the devils we know…"

Myndo brooded silently. *You're a bunch of weak-kneed farmers' wives. You chase after the chicken you want for dinner, hoping it will die. You wait and plot and plan when all you really need is a sharp axe.* She watched the Primus carefully. *When I take your place, ComStar will become a force greater than anything you can imagine. The Word of Blake will become known for the truth that it is.*

The Primus smiled but without a trace of warmth or pleasantness. "If you do not want to be embarrassed, Precentor Dieron, I suggest not calling for a vote on Interdiction. It seems that we choose to stand by our earlier agreement."

Myndo nodded. "Very well. I am content to wait until House Davion attacks Sarna—but no later." *Now all I need do is restructure enough spy reports to make Sarna look very tempting.* Into her mind, unbidden, came an image of Hanse Davion. *Perhaps, with the Fox doing the planning, I will need do no work at all...*

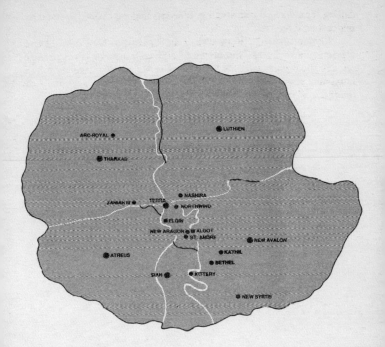

MAP OF THE INNER SPHERE
SHOWING MILITARY ADVANCES
AS OF 3029

BOOK I
TRUTH

The pure and simple truth is rarely pure and never simple.
—Oscar Wilde

1

New Avalon
Crucis March, Federated Suns
3 March 3029

Hanse Davion squinted his ice-blue eyes against the harsh glare of the lights, while around him, the applause from the reporters jamming the small auditorium thundered. Tall and regal in his maroon dress uniform, the Prince of the Federated Suns stood at the wooden podium, smiling as he waited for the ovation to die down. When it gave no signs of abating, he raised his hands to quiet the enthusiastic crowd.

"Please, let us at least have the appearance of an objective press...." He joined in with the journalists' laughter at the remark, then set his face in an expression of calm dignity. "I have a statement, ladies and gentlemen, before I take questions."

Hanse's left hand smoothed his closely cropped auburn hair. "Few would argue that warfare is mankind's oldest profession—and oldest obsession. Wars have decided the course of history in the seven thousand years of recorded time, and the art of warfare was no doubt forged in a crucible of even greater antiquity."

Hanse paused for a moment to drink from the glass of water set beside the podium. "The history of warfare often glorifies the feats of courage that win battles, or the valiant efforts of those who fought and lost. Historians freely second-guess an order given by this or that general, but they seldom count the Human factors entering into the equations. The barbarity of war can be reduced to statistics, but individuals feel the pain of losing a son or father or brother in emotional rather than mathematical terms.

"Even wars fought in accordance with the Ares Conventions—warfare that minimizes the impact of battles on civilian populations—are not without loss and pain. Yet it is a rare death that affects a whole nation. Today I have the sad duty of informing you, my people, of just such a death."

Hanse watched the reporters glance quizzically at one another. *No, your sources have not leaked this piece of information. The only way you will hear it is from my mouth.* Hanse let his lower lip tremble and injected a huskiness into his voice.

"Today we received confirmation of the death of Duke Michael Hasek-Davion." The Prince paused as the reporters' shocked outbursts echoed off the room's walls, then resumed his narrative as silence fell over the assembly. "He died—actually was brutally murdered—at the hands of Maximilian Liao. I take full responsibility for Michael's death. He died pursuing a policy he believed I favored.

"It is no secret that Duke Michael and I had our disagreements in the past, but they were not so dark and divisive as you, the members of the press, characterized them. There is a universe of difference between being fierce rivals and the relationship I shared with Duke Michael. You saw him as my enemy. I saw him as loyal opposition." Hanse sighed heavily. "He will be sorely missed, and his death will not go unavenged."

The Prince's expression did not change, but his voice rose to its normal range. "Liao's assassins were also ordered to destroy another individual in their efforts to please their mad master. In a move that can only be described as psychotically paranoid, Liao ordered the death of Colonel Pavel Ridzik. With the Maskirovka's usual efficiency, they failed to kill the Colonel, but maimed and murdered hundreds of innocent bystanders when the hit team exploded an entire city block trying to get one man."

Hanse allowed the hint of a smile to pull at the corners of his mouth. "Driven by concern for his people, the people of Tikonov, Colonel Ridzik sought us out. After a series of negotiations, we have agreed to recognize the Tikonov Free Republic and to terminate all hostile operations within its borders in return for a pact of mutual protection and defense. Once again, all the people of the Successor States have proof of our support for political freedom and each individual's right to pursue his or her destiny."

The Prince looked out over the press corps, then smiled wryly. "You will no doubt ask why we are at war with the Capellan Confederation if this is so. Why not let them live in peace? I ask, can

4

anyone be truly free when so unscrupulous a leader lurks nearby? Liao thought nothing of destroying a whole city block to kill one man. Can the concepts of personal liberty and freedom mean anything to such a mind? The answer, quite simply, is no. We will do what we must to bring an end to Liao's madness."

The Prince set aside his prepared text, then braced his hands against the edges of the podium. As reporters shot to their feet for questions, the Prince pointed to a slender man in the center of the pack.

The other reporters sank quietly into their seats as the man introduced himself. "Joe Adams of the Information Network. Highness, how was Duke Michael killed, and how was news of his death transmitted to you?"

Covering his mouth with his fist, Hanse coughed lightly before answering. "We have nothing even approximating an autopsy, Mr. Adams, but preliminary reports indicate death was the result of a gunshot wound to the head. It is possible he was beaten beforehand. As for how we learned of his death, we received a communique from ComStar officials to arrange a transfer of the body from Liao hands to ours on Spica."

Again, the reporters stood up en masse, but the Prince singled out a dark-haired woman near the front. "Yes, you, Ms. Watkins."

The reporter glanced down at her compad's LCD display, then smiled at the Prince. "You said you accepted responsibility for the death of Duke Michael Hasek-Davion. Could you explain why?"

Hanse hesitated for a moment, then exhaled heavily. "Michael, concerned about a Liao slash at the Capellan March, took it upon himself to travel to Sian. He wanted to negotiate a settlement with Maximilian Liao, but things obviously turned sour on him. The reason I accept responsibility for his death is because I did not attend fully to Michael's concerns about the Capellan March. This happened because of my preoccupation with the war, but that does not absolve me of guilt."

A sandy-haired reporter won the shouting match to get the next question in. "Alf Cordes, New Avalon Broadcasting. How can you embrace Colonel Ridzik as a guardian of freedom when he was the author of the Truth Massacre in which three thousand men, women, and children were butchered by MechWarriors? We know Colonel Ridzik is an ambitious man, and quite probably engineered the death of Tormax Liao to ensure Maximilian's accession to the Capellan throne. Are you not afraid to let such a man get close to you?"

Hanse Davion's eyes narrowed to slits. "Mr. Cordes, I am well aware of Colonel Ridzik's record. I could stand here sharing with you

5

a host of rationalizations, but I will spare you. Colonel Ridzik's support means we are able to reduce garrison forces, which ensures fewer casualties both on the front and behind the lines."

Hanse allowed himself the hint of a smile. "As for being afraid of Colonel Ridzik—I have always respected his abilities as a leader and a politician. I am not afraid of him. I am wary of him. There is, I assure you, a world of difference between the two conditions."

The Prince pointed to a reporter in a wheelchair for the next question, a genuine smile brightening his face. "Yes, Brandon. You're next."

The reporter smiled. "Thank you, Colonel, I mean…"

Hanse waved away the gaffe. "Not to worry, Brandon. I'm just glad someone remembers my days in the regiment."

Brandon Corey let the other reporters' laughter die out before framing his question. "Highness, recalling your days in command of the Davion Heavy Guards, would you have imagined that an assault the size and scope of your Capellan invasion could be so successful?"

Hanse Davion smiled. "As ever, Brandon, your questions do not allow for simple answers. I must admit that as the commander of the Davion Heavy Guards, I never envisioned a military strike of these dimensions. That is because military academies throughout the Successor States have preached the idea that a strategic advance is impossible."

The Prince raised his right hand to forestall questions while he continued his explanation. "In the six centuries since BattleMechs first strode onto a battlefield, combat has become rarefied. When we look at a BattleMech, we see a ten-meter-tall amalgam of metal and munitions. Too often, we see a 'Mech as a chivalrous knight's armor and charger all bound together, and we imagine battles as fought between individual pilots, not faceless squads and divisions of soldiers.

"It dawned on me, during a casual conversation with Colonel Ardan Sortek, that we'd overlooked a central fact about BattleMechs." Hanse held his left hand out palm up, then curled the fingers in to form a fist. "To Napoleon…to Patton…to Rommel, a BattleMech would have represented the strength of a company or a division. Those generals, armed with communications technology that looks infantile compared to ours, easily commanded companies and divisions. They controlled armies composed of hundreds of thousands of individual warriors just to get the firepower of one of our 'Mech companies. If they could do that then, I asked myself, why can't we do it now?"

Corey leaned forward in his wheelchair. "That is when you

decided to conquer the Capellan Confederation?"

Hanse shook his head. "That's when I decided we would organize the Operation Galahad exercises in 3026 and '27 to test out the idea. When those exercises indicated that large numbers of troops could be moved effectively, we looked at dealing with the Liao threat."

A man behind and to the left of Corey stood quickly, and the Prince let him speak next. "Ron Kilgore, Nebula News Network. Reports of Liao attacks on a number of Federated Suns worlds have begun to filter back from the front. Have you any comment about them?"

The Prince stood stiffly. "You know well, Mr. Kilgore, that military security bars me from discussing troop deployments and strengths with you, but your question does need to be answered. Yes, Liao forces hit several of our worlds in both the Draconis March and the Capellan March. Their objective was to capture or destroy supplies being held on those worlds in preparation for staging our next advance. Liao's intelligence service, the Maskirovka, had interpreted certain bits of data to suggest that this would be a crippling attack. However, it was our Ministry of Intelligence, Information, and Operations who fed them the information. In intelligence circles, that's known as bait."

The Prince smiled as the reporters laughed. "Let me assure you that though Liao forces did land, none of them got away again."

Hanse nodded to another reporter. "Mr. St. James."

"Thank you, Highness. Last September, in your first press conference concerning the invasion, you said, 'It will continue as long as it must.' Do you now have a better idea how long that will be?"

Hanse Davion shook his head resignedly. "At one time, I thought we could subdue Liao by taking away the industrial worlds in the Tikonov Commonality, but he does not seem to realize he has lost his ability to wage an effective war. Indeed, the attempted assassination of Pavel Ridzik and the murder of Duke Michael Hasek-Davion point out that our assessments of Liao's mental stability have been far from the mark. Now Liao seems more like a rabid animal that must be put down than a shrewd leader of men."

Hanse frowned. "Please understand that this war is a hardship for me, just as it is for every one of my subjects." He looked up and out beyond the auditorium's wall. "This war keeps me apart from my wife. This war has cost me my brother-in-law, Michael. And every day I must send men and women off to die, which is a painful duty."

A woman with short black hair stood. "Highness, we have heard rumors that Justin Xiang, a man you exiled two years ago, now serves as Maximilian Liao's advisor on intelligence matters dealing with the

Federated Suns. Xiang is the son of your Quintus Allard, Minister of Intelligence, Information, and Operations. Is it true that you launched this invasion as a preemptive strike to prevent Liao from doing damage based on secrets known to Xiang? And if he has hurt the Federated Suns, will you sack his father?"

The Prince cleared his throat, but the look of contempt remained on his face. "Based on how the Capellan forces fell into our ambush, Justin Xiang must be an impotent advisor to Maximilian Liao. Xiang might once have been considered a capable company commander. As an intelligence advisor to Maximilian Liao, he could easily be considered an asset to the Federated Suns. As for Quintus Allard, it was he who planned Operation Ambush and carefully orchestrated its successful execution. I have the utmost confidence in him, and he will remain at my side until the day he chooses to leave my service."

A grizzled older man stood to ask the next question. "Shifting from the Liao front for a moment, Highness, we've heard rumors that a Liao unit, the Northwind Highlanders, landed and drove two Kurita regiments off the planet Northwind. Could you comment on this, and tell us if there are any plans to liberate the world from the Liao forces."

Hanse half-smiled. "Again, for reasons of military security, I cannot answer you fully. Suffice it to say that the arrival of the Northwind Highlanders on the world their forebears left centuries ago was not unanticipated or unwelcome."

With that, Hanse Davion held up his hands. "No more questions," he said. "I have much work to do. But we will do this again...soon. I do respect your right to know the truth, and I will share it will with you as often I can." Ignoring the shouted questions, Prince Hanse Davion turned from the podium and retreated through the doorway behind him, deeper into the sanctuary of his palace.

2

New Avalon
Crucis March, Federated Suns
3 March 3029

As the CID guards closed the auditorium doors behind him, the Prince looked up to see his white-haired Minister of Intelligence, Information, and Operations waiting for him. "Morning, Quintus." By the dark look on the other man's face, the Prince knew something was wrong. "What is it?"

"I now know why we did not find Morgan Hasek-Davion this morning," Quintus said. "A holovid disc arrived during the night from the ComStar station here in New Avalon City. The label read, 'M. Hasek-Davion.' It was delivered to Morgan about three hours before dawn."

Hanse felt an icy hand claw at his gut. *Dear God, no! Morgan was not meant to see that disk, at least not before Quintus and I had gone over it.* The Prince swallowed hard. "Where is he?"

Quintus pointed down the hallway. "He's with Melissa. Kym Sorenson is there as well—your wife summoned her. Morgan's feeling betrayed, Highness, and very angry."

Hanse nodded, then started along the corridor with long-legged strides. As Quintus caught up with him, the Prince asked, "Does Morgan know about Kym? Does he know his lover is one of your agents, and that she's keeping an eye on him for us?"

"Not a clue," Quintus said. "Kym's too good for that. But if he found out, it would devastate him."

9

The Prince nodded. "You and I are the only ones who know. I've not even told Melissa."

The two guards at the door to Hanse's personal chambers snapped to attention. The Prince acknowledged them with a nod, then opened the door and passed through. Quintus followed him and closed the gold-leaf trimmed door with a secure click.

Melissa Steiner-Davion, her blond hair a radiant frame to her beautiful face, met her husband at the door. Hanse did not hear nervousness in her greeting, but he felt it in the tremor of her moist palm as she grasped his hand. *That's fear I see in her eyes. Morgan must be in great pain, but it's pain I cannot relieve.*

Melissa kissed him lightly on the cheek. "He's angry, Hanse. Take care. He strikes out blindly, but you can help him."

Hanse nodded to his wife, then walked across the small foyer and into the larger sitting room. There he saw Morgan Hasek-Davion seated on a couch staring at the holovideo monitor. Normally tall and noble-looking, Morgan had slumped down on the cream-colored sofa until his back rested on the seat cushion and his long legs extended into the center of the room. His reddish-gold hair, worn long and unbound, hooded his strong-featured face.

Beside him, clinging to his right arm and stroking his hair, sat Lady Kym Sorenson. Worry and fear drained the usually bright look from her pretty face. The way her blond hair was gathered back from her face and her casual dress told the Prince she'd come immediately when called. *I wonder if it was something more than duty that prompted her quick response?*

Morgan's head snapped around, his green eyes angry. "You! You knew, didn't you? You knew and you didn't tell me!"

Hanse glanced at the monitor. It showed a reporter giving a summation on the press conference. He looked back at Morgan, then shook his head. "I tried to find you and tell you before I had that conference. I didn't want you to hear it that way, but I had to make a statement because the Maskirovka had already begun leaking information to media outlets in the Capellan March. Where were you?"

Morgan snarled like angry dog. "I was out...walking!"

Hanse narrowed his eyes. *Another nighttime sojourn in the Peace Park, no doubt.* "You didn't leave word with the Palace where you were. You are my heir...that is required of you!"

Morgan's voice dropped to a rime-laden whisper. "I had other things on my mind! I had seen this!" Morgan pointed a remote control at the holovid monitor and hit a switch. The reporter flashed away as if carved up by countless invisible razors.

The monitor focused a scene aboard a DropShip. From the gold insignia on the interior hullplates, the Prince easily identified the craft as belonging to ComStar. As the camera moved back, people came into focus. A ComStar Acolyte, wearing the yellow robe characteristic of his rank, stood in the center of the ship's shuttle bay. On his right stood seven men in the uniforms of Michael Hasek-Davion's Fifth Syrtis Fusiliers. An eighth man, dressed in a dark blue suit of civilian cut, waited with the soldiers at one end of the strip of red carpet.

In the background, a hatch opened in the side of a dart-shaped silver shuttle bearing the Capellan Confederation crest of a sword-clenching fist against a green triangular field. A stepped ramp slowly unfolded and touched the deck just shy of the red carpet. The camera moved in for a close-up as the first Liao representative descended the steps.

Quintus Allard, who had just entered the room to join his Prince, stiffened as the camera focused on that individual's face. Quintus looked up at the Prince and nodded. "It's Justin."

Hanse Davion flicked a glance at Kym Sorenson, but she gave no clue that she recognized or cared who the black-clad Capellan was. *Ah, Quintus, you chose this woman well. Though her mission of watching Justin during his time on Solaris VII ended with her betrayal and a broken jaw, she gives no sign of knowing him at all. Nerves of steel and ice-water for blood. How do you manage to find so many people suited to such difficult duty?*

Justin Xiang reached the bottom of the steps, then stood back. His black suit, cut in a conservative Capellan pattern, had no lapel or decorations other than the flat black buttons running up the front. Justin's trousers had razor-sharp creases and hung over the tops of his boots. The Capellan spy wore a black glove on his left hand and carried a white envelope in his right.

He glanced up the stairs, and the camera panned to follow his gaze. The first pair of pallbearers, dressed in suits that matched Justin's in everything except color, descended the steps. The deep, rich brown of the mahogany casket contrasted sharply with the white uniforms of the pallbearers, yet was only a shade or two darker than their flesh. The camera focused on each man, but their half-closed almond eyes and expressionless faces revealed nothing.

The first two men down the steps worked hard to keep the casket level. With strict military precision, the Capellan honor guard carried the mortal remains of Duke Michael Hasek-Davion to the DropShip's deck, then waited for Justin to lead them down the carpeted strip.

Justin preceded them at an even pace, stopping at the ComStar

11

Acolyte. The Federated Suns representative left the Fusiliers behind as he stiffly walked to his place opposite Justin Xiang.

Xiang bowed to the Acolyte. "The Peace of Blake be with you." Xiang then bowed to his counterpart from the Federated Suns, but the gesture showed none of the respect he had given the Acolyte. "Hello, Ambassador Robertson."

The Prince's robust representative gave Xiang a curt nod. "How nice of the Chancellor to allow his lap dog to honor us."

Xiang stiffened, but refrained from slashing back. "The Ares Conventions require the repatriation of all spies, living or dead. Treason is not tolerated in the Capellan Confederation. That which was once Duke Michael Hasek-Davion is yours to do with as you wish." Xiang hesitated for a moment and softened his voice. "The Chancellor wanted to leave the body for carrion birds to pick clean, but I prevailed upon him to return the Duke to you."

The stern look on Robertson's face eased. He nodded slightly. "Thank you, Citizen Xiang. It is good to know you still respect some of our customs like any civilized man."

Xiang's dark, almond eyes flashed with emotion. "There are many things I respect about the Federated Suns, Lord Victor. But you should not imagine that my respect in any way dilutes my desire for vengeance after being humiliated and exiled by Hanse Davion and my father."

Xiang stripped the glove from his left hand, letting the fleshlike garment fall to the carpet. The camera focused on his hand as he brandished it. The light from the holo's harsh spotlights glittered off the metal seams. "I gave a piece of my flesh, and my whole heart and soul for the Federated Suns, but I got nothing in return. Your Prince turned against me, and I am more than happy to reciprocate."

Xiang thrust the envelope into Robertson's hand. "These are all the documents we require to return the body to you. We even included the original of Michael's death warrant. I'm sure the Prince will frame it."

Robertson accepted the documents as Xiang turned away. Both men signaled their soldiers to move forward. Directly at the center of the carpet, opposite the spot marked by the ComStar Acolyte, the Fifth Syrtis Fusiliers accepted the body of their slain master in silent dignity. Only their taut expressions and fury-filled eyes showed their hatred for the Capellans.

Morgan hit the remote control switch. "You told me a number of days ago that you'd received word that my father was injured, but that you could provide no details. Then I get this delivered by messenger.

12

I nearly went mad when I watched it! And when I come here to find out what you know, I'm told you're giving a press conference!"

Morgan shot to his feet and came eye to eye with his uncle. "My God, Hanse, why didn't you wait? Why didn't you speak to me first?'

Morgan thrust a finger at the monitor. "You told the reporters you accepted responsibility for my father's death. You should have stopped him. You shouldn't have allowed him to go to Sian."

Hanse raised himself to his full height. "Allowed him to go? I did no such thing. Your father went of his own accord, and Liao killed him for very good reasons."

Morgan hesitated. "But you said…"

"Damn what I said! Those were reporters. They have no idea what really goes on in the world. They ferret out the truth beneath the headlines we give them, but they never realize that what they see as bottom is merely the roof on the level below that!"

Hanse looked at both Morgan and Lady Kym. "What I tell you now cannot go beyond these walls." Hanse pointed at the couch. "Sit down, Morgan." His nephew shook his head, folding his hands behind his back like a MechWarrior standing at ease. Hanse softened his voice. "Please, sit down."

Morgan seated himself as Hanse crossed to the holovid monitor and shut it off. "That packet of papers contained enough information for Quintus to fit the last few pieces of a puzzle together. We knew, for a host of reasons, that military information was being leaked from our forces to the Maskirovka. We also knew, because of the speed with which the information was received on the enemy side, that the information came from someone close to your father. We knew how long it took information to reach Liao because Alexi Malenkov, Justin Xiang's aide, works for Quintus Allard."

Hanse held out both hands to stop the question on Morgan's lips. "We believed the mole was your father's good friend, Count Anton Vitios."

Morgan shook his head. "That's impossible. Vitios's family died in a Liao raid on Verlo. He's got a pathological hatred of anything Capellan." Morgan glanced over at Quintus Allard. "We all saw that when he prosecuted your son for treason."

Quintus nodded. "We believed, as some of our psychologists did, that Vitios went round the bend when he began to believe that neither the Prince nor your father was doing enough to fight Liao. By giving Liao information, he could manufacture weaknesses that would prompt Liao to make disastrous attacks. We discovered, in fact, that troop strengths for your father's units were listed as being under-

13

strength when passed to Liao."

The Prince nodded slowly. "We used this information leakage to set up our ambush of Liao troops back in January. It was an unmitigated disaster for Liao. It was not until after the attacks had been organized, and Liao troops sent on their missions, that we sent information to your father reporting what we had done. Instead of arresting Vitios, your father fled to Sian."

Openmouthed, Morgan stared at Hanse Davion, then slowly shook his head. "No, that's not possible. My father would never do anything like that." Morgan shuddered. "You're saying my father betrayed the Federated Suns."

Hanse looked down at Morgan and felt his chest tighten. *Yes, it hurts to hear it. It is well that we keep the whole truth from you.* "It was not treason, Morgan, though it might seem like it. Michael had negotiated a truce with Liao. No, he did not have my sanction to do so, but your father was semi-autonomous in the Capellan March and he did what he must to protect his people. His action angers me, but I can understand it."

Morgan rubbed his forehead with his left hand. "So my father went to Sian to persuade Maximilian Liao that he had not knowingly violated their agreement..."

"And Liao, having just learned of the attacks and their results, blamed your father for the failures. Liao did not take into account the fact that he could not have recalled his troops in any event. Because the Liao forces traveled through uninhabited star systems, the ComStar network could not have been employed to warn them about the traps."

Hanse squatted in front of Morgan and looked up into his eyes. "Your father made an error in judgment, not in loyalties. Had he come to me, I would have credited him with an incredible stroke of genius in using Liao's Maskirovka against him. He chose not to trust me, and he died for that mistake."

The Prince straightened up. "The body is being taken back to New Syrtis. Political control of the Capellan March has been transferred to your mother. Military control will go to Marshal Vivian Chou. I have a command circuit ready to take you to New Syrtis."

Morgan shook his head slowly. "With all the JumpShips you have committed to the war, the circuit to New Syrtis cannot be complete."

"No, it's not. The trip to New Syrtis will take a month because each JumpShip must make two jumps. That adds four weeks for recharging the Kearny-Fuchida drives during the trip."

Morgan sighed heavily. "I would arrive too late for the services."

14

He stood. "Uncle, give me the Fifth Syrtis Fusiliers and let me avenge my father."

Morgan's plea stabbed into Hanse's heart. *Dammit, Morgan, I cannot honor your request. The Fifth Syrtis is riddled with men who would avenge Michael's death by coming after me. I cannot trust you with a pack of vipers like that. With you at their head, they might succeed in fomenting a revolt in the Capellan March. Your father could use them to reach out from the grave and do to me in death what he could never manage in life.*

Hanse shook his head. "We have gone over this time and again. Until Melissa bears me a child, you are my heir. I will not give Liao a chance to extinguish the hopes of House Davion and House Hasek. I know it chafes like a coffle, but your duty is to remain here, hale and hearty, ready to lead if I need you."

"No, Hanse, this is not like the other times." Morgan balled his fists. "Before I wanted to fight Liao to bring glory to House Davion. That was my motivation and my desire, but my father's murder has changed things. Now I must avenge his death."

Hanse narrowed his eyes. "If I refuse, will you strike out on your own, make your own deals, and fight your own war?"

Morgan started to answer, then stopped as Hanse's trap opened up before him. He let his fists drop limply to his side. "No, Prince Hanse Davion, I am not so much my father's son to do that. I serve you in whatever capacity you demand of me." He bowed his head. "Now, my Lord, if you will permit me, I would beg your leave to mourn my father."

Hanse nodded silently and reluctantly let Morgan Hasek-Davion leave the room. *Mourn him, Morgan, but learn a lesson from his death. Your loyalty must ever be to the Federated Suns. If you falter, if the people who supported your father are able to seduce you, then you will suffer your father's fate.*

3

Justin Xiang slapped a new power pack into the Magna laser carbine, then looked around the corner. He snapped his head back as the two silhouetted figures deeper in the corridor triggered a ruby burst at him. He crouched as best his exoskeleton would allow, then dove into the corridor, rolled and came up on one knee. His finger tightened on the trigger.

Hot scarlet darts of laser fire raked across the corridor. One bolt hit a guard high in the chest, flaring like a meteor against the man's ablative vest. The guard stiffened, then dropped flat on his back. The other guard caught three bolts stitching their way from his right hip to his left shoulder. The impact spun him around, then dropped him into a rigid heap.

Justin ran up the corridor and knelt beside the men he'd shot. He pushed their guns beyond their reach, then turned and signaled to the men hunkered down behind him. Two of them swept on past him and took up positions on either side of the door to the exterior. *Not bad, so far. We've only lost three out of our dozen. I can stand 25 percent casualties.* He narrowed his brown, almond-shaped eyes. *Even more—this mission is that important.*

The other six team members moved up to Justin's position. The rear guard kept their weapons pointed back down the corridor to cut off any pursuit. The other three people—known to the assault team as "mules"—sought out what cover they could find. The samples filling the satchels on their web belts made for a bulky outline, but they managed to make themselves small targets nonetheless.

Justin turned to the two men at the facility's entrance. He nodded, sending them through the doorway. One twisted, stood, then fell back against the door jamb as he took fire from outside. The second man jerked himself back through the doorway, but his legs no longer worked.

"They've got a *Locust* out there!"

Dammit! All the 'Mechs were supposed to be drawn off by our diversion! Justin whirled. "Ling! Maximovitch! Get those V-LAW rockets ready. Be at the door. I'll draw it off."

Justin took a hand-held short-range missile launcher from one of the mules. Glancing through a transparent spot in the launcher, he saw a small piece of the red designator band running around the warhead. *Good. An Inferno round. It won't kill the* Locust, *but the jellied fuel it'll spray all over will screw up its infrared sensors. Scanning for heat patterns must be how it knew I had two men on either side of the doorway.*

Justin handed his carbine to one of the mules, then pointed toward the sprinklers running along the center of the ceiling. "If you please, Mr. Chung, let's cool this place down."

One shot started the whole line of sprinklers spraying. Justin let the water soak his clothing enough to kill his IR outline, then bolted for the doorway. Once he hit sunlight, he cut to the right, away from where the team's 'Mechs waited, and back toward the *Locust*.

Fool! You expected us to go for our 'Mechs to fight you! Justin brandished the missile launcher like a gauntlet to be thrown down in challenge. *That's an error you'll not soon make again!*

The *Locust* tried to pivot quickly, but the awkward-looking 'Mech was not built for swift lateral movement. The stubby wing on the ten-meter tall 'Mech's left side geysered spent machine gun shells as the pilot tracked the weapons pod after Justin, but the Maskirovka agent sprinted beyond the edge of the machine gun's arc. The pilot, while continuing to turn his 'Mech, swung the *Locust*'s underslung laser into line with the running man.

Justin dropped to his knees, skidding to a halt only three meters from where the laser's hot burst sizzled through the air. As waves of heat washed over him, Justin rose to one knee. He settled the missile launcher's heavy weight on his right shoulder, clamped his metallic left hand to the barrel, then let the missile fly.

In the space of a heartbeat, the Inferno rocket crossed the twenty-five meters to its target. Instead of slamming into the ferro-ceramic alloy armor covering the *Locust*, the missile blossomed like a horrific, fiery flower. Tendrils of thick, syrupy chemicals shot out over the 'Mech, coating it like honey, then burst into flames.

Crouching in the doorway, Ling and Maximovitch appeared. Their missiles flew straight through the conflagration and exploded against the *Locust*'s hull. Both missiles splashed a black cloud over the 'Mech, but the fire quickly consumed the paint as additional fuel.

Justin raised his left fist in congratulations. Discarding the empty launcher, he pressed his right hand to his throat mike and keyed a channel to his partner. "That should be it, Tsen. We're clear. What was our time?"

Tsen Shang's rich voice came back immediately, but seemed to lack some of the emotion Justin might have expected. "Twelve point two-three minutes. You shaved a minute and a half off the last time."

Justin smiled. "And we got one more person out this time. The mission worked even without gassing the whole complex. This operation is definitely viable."

"Roger." Irritation rimmed Tsen's voice. "The Chancellor wants you to report to him immediately. Don't bother cleaning up. It won't matter to him."

"Roger."

Justin dropped his hand from the throat mike, then frowned. Tsen Shang had been acting strangely ever since his counterattack against the Davion storehouses had turned out to be a big trap. He was blameless though, because he'd been forced to use Michael Hasek-Davion's intelligence reports to plan the assault. There was no way Tsen could have known the information had been tailored by Davion's own Intelligence Ministry. No one could have guessed it.

Justin shrugged his way out of his equipment harness, letting it clank to the ground. He pointed it out to one of the men returning from extinguishing the fire on the remotely controlled *Locust*. He considered freeing himself of the exoskeleton's grip, but decided there was not time. Unless someone shot him with a down-powered laser blast, the suit would not stiffen up to simulate a wound—thereby causing a problem.

The downturn in Tsen Shang's attitude rubbed at Justin's consciousness like an ill-fitting boot against the heel. He had expected Shang to be glad Justin had persuaded the Chancellor not to execute him or exile him to Brazen Heart. Instead, it only seemed to make Shang more sullen. Justin knew it, too. Romano Liao had something to do with the other man's mood swings. He shook his head. *She's definitely a candidate for retroactive birth control.*

Justin had first met Tsen Shang two years before on the Game World, Solaris VII. Tsen, a Maskirovka agent, had posed as a wealthy Capellan noble sponsoring a team of heavy 'Mechs in the gladiatorial combats on Solaris. Justin, newly exiled from the Federated Suns, had fought well and changed the fortunes of the Capellan Confederation in the games. Based on some of Justin's actions, Tsen Shang quickly realized that the son of Davion's Intelligence Minister could be a valuable asset to the Capellan Confederation. Shang abducted Justin, and Maximilian Liao himself recruited Justin into the Maskirovka.

Justin and Tsen worked closely together and developed a plan for streamlining the Maskirovka to make it more efficient. Maximilian Liao accepted the plan, put it into place, then appointed Justin and Tsen to head up the omnibus "Crisis Team." That saddled both men with great responsibility and brought them into close contact with the Capellan royal family.

Justin smiled as he walked from the simulation range toward the Spring Palace. *Very close contact, indeed.* Romano went after Tsen like a vampire after a Spican bloodfish. *She wanted him as her own pet Maskirovka agent, and she got him. I suspected she would eventually direct him against me to solidify her powerbase, but my involvement with her older sister made Romano hate me so much she stepped up her efforts. Shang is caught between our friendship and her manipulation. Unfortunately, Romano is winning...*

Justin forced himself to pause for a moment. He drew in a deep breath, letting the clean, fresh scent of spring wash away the last vestiges of Inferno stink. He glanced beyond the boxy palace to the distant line of tall pines. The darkness of the woods looked so inviting that he momentarily considered bolting for its sanctuary.

Reluctantly, he rejected that plan. *A split between Tsen and me is probably inevitable. And his discovery that my aide Alexi Malenkov was spying on Romano did nothing to put me back in his good graces. He probably told Romano about the surveillance, but she hasn't tried to have me killed. It must be that my anger at her attempted assassination of my father frightened her. She's not gotten Tsen to oppose me outright yet, but his sour attitude about Operation Intruders Communion probably means his resistance is weakening.*

"Justin, wait!"

The sound of Candace Liao's voice brought a smile to Justin's face. As tall as he, she quickly closed the distance between them with long-legged strides. Her gray eyes flashed mischievously as she took Justin's right hand, and her long black hair fell forward of her shoulders to frame her lovely face.

19

Justin squeezed her hand, then kissed her on the lips. "Good morning." Justin squinted up at the sun like a mariner measuring its arc. "What are you doing up this early?"

Candace gave him a mock-pout. "You should have awakened me. I told you I wanted to watch the rehearsal of your operation."

Justin smiled teasingly. "That is not what you mumbled this morning when I crawled out of bed."

Candace raised an eyebrow. "You never tried to wake me up."

Justin laughed. "I did so. You, my Duchess, had ordered me to do just that, and I made a valiant attempt at fulfilling my duty. This morning, however, you countermanded that order."

"What did I say?"

Justin slipped his arms around her. "It was either 'good luck' or 'gimmee covers.'" He kissed the tip of her nose. "I translated that into your desire to sleep in."

Tension tightened the corners of her eyes. "I appreciate it, lover, but you should not have done it. There are things I should have accomplished already today."

Justin shook his head. "Ease off, Candace. I know you're worried about what Hanse Davion is going to do in the area of your St. Ives Commonality, but we've absolutely no indication that he's planning a strike against your holding."

Candace disengaged herself from Justin's arms. "That's hardly reassuring, Citizen Xiang. As I recall, Hanse Davion's invasion came as a complete surprise."

Justin bowed his head. "Touché, Duchess. I would point out, however, that we had ample clues of buildups along the border. Our error was in assuming Davion meant only to conduct another one of his Galahad exercises. That's what communications from Michael Hasek-Davion were telling us. We only expected Hanse to flex his muscles, but he struck out at us instead."

Candace's anxiety ignited anger. "Because of my father's ineffectual attempts at a counterstrike, the St. Ives Commonality has been stripped of JumpShips. We couldn't get reinforcements into it even if Davion did attack."

Justin sighed heavily. "That's all right. We don't have any reinforcements. Your father's already issued orders calling up all reserve units on all planets, and for the training of the citizenry to fight the invaders. That may slow Davion down, but it's not going to turn the tide."

Justin's steel hand curled into a fist like a flower wilting in timelapse photography. "My assault will make the difference. Once

20

we hit Bethel and the secret New Avalon Institute of Science facility there, we'll be able to meet and defeat Davion's forces." He met her chilly stare. "The JumpShips from St. Ives are being stretched into a command circuit that will deliver my forces to Bethel and bring them back quickly."

Candace nodded stiffly. "I understand the importance of the command circuit and the raid, but I wonder if it will be in time to save the Capellan Confederation."

Justin shook his head slowly. "I cannot answer that, but I do know you need not fear for your St. Ives Commonality. Alexi showed me a report that indicated the Fifth Syrtis Fusiliers were pulled from Kittery. They were aching to avenge Michael Hasek-Davion's death. If Hanse has moved them from Kittery, he's planning to use them elsewhere. As long as you have no JumpShips in St. Ives, Hanse knows you won't be hitting him. He will wait."

"I hope, for the sake of my people, that you are correct."

Justin smiled cruelly. "I hope so, too. I want Hanse Davion looking ahead, so far ahead that he'll not see what I'm going to do to him. Once Operation Intruders Communion is complete, we will use his own technology against him. It will be glorious."

Candace stepped close, caressing Justin up over the chest and shoulders as she slipped her hands around his neck. "I believe you, my love, and I dearly wish to share your victory, but I urge you to be cautious. There are those who will mark you as a target. Pavel Ridzik was once my father's trusted advisor, much as you are now. Do not let your personal desire for revenge make you blind to those who might wish to eliminate you."

Justin looked into her quicksilver eyes as his arms enfolded her. "I'll be careful."

Candace smiled happily. "I have ways to insulate you from some things, and your position in the Maskirovka will shield you as well. We both realize who your biggest threat is, and we also know she has great access to my father." She kissed his lips lightly. "As long as we are together, Justin Xiang, she will be unable to hurt either one of us."

Justin nodded quietly. *That's the game then, isn't it? Candace and Romano both sense their father's weakness, yet each realizes that only he can eliminate the other as a rival for power. This is a dangerous place to be, Justin, but it is the place where your duty has placed you. Make the best of it, because second-best in this arena ends up in a box.*

He smiled at Candace and gave her a squeeze. "Together, we're invincible."

4

Justin followed Candace Liao through the black-lacquered doors into the cool, dark briefing room. The doors closed behind them with the whispered hiss of vapor jets, then locked with a loud click. Justin stepped forward to the nearest end of the black lozenge table. He drew a chair out for Candace, then bowed to Chancellor Maximilian Liao.

The Chancellor, seated in a high-backed black marble chair, nodded his head wearily. The wisps of gray and white imperfections in the throne mirrored the light streaks threading Liao's unruly hair and long, slender moustache. The only color on the Chancellor's drawn face was in the purple shadows beneath his eyes.

Justin shivered. *When I first saw him, I thought of a spider, all gangling arms and legs, sitting in the middle of a cosmic web. Now he looks like a scarecrow in some barren, wind-scourged field. Hell, wearing that black uniform, he looks ready to die this instant.*

Seated at the table's far end, Tsen Shang nervously shuffled some papers. Tall and dark, he looked much like the Chancellor must have in his younger years. At Romano's urging, he'd grown a moustache just like Liao's. In a fit of independence, however, he'd refused to pare back his fingernails. In keeping with the current fashion, Shang wore the fingernails on the last three fingers of each hand at a length of ten centimeters. Black polish hid the carbon fibers reinforcing the nails, but Justin remembered well the time Tsen had slashed through a leather jacket with the razored edges of the fingernails. *Candace is right. I*

22

must be cautious. When Romano breaks down Tsen's last feelings of friendship toward me, he will become a most dangerous enemy.

Seated at her father's feet, Romano glared at Justin like a feral cat. Her green eyes dripped unholy menace and the sneer on her face only deepened when she looked at her sister. Her reddish-brown hair framed a face that would have been beautiful if not for the malevolence that distorted it.

Justin looked up at the Chancellor. "You have summoned me, Celestial Wonder?"

Liao nodded curtly, folding his hands together agitatedly instead of steepling them confidently, as was his habit. "Disturbing things, Citizen Xiang. Most disturbing things."

Justin glanced at Tsen. "What have we got?"

Tsen laid his papers down on the table's shadowy surface. "Davion forces have not advanced yet, but they are building up all along the Second Try-Highspire line."

At the mention of her old holding of Highspire, Romano bristled angrily. Maximilian reached down and stroked her red-brown hair with a bony hand. Like a child being comforted, Romano leaned the side of her face against her father's leg.

Justin nodded. "We've no idea when they will strike?"

Tsen shook his head. "We've issued orders calling up all reserves. The militia is being reinforced with older MechWarriors, and we've told everyone that we have troops on the way to bolster the defenses. We've initiated the creation of Youth Squads and are training them with Inferno and SRM launchers. We expect them to use the city terrain to good effect to harass the invaders. Davion's people will find it far more costly to take our worlds than during the first wave of assaults."

Justin smiled. "Good. What's the problem?"

The Chancellor frowned darkly as he pulled a folded sheet of paper from his tunic. "This message arrived today from Colonel Archibald McCarron! He says he's moving his remaining four regiments from their garrison worlds to Palos! I gave no such order!" Color flooded Liao's face as his fist crumpled the message. "At my request, Tsen Shang checked and found that the order went out over your signature."

Despite the Chancellor's wrath, Justin sat back in his chair. "Good. Very good."

"What?" Shang shook his head in disbelief. "Palos is a hideous place to deploy a crack mercenary unit like McCarron's Armored Cavalry. Are you mad? Stripping them from the Capellan March border leaves us open to an assault on Sian."

Justin pressed his hands to the tabletop as he stood. "No, gentlemen and ladies, I am not mad. I have merely averted a catastrophe." He glanced at Shang. "What happened to McCarron's first regiment?"

The distrust in Shang's eyes dropped away as he thought about Justin's question. "Davion forces destroyed it utterly in battles on Arboris and Basal."

Justin nodded, the hint of a wry smile tugging at the corner of his mouth. "No quarter asked or given because of McCarron's raid into the Federated Suns six, seven years ago. McCarron's Armored Cavalry severely embarrassed the Federated Suns then, and Hanse Davion returned the favor in the first part of his attack. How do you think that makes McCarron feel?"

Shang allowed himself a smile. "He's anxious to prove he's top dog again, and he wants revenge."

Justin lightly tapped the table with his metal fist. "Exactly." He glanced up at the Chancellor. "McCarron's always been a loose cannon. We've granted him duty on worlds that don't need protecting because it puts him in striking distance of worlds that do. Inefficient perhaps, but it works to keep a top-flight merc unit fighting for us at reduced rates.

"Well, this little action of McCarron's is on his own tab. He wanted to hurt the Federated Suns, and he was going to do something whether we gave him permission or not. I recognized this and cut him some marching orders."

The Chancellor's dark eyes half shut, then he nodded slowly. "I see the wisdom in your action. You guided a flood you knew you could not stop. Still, I would debate the wisdom of posting them on Palos. That world may produce the finest champagne in the Successor States, but it is not a military target worth defending."

"I agree, Universal Master. McCarron's Armored Cavalry is really on Sarna."

Justin's words shocked everyone in the room. The Maskirovka analyst slowly nodded his head in response to the unspoken question. "Yes, McCarron and I worked out a code. He is on Sarna, but his message says he is on Palos. That is where Hanse Davion's people will believe him to be. From Sarna, McCarron can hit any world Davion is likely to attack in his next wave."

Candace swiveled her chair around. "Do you believe there is a spy in our midst?"

Justin pursed his lips and thought for a moment before answering. "I don't know for certain, but I feel we are dealing with a traitor."

24

Shang's head came up. "Why?" His question, voiced without hostility, told Justin the same idea had been nibbling at the edges of his mind.

Justin straightened up. "The first thing that made me suspicious was how easily Pavel Ridzik seems to have eluded the assassin we sent to deal with him. She was perfect. She played to his libido and he stopped thinking. The bomb she used leveled half a block, but he'd already managed to escape the restaurant and the immediate vicinity. He had to have been warned, and his quick alliance with Hanse Davion suggests repayment of a debt."

Shang nodded in agreement. "The problem is that we had a long chain of agents working on that case. Any of them could have let the word slip."

Justin wavered. "Perhaps, but I think the leak comes from here in Sian. Davion might have learned Ridzik was to be hit by someone in a chain, but only a leak at the beginning would have given him the time to arrange for Ridzik's evacuation."

"Point taken." Shang looked up at the Chancellor, and Maximilian nodded.

Justin continued. "In addition to that incident, I got to thinking about what Michael Hasek-Davion claimed before he died. He said Hanse had been giving him false data. We discounted that idea because we knew Michael had given us less than 100 percent-reliable information. But what if he was telling the truth for once? Hanse would need someone inside the Maskirovka to make certain any good data we got was diverted while our reliance on Michael's information crippled us."

Romano sat forward like a cat readying to pounce. "Who? Who could it be?"

"It is easier, my Lady of Highspire, to tell you who I do *not* suspect." He glanced around the room. "I trust everyone here, and Alexi Malenkov, but no one else."

Candace stiffened. "Not even the Chancellor's wife?"

Justin hesitated. *Tsen, Alexi, and I know that Elizabeth Liao had an affair with Pavel Ridzik, but that information was to have gone no further.* A glance at Romano shook his confidence, but the expression on the Chancellor's face quickly drew all his attention. *What is going on?*

Pain and confusion fought for control of the Chancellor's countenance. "Leave her out of this. She will come back."

Romano twisted around. "Father, divorce her. Sentence her to Brazen Heart. You always forgive her when she deserts you, only to return penitent. Wash your hands of the slut!"

Maximilian Liao stiffened with anger, which seemed to infuse his body with life again. "I will not be lectured to by a spoiled whelp, Romano. I am the Chancellor of the Capellan Confederation! I have proved my worth to my nation over and over again! What I wish to forgive and forget concerning the woman I married after your mother died is my business. It is not a subject I choose to discuss with a petulant, landless noblewoman!"

Most others would have withered under Liao's harsh rebuke, but not Romano. She calmly blinked her green eyes at him, catlike as ever. She lowered herself to her place at his feet, but refrained from leaning against him.

Justin looked up at Liao's angry face. *If the Chancellor's wife has taken off again, we must find her. Prince Hanse Davion would have a field day with her defection.* He narrowed his eyes. *It will have to be suggested, but not here and not at this time. I'll put Alexi on it quietly.*

Tsen filled the awkward silence with a question. "What have you done about this traitor idea?"

"I've had Alexi double-checking some communications records, but it's a big job for just one person. I've been busy delivering Michael's body and preparing for Operation Intruders Communion."

Maximilian Liao closed his eyes like a sunning lion. "Tsen Shang, you will take over the investigation of the possible spy in our midst. He or she will be found and taken alive. I will have Davion's entire network on Sian."

"Yes, Celestial Wisdom." Shang nodded his head, then looked over at Romano as she tugged on his sleeve. The virulence in her eyes clearly shocked him. He tried to shake his head to divert her will, but she would have none of his reluctance.

Romano stared daggers at Justin. "This extravagant 'command circuit' you have created for your personal quest is using up far too much in the way of JumpShip resources. We cannot transport troops efficiently because of it. You are costing us this war."

Muscles bunched at the corners of Justin's jaw. *Bitch! Your games could prove very costly.* He drew in a deep breath to purge himself of rage, then exhaled slowly. "Your lack of sufficient foresight again betrays you, Lady of Highspire. We all realize a JumpShip must recharge for up to two weeks at a star before it can make one of its thirty-light-year jumps. Though this mode of transport is faster than any other we know, the recharging delays make the trip from Sian to Bethel longer than two months. At the current rate of Davion advances, that would put his troops here at the same time I completed my round trip."

Justin leaned forward over the table. "The command-circuit idea, created by Hanse Davion to facilitate the swift movement of troops, means we have a charged JumpShip waiting at a star to continue the next leg of the journey. That means the six-jump trip to Bethel can be completed inside three days."

Romano stared at Shang. Helplessly, Justin's partner turned to him. "No one denies the need for a command circuit to get you to Bethel, and the six JumpShips employed in it are well-used. What we have to ask"—he glanced at Romano—"is why you need eight ships to return by a different route. Those eight ships could be better spent ferrying troops to the front."

Justin smashed his steel fist into the table, cracking the table's black petrochem coating. "Come on people, get with the game here." Justin shook his head at Shang, whose face flushed with anger, then addressed himself to the Chancellor. "We have discussed the need for my speedy return by another route over and over again. Once Hanse Davion discovers we have successfully raided his secret base and have stolen the formula for the new, superstrength myomer muscles, he will stop at nothing to prevent my return to Sian. He might even order JumpShips destroyed!"

Even as he spoke the words, Justin felt an involuntary shiver run down his spine. *No one talks about destroying JumpShips, not even in jest. They are the pinnacle of lostech, desperately needed to speed men between the stars. Everyone knows that they can be repaired and even manufactured, but the science of what makes them work has been lost. Destroying a JumpShip would be a sacrilege!*

The horror of losing something that could not be replaced did not deflect Romano. "Not only do you tie up extra ships, now you tell us the ones you used may be destroyed." She looked up at her father. "This is a fool's mission." She stabbed a finger at Justin. "He beggars us just to exact his own revenge upon Hanse Davion."

Justin laughed harshly. "Your mind is too small to see the true depth of my feelings toward the Prince. Do you honestly think I will consider myself revenged because of a strike into the Federated Suns? No, Lady Highspire, not in your wildest dreams. I want the myomer fiber formula so we can transform our current 'Mechs into an unbeatable force. The new fibers will triple our 'Mech strength. The new muscles will allow our 'Mechs to carry more armor and weaponry. With these new machines, we'll be able to stop the Davion advance, crush Ridzik's fledgling nation, and force the invaders back into their own territory." He smiled at the Chancellor. "Deep into their own territory."

Romano frowned suspiciously. "If these myomer fibers are so

powerful, and far enough along in development for us to steal them, why doesn't Hanse Davion equip some of his own BattleMechs with them? How do we even know they exist?"

Justin's smile did not waver for an instant. "The myomer project was a hobby for Professor-General Sam Lewis. He used to like to talk about it with MechWarriors and even mentioned it in a commencement address at Sakhara Academy five years ago, but no one ever took him seriously. After all, the man's known for Kearny-Fuchida drive research, not myomer fiber work. People figured he was talking about advances we might see someday, yet rumors of strange new fibers were always running through the Armed Forces of the Federated Suns during my tour with them.

Justin looked up at the Chancellor. "One of the few positive things to come out of our January counterstrike was the discovery of information on the planet Axton. That information included the location of a secret NAIS outpost on Bethel, where Lewis was also reported present. Once the war began, Lewis was called back from Bethel to New Avalon Institute of Science to supervise some new work with the Kearny-Fuchida drive research project to help minimize ship losses in the fighting.

"After he left Bethel, Davion security at the base relaxed considerably. I activated a deep-cover agent we had in place, and he learned that one of Lewis's assistants had continued to play around with the myomer project even though he'd shifted to other duty. He has achieved a breakthrough that strengthens the pseudo-muscle fibers, but hasn't been able to communicate this to Lewis because of the heavy security surrounding the Professor. What it means is that Hanse Davion and his people don't yet realize what they've got, and that's why we must act quickly. The time to strike is now!"

Romano started to protest, but Maximilian Liao raised his hand to silence his daughter. "We will have no more discussion of this. The plans have been made and will not be changed at this point. When do you leave?"

Justin licked his lips. "In the morning. We'll jump a week from now and be back ten days after that. Within a fortnight, you will see the genesis of a new 'Mech race—a race of giants under your control."

Shang looked up. "Justin, you'll be pleased to know we finally got word concerning the force you'll face on Bethel. It's the Davion Light Guards First Regiment, Delta Company."

A predatory grin spread over Justin's face. "Still commanded by Andrew Redburn and built from those whelps in the training battalion I left behind?'

Shang nodded.

"Excellent!" Justin rubbed his right palm over the cold metallic knuckles of his left hand. "More than one debt can be repaid on this mission."

The Chancellor, his fatigue banished, smiled like a vulture. "The pride of the Confederation goes with you, Citizen Xiang. You will not know defeat."

5

Sian
Sian Commonality, Capellan Confederation
20 March 3029

Deep within a quiet woodland hollow, Justin Xiang mirrored Candace Liao's series of *t'ai chi chuan* exercises. The slight breeze whispering through the venerable pines was just enough to mask the noises of civilization from the palace complex two kilometers to the south. Only a few of the dying sun's rays stabbed through the labyrinth of tree trunks, and those that did splashed coppery highlights on the sweaty flesh.

Perspiration burned into Justin's eyes, and weariness filled his muscles with fire, but he refused to call a halt to the exercises. *It's been only a year and a half since Candace started practicing* t'ai chi, *but it has calmed her and given her so much grace.*

He glanced at her left shoulder. Several strings of white scars puckered the ruined flesh over her deltoid muscle, which Justin knew was more myomer than natural. *Thirteen years ago, she'd injured that arm ejecting from a badly damaged* Vindicator. *She's worked hard to repair it, and now it's almost returned to a normal range of motion.*

Candace drew her limbs together, letting her hands hang at her side, and bowed to Justin. "I can continue no more."

Justin returned her bow somewhat less gracefully. "Forgive me. I was daydreaming, and it spoiled my concentration."

Candace knelt on the carpet of rust-colored pine needles and pulled two white towels from a tan canvas bag. She offered one to Justin. "What were you thinking?"

30

Justin shrugged as he wiped the sweat from his face. "I was reminded of old folktales in which a wound would not heal unless the person who inflicted it wished it so." He glanced at her shoulder.

She nodded thoughtfully. "And have you wished my shoulder to be whole?"

"Yes, and my wish is coming true." Justin hung the towel around his neck and held on to each end with a hand.

Candace looked up at him. "What about your arm? Has the person who inflicted that wound wished it to be healed?"

Justin shook his head slightly. He held out the blackened steel arm for inspection. From his elbow down, its form closely matched the flesh-and-blood limb it was meant to replace, but the cold lifelessness mocked its mission. Concentrating, Justin opened the hand and rotated it around in a wrist-roll.

"I'm afraid the man who did this can no longer wish anything whole." Justin's metal hand snapped shut into a fist. "My metal friend exacted its own revenge when I learned who had maimed me."

Candace shuddered slightly. "Perhaps I asked the question incorrectly. I meant to ask about the scar you carry around on the inside. There are times I think your hatred of Hanse Davion will consume you, and I do not want that to happen."

What are you saying? Justin frowned. "Do you not want me to raid Bethel?"

Candace reached up and drew Justin down beside her. She took both his hands in hers. "We can both see the effects of unbridled hatred in my sister, Romano. It has infected her and made her malignant. I understand and share your anger at the Prince for the injustices he allowed against you. I understand your desire to embarrass and humble him."

Justin stiffened. "Do you really understand it all, Candace? Do you know everything? Did you know that while I was on Solaris, he had my father arrange for one of his spies to become my lover? Did you know she sent reports on everything I did? Did you know Prince Hanse Davion offered a man a title, a regiment, and a world to kill me in the games on Solaris?"

Justin stood abruptly and stalked a few steps away from her. "What do I feel for the Prince? I hurt from betrayal. I did everything I could for him, just as I do everything I can now for the Capellan Confederation. He forced me away from my family. He stole my name, my dignity, my livelihood, and my self-respect." Justin spun back. "I had always thought, foolishly perhaps, that I made a difference, that I counted for something."

Justin shook his head. "In a split second, the Prince showed me I was nothing. I was insignificant. In a fit of pique, he destroyed me." Justin looked at his left hand and chuckled. "At that time, I had no control over this limb. And that's what prevented me from slitting my other wrist—I couldn't hold a razor blade steady enough to do the job."

He stared hard at Candace. "Do you think the Prince could ever wish that wound healed?"

Candace stood, her eyes flashing silver. "If he did, would you let it heal? If he held a hand out in friendship, would you take it?"

His face shrouded in shadow, Justin stared at her. His voice dropped to a deadly whisper. "No games, Candace. Say what you mean."

Candace folded her arms across her chest. "For all your brave talk about how this Bethel raid will seize technology that will make our forces the masters of the battlefield, you know that's unlikely. You want to embarrass Hanse Davion by hitting a base he believes is hidden away. I understand that, and I applaud it. A strike into his territory will bring the war home to his people. That's good! They need to understand this is more than staged battles on Solaris. And perhaps this new myomer fiber will make our dwindling supply of 'Mechs better able to hold what we have left."

Justin exhaled slowly. "Be wary, Duchess, for you skate along the edge of treason."

Her laughter was harsh. "Do I? Is it treason to see the future and adapt to it? You know as well as I that we will never gain back even a tenth of what we have lost. Tikonov is gone forever, and with it, goes some of our most important 'Mech production facilities. The future's not written in crabbed handwriting on the wall. The Prince has made his message clear in two-meter-high, glowing holographic letters: The Capellan Confederation must die!"

Justin hung his head heavily. "What you say is true. Though my anger at Hanse Davion fills my eyes with a bloody red haze, it does not make me blind. You have drawn a plan of action from your analysis?"

Candace nodded. "In the storage area beneath your 'Mech's command couch, you will find a holodisk on which I have recorded a message for the Prince. I inquire as to what terms he would like for our surrender."

"Surrender." Justin spoke the word as though it were something sour in his mouth. "There are those who would consider this an act of high treason and would see you punished for it."

Candace lifted her head. "If they want to say it is treason to desire safety for my people, I am guilty. If they want to say it is treason to

32

preserve something of the Capellan Confederation, I am guilty. The question is, are you one of those who would see me punished for this action?"

Justin swallowed hard. "I am not as inhuman as this prosthesis might suggest, and well you know that. On an intellectual level, I know you are correct. On an emotional level, my love for you and my loathing of Hanse Davion do battle. If it is your desire, I will take Hanse Davion's hand whenever he extends it to me. Until that time, however, he is my sworn enemy."

Justin reached out to her, and she came to him. "I will leave your holodisc in the Bethel facility. After we've raped the Prince's research base, though, I would not venture a guess about his reaction."

He kissed her on the forehead. "As for any hint of treason, do not worry yourself. In my mind, your fate and that of the Capellan Confederation are inexorably linked. I accept as my sacred duty the safeguarding of both." *I will keep you safe from all adversaries, my love, but who will protect me?*

6

Romano Liao glanced at Tsen Shang's reflection in her vanity table mirror as he entered her bedroom. "So, did you see him off?" Her sing-song voice for once seemed to carry neither challenge nor edge to it.

Tsen nodded. "I just returned from the spaceport."

"And was my sister there as well?"

"Yes. She almost went out to be with him on the JumpShip until they left the system."

I'll bet she did. She's become positively domesticated since she started sleeping with Xiang. I doubt she knows a war is on. Romano smiled at Tsen, then dabbed gloss onto her lips with the tip of her little finger. "Why did she choose to stay planetside?"

Tsen shrugged as he dropped into a Louis XIV chair set against the pale green wall behind her. "I think Justin asked her to stay here. He said none of the others on the raid would have their paramours with them and it might cause trouble."

Of course, she listened to Justin. He must know some special tricks with that metal hand of his... "Why is it, Tsen darling, that everyone does what this renegade from the Federated Suns tells them to do?"

Tsen frowned. "I don't understand you."

Romano scowled for a moment, then composed a more kindly expression as she turned to face her lover. "You and I have discussed the wastefulness of Xiang's return command circuit. You agreed with

34

me that those JumpShips could be employed more usefully elsewhere. You told me they could have been used to move troops up to retake Highspire. Yet you did not fight him in the meeting yesterday. What power does he have over you?"

Tsen stiffened. "He has no power over me."

Sarcasm set off on every syllable of Romano's riposte. "Doesn't he? You were upset that Justin had given orders to McCarron's Armored Cavalry, but your protest died. You should have seen yourself. You glowed as Justin asked you questions and you answered them correctly. You performed tricks like a trained ape."

"No!" Tsen shook his head violently. "You don't understand. Justin's plan is a good one. His reasons for needing the extra JumpShips are valid. His orders for McCarron's Armored Cavalry made sense. Justin thinks his plans through—there is very little for me to protest."

Romano gave a lilting laugh. "How foolish you are, my dearest, to believe I do not see what Justin is doing to you. You believe he keeps you around because he needs your help, and you believe you owe him because he prevented my father from having you shot after your plan led us into Hanse Davion's trap." She paused as Tsen's shame burned on his face.

Romano smiled like a mother showing sympathy for a child's scraped knee. "Lover, you must see this as well. You coordinate a massive operation—a task that is difficult in and of itself—and it meets with disaster. Justin Xiang sends a raid off to a nothing planet and claims a great victory. He also arranged the assassination attempt on Pavel Ridzik, but it failed and he now blames Davion spies for it. You live within your shame, but he refuses to let any errors spot his record."

Tsen stared at the carpeted floor. "What are you saying, my lady?"

"I am saying that Justin is using you to make himself look better. You must show initiative." As Tsen's head came up, she saw the gleam of an idea in his eyes. "What? What have you got, my love?"

Tsen Shang smiled easily. "I will find that spy and deliver his head to your father..." Tsen's voice trailed off, his smile dying as Romano frowned darkly.

"No, Tsen. You think in terms that are far too small!" She reached back onto her vanity, grabbed a cut-glass bottle of perfume and hurled it at him. It exploded against the wall behind him, splashing him with musk and glass slivers. "What difference will a measly spy make? What is one spy when Xiang claims the salvation of the Capellan Confederation? You need a bold stroke to eclipse his glory!"

Tsen hung his head. "There is nothing that I could plan."

"Ha!" Romano lanced Tsen with a stare like cold malachite. "You yourself told me that JumpShips are crucial for a war. That's exactly the reason Xiang's plan is wasteful. Why not cripple the Federated Suns' JumpShip fleet? Why not strike at the Kathil shipyards?"

Tsen looked at her with utter disbelief. "That's impossible!"

Show me spine. Prove your worth to me now, or you'll end up sharing the hole where I've had my father's wife planted. She narrowed her eyes. "Impossible? What would Justin Xiang say to that plan? Would he say impossible? Would any man say impossible?" She stood and let her silken gown slip from her body... "Perhaps I should just seduce Justin Xiang and forget about you..."

Tsen shot to his feet, dark eyes blazing with fury. "No!" He half-turned, slashing the satiny upholstery of the chair into ribbons with the nails on his right hand. "I am not to be cast aside that easily, Romano."

She watched him, knowing better than to comment. *I have seen him like this before. He fought within himself the same way on the night when he told me—in direct conflict with an order Justin had given him—that the whore my father called a wife was rutting with Pavel Ridzik. That weakened his loyalty to Xiang, and now it will be broken. My father gets Maskirovka reports from Xiang, and now I will get mine from Tsen Shang.*

Tsen's head came up slowly. "It is possible for an attack to be arranged on the Kathil shipyards. I will need to plan it alone so the spy in the Maskirovka will not learn about it."

Romano nodded as he spoke. "Yes, and reveal the plan to my father at a point when no one could get word out in time to warn the Prince."

Tsen chewed his lower lip. "That will mean we must have a command circuit going to Kathil. If the troops move by conventional means, they'll arrive too slowly."

Romano stepped toward him. "No matter. We can divert some of the JumpShips from Xiang's circuit after he has used them. Instead of calling them back, we'll post them to new positions."

Tsen smiled. "And we will need crack troops."

Her breath coming quickly, Romano whispered, "We'll have the best. I'll order my father's Death Commandos to carry out your strike." She reached out and wrapped her arms around Tsen's waist.

Lost in thought, Tsen's eyes nearly closed. "It may just work."

She pulled him close and pressed her body against his. "It will work, lover. With this victory, you will ascend to your rightful place within the Maskirovka." Stroking his hair, she glanced over his shoulder and smiled confidently at her own reflection in the mirror.

7

Captain Daniel Allard gratefully accepted the actuator wrench from the dwarf standing just inside the 'Mech bay. "Thanks, Clovis. The only time I need one of these things is when I can't find one." Dan used his forearm to wipe away the sweat pasting light brown curls to his forehead, then used the crescent-shaped tool to hook a myomer muscle into a BattleMech's finger joint. "Yeah, that fixes it. Better making repairs now than in combat."

Clovis's brown eyes twinkled as he lifted himself onto a crate and sat eye to eye with the MechWarrior. From behind his back, he produced a cold bottle of beer and handed it to Allard. "This is just one of the ways I can think of to repay the Kell Hounds for helping us out." Clovis looked out across an open field of ochre grasses toward where the Kell Hound MechWarriors were working. "Styx was the first time I'd seen 'Mechs in action. Somehow, here, the machines don't seem the same."

Dan nodded. *MechWarriors are trained to think of their machines as destroyers. "Ten meters tall and full of nasty" is how I remember one instructor describing them. It takes someone with Morgan Kell's vision to see this use for a 'Mech.*

Out across the field, the humanoid war machines worked amid a boxy lattice of steel girders. In the distance, they almost looked like robot children laboring to build a secret clubhouse, yet Dan knew the structure rose two full stories above the plain. Lasers normally used to pierce and destroy other BattleMechs had been powered down so they could be used to weld the metal beams in place. *After what we just did to the* Genyosha *base on Nashira, watching the 'Mechs build the town of New Freedom for the Styx refugees seems ironic.*

Clovis raked a stubby-fingered hand back through his long black hair. "Getting all these buildings constructed would have taken us many months and would have cost lots of ComStar bills. This is amazing."

Dan nodded, then gulped down some more beer. "You and your mother drove a hard bargain, Clovis. We get access to the *Bifrost* so it can jump us around, and you get a city."

Clovis raised an eyebrow. "You know as well as I do that Morgan might have argued for more if Duke Aldo Lestrade hadn't tried to throw us off this planet. He gave us two months to try to improve the site, but I doubt he expected much. And here we are, almost finished, and it's two weeks ahead of his deadline."

Dan nodded. "You're right—Morgan would do just about anything to irk Lestrade." *Aldo Lestrade's meddling in Lyran Commonwealth politics had caused plenty of trouble. His attempted assassinations of Archon Katrina Steiner had failed, but his last attempt to ruin the alliance between the Lyran Commonwealth and the Federated Suns nearly killed Melissa Steiner. It also cost Morgan his brother Patrick.*

Dan took another long drink. The cool liquid vanquished his thirst and reminded him of things more sociable than Lyran politics. Lowering the bottle, he fixed Clovis with a mischievous stare. "Clovis, have you asked Karla Bremen to the dance next weekend?"

The little man stiffened, then shook his head. "No."

Dan frowned. "Blake's Blood! You've done nothing but moon over her ever since you heard she'd broken up with that guy...what was his name?"

Clovis picked up the actuator wrench and turned it over in his small hands. "Thor. His name was Thor."

The image of a huge man flashed through Dan's mind as Clovis spoke. "Yeah, that was it. Well, why don't you ask her?"

The dwarf looked down. "She'd not go with me. She doesn't even know I exist."

Dan drank more beer, then set the half-empty bottle down on the crate beside Clovis. "That's not true, and you know it. I saw you talking with her the other day. She was smiling and laughing."

Clovis's face darkened. He carelessly drummed the steel wrench against the wooden crate, splintering off little pieces of it. "Yeah, we spoke. She wants me to show the children in her classes how to work computers. Show-and-tell-computer time. Nothing big or special."

Dan scowled. *Something's going on here. I've never seen Clovis so morose.* "I don't know, Clovis. If I were you, I'd capitalize on that opportunity…"

The dwarf's long black hair fell forward as he nodded his head. "I have. I agreed to teach the kids…"

Dan shook his head. "You don't understand. I mean you should ask her to the dance." He cocked his head at his friend. "If you don't, I just might. Maybe I'll even act like a jerk and let you rescue her…"

Clovis's brown eyes blazed with anger. "You don't get it, do you? I could no more rescue her from you than I could fly without wings. She'd prefer you, even being a jerk—which I don't think you could manage—to a half-man."

"Clovis, I'm sorry," Dan said. "I didn't mean to hurt you. I just hate to see you feeling low. The worst she could do is say no."

Muscles bunched at the corners of Clovis's jaw. "I know you meant well, Dan, but I just don't want to talk about it. It's not so bad for you because you know someone special like your Jeana will say 'yes' someday." He glanced down at the hole he'd chopped into the crate. "I don't know that."

At Clovis's mention of her name, Dan's hand strayed to the meter-long strip of green silk tucked into his belt. "Jeana is special to me, Clovis, but she might not be to someone else. More women have been special to me than I ever was to them, and you'll be special to someone, too. But you'll never find out who she is until you open up and take a chance."

Clovis shot Dan a sidelong glance. "Bet you wouldn't set me up with your sister Riva, would you?"

Dan grinned broadly. "Got a couple of ComStar bills? I'll send a message out to her now to come get you." Both men chuckled over the idea of Riva Allard traveling for months to reach Lyons for a date, but their laughter died as two of the Kell Hound infantrymen approached them with a visitor in tow.

"Captain Allard?"

"Yes, Sullivan, what is it?" Dan looked at the yellow-robed visitor and narrowed his eyes. *What is a ComStar Acolyte doing here?*

Sullivan's expression did not hide his irritation. "Sir, I explained to the Acolyte that he could just leave his holodisk with us and we'd see it would get to Colonel Kell, but he insisted…"

Dan nodded understanding. "You and Murphy can return to your posts. I'll take care of our guest." He turned to the Acolyte. "What can

I do for you?"

The pinch-faced man narrowed his eyes. "I must see Colonel Kell. I have a message for him."

"Indeed." Dan glanced at Clovis and admired his manly effort to keep from laughing out loud. "Corporal Sullivan said you had a holodisk."

The Acolyte scowled. "Whatever it is, it is for Colonel Kell, and for him alone. Those are my orders. Such were the wishes of the person sending…"

"And paying for…" quipped Clovis.

"…the message." The Acolyte glowered at Clovis, who merely ignored him.

Dan frowned. "If you insist, I can call the Colonel in."

The Acolyte nodded curtly, so Dan picked up Clovis's radio from a crate and keyed in to Morgan Kell's 'Mech. "Dan here. Sorry to interrupt, Colonel, but we've a messenger from ComStar. He's got a holodisk for you and refuses to release it to anyone else."

Static hissed through the radio's speakers for half a second before Morgan Kell's deep voice replaced it. "What's your read, Dan?"

Dan raked the Acolyte over with an openly appraising glance. "He seems to fit, but I'm uneasy about this message. I'd bet on it being bad news instead of good."

"I'll head in. Can you round up the staff?"

Dan frowned. "Conn and Second 'Mech Battalion are still over at the quarry. It would take them two hours to get here. Salome and Cat are there in the work group with you. Scott Bradley's here in the bay."

"Good. Get them. Have Clovis join us as well."

"Roger, Colonel. Out." Dan grinned at the Acolyte and pointed toward the construction site. "If you want to walk out and meet him…"

The Acolyte took two steps toward the bay opening, then stopped short. He shook his head, nervously stuttering through his words. "N-no, n-not necessary."

Dan laughed. Coming at a dead run across the field, the thunderous steps of Morgan's *Archer* sent heavy tremors through the ground. The titanic 'Mech swung its ponderous fists as a man might, but the I-beam clutched forgotten in the left hand was eloquent witness to the machine's incredible strength. The hunched shoulders and forward thrusting head gave the *Archer* a bestial look even more threatening than its sheer size.

Dan slapped the stricken Acolyte on the shoulder. "Hope this is worth it, buckaroo, because the Colonel…well, he doesn't like disappointments."

40

Dan watched Morgan Kell slip the holodisk into the player. *On a scale of 1 to 16, Morgan's anger ranks about a 32*, he thought. Dan could tell Kell didn't appreciate the Acolyte's antics, especially when he learned the message was from Aldo Lestrade.

Seated against the back wall, Dan had a full view of the rectangular briefing room. A long table filled it, and twelve chairs surrounded the table. The four other people at the meeting had seated themselves near the middle of the oaken table, and all faced the far end of the room where Morgan fiddled with the holodisk viewer.

Morgan straightened up to his full height and forced his anger out with a deep breath. His cooling vest and shorts revealed a muscular body that was relatively unscarred for a MechWarrior his age. Kell's long black hair and thick beard were shot with gray, but only enough to give him an air of nobility. His dark brown eyes sparkled with a vitality that seemed to promise this man could live forever.

Morgan smiled at the officers present. "Forgive the theatrics of calling you from the field for this. The ComStar Acolyte's actions suggested it might be important. Even though the message is from Aldo Lestrade, it might have some value. In any event, I would apprise all of you of its contents in the end, so we might as well share the shock together."

Morgan hit a button on the disc player's remote control. The black screen lightened to reveal the simple rectangular crest of the world of Summer, then dissolved to a picture of a rotund little man seated behind a massive desk. His salt-and-pepper hair lay flat on his head like a bad toupee and did not move as he patted it into place with his plastic left hand. Lestrade stared intently into the camera,

"Colonel Kell, I will dispense with all pleasantries because I know you would find them fatuous. We do not like each other, and I am content to maintain our relationship at the distance this mutual hatred engenders."

Lestrade leaned back in his high backed leather chair. "It has come to my attention that you and your mercenary unit have taken up residence on my world of Lyons. I understand that you are staying in the refugee colony the Archon encouraged me to permit on that world." His choice of words and manner of speaking left Dan no doubt that Lestrade did not like the Styx colony at all, and only permitted it because of pressure from the Commonwealth's Archon, Katrina Steiner.

The camera pulled back to reveal more of Lestrade's office. The walls were made of unfinished gray stones that appeared to have been put together in an almost haphazard manner. Dan squinted at the image. *That must be the Lestrade castle. Wasn't it moved stone by stone from Terra about five hundred years ago? I'm surprised to see it's survived the Kurita raids Lestrade is always complaining about.*

Lestrade left his seat and limped around to the front of his desk. "Though I can appreciate your desire to return behind the lines after a raid deep into the Draconis Combine, I do not want you on any of my worlds. The Archon may have appropriated my troops to fight Hanse Davion's war against the Draconis Combine, but I want no part of the war. You and your Kell Hounds are a threat to the peace and well-being of the Isle of Skye. I hereby order you to leave it."

The camera moved in as Lestrade graced the viewers with a plastic smile. "I can appreciate the time it might take for you to move a mercenary unit. You have two weeks from the receipt of this message to be gone from the Isle of Skye. Have I made myself clear?"

Morgan shut off the viewer as the screen faded to black. He turned in his seat and leaned forward over the table. "Disgustingly frank for Lestrade..." he said. "Well, he says we've got to get off Lyons in two weeks. Comments? Salome."

Morgan's flame-haired second in command, Major Salome Ward, looked around at the small group. "Since all the troops have left Lyons for the attack into the Draconis Combine, our departure would leave the planet defenseless. I realize that Lyons seems far behind the lines, but just one 'Mech battalion jumping in from an uninhabited star could wreak havoc."

Major Scott Bradley, the dark-haired MechWarrior seated across the table from Salome, frowned. "Why hit Lyons?" He smiled apologetically at Clovis. "Not to run down your new home, but the object of modern warfare is to destroy the enemy's ability to wage war. Lyons, in that sense, is not a military target. Were the Combine able to spare troops for raid, then this world's agro and water supply might make it a target, but I think the Combine has some other worries."

Morgan nodded. "I agree with you, Scott, that the Combine has other problems, especially in the Rasalhague District, but the Lyran offensive's punch down in the area came just slightly rimward of here. I would not consider the Isle of Skye's border at all secure. If the Combine wished, it could come through here, then swing out to trap troops in a pocket centered on Marfik."

Dan shook his head. "What troops does the Dragon have to perform such a maneuver? Most of the Dieron Military District's troops, including the *Genyosha*, made that assault on the Terran

Corridor and got pushed back."

"True, but Davion has not attacked into the Dieron District to pin down those troops. For all we know, they're massing on Yorii or Imbros III for a strike at Lyons." Morgan looked over at the black man seated between Salome and Dan. "What do you think, Cat?"

Cat Wilson knit his fingers together and rested his hands like a cap on top of his shaved head. "I think I don't trust Lestrade as far as I could throw this planet. He thinks he's got an ace up his sleeve somewhere. His wanting us out of Lyons could be a simple move to reassure Kurita that he, Lestrade, is not part of the war. As much as the man is a lying, scheming, power-hungry sycophant, we should remember that a Kurita raid cost him his left arm and left leg. I doubt that the idea of another Kurita assault on his holdings appeals to him."

"Point well taken." Morgan looked past Scott Bradley toward Clovis. "You're the mayor of New Freedom. What do you think?"

The dwarf smiled affably. "Remember, I'm only the acting mayor. Once my mother stops running you around in the *Bifrost*, she'll take over again." Clovis glanced at Cat. "My mother has told me stories of the raid in which Lestrade lost his arm and leg. She used to work in the castle on Summer and had to flee for her life during that raid. From what she's said, Lestrade probably murdered his father, and almost certainly arranged the accidents that killed all his siblings so he would inherit the throne. That doesn't offer much of a recommendation for his character, but I'd have to side with Cat. I don't think Lestrade would want a raid from the Combine in the Isle of Skye. And even if he did, why Lyons? It would make no sense."

Clovis looked back at Morgan. "Isn't this something of a moot point? You were going to be leaving Lyons within the month anyway. Right?"

Morgan nodded. "That's our plan. We've got a meeting scheduled for Ryde at the beginning of June. Whether or not we would have left Lyons on our own, part of me hates to appear to be following Lestrade's order. I suppose it can't be helped in this case. We cannot afford to be late arriving on Ryde."

Dan clenched his teeth. *Morgan calls it a meeting, but all of us know what it really will be. Morgan and Yorinaga Kurita will once again do battle to determine who between them will live or die. While this war engulfs all the Successor States, Morgan Kell and Yorinaga Kurita are also holding their own little war. Were Morgan not preoccupied with—hell, obsessed with—his private conflict, he'd drop the Kell Hounds in on Aldo Lestrade just to deliver an answer to that madman's order.*

"So, we'll get the Kell Hounds out of here on time, just to keep Lestrade happy," Morgan went on, his countenance darkening. "But if our compliance plays into one of Lestrade's schemes, I swear the Kell Hounds will make the Duke regret it for what little of his life he'll have left."

8

Tharkad
District of Donegal, Lyran Commonwealth
20 April 3029

Jeana Clay hit the pause button on the holodisk recorder as she turned toward the door. The instant the Archon entered, Jeana rose from her chair and crossed the room quickly. Before the guards had closed the door, she threw her arms around Katrina Steiner. "Hello, mother. How good to see you today."

Jeana's voice—a perfect match for that of Melissa Steiner-Davion—did not betray her unease. *Why has the Archon come to my chambers? Has something happened to Melissa?* Jeana pulled back from the tall, platinum-haired matriarch and gave her a respectful bow. "Forgive me, Archon, but I did not expect you."

The gray-eyed woman smiled easily and waved Jeana back toward her chair as she seated herself on the edge of the bed. "There is no emergency. Don't be alarmed. According to the holodisk I received this morning from the Federated Suns, Melissa is well."

Jeana caught a glimpse of her own reflection in the mirror on the closet door. The long golden hair and carefully sculpted features matched Melissa's face in all details. The gray eyes, given to Melissa by genetics and Jeana by contact lenses, stared back at her from the mirror. *I wonder if I'll ever get used to wearing another's face.*

Jeana turned to the Archon. "Is Melissa pregnant yet?"

Katrina Steiner shook her head. "No, you are not pregnant yet." They laughed together, but the Archon's smile turned pensive. "Your look, your manner, your laugh. There are times when I think you and

Melissa conspired to switch places and fool all of us."

Jeana shook her head. "No, Archon. Your daughter has been with her husband since we left Terra after the wedding."

Katrina looked fondly at Jeana. "I had a message from Morgan Kell today. He says the Kell Hounds have been ordered off Lyons and will be proceeding to Ryde. If I read between the lines correctly, he thought you would be interested in this information. He also said to tell you, 'The Sanglamore Sash has kept Dan quite safe.'"

Jeana felt her heart leap. *Please, God, let it continue to do so*. She looked up at the Archon, then blushed. "I gave Dan Allard the sash I got when I passed my final 'Mech test at Sanglamore …"

Katrina Steiner nodded knowingly. "I noticed you were quite taken with him during the festivities before the wedding. I know we're not really mother and daughter, but I also realize you've got no one to talk to about such matters. If you wish…"

Jeana smiled. *My father was right to help you escape Alessandro Steiner's trap so many years ago. You actually do care about your people.* "It is difficult." She pressed her lips together into a think-line. "I wanted very much to tell Dan who I was and what I did, but I could not violate security like that. If people knew your daughter was in the Federated Suns, your political enemies could accuse you of selling out the Commonwealth to Hanse Davion."

Jeana looked up into the Archon's steel-gray eyes. "What makes Dan so remarkable is that he did not press me on the subject. He just wanted to know if I was happy, and if so, he said that was enough for him. I know it's crazy because we've had so little time together, but it seems like I've known him all my life."

"You love him very much, don't you?" Katrina asked softly.

Jeana nodded. "I remember the first reception on Terra. It seems like we danced forever. He was so gentle, yet so strong." Jeana covered her mouth to smother a giggle. "Archon, I don't know if you've noticed, but all MechWarriors from the Federated Suns wear ceremonial spurs on their boots. They're just small things, with no rowls, and are said to recall the old days when cavalry troops moved quickly and hit hard— just like 'Mech regiments."

The Archon laughed. "Silly superstition. Just like a Sanglamore Sash, right?"

Jeana blushed. "Touché, Highness. Anyway, while Dan and I were dancing, the hem of my gown caught on a spur during a turn. I began to stumble, but Dan managed to lift me up and continue the dance without so much as losing a beat of the music. Then he spent the next minute or two apologizing for his clumsiness in getting his spur caught. Not often you find strength, agility, intelligence, and consideration wrapped up in so handsome a package."

The Archon nodded. "And in a MechWarrior, even more rare." Katrina stared off over Jeana's shoulder. "It does not surprise me that Morgan selected him to join the Kell Hounds."

Jeana noticed a change in the Archon's voice. "What's wrong? Forgive my presumption, but you seem apprehensive."

Katrina Steiner raised an eyebrow. "You have my daughter's perceptiveness as well as her face. I am worried...about Morgan. He left the monastery on Zaniah when he learned Yorinaga Kurita had returned from exile and killed his brother, Patrick. I think Morgan's preoccupation with Yorinaga may be clouding his judgment."

Jeana chewed her lower lip. "It almost sounds as though Morgan is engaging in a vendetta like a Leutnant fresh out of Sanglamore or Nagelring."

Katrina rose and moved to the doors leading out to the balcony overlooking the Triad's garden. "I've known Morgan Kell for twenty-three years. Morgan was there with me and my future husband, Arthur Luvon, when your father whisked the three of us to safety. Morgan, Arthur, and I traveled a long way and saw many things in the year we spent running from Alessandro Steiner's assassins.

"I learned a great deal about Morgan in that time. He might have been considered reckless and daring, but he was never one who wanted to engage in personal competition with an enemy. Morgan was more the type to fight as hard as he could, then offer the winner or loser his hand in friendship and respect. You're a MechWarrior just as I was. You know what I'm talking about, don't you?"

Jeana rose from her chair and walked over to the Archon. She slipped her arm around the other woman's shoulder and gave her a hug. "Yes, I've seen MechWarriors like that, and I've the utmost respect for them. Still, Morgan changed after Mallory's World back in 3016. He quit the regiment he and Patrick created, scattered all but a battalion of the Kell Hounds, and then retreated to a monastery for eleven years. That's not at all like the Morgan you describe."

Katrina nodded wearily. "I think that's what scares me so. If Morgan were merely acting like a kid, trying to prove how tough he is at his age, I'd sponsor him in the games on Solaris. The problem is that Morgan's not acting like a kid. Everything—his return, reforming the regiment—seems directed at a final confrontation with Yorinaga Kurita." Katrina looked at Jeana with tears beginning to well in her eyes. "I think Morgan knows exactly what he's doing, and I think it will kill him."

Jeana hugged Katrina more tightly. "No one wants to see a friend heading toward disaster and not be able to do something about it."

The Archon shook her head. "I guess I'm just being too selfish. Morgan and Patrick used to remind me so much of Arthur that I could see his spirit living on in them. The Kell Hounds, the name of their unit, was the name Arthur used to call the two of them as kids. They used the name in his memory." Katrina swallowed hard. "If I lose Morgan, then I'll have nothing left of my husband."

"But you always have your daughter, Highness. Think how proud your husband would have been of Melissa, and how he would have applauded her marriage to Hanse Davion."

Katrina drew a handkerchief from her pocket and dried her tears. "Thank you for reminding me of that and for enduring so much in your role as Melissa. You serve the Commonwealth well."

Jeana bowed deeply. "You honor me more than you know."

Katrina took Jeana's hand. "You may not be my daughter, but I don't think I could have spoken as openly even to her. Thank you even more for your friendship, Jeana."

A quick knock at the door preceded its opening by half a second. A tall, black-haired young woman poked in her head with a smile. "Mel, do you still want to go…Oh, Archon, forgive me. I…"

Katrina smiled warmly. "It's all right, Misha. Melissa and I were just chatting about the difficulties of being parted from one you love."

"Speaking of which, my friend," Jeana said teasingly, "have you heard from your Captain Redburn?"

Misha swung the door shut behind her, then crossed and sat on the bed. "I received a holodisk from him that's two months old. The Federated Suns military censors let most of the message get through. He sounds healthy enough. He's in a new 'Mech—I gather from vague references that it's a captured Liao *Centurion*…"

Jeana sat down next to Melissa Steiner's closest friend and took Misha's right hand into her own. "What happened to his old 'Mech?"

Misha shrugged. "I'm not sure, but sifting through the press releases and stories coming from the Liao front, I gather he lost it on St. Andre in the first wave of assaults. I've seen hints about a training battalion that has proved to be very effective as a strike force. Putting that together with some things Andy said before the war started, that must be his unit."

Katrina narrowed her eyes. "I think I may recommend that Simon Johnson of the Lyran Intelligence Corps put you to work breaking down Kurita intelligence, or maybe seeing what you can glean from the information we make public. I daresay Quintus Allard would be alarmed to hear what you've deduced about the Davion war effort."

Jeana gave Misha one of Melissa's smiles. "Mother, you've dealt with Misha's father long enough to know it's impossible to keep a secret from someone in the Auburn family. Court historians extraordinaire!" She patted Misha's hand. "The Auburns are the only thing that keep us Steiners honest."

Misha smiled. "True enough." She looked up at the Archon. "If you think I could be of use in the LIC, I'd be happy to assist, but I'm not sure I want to work with Simon Johnson. That spymaster is so tricky. I always feel I cannot trust anything he says."

Katrina nodded. "We'll save you as our secret weapon then. In the meantime, I'm interested in your thoughts and theories about Kurita. Keep me posted."

Misha smiled. "I promise, Highness."

The Archon moved to the door. "I'll let you two get on with whatever you had planned for this afternoon." She held her hand out to Jeana and drew her daughter's double into a hug. "Have fun, Melissa. And thank you for our chat. It was just like old times."

9

Furillo
Bolan Province, Lyran Commonwealth
25 April 3029

"The question is, Ryan Steiner, do you want to be Archon?"

Ryan Steiner raked long, slender fingers through his thick blond hair and stared back at his questioner. *Your tone, great-uncle Alessandro, suggests that 'yes' is the only proper answer. It's the answer I'd give in a heartbeat, too, except that I know you hope for a return to the throne.* He narrowed his eyes and imagined he saw disgust flicker across Alessandro's gray eyes. *It's true that my eyes are darker than those of most Steiners, but that doesn't mean I'm as weak or defective as you seem to imagine.*

Ryan nodded his head to the older man seated across from him in the solarium. "Yes, Archon, I do desire the throne."

Alessandro's smile at Ryan's reply brought some life back into the ex-Archon's tired, wrinkled face. It had been twenty-two years since Katrina Steiner had deposed him. Ryan knew that Alessandro had been more subtle than some others in attempting to take back his power, but none of these schemers had been very effective. Ryan wondered what plot his uncle had in mind now and why he was trying to work his great-nephew into it.

As if reading Ryan's mind, Alessandro waved him to one of the wicker chairs arranged to face a holodisk viewer. Above them, through the solarium's glass roof, the stars burned with a fierce cold light. Ryan smiled as he saw that the larger of Furillo's dual moons had moved into the constellation Serpentarius. *I've always considered that*

50

a good omen. Perhaps the old man's plan will work.

Alessandro leaned forward, placing his elbows on his knees. "As well you know, I have plotted my return to the Archon's throne for almost as many years as you have been alive." The old man smiled ruefully. "Over the years, dozens of my plans have failed, but I have not lost heart. Practice makes perfect, they say, and I have had enough practice to perfect a hundred different ways to take power. I still have supporters scattered throughout the Commonwealth, and I have secrets that can coerce cooperation out of the most difficult of enemies."

The wrinkled old man looked up at the stars as if he hated them. "What I no longer have, Ryan Steiner, is time. I'm only seventy-two years old, but life has caught up with me. The doctors think they can trace it back to a dose of radiation I took in a 'Mech battle forty years ago." Alessandro looked up into the starry night and spoke as though defying the universe itself. "My body is consuming itself, but I have refused to let the doctors do anything. I will not die half a man."

Ryan felt his mouth go dry. *Dying? He must have known for some time. That's why he's had me here "helping" him. He's not needed my aid as much as he is grooming me to replace him.* "I am deeply saddened to hear this news, Archon."

Alessandro's features sharpened into a viperlike expression. "Please, Ryan, do not pity me. That I will not have. I have brought you here to be forged into a weapon for use against my enemies. Right now you need another lesson, and there is no subtle way to teach this one to you." Alessandro picked up a remote control and pointed it at the holodisk viewer. "Watch this."

The screen brightened to reveal the regally handsome face of a man who might have been twenty-five years younger than Alessandro, but who was the Archon's junior by only sixteen years. The man's gray eyes and platinum blond hair marked him a Steiner; the scar tugging at the corner of his right eye marked him a MechWarrior. His deep voice rumbled undistorted from the speakers. "Greetings, Alessandro."

Ryan smiled without realizing it. *Uncle Frederick! When did you begin to address the Archon so cordially.*

Frederick's image smiled to put the viewer at ease. "We have quarreled for too long. I still recall your visits to our home when I was but a child. I always wanted to be like you, and growing up, I cherished the picture taken of the two of us upon your graduation from the Nagelring Academy. I recall you promised me your 'Mech command when I became old enough to earn it, and I labored from that point to be worthy of your bequest."

Frederick's hand absentmindedly strayed to the scar on his temple. "The time has come for us to put down our differences and unite to oppose the Witch. She's already given her daughter to Hanse Davion, and I fear she will give away the rest of the Commonwealth as well. She's openly embraced his war and sends our citizens to die in order to keep the Dragon from Davion's neck. I am certain this situation alarms you as much as it does me."

Frederick lifted his head high. The camera slowly withdrew to show him in the gaudiest of medal-laden uniforms possible within the Lyran Commonwealth. Though he had earned each medal honestly, he looked more like a whore piling on jewelry than a heroic warrior.

Ryan narrowed his eyes. *He flaunts evidence of his service to the Commonwealth while he discusses treason.* A glance at the disgusted expression on Alessandro's face told Ryan that the Archon's thoughts must parallel his own.

Frederick continued his monologue. "We are in a time when simple events could change everything. The Commonwealth is nearing a point of dissolution because of the Davion question and this war. Were something to happen to the Archon, the social upheaval could destroy the Commonwealth. Neither of us wants to see that happen.

"You, Alessandro, still hold considerable sway within the Commonwealth. Unfortunately, your age calls into question your ability to create a government that could stabilize the Commonwealth. This is not a concern in my case. Though we both know you would do your best, I submit that your age is not in your favor in this area."

Frederick tried to smile beneficently, but his craving for power distorted the expression. "It is time, uncle, for you to pass the mantle of leadership to me. I require from you a pledge of support so that the Commonwealth we both love can continue, despite the grave mistakes made by the Witch. It is now time for my generation to regain control of the Commonwealth, and it is your duty to support me.

"Please reply soonest. There may be no time to waste."

Alessandro froze the image with Frederick's mouth hanging open, making him look stupid. Smiling, the older man turned to Ryan. "What do you think?"

Ryan frowned. "The message is openly antagonistic and arrogant. Frederick hints at some disaster that might befall Katrina Steiner. Because Uncle Frederick does not think in terms of subtleties, I have to assume Duke Aldo Lestrade lurks somewhere in the background. That leads me to have little confidence in the successful completion of the plot."

Alessandro nodded solemnly, his pleasure at Ryan's analysis

shining in his eyes. "Had Frederick said, 'Alessandro, I'm taking the Tenth Lyran Guards to Tharkad to kick Katrina out of office,' I might have supported him. Aldo has already failed at least three times to assassinate Katrina, and I cannot see any indication that he might succeed this time."

Ryan straightened up in his chair. "You think he'll try to kill her again?"

Alessandro nodded. "Do neutrinos precede visible light in a supernova? As long as Katrina is alive, there is no one who will depose her. Her grip on power is too strong. People would rally to her defense. Katrina Steiner will rule the Lyran Commonwealth as long as she lives. Even if Frederick does not understand this, I am sure Lestrade does."

Ryan eased back in the chair. "What do you think Frederick meant when he hinted at dissolution of the Commonwealth? Do you think that has something to do with Lestrade's separatist movement in the Isle of Skye?"

Alessandro smiled broadly. "Very good question. It would be my guess that Lestrade will use any Kurita strike as an excuse to declare the Isle of Skye independent and a non-combatant. Pavel Ridzik has done something similar, and ComStar nearly beat the Federated Suns in declaring support for his realm. I would guess Lestrade has spoken to some ComStar officials about this already."

Ryan narrowed his eyes. "Why would ComStar support such independent nations?"

Alessandro shrugged carelessly. "Being pacifistic, perhaps they imagine they can extinguish the war one small nation at a time. They can also get a smaller government to grant them concessions—like paying for communication network upgrades—much more easily than with a larger nation. Maximilian Liao is notorious for leaving deep fingerprints on each C-bill his government spends."

Ryan smiled at the joke. "So we know Frederick will take power after something has happened to Katrina, and we know Lestrade will make the Isle of Skye independent. It strikes me that the latter should happen before the former, then Frederick could bring the Isle of Skye back into the fold to gain some instant appreciation from the people."

"Very good, Ryan. Very good." Alessandro watched his grand-nephew carefully. "So what do you imagine my reply is to Frederick?"

Ryan pursed his lips. "You refuse to support him."

Alessandro shook his head. "No. Wrong. If you want to be Archon, you must learn how to use your enemies. Here I have a situation where Frederick is pitted against Katrina. If Frederick fails, he is eliminated. If he succeeds, Katrina is eliminated. My role is to serve as a catalyst because either outcome is good for my, ah, your political future."

Ryan nodded slowly. "You tell Frederick you support him, but you do not, in fact, give him any help. If he succeeds, he will be weak. Then you can use your influence to support me in a drive to depose this bloody-handed murderer."

The Archon smiled. "Melissa will be torn between her husband and her homeland. You will rally all the anti-Davion support in the Commonwealth, and through a carefully orchestrated public relations campaign, we will win you support. You will be Archon while Melissa is left to live with her husband."

Ryan raised an eyebrow. "What if Frederick's plan goes sour?"

Alessandro licked his lips like a hungry cat. "We will be sure the Archon sees a copy of the holodisk you just saw. It will be enough to reveal Frederick for the bumbler he is, and it will be enough for Katrina to rid herself of him. She will then be indebted to us, bringing you one step closer to becoming Archon."

The younger Steiner frowned deeply. "Why would you help her? You hate her. For over twenty years, you've tried to get rid of her. You even tried to have her killed on Poulsbo the year I was born. I'm confused."

Alessandro sat back, steepling his fingers as he did. "I see you have come to believe all the stories that my rivals have circulated over the years. I have opposed Katrina Steiner, but not because I do not believe she makes a fine Archon. I saw her leadership abilities long ago and would have designated her as my heir instead of Frederick."

Ryan could hardly believe his ears. "But you tried to have her killed on Poulsbo! That's hardly a sign of support for your Heir-Apparent."

"No, Ryan. I did not send Loki operatives after her on Poulsbo. That story is a complete and utter fabrication." Alessandro's eyes focused distantly, and he chuckled to himself. "Do you know what Heimdall is?"

Ryan stiffened as a chill ran down his spine. "It's supposed to be an anti-government movement. It's very secretive, but rumors suggest many highly placed members of the government are linked with Heimdall." Ryan hesitated. "It is said that Heimdall kept Katrina safe from your assassins on Poulsbo."

Alessandro sighed heavily. "It is true: the victors write the history. What you have said about Heimdall is true. A number of nobles formed the organization to combat excesses in the government ages ago—only members of that God-cursed group know when it was actually formed. It just so happens that back in 3005, I learned the identity of a Heimdall leader. It was Arthur Luvon."

Ryan's jaw dropped open. *Katrina's husband and Melissa's father!* "The Duke of Donegal?"

Alessandro nodded solemnly. "I sent Loki operatives out to kill him while he visited Poulsbo. I had no way of knowing that Katrina and Luvon's cousin, Morgan Kell, would all be at dinner on the evening selected for the termination. Somehow they escaped the trap and assumed Katrina was the target. Over the next year, this view became reinforced in Katrina's mind and in the mind of the public. When she returned from hiding, our relationship was in tatters and she had fallen completely under the influence of Arthur Luvon. How could I explain to her that I had not meant to kill her, but the man she loved? Had I told her the truth, I think her vengeance would have been swifter and less merciful."

Ryan watched Alessandro deflate as weariness caught up with him. *Part of him welcomes death and even wishes Katrina had killed him after she stripped him of office. Another part of him, the part pushing me as a rival for Melissa, relishes the fact that he has lived long enough to prepare his revenge for what she did to him so many years ago.*

Ryan smiled. "The lesson you spoke of earlier…I think I have learned it. If I am to be Archon, I must learn to pit enemies against each other. I must trust no one's word unless I have some evidence that this person will keep it. And in a political bargain, I must always look for a thumb on the scales. Everyone is out for himself."

Alessandro smiled broadly. "You do see what I have been teaching you. Remember, there is nothing in the universe more desirable than being Archon. Winning that post does not so much depend upon your being able to outrun opponents. What it requires is that you cut down the competition as ruthlessly as possible."

Ryan returned Alessandro's smile. "Then let us begin with Uncle Frederick…"

10

Akira Brahe turned to study his father's strong profile in the light of Nashira's bloody moon. The face looked like it might have been chiseled from stone. *How can he look out over this destruction and maintain an expression so devoid of emotion?* Yorinaga Kurita narrowed his dark, almond-shaped eyes. *It is as though he is trying to make sense of what the Kell Hounds has done to Nashira in their assault.*

From high atop the *Genyosha* base's command center, Akira followed his father's gaze over the damage left by the mercenaries. Every building in the base, save the one where they stood, had been flattened with a vengeance. Some had vanished without a trace. With the others, the debris was not scattered randomly as it would have been if a battle had raged at the base, but was concentrated at the site where each building had stood.

Akira frowned heavily, irritation and anger like sparks in his tawny eyes. He nervously ran the fingers of his left hand through his close-cropped bronze hair. "It makes no sense, *sosen*. Why would the mercenaries do this?"

Yorinaga turned slowly toward his son. "No sense? Explain to me what confuses you."

Akira, stung by his father's tone, stiffened. "Do you *ask* this as my father, or order it as the *Tai-sa* of the *Genyosha*?"

Yorinaga bowed his gray-haired head. "*Sumimasen*, Akira.

56

Forgive me. I did not mean to rebuke you or seem to question your abilities." Yorinaga looked again at the pattern of destruction. "It is just that I desire to see all this with your eyes. Perhaps your eyes are less blind than mine."

Akira nodded. "I wonder about more than just what the Kell Hounds did to our base. It makes sense to me that they would destroy it. They would have expected us to be here, and we were not." Akira waved a hand to take in the full circle of ruins. "The strange thing is that their actions were inconsistent with what our Internal Security Forces tell us about the tactics of mercenary scum."

Akira licked his lips. *The ISF tells us all mercenaries are without honor, but I did not see that on Northwind when fighting against Team Banzai or even the group masquerading as the Kell Hounds Third 'Mech Battalion, Bradley's Bravos. They fought for more than money. They fought like true warriors.*

Yorinaga allowed himself a brief smile. "I am certain reports of this incident will cause some confusion in the court at Luthien. While we are out attacking Northwind because the ISF reported the Kell Hounds are there, the Kell Hounds have penetrated Combine security and learned of our home base. They hit it, only to find we are not here, while we discover they are not at Northwind."

Akira smiled. "Luthien will also have to puzzle over why the Kell Hounds ordered all the civilians to clear out from the base, and why they gave them five hours to move all of the *Genyosha's* personal effects from the buildings they intended to destroy." Akira looked down at the building on which they stood. "And they'll wonder why the command center was spared."

Yorinaga narrowed his eyes. "Morgan Kell ordered the civilians out and allowed them to move our possessions because he wanted it clearly understood that his war has nothing to do with the Draconis Combine, or even the *Genyosha*." Yorinaga looked at his son. "And the reason he left this building standing is because it was from this point that he orchestrated the base's ruin."

Yorinaga pointed toward a pile of debris. "See where the natatorium stood? Notice how the stones seem scattered randomly, but fall in a cross-shaped pattern beside that largest pile?"

Akira shrugged. "I supposed some Christians had arranged those stones in memory of a comrade they believed trapped in the building when it was destroyed."

The *Genyosha's* leader smiled. "Your assumption was correct, but you attribute it to someone here on Nashira. You will recall that the ISF learned that Morgan Kell retreated to a Christian monastery on

Zaniah while I was in exile on Echo. Kell ordered the stones laid in that pattern to mark the place where his brother died."

Akira frowned, trying to remember the name of the world where Patrick Kell had been slain. *That happened back before I joined the* Genyosha. "Styx? That system is just a collection of asteroids." Akira smacked his right palm against his forehead. "Just as the natatorium is reduced to a collection of blocks."

Yorinaga smiled, pleased with his son's perception. "This building represents Terra, and the rubble piles mark the location of worlds to a rough distance of 130 light years out."

Though never schooled in astronavigation, Akira had learned enough from talking with JumpShip crewmembers to recognize the placement of some worlds. "Why, *sosen*? What earthly purpose could this star map have?"

Yorinaga drew in a deep breath. "As you have guessed, the sort of blind stabs we, the *Genyosha,* and the Kell Hounds, engaged in back in January could continue forever. We might never be at the same place at the same time, and Morgan Kell took precautions against that happening again."

Yorinaga pointed at a ruin off toward the northeast. "That pile represents the Steiner world of Ryde. Around it you can see three smaller piles of bricks—these taken from buildings other than the one transformed into Ryde. They represent the world's three moons."

Akira nodded. "They are positioned in a manner that indicates when the *Genyosha* should appear there?"

"In June," Yorinaga said. "Only a month from now. We can just make it in time."

Akira drew himself up to his full height. "*Sumimasen, Tai-sa,* put it down to my mother's Scandinavian blood or to my poor training with the Eleventh Legion of Vega, but how do you know this will not be a trap?"

Yorinaga shook his head slowly. "Morgan Kell would not do that. No, this is the last act in a play that began sixteen years ago on Mallory's World."

The garish light of Nashira's red moon painted scarlet highlights over Akira's face. "That would be 3013. I thought your fight with Morgan Kell took place in 3016."

Yorinaga closed his eyes and tried to relax, but Akira saw the tension in his father's slender frame. "Kell and I first opposed each other in 3013. My battalion of the Second Sword of Light had succeeded in trapping the command company of the Fourth Davion Guards in a maze of canyons. Our aerowing controlled the skies over this area, which prevented the Davion Guards from jumping scouts onto the ridgelines to find a way out. With the fighters to spot for us, we knew where to hunt for our quarry, but without scouts, they did not know where to run or hide."

Yorinaga massaged his forehead with his left hand. "If ever there was a glorious battle, this was it. Prince Ian Davion, on sheer strength of personality, kept his troops together. He sprang ambushes on us, but never let his rear guard get trapped. On the few occasions when we engaged his people in a real firefight, the Prince's *Atlas* was always the last 'Mech to withdraw.

"We finally trapped the company in a canyon that tapered down into a narrow route out. Prince Ian held my people back, delivering salvo after salvo of long-range missile fire that savaged the 'Mechs of my command. When his missiles were exhausted, he used his autocannon and medium lasers to halt our advance as his command trickled out of the canyon."

Yorinaga's eyes snapped open. "You should have seen it, Akira. That *Atlas* shrugged off our assaults as though they were pesky flies. Armor flew from the 'Mech in sheets of molten debris, but Ian Davion made no move to retreat. Here he was, leader of the Federated Suns, almost as important as Takashi Kurita himself, but he would not turn and run. Seldom is such a warrior born outside the Combine."

Yorinaga's nostrils flared as he remembered, and Akira listened, spellbound. "I ordered my troops back, then brought my *Warhammer* forward to engage the Prince. We both knew I would kill him, but I believe he took comfort in knowing I would give him a warrior's death.

"He was magnificent in battle. He moved his *Atlas* with an agility I've seen in only a handful of MechWarriors. His last volley with the autocannon all but tore off my *Warhammer*'s left arm and his lasers raked over my armor like the claws of some angry beast. He was spectacular, but I was better."

Yorinaga was fully caught up in the memory. "I pushed my *Warhammer* to the limit and beyond. I fired my particle projection cannons in tandem, ignoring the waves of heat building up through the cockpit. Sweat poured into my eyes in a stinging flood, but I kept my sights on the *Atlas* by feel and sense more than by vision. My 'Mech and I moved almost as one as we drilled PPC beams through the *Atlas*'s armor. Explosions in the 'Mech's chest flashed like lightning trapped in a thunderhead, and I knew the machine was all but dead. Prince Ian would have ejected, I am certain, but one of my short-range missiles had exploded against the *Atlas*'s head and sealed the canopy. Leaking black smoke from a dozen mortal wounds, the *Atlas* teetered, then fell to its back on that armor-littered canyon floor."

Yorinaga's voice cut off abruptly. Akira studied his father's shadowed face. *I've never seen him look so angry, so outraged, so humiliated...*

When Yorinaga spoke again, his voice was choked into a hoarse whisper. "I moved in to see if the Prince yet lived. If so, I would capture him. If not, I meant to bring the Dragon proof that his hated enemy was truly dead. I never got the chance.

"Two companies of the Kell Hounds appeared on the ridgeline as if by sorcery. A voice, one I would come to know as Morgan Kell's, broke into our tactical channel. 'Leave him alone.' It was a warning and a challenge and a plea all wrapped up in one, but I ignored it.

"A *Shilone* fighter from the air lance covering us screamed down out of sky and lined up for a pass at Kell's *Archer*. Instantly, the *Archer*'s missile racks vomited out two clouds of LRMs. The missiles rose on vapor trails that all converged on the attacking fighter. Their combined explosions rivaled the sun for half a second, then the *Shilone*'s flaming wreckage slammed into the canyon wall, showering the battlefield with thousands of firebrands."

Yorinaga's voice seethed with anger and disgust. "The jump-capable Kell Hound 'Mechs dropped down into the canyon. With one shot, Salome Ward's *Wolverine* snapped my *Warhammer*'s left arm off. Kell's *Archer* launched flight after flight of LRMs at the troops behind me, yet staggered his assaults so they could withdraw if they wished. His air lance reclaimed the skies over the canyon, preventing us from rising to the ridges to oppose them.

"Clearly, he wanted nothing more than to save the Prince. He did not press his advantage against us as we had in hounding Ian Davion to his death. He stole all the glory and honor from my greatest victory."

Akira swallowed past the thick lump in his throat. "What happened later, in 3016? All I know are vague rumors. When the ISF came to our home and arrested Mother and me, they only said you'd disgraced yourself and the Dragon. They laughed and said we were to become slaves...if we were lucky." Akira looked into his father's eyes. "What could you have done that was so terrible?"

Yorinaga eyes slitted. "For killing the Prince, Takashi Kurita promoted me to *Tai-sa* of the Second Sword of Light—a great honor. I would control the Dragon's personal regiment. I was given free rein to plan operations and direct our battle for Mallory's World. I spent three years developing my master plan, but throughout that time, I had but one goal. I was not out to conquer Mallory's World as much as I desired to crush the Kell Hounds and avenge myself upon Morgan Kell.

Yorinaga looked at his son. "Everything was perfect. The Thirty-sixth Dieron Regulars managed to pin down the Kell Hounds' Second 'Mech Battalion, leaving the First trapped high in the mountains. I had selected the First 'Mech Battalion as my primary target because Morgan Kell commanded the Second Battalion and I wanted him to know I had crushed his brother's half of the unit when I came for him. He surprised me, however, and was present, with his Command Lance, consulting with his brother."

Akira felt uneasiness roiling in his gut. *The calmness my father has shown since leaving exile is unraveling. This is the man I remember from my youth, but I'm not sure I prefer him to the Yorinaga I have come to know as the commander of the* Genyosha.

Yorinaga tucked his hands into the sleeves of his *kimono*. "One of my scouts recognized Morgan's *Archer* and reported his presence back to me immediately. He also noted how the Kell Hounds had dug themselves into a nasty position. Our only routes to them were along alleys in which the mercenaries could concentrate their fire. Our assault would be difficult, but we were the Second Sword of Light—Takashi Kurita's own regiment. We would not be defeated.

"Then something remarkable happened. Morgan Kell marched his *Archer* from behind the fortifications and began to recite his lineage. I felt blood pounding in my temples as I listened to his voice. He was calling me out to engage him in single combat. He was willing to put his life on the line to save his people, and I accepted his bargain!"

Yorinaga's eyes flashed as he remembered the battle. "You should have seen it, Akira, for it was an incredible battle. Kell and I both closed. His medium lasers stabbed again and again at my *Warhammer*, and I answered with staggered blasts of PPC fire. Armor melted and ran like wax from both our 'Mechs, but all the wounds were superficial. Morgan danced his *Archer* around, avoiding my shots while managing to sting me repeatedly.

"He was good, very good, but not good enough. I knew I'd not kill him unless he could be lured into making a mistake, so when two of his shots hit my right PPC, I switched the weapon to standby and did not use it in our next series of exchanges. Realizing my weakness, Kell swung his *Archer* around and came in for close combat."

Yorinaga's hands left his sleeves and dropped into the position they would have occupied in a *Warhammer*'s command couch. "I brought the right PPC up and fired. The particle beam sliced through the *Archer*'s right shoulder like a cleaver, severing the arm cleanly. Kell's *Archer* stumbled to its knees and waited for me to execute it."

Yorinaga's face reflected the pain of that moment. Akira longed to comfort his father, but he knew that would cost the older man face. *This is his struggle. I will respect that.* He waited silently for his father to continue.

Disbelief edged into Yorinaga's voice. "In my exultation, I took no notice of the fact that my targeting crosshairs did not blink when I dropped them on the *Archer*'s form. The computer refused to lock onto the target, but that mattered not at all. This was not combat. This was an execution. Why would I need computer assistance? Without care and too much emotion, I fired every weapon I had at the *Archer*."

Yorinaga stared up at the Bloodmoon. "Every weapon missed. PPC beams flashed wide of the target, reducing the ground they hit to molten glass. My SRMs flew out in a haphazard spread, bracketing the *Archer* but doing no damage. My lasers shot short or high at their own whim, and my machine guns chattered away impotently. Panic rose in me as the heat buildup spiked within the cockpit, but it was not the heat that alarmed me. Somehow I had missed my foe!

"Suddenly, the *Archer*'s missile pods popped open. Two flights of LRMs leaped forward. Even though the warheads did not have time to arm themselves, the missile impacts battered me. It was like taking shelter in a tin shack to avoid a hailstorm. The missiles crushed armor and spun my *Warhammer* about in a full circle, but somehow I managed to keep my 'Mech upright."

Yorinaga's hands tightened into fists. "When my vision cleared, I fired everything at the *Archer*, but again nothing hit it. The one-armed 'Mech struggled to its feet, continuing to ignore my assaults. Then Morgan made his *Archer* bow to me."

Yorinaga fell silent as though this last statement somehow explained everything that needed explanation. Akira felt a chill run the length of his spine. *There's the conflict. My father both hates and respects Morgan Kell for what he did. With that bow, Kell acknowledged my father as the superior fighter, but robbed him of his victory.*

Akira kept his voice low. "It is said you opened your canopy and threw your *katana* and *wakizashi* to Kell." *Those blades had been in the Kurita family for over three hundred years, and you received them from the Coordinator's hands. What made you do that?*

Yorinaga nodded wearily. "I felt I had no choice. After doing everything possible to kill Morgan Kell, I had failed in that duty. I had ceased to be a faithful warrior right then and there. I had to acknowledge him as my superior."

Yorinaga's head came around. "And it is true, I did utter a haiku:

Yellow bird I see.
The gray dragon hides wisely.
Honor is duty.

Many took it as my death haiku, but it was not. In Morgan Kell, in his ability and intelligence and understanding of our way, I saw something that could destroy the Draconis Combine."

Akira frowned. "I don't understand."

"Neither did I, fully, not until years and long meditations later." Yorinaga hesitated, as though reluctant to reveal a damaging secret, but the look in his son's eyes seemed to make him continue. "With *Bushido*, we find the discipline to become fearless warriors. Honor is all-important, and our concept of self is secondary to state and family. We are but an extension of the Dragon, and our actions honor or shame the Coordinator."

Yorinaga nodded slowly. "Morgan Kell understood this. He used my desire for honor to save his men. Had I killed him, I would have allowed them to mourn their slain leader, and I would have accepted their pledge of neutrality. The Kell Hounds' freedom would have been purchased not with Morgan's blood, but with the honor he showed me in that situation.

"When he bowed to me, he trapped me. We had agreed to fight so that the victor could be merciful to the vanquished. I had lost, and because *Bushido* bound me to do so, I was forced to withdraw. To do otherwise might have won the battle, but it would have shamed Takashi Kurita. He could live without Mallory's World, but could he live without honor?"

Yorinaga swallowed hard. "I returned to Luthien and reported what I saw and felt to the Coordinator. I then resigned my commission and asked to be allowed to commit *seppuku*. The Coordinator exiled me to the zen monastery on Echo V while continuing to refuse my request. Eleven years later, he finally agreed to grant it, provided I first create and lead our elite unit, the *Genyosha*."

Akira pointed off toward the rubble representing Ryde. "We will meet the Kell Hounds then?"

Yorinaga nodded gravely. "Yes. Just as Morgan Kell studied to know me and use that knowledge against me, so I studied him while on Echo V. I know him…I share his abilities. Kell and I will meet again on Ryde, Akira. And there we will destroy one another."

BOOK 2
DECEPTION

It is double the pleasure to deceive the deceiver.
—Jean de la Fontaine

11

Bethel
Capellan March, Federated Suns
9 April 3029

Justin Xiang stood in the middle of the 'Mech bay in the *Leopard* Class DropShip *Ganju* and stared up at his BattleMech. Over five times his height and massing fifty tons, the *Centurion* known to Solaris VII fight fans as *Yen-lo-wang* towered above its master. Humanoid in configuration, its left arm ended in a mechanical hand while the muzzle of an autocannon formed the right arm's terminus. The 'Mech's faceplate had been opened upward, and a rope ladder spilled down the machine's breast to the deck.

Justin smiled to himself. *You saw me safely through my battles on the Game World. Let us hope you'll make this raid work, too.* Justin had just reached out for the ladder when he heard someone call his name. He turned, the smile still on his lips.

Alexi Malenkov, Justin's chief aide on the crisis team, jogged awkwardly in his direction. A black jumpsuit covered the lanky blond from hooded head to feet and gloved wrists. A mirrored faceplate rode clipped to his shoulder, but when in place, would give Alexi complete night vision in addition to cleaning the air of all harmful gases and smoke. A bulky backpack contained his parafoil, and a rucksack belted to his middle contained all his weaponry, except for the needle pistol riding in a holster beneath his left armpit.

Justin's smile grew wider. "I think, were we to drop you alone on the facility, the Feds would surrender straight away," he said, chuckling at the sight of Alexi. "You look pretty fearsome."

Alexi joined in the laughter. "Thanks. After this raid, I'll go into holovids. There's got to be a commando series coming out of this."

Justin nodded. "Malenkov the Mercenary. I can see it now: dolls, holovids, clothes. Probably earn more than the guy who does the *Immortal Warrior* series. Hope you remember your friends when you get rich."

Alexi nodded confidently. "No problem." His smile slowly died as a frown creased his brow. "A couple of our people seem to be a little too anxious about notching their guns, though. We'll be down and in gassing the lab while you and the other three 'Mech pilots bring your 'Mechs up. What do you want me to do with any trigger-happy folks?"

Justin frowned. "Our people have to return fire if they're opposed, but if they start shooting things up, you'll have to kill them." Justin pointed toward the *Centurion*. "Once I strap in, I'll remind everyone we're here to steal the golden egg, not kill the goose. When we've driven Davion back, we'll want to use these people to our own benefit."

Alexi flashed Justin a thumbs-up. "Got it. Good luck."

"And to you, Citizen Malenkov." Justin punched Alexi lightly in the shoulder. "Shoot straight, but keep your head down."

Alexi turned away, leaving Justin to mount the ladder to his 'Mech's cockpit. Nimble as a monkey, Justin ascended the ladder and reached the cockpit despite his mechanical left hand. Once inside, he settled into the command couch and touched a button on his right that reeled in the ladder and dropped the faceplate down into position. With a hiss, the cabin pressurized itself.

Justin unzipped his black jumpsuit, revealing the cooling vest he wore beneath it. Plastic tubes of coolant ran between the goretex material next to his skin and the vest's outer layer of ballistic cloth. Justin snaked out the vest's power cord and snapped it into a socket on the left side of his couch. He felt the ticklish sensation of fluid moving through the tubes as the vest pulled heat away from his body.

Through slits on the thighs and upper arms of his jump suit, Justin pressed medical monitoring electrode pads to his flesh. He then opened a panel on the right side of his couch and pulled out four cables. He clipped one end of each to the pads, then snaked the cables up through the appropriate loops on his cooling vest. He let the plugs hang limp at his throat.

Reaching up and behind himself, he pulled his neurohelmet from the shelf above his command couch. He settled it down over his shoulders, adjusting it to rest comfortably on the vest's padded shoulders, with the neurosensor ring pressed snugly against his head. With the triangular faceplate centered, Justin presed some velcro tabs to keep the helmet in place, then plugged the four sensor wires into the sockets on the helmet's throat.

He grinned to himself. *It's been far too long since I've been in a 'Mech. What I have been doing is vital to the war effort, but being denied a 'Mech is almost unbearable. I'm a MechWarrior first. Nothing will ever take that from me.*

Justin reached over to his metallic left hand with his right and tugged back on the middle and ring fingers until they pressed nearly flat against the back of the hand. With a click, a small compartment cracked open at Justin's left wrist. He slid the panel back, allowing a ribbon cable to spring out like a striking snake. Justin snapped the connector into a socket below the joystick on the command couch arm.

With his right hand, he punched a button on the console to his right. The computer's voice echoed within his neurohelmet. "I am *Yen-lo-wang*. Who presents himself to the King of the Nine Hells?"

"Your humble servant, Justin Xiang."

Light static played through the speakers before the computer replied. "Voiceprint pattern match obtained. Proceed with your supplication."

Justin narrowed his eyes. "Vengeance is justice when visited upon the unjust. Grant me the power to dispense justice."

"Authorization confirmed. All I have is yours to use." As the computer's voice died, all the 'Mech's screens blossomed into color. The computer filled the primary monitor with a green and gold tactical readout of *Yen-lo-wang* and its unusual weaponry array. The *Centurion* had been modified for combat on Solaris. In place of the LRMs normally found in a *Centurion*'s torso, Justin had an autocannon magazine. The Luxor autocannon in the 'Mech's right arm had been replaced with a heavier Pontiac cannon that gobbled up ammo at double the Luxor's rate of fire—hence the need for the additional magazine.

Justin glanced at his inert left hand and the colorful cable running from his wrist. *Just thinking about moving the hand to manipulate the targeting joystick accomplishes the job for the lasers, fore and aft. Right hand takes care of the autocannon. With any luck, though, our little ruse will mean no 'Mechs show up and I won't have to shoot anything.*

Justin punched up a radio link with the DropShip's DropMaster. "What is the situation out there, Master Chung?"

The older man's seamed face appeared on an auxiliary monitor. "It would appear, Citizen Xiang, that your assessment of Captain Redburn is correct. We show the ion-trail of an *Overlord* DropShip in a low arc heading for the reactor assembly plant. We are continuing to send and receive messages to and from the Maskirovka cell in that area. Redburn took the bait. You are to be congratulated."

Justin smiled to himself. *I taught Andrew Redburn a great deal as his commanding officer. Andy's getting his people into place in preparation for the Fourth Tau Ceti Rangers' diversionary drop.* "As nearly as you can tell, the *Ganju* has remained safely hidden in the Rangers' DropShip scanner shadow?"

"Roger, Citizen." Chung glanced at a monitor, then looked back at the communications camera. "All radio traffic appears normal, and I've heard no mention of anything other than an *Overlord* incoming. We're ten minutes to atmosphere and fifteen to split off. Davion's people have sent up no fighter cover, so I would anticipate a smooth run at the target."

Justin nodded. "Good. Keep me informed. Out." Justin hit a switch that transferred him to the tactical frequency all twelve of his people were monitoring. "Look sharp, people. We're about twenty minutes from the paradrop and twenty-five from unlimbering our 'Mechs. Let me stress once more that this is not designed to be a 'wet' mission. Yes, we've practiced it with opposition just to keep us sharp, but we're not on a search and destroy mission. The Chancellor wants these scientists kept alive so we can use them later, after we throw the invaders back."

Ling's voice broke into the circuit. "Why don't we just take them with us?"

Justin narrowed his eyes. *Citizen Ling asks too many questions.* "We are to leave them here because to take them with us would necessitate moving the whole lab. The Chancellor believes it is better to steal the eggs than to pay for the goose's upkeep. That is beside the point, however. Keep yourselves ready for a fight, but you are not to murder those who have been overcome by the gas. Understood?"

Verbal confirmation came from everyone as the *Ganju* bucked through its first impact on the atmosphere. "Jumpers report to the jump bay. MechWarriors finalize all facets of your preparation. This is it, gentlemen and ladies." Justin smiled cruelly. "This is the beginning of the end for Hanse Davion."

Sparks showered and shot from *Yen-lo-wang*'s legs as the 'Mech strode through the NAIS facility's electric fence. Justin pointed toward the darkened road that ran off to the west. "Kwok, Ivanov, head off that way and secure that approach with your *Raven*s. Livinsky, watch our backtrail to the *Ganju*. When the team comes out, it will be your responsibility to buy the time to get to the ship if we have trouble. Make sure your *Vindicator* is in position to do just that."

"Roger, Justin."

Marching the *Centurion* over to the three-story glass and brick building, Justin saw an individual on the roof wave his hands in an "all clear" sign. Justin nodded, bringing the *Centurion* up to the building. *They've pumped that gas in for five minutes. Everything should be under.*

Justin took one last look at the holographic display the 'Mech provided him of the whole area. *The Prince and my father are to be congratulated. This place is hidden in plain sight. It functions like a normal electronics plant—an electrified fence for night security and a checkpoint for daily visitors—but it's not built up enough to attract unnatural attention. That a 'Mech company is billeted closely enough to react to a raid seems like careful planning on the part of the plant's owner instead of any governmental attempt to protect it.* Justin smiled. *It's just too bad we knew where to look.*

He punched a button on his console, opening the *Centurion*'s faceplate. He unsnapped his cooling vest from the couch and released his left-wrist cable from the couch's arm. He stuffed the cable back into its compartment and snapped it shut. Unplugging the sensors from his neurohelmet, he shoved it back up into place, then zipped up his jumpsuit.

Before he slid from the command couch, Justin opened the compartment below it. From there, he withdrew a needle pistol and shoulder holster. He donned them immediately, adjusting the holster to fit snugly beneath his left armpit. Feeling around in the compartment carefully, he found the other item taped to the compartment's roof. He pulled it free and stripped the tape from it.

Candace's holodisk for the Prince. The item, barely twelve centimeters in diameter, could contain over an hour of holovid message on its bottom rainbow surface. The blue and white crest of St. Ives had been emblazoned on the obverse, and the bold labeling made Justin uneasy. *I will have to be careful with this or someone will wonder why I'm leaving it behind.*

Justin slipped it into the slender pocket on his jumpsuit's right thigh. He pulled the jumpsuit hood up over his head, then reached behind the command couch to another storage area. From there, he pulled one of the mirrored facemasks Alexi and his men had already donned. Tightening it into place by pulling on the straps, Justin crossed to the *Centurion*'s chin and leaped the one-meter gap to the lab's roof.

Justin caught up with the other eight commandos at the doorway

71

leading down into the lab. It already stood open, and two men had reached the bottom of the stairs without injury. Silently, the others followed, tension winding inside them like a viper.

Justin watched the two pointmen move into the brightly lit corridor. He found himself tensed against the sound of gunfire. When neither man evaporated in a hail of plastic flechettes or bullets, Justin started breathing again. Both men signaled that the corridor was secure.

Justin smiled as he stepped into the passageway. Lab Techs lay in the corridors as if it were naptime in a nursery school. Halfway up the corridor, a number of fluids puddled into an oily slick where a Tech had dropped a tray of samples. As the puddle neither smoked nor bubbled, Justin simply ignored it.

He pointed to the doors up and down the corridors. "Fan out in pairs. Eliminate dangerous situations—shut off burners or boiling things and don't go wrecking anything. Use the cameras you were issued to document anything interesting. Scour this level and look for the stuff our scientists showed us as being a clue to a myomer experiment. Let's do it fast. We don't want to take more time than necessary."

The black-clad Maskirovka agents spread out like living shadows through the facility. Though the third and second levels were filled with wondrous machinery, none of it yielded their quarry. On the first level, though, back in a lab tucked in a corner, Ling reported success.

Aside from the two people posted at the door, the team crowded into the small lab. Standing over the snoring body of a white-haired researcher, Ling pointed at a thick, black bundle of myomer fibers. Two meters long, it was anchored at one end to a steel I-beam and attached at the other end to a piston-like, spring-loaded tensometer. A digital display on the piston reported the tension to be at 4,000 kilograms.

Justin glanced at Alexi. "That's a finger flexor. That muscle's four times as powerful as the fibers on my *Centurion*! Can you imagine what a full arm muscle or leg muscle could do?"

Alexi shivered. At a nod from Justin, he worked the piston's controls and reduced the tension to nothing. The myomer fiber fattened as it grew shorter. Alexi unhitched it from the piston, then shook his head. "Justin, this stuff is so light. Using this, we'll be able to add more weaponry to our 'Mechs."

Maximovitch, poking around in a container of holovid disks, laughed aloud. "Looks like I've got documentation on two series of tests run with this stuff, as well as the notes on its development."

Justin nodded. "Good, Georgi. Take them." Justin directed one other commando toward Alexi. "Li, I want you to carry the muscle. We had planned to cut it up, but that's when we thought it would be heavy. The rest of you form up out in the hallway and head toward the front of the building. It's time for us to get out of here."

Justin waited for the others to leave the lab before he crossed to the container Maximovitch had rifled. He pulled Candace's holodisk from his pocket and dropped it in with the others, then cried out as a horrible, high-pitched wail screamed through his skull.

Both hands went to his ears, but the sound died quickly enough for him to hear a needle pistol being cocked. He turned slowly to face Anatol Ling and stare down the barrel of the agent's pistol. Raising his hands, Justin let steel fill his voice. "What is the meaning of this, Ling?" *I hope someone picks up the broadcast and comes to investigate.*

Justin's distorted image pendulumed back and forth across Ling's curved faceplate as the agent shook his head. "The squeal was a jammer, Xiang. No one can hear you." Waving the gun's muzzle, Ling forced Justin back and away from the holodisk collection. "Well, well, what have we here? Treason on the part of the Duchess of St. Ives?"

Justin stared at the pistol. *Ten meters between us. I can cross that distance before he gets a second shot off, and the needles don't have the mass to stop my charge.* "You're working for Romano Liao, aren't you?"

Ling's nod was almost respectful. "You are quick, Xiang. Yes, she wanted to make sure you would not return from this mission. I think, however, she will be more interested in hearing about this disk than a description of your death. She wanted me to shoot you first in the groin, you know. Your death will earn me her thanks, but this disk…"

As Ling shifted his pistol from his right hand to his left preparatory to grabbing the disk, Justin reacted. Moving to his own left, he cut the distance between them in half by the time Ling's finger tightened on the trigger. Fire exploded from Justin's flank as needles raked like barbed claws through his vest and flesh. The pain shocked him and cost him a second as Ling thrust the gun at Justin's stomach and pulled the trigger again.

Two gunshots sounded as one. Ling's faceplate fragmented into a thousand mirrored splinters as a cloud of darts slammed into the left side of his face. Already dead, he spun away from the impact, crashing against a slate-topped lab table. He slid to the ground in front of where Justin Xiang knelt with both arms clutched around his midsection.

Justin looked up as Alexi dropped to his knees beside him.

Concern and fear shot through the Tikonov native's voice. "Take it easy, Justin. We'll get you out. You'll survive."

Justin nodded heavily, then coughed. "Yeah, I will. My flank feels like it's on fire, and my stomach hurts like hell." Hearing Alexi gasp, Justin forced himself to laugh. "It's not as bad as you think, Alexi."

Malenkov patted Justin's shoulder reassuringly. "You're in shock. He shot you twice at pointblank range, Justin."

Justin could hear what Alexi was thinking. *Needle pistol shot in the stomach at that range, my insides should be paté.* Justin eased his left hand out as he straightened up. "I'm fine, Alexi. If I'd not been so close, I'd have been in trouble."

Justin opened his left hand, revealing a myriad of crisscrossed silver scars on the metal palm and fingers. "Instinctively, I grabbed for his gun to redirect it. My hand blocked the blast at the muzzle before the darts could spread. The impact drove my fist back into my stomach, knocking my wind out, but I'll be all right."

Alexi looked down at Justin's right side. "What about the first shot?"

Justin shrugged and slowly stood. He steadied himself against the wall. "Flesh wound. Needles cut some coolant lines, and that stuff stings like hell in the lacerations, but no real damage. Just some more scars."

Justin caught Alexi looking at the holodisk from Candace, but the slender man only shrugged. "You're my boss, Justin. You know what you're doing. I know you're not the spy I'm looking for, so I trust your judgment."

Justin cocked his head to the side. "Then why did you come back here?"

Justin heard Alexi's smile in his voice. "Didn't trust Ling." Punctuating his remark, Alexi stepped on Ling's jammer and destroyed it.

Radio chatter suddenly filled Justin's ears. "Xiang, come in! Kwok and I have four 'Mechs coming in. Two read as *Valkyrie*s, one *Jenner* and a *Centurion*. We're moving to engage."

"Roger, Ivanov. Hold them. I'm coming up." Justin pointed toward the lab's door. "Alexi, get everyone out and back to the ship. We'll hold the 'Mechs off, then join up. Got it?"

"Check." Alexi hesitated. "And Justin?"

"Yes?"

The tall man pointed at Ling's body. "I'm glad we got that Davion assassin before he got you."

Justin nodded. "Amen to that. See you on the ship."

12

Captain Andrew Redburn stared at the auxiliary monitor in his *Centurion*. "Say that again, Captain? What the hell are you telling me?"

The Captain of the *Overlord* Class DropShip gritted his teeth against the anger in Redburn's voice. "I said we've been had, Redburn. They had a goddamned *Leopard* hiding in the *Overlord*'s shadow. It's broken off and is heading back toward your base."

Andrew slammed his fist against the arm of his command couch. *Andrew, you're a flame-brained idiot! Sure, you learned how to anticipate the landing zone for incoming enemies, and you got your people here, but who taught you that little gem? Justin Xiang Allard!* Andrew stiffened and clenched his fists so tight they went white. *Dammit! Justin must have planned this little raid, and he knew I'd take the bait like a raw recruit. Maybe he's even on the* Leopard.

Redburn looked at his primary monitor and saw that all of Delta Company, save himself and three others, had already gotten off the *Defiant*. "Listen up, Delta Company. We've got a *Leopard* heading back toward our base to rip things up while we're here. Bisot, de Ridefort, St. Armand, and I haven't unloaded yet, so we'll head back. Drew, since we're pulling two of your *Valkyrie*s, fold your lance in with Archie's fireteam."

"Roger, Cap."

Redburn shifted radio frequencies to the command frequency he shared with his second in command, Leftenant Robert Craon. "Robert, this is your play. You've got twenty-three 'Mechs in perfect working order. Their *Overlord* can carry thirty-six 'Mechs, though it's probably light. Hit and run until you can size them up, then hurt them. If they decide to break off, let them run. But guard any salvage."

Craon's voice came back strong and nearly devoid of nervousness. "Copy, Captain. Be careful."

Andrew nodded slowly. "Words to live by." Punching a button, Andrew brought the *Defiant*'s Captain back on screen. "Captain, how about boosting us back to the western perimeter of our base, low arc, high speed."

The older man smiled. "Course plotted and locked in. We'll be there in just under fifteen minutes."

Andrew shuddered as he felt the vibrations of engine ignition thrum through the ship. Sweat trickled down his spine. *They've got to be going for the lab, but how could they know about it? The garrison officer I took over from said the true identity of the lab had been passed only from commanding officer to commanding officer. Couldn't have the garrison too big because Bethel is a nothing world. All they do is raise some grain on the plains and there's that infant wine industry here in the mountains.*

Andrew keyed the radio connection to the three other pilots in his hastily formed lance. "Listen up, campers. This could be nasty. A *Leopard* peeled out of the *Overlord*'s sensor shadow and has headed off toward our base." Andrew drew in a breath. *Better make this sound good.* "TerraDyne put out some press releases a couple of months ago talking about a breakthrough in miniaturization. Had an alert about it because they thought some local Maskirovka might take an interest. It looks like someone on Sian bought the story bigtime."

Odo St. Armand's voice crackled into Andrew's neurohelmet. "What are we looking at, Cap?"

Andrew punched some commands into his computer and patched his primary monitor into the ship's computer. The computer filled his display with a representation of the *Leopard*'s deceleration, handling, and energy output levels. "According to the computer, it looks like it was running with 'Mech weight, something slightly heavier than we are. Given Liao preferences, maybe a *Centurion*, a *Vindicator*, and a couple of that new thing they have…the *Raven*?"

Andrew typed in another request for information, and the computer gave him a tactical readout on the *Raven*. Birdlike, the 'Mech sported two medium lasers on its right wing, a six-shot SRM pod on the right side of its body, and an Electronic Counter-Measures package on its nose. Below that, the computer confirmed that his estimate of enemy strength would fit within the parameters suggested by the *Leopard's* flight data.

Andrew smiled. "The computer says there's an 80 percent chance my configuration is correct. The *Raven* has tissue paper for armor, but the ECM pods make them tough to hit. Watch for them to ambush us. The *Vindicator's* the only one of their 'Mechs that can jump. Its PPC will make short work of your *Jenner*, St. Armand, so steer clear unless you can get inside."

"Roger, Cap." St. Armand laughed aloud. "I'll take out the *Raven*, guys, if you want the *Vindicator*. I figure the Captain will want to go mano-a-mano with the other *Centurion*."

Redburn chuckled lightly. "That sounds fine, St. Armand. We'll see if their new *Centurion*s work any better than the one I'm sitting in." Suddenly, a memory clawed its way up from where he consigned nightmares and unpleasant thoughts. Two years before, on a ship traveling from the Lyran Commonwealth to the Federated Suns, Andrew had seen the holovid of a battle on Solaris. *Justin took part in that battle, and he fought in a* Centurion.

The instant the thought occurred to him, he knew that Justin was the pilot of the Liao *Centurion*. Conflicting emotions swirled through Andrew's mind. Mostly he was angry because he saw this assault on his planet as a personal insult. *He's struck back at his father and at the Prince. Just over a year and a half ago, he sent assassins to kill me and the staff of Delta Company. He rejoiced, no doubt, when he found we were here protecting his prize.*

Andrew ground his teeth, then felt his stomach flip-flop. *No, that can't be what happened. If nothing else, the Justin Allard I knew was not a murderer. He'd not have sent assassins. I didn't believe it then, and I have no reason to believe it now.* Nausea soured the taste in his mouth. *How could I think such horrible thoughts about a man who was my friend?*

A third emotion seared into Andrew, and his mind recoiled against all its implications. *Whether or not he's the same man you once called friend, he's still a better MechWarrior than you'll ever be. You saw what he did with a* Valkyrie *in combat with a* Rifleman. *Sure, the* Valkyrie *lost the fight, but there was enough armor blown off that* Rifleman *to build a* Jenner. *You'll be going up against him in evenly matched* Centurions, *which means you're still outgunned. He's forgotten more about MechWarrioring than you'll ever know.*

Captain Porter's face appeared on Redburn's primary monitor again. "We're coming in, Redburn. Get your people ready!"

Porter's voice shocked Andy out of his brooding. "Ready or not, gentlemen. We're on."

Porter had the 'Mech bay doors halfway open before the ship hit the planet's surface. The DropShip settled roughly to the ground, and St. Armand's *Jenner* cleared the hatch before the ramp had fully extended. De Ridefort and Bisot likewise used their jump jets to leave the ship's hold. They set themselves up in a defensive perimeter as Redburn's *Centurion* lumbered from the *Defiant*.

The *Centurion* pointed west with its autocannon. "Let's move it, but stay with my speed." Redburn started his 'Mech sprinting down the road at 68 kph, its maximum speed. "You quick things can use your speed when we get into combat. Won't be long now."

Gerald de Ridefort's bass voice rumbled through the speakers in Andrew's helmet. "Rules of engagement, sir?"

Andrew swallowed hard. "If it moves, kill it. We'll sort things out and apologize later."

Around a bend in the road and up a slight incline, the *Valkyrie*s began to outstrip the *Centurion*. From a dark copse on the left, Andrew saw a series of bright, arrowlike flashes as the two hidden *Raven*s let fly with SRM volleys. Explosions battered de Ridefort's *Valkyrie*. Two missiles blasted armor from the 'Mech's thick left thigh while another wreathed its right ankle in a halo of orange flame. The last missile detonated beneath the *Valkyrie*'s pointed chin, snapping the head up and around as it chipped armor plates away. The missiles that had missed peppered the hillside with brilliant bursts of vermilion and gold.

As de Ridefort's *Valkyrie* stumbled back away from the ambush, Andrew turned his *Centurion* to face the shadowed grove. The *Centurion*'s autocannon swept up and locked on target as the targeting crosshairs shot like a meteorite across Andrew's holographic display. The golden cross flashed once, confirming target acquisition, and Andrew hit the trigger.

The Luxor autocannon growled like a wild beast as it vomited fire and metal. Phosphorescent tracer rounds drew frozen lines of light from the gun's muzzle to the target, then shot off at sharp angles as their fragments ricocheted through a cloud of armor debris. Silver light flared vividly from one *Raven*'s right side as autocannon shells ripped its right wing off and sent it sailing through the night sky.

St. Armand's *Jenner* lanced four medium laser beams through the woods, igniting the trees they touched. Three of the ruby energy lances burned into the as-yet-undamaged *Raven*. Two beams carved armor from its left leg in long liquid ribbons, exposing the myomer muscles

78

and ferrotitanium bones beneath them. The other beam gashed a molten scar across the 'Mech's vestigial left wing.

The second *Raven,* the one Andrew's computer had tagged as Beta, fired its two medium lasers at Bisot's *Valkyrie.* The beams raked like claws down the breast of his 'Mech. Liquefied armor ran down the furrows they ripped in the 'Mech's ceramic flesh, but failed to penetrate the *Valkyrie's* thick hide.

In tandem, Bisot and de Ridefort—who had regained control of his reeling 'Mech—trained their lasers on the Beta *Raven.* Their lasers shot out in stuttering pulsed beams. De Ridefort's shot missed, but Bisot's aim was true. His laser stitched fire along the *Raven's* left flank, slicing off armor plates like a whittler carving wood.

The Alpha *Raven* launched another SRM flight at de Ridefort's *Valkyrie,* but the missiles passed harmlessly wide of their target. Despite apprehension about the harm that heat build-up could do to his 'Mech, Andrew linked the target for his LRMs to that of his autocannon. *This has got to stop now.* Dropping the crosshairs onto the Alpha *Raven,* Andrew let go with missiles and cannon fire.

The *Centurion's* LRMs corkscrewed through the pitch-black night, then shattered the darkness with the lurid strobes of half a dozen explosions. Armor shot away from the *Raven's* left leg and arm like leaves tossed about in a strong wind. The autocannon's storm of shells peeled the armor from the *Raven's* left torso as though it were so much *naranji* rind. The *Raven* swayed, staggered by the savagery of the assault, then sank back on its haunches.

Beta *Raven* loosed a volley of SRMs at Bisot's *Valkyrie.* The missiles lanced up at the humanoid 'Mech in a straight line. One blasted into laser-weakened chest armor, while two exploded against the *Valkyrie's* left arm. The fourth and final missile detonated against the *Valkyrie's* head, but Bisot weathered the blast that sent armor shards flying.

St. Armand's *Jenner* again concentrated its fire on the Beta *Raven.* Only two beams hit target as the *Raven's* pilot moved to disengage. One light-spear stabbed through the tattered armor on the 'Mech's left wing and burst out the other side. Sparks erupted from the wound, and the wing twisted awkwardly toward the ground as its controlling myomer fibers melted.

The wing's damage and uncontrolled rotation threw the *Raven* off-balance. It pivoted on its left leg just in time for the *Jenner's* second beam to rip a line through the armor on its right flank. De Ridefort and Bisot added their lasers to the assault, neatly slashing into the troubled *Raven.* Bisot's shot drilled into the 'Mech's right leg, jamming some half-melted armor into the reversed knee-joint.

The *Raven* stumbled back toward the right as its damaged leg missed a step. When the motion exposed the *Raven's* naked left flank to de Ridefort, he speared laser fire through the 'Mech's vitals. The coruscating scarlet beam touched off a series of explosions in the *Raven's* SRM magazine. Like a string of firecrackers, the detonations flashed one after another until the roiling fireball ballooned into a brilliant sun. Its dazzling white light reduced the *Raven's* skeleton to a silhouette, then consumed it hungrily.

Andrew sent his *Centurion* racing up the hill as the Alpha *Raven* reared back up to its feet and headed back down the hill. *We've lost too much time already to go after it. We have to reach the factory.* Andrew keyed up the *Defiant's* frequency. "Porter, we have one heading back toward you. Kill it." Andrew switched back to his command frequency before Porter answered him. "Remember, men, they have a *Leopard* out here, so don't do anything foolish."

Cresting the hill, Andrew shifted his scanners from starlight to infrared. The holographic display changed from black with dark green highlights to a surreal rainbow landscape, with men and machines radiating white and yellow heat tracings. Off to his right, he saw the outline of a *Vindicator* and half a dozen bobbing balls of glowing light he recognized as running men. Over at the factory, he saw a *Centurion* standing next to the building and watched as a man-form leaped from the lab's roof into the 'Mech's open cockpit.

"Bisot, de Ridefort, the *Vindicator* is yours. St. Armand..." Andrew's voice died as his spirit rebelled against ordering a 'Mech to attack infantry.

"I'm off varminting, Cap," came St. Armand's voice.

The *Vindicator,* which looked like a Human giant except for the particle projection cannon that formed its right forearm, moved to block the *Jenner's* pursuit of the runners. It raised the PPC and let fly with an azure bolt of man-made lightning, but the jagged energy burst shot wide of the birdlike *Jenner*. The beam drilled into a pine tree, instantly igniting it into a torch, then exploding it into a million flaming splinters.

Both *Valkyries* launched LRM volleys at the *Vindicator*. Missiles blasted up and down the PPC's barrel, stripping it of armor and exposing the glowing blue charging coils. Five missiles smashed into the *Vindicator's* left breast, blasting the the armored hatches protecting LRM launch tubes off the 'Mech's chest, but failed to do more serious damage. Two other explosions gouged deep wounds into the armor on the 'Mech's right leg, but the armor remained unbreached.

Andrew turned his attention to the *Centurion*. He punched up the old tactical frequency he'd shared with Justin Allard when Justin had commanded the First Kittery Training Battalion, the group that had become Redburn's Delta Company. "It's you, isn't it, Justin?"

The answering voice sounded flatter and more inhuman than a computer construct's voice. "Run, Andrew. I owe you nothing. You have no hold over me that will save your life." The Liao *Centurion*, its faceplate locked down securely, turned to face Andrew. "I slew men with twice your skill on Solaris, Captain. Do you really want to die here and now?"

You bastard! Andrew dropped his LRM sight on Justin's *Centurion* and answered with an LRM flight. Half the missiles blasted craters through the armor over *Yen-lo-wang's* right breast. Semi molten ceramic shards shooting away from the 'Mech painted glowing gold trails across Andrew's IR display while the wounds on the 'Mech burned like red-orange embers.

The other five missiles wreathed the *Centurion's* head with a firestorm halo. Armor spun away through the night as the explosions staggered *Yen-lo-wang*. The 'Mech stumbled back into the lab, crushing a wall and shattering windows along the third floor. Andrew clearly recognized Justin's masterful hand on the controls as the *Centurion* rebounded off the building, dropped to one knee and steadied itself with left hand pressed into the ground.

Justin's haunting laughter robbed Andrew of any exultation. "So the puppy has developed teeth. Very well, Redburn. Come on." Justin's voice dropped to an arctic whisper. "I've never felt stupidity is a reason to grant a foe mercy."

Andrew ground his teeth together. *How could I have thought of this man as a friend?* Andrew set his 'Mech in motion, charging forward well inside of his LRM range. *I want this fight to be down and dirty, not impersonal like a missile duel.* Andrew impaled *Yen-lo-wang's* image on the autocannon's crosshairs, then tightened up on the trigger.

The autocannon's stream of metal fury blasted into *Yen-lo-wang* just below the medium laser muzzle in the center of its chest. Armor flew like wood chips beneath the bite of an ax, and a white plume of heat jetted across Andrew's display. The Captain smiled broadly. *Punched through and hit some engine shielding.*

Justin's laughter shifted to allow some grudging respect. "Damn, and me with a damaged cooling vest. Good, Andy, but not good enough. Good-bye."

As *Yen-lo-wang* raised the muzzle of its autocannon toward him,

Andrew's stomach boiled. *Something about that 'Mech, some way he modified it on Solaris. No, no! It's got a Pontiac!* The screaming whine of *Yen-lo-wang's* autocannon filled the night. Depleted uranium slugs hammered into the *Centurion's* right thigh. Crushed armor plates crumbled to dust with a grinding and crunching that sounded to Andrew like an animal gnawing on the limb. Andrew felt his 'Mech shudder as more shells shredded the thickly corded myomer muscles in the *Centurion's* thigh, then his heart sank.

The projectiles ate through the ferrotitanium femur like a disease. With echoes of the gunshot-like snapping still reverberating through the cockpit, Andrew fought to keep his machine upright. Hopelessly unbalanced as the 'Mech's leg cartwheeled away behind it, his *Centurion* pitched to the right, slammed to the ground on its side, then rolled onto its face.

Sparks shot through the cockpit like fireworks. Two monitors went dead and a third displayed, with clinical objectivity, the damage to the *Centurion*. Its right leg was gone, and landing on the autocannon had damaged it. Internal systems showed damage, and the computer reported that because of the *Centurion's* position, the ejection system could not work.

Andrew felt the heavy vibrations from *Yen-lo-wang's* approach. He braced himself for the coup de grace. *Fire and steel. That autocannon will reduce this cockpit to radar chaff.*

Justin's voice filled his neurohelmet. "I assume you're still alive, Andrew, and I will leave you thus. On Solaris, I did that favor for one enemy. Don't make his mistake and come after me again." Justin paused, then added a stinging afterthought. "And stay away from Solaris, too. You wouldn't have lasted this long fighting there."

Andrew stabbed his index finger onto the solar system's tactical display. "Look, Porter, you yourself said we can catch them. They've only got a four-hour lead on us. We head out at 2.5 Gs, fly close enough to the third planet—that gas giant—to get a slingshot effect and we'll reach their JumpShip before they will." Andrew raked fingers back through his thick auburn hair. "Why can't any of you see this?"

Robert Craon exchanged glances with Captain Porter. "Captain Redburn, we can see what you're saying, but it would be a suicide mission. The *Defiant* would be pitted against another *Overlord* and a *Leopard*. All the Liao *Overlord* has to do is snipe at the *Defiant* as Captain Porter tries to catch the *Leopard*. It won't work."

Andrew looked daggers at his aide. "Then we'll make it work!"

The door to the tactical center slid up into the ceiling. Andrew snapped his head around and instantly recognized the slender outline of TerraDyne's chairman. "This is a closed meeting, Anderson. No civilians."

Anderson said nothing as he stepped into the room and allowed the door to close behind him. He flipped a plasticized identification card onto the display. It bore a picture of his face, a retinal pattern, and the Counter Intelligence Division legend across the top. The name on it, however, read "Richard Dorvalle."

Dorvalle looked at Porter and Craon. "You are dismissed. I was never here."

The two of them looked at Redburn. Andrew opened his mouth to protest, but the anger and defiance that had been driving him evaporated. Wearily, he nodded assent. As they dutifully passed out the door, Redburn fixed the spook with a piercing glance. "So, what's really going on here?"

Dorvalle kept his angular face emotionless. "That is not really important, Captain Redburn. What is important is that I have had a communication from the Prince, who asks me to pass on his congratulations to you."

Redburn leaned heavily forward on the tactical display. The computer updated the configuration, setting the *Leopard* and *Overlord* yet further from Bethel. "And what did I do to please him? I was unaware that having a traitor disable your 'Mech is regularly rewarded with a medal or thanks."

Dorvalle's face hardened. "Come off it, Redburn. Self-pity does not become you. You impressed the Prince by actually splitting your command and heading off after the *Leopard*. Your main body tied up the Fourth Tau Ceti Rangers and bagged a couple of heavy 'Mechs. Your people nailed two *Ravens*—which we're sending back to the NAIS for study, by the way—and a *Vindicator*. You also identified the pilot of the *Centurion* you faced."

Andrew shook his head. "What is it with you spies? You're trying to console me by pointing out a silver lining on a very dark cloud. Didn't you miss something? They got into the lab and got back out. As far as security is concerned, that lab is a hemophiliac that just tangled with a *chotodar!*"

Dorvalle actually allowed himself a smile, albeit a small and controlled one. "That, Captain, is the reason the Prince is most pleased, and the reason you will not pursue the *Leopard*."

Everything suddenly landed on Andrew like a ton of bricks. He stepped backward to the wall, then slumped down at the base of it. "It was all a set-up? I let a *Vindicator* put a *Jenner* pilot in the hospital with a broken arm and leg, and left two *Valkyrie*s held together with baling wire and spit for a set-up? Why the hell didn't you just give the information away, or let me know so I could have held my people back?"

The spy shook his head slowly. "If we didn't put up the appearance of a fight, Liao would never believe the information he got is valuable. This isn't a game, but there are times when we have to trick the other side into doing what we want them to do. It worked with Operation Ambush, and it worked here. It could have cost lives— thank God it didn't—but the payoff could end the war early and save countless lives."

Andrew sighed heavily. "Good. I'm glad. I'm glad the final laugh is on Justin Xiang, and that the Prince has avenged himself upon Justin." Andrew ground his palms against his eyes. *Next time, it'll be my turn. And then, Justin, the last laugh will be mine. May it ring in your ears as you die.*

13

Lyons
Isle of Skye, Lyran Commonwealth
15 May 3029

Clovis Holstein hugged the little girl to his chest and rocked her gently as the explosion's thunderous tremors faded. Brushing the dust from her hair, he forced a soft levity into his voice. "Gotta get this dirt out of your hair, Sarah, else you'll be looking like your grandma." He felt the child stiffen when he mentioned her grandmother, so he hugged her tighter. "Hush now, Sarah. No tears."

Through the shelter's dust-laden air, in the dim light of a single bulb, Clovis studied the dirty, tired faces of thirty children. *If just one starts crying, they'll all fall apart.* He glanced over at the older children and gave them a reassuring smile. *If they'd not held up as well as they have, Karla and I would have fallen apart. Two days. How much longer will the Combine keep that company blasting our township to rubble?*

Clovis let Sarah slide from his lap and gently laid the four-year-old-child down next to her eight-year-old-brother. "Rex, take care of your sister." As the tow-headed boy nodded bravely, Clovis stood and dusted himself off. He picked his way across the shelter's floor, carefully avoiding children trying to sleep, and caught Karla Bremen's attention.

With a smile on her pretty face, she gave no sign of the concern and worry that had plagued her since she and Clovis had led her schoolchildren down into the bomb shelter. Clovis brushed his long black locks back away from his face as she crossed toward him, then

85

stopped. *Preening yourself again, Clovis? You idiot! Your desire to impress her is what got you into this position!*

Because New Freedom was small, all the students had worked in a single classroom set up in what the Kell Hounds had previously used as a mission briefing room. When elements of the Third Dieron Regulars hit the town, Clovis had been teaching the class about computers. He and Karla immediately guided the children to safety in the shelters below the 'Mech hangar. The arrival of the Combine troops had transformed the beginning of Clovis's dreams into an ongoing nightmare.

Karla, slender and two heads taller than Clovis, squatted down to speak with him. Despite the dirt on her cheeks, nose, and forehead, Clovis thought her most beautiful. Looking around to make sure none of the children were watching them too closely, Karla let her smile evaporate. "Clovis, I'm worried. I thought you said they'd be gone by now."

Clovis swallowed hard. He rested his stubby-fingered hands on her shoulders, brushing her medium-length brown hair back from her once-white blouse. "What I said before makes no difference. We have enough food down here for a month or more." Clovis faltered. *This shelter was meant to house fifty adults. We can survive here for a long time.*

Karla nodded. "I know. It's just the pressure and all the unanswered questions the children ask. They all want to know if their parents are alive. What can I tell them?"

Clovis could not meet her blue-eyed gaze. "Lie to them. Tell them everyone is fine and hiding in other shelters like this. For now, it will calm them enough to sleep." Clovis shrugged. "The truth will still hurt later, but truth isn't what they need right now."

Clovis reached out to cup Karla's chin in his right hand and tilt her head up. "Listen. You're going to have to hold them together." He glanced upward. "I've got to go see what's happening."

Karla shook her head incredulously. "You can't abandon me here."

Clovis turned away and buckled on a gunbelt with a Smith and Webley Foxfire in the holster. Most warriors referred to the weapon sarcastically as the "purse pistol," because it seemed too small and delicate to be deadly. Clovis drew the pistol, which fit his small hand perfectly, and charged it with a snap. He slid it back into the holster with a fluid motion that only came with long hours of practice.

His back still turned, Clovis tried to sound confident. "I have to go up there, Karla. I have to find out what's going on so we can help figure out what we're going to do."

Karla reached out and grabbed Clovis by the shoulder, spinning him around to face her. "You can't leave us! What sort of man would desert thirty children…" Her voice trailed off as she read the anguish twisting over Clovis's features. "Oh, God, Clovis. I'm sorry…I didn't mean…"

Clovis clenched his jaw and waved away her concern. "You're right, no *man* would abandon thirty children. No *man* would have found himself in this predicament. A real man would have led everyone to safety far away from here. Being only half a man, I ushered everyone into this rathole, and now the cat sits up there, waiting for us to come to it."

He looked into her azure eyes. "You don't know how, before all of this, I wished for some way to show you what sort of person I really am. I used to fantasize rescuing you from a dangerous situation…Yes, even trapped in this body, I can dream of being a knight in shining armor." Clovis snorted derisively at the image. "Then this happens and the opportunity I wished for lets us both see what I truly am. The word *pitiful* seems so appropriate."

Karla stared at Clovis silently. "Clovis, I don't see you as pitiful…"

"Save it!" he snarled angrily, jerking a thumb back toward his own chest. "I know what I am, and I know how everyone sees me. I'm an oddity. I'm a court jester. I'm a freak of nature that people befriend just to prove how open-minded they are, but they never want to get close. They don't care because I'm not a real person. I'm a resource, but in this situation, I'm not very useful. Face it. You'd never have spoken to me if you hadn't wanted me for your class."

Karla slapped Clovis hard across the face. "Clovis Holstein, I will not be spoken to in that tone or with those words! You insult me, and you insult all those who are your friends. "

She pressed her right hand against Clovis's livid cheek to stroke away the sting. "You think people only see you as small, but that's not true. Maybe they're more aware of your physical proportions at first, but that changes after a while. I've got dark hair and light eyes and I always think people find me strange because of that unusual combination. You've got no monopoly on such feelings."

She frowned heavily. "How can you say no one cares about you or wants to be a true friend? I remember seeing you at the community dance a month ago. I envied how you got along so easily with everyone. You, Dan Allard, and Cat Wilson laughed and carried on like three close friends, and it certainly didn't look as though your friends were just politely tolerating you."

Clovis looked down at his feet. "Perhaps I do have some friends, but that's beside the point. You wouldn't have gone to the dance with me."

Karla narrowed her eyes. "You didn't ask me, did you?"

Clovis's look challenged her. "Would it have made any difference if I did?"

She sighed. "I won't lie to you, Clovis. You don't fit the image of my dream man."

The dwarf shook his head. "And Thor does?"

Karla Bremen moistened her lips. "Clovis, I'm not a teenage girl looking for a date for the big dance. Yes, at one time, Thor closely matched what I wanted, but I've changed since creating that image. There are some things more important to me than looks." She glanced back over her shoulder to the room where the children lay huddled together. "The care and feeling you've shown over the past couple of days have touched me. You have strength, you have heart, and as much courage as anyone who ever strapped himself into a 'Mech."

Clovis studied her face. "Are you saying there's a chance for me in your life?"

Karla nodded. "It's not a contest with me as the prize. It's working together to see if we have what it takes to form a lasting partnership. I make no promises, other than to be honest with you, and you'll have to accept that. If we're to have a relationship, it will have to grow of its own accord."

Clovis smiled as the tension between them eased. "Hope for the best, but prepare for the worst, as they say at the fights on Solaris."

Karla laughed sincerely. "A wise idea. You've no idea how awful is my cooking nor how voracious is my appetite for truly bad holovids."

"I'll take my chances." Clovis looked back toward the room containing the children. "You'd best get back to them. I still have to go up there and see what is going on."

She hesitated, then said softly, "Be careful, Clovis."

Slinging a satchel full of electronics repair tools over his shoulder, Clovis laughed lightly and headed toward the shaft leading upward. "Take heart, fair damsel. Beset by the Dragon we may be, but no knight in shining armor would ever leave a lady in peril."

During the long climb up toward the surface, Clovis forced himself to concentrate on the mission at hand. *Can't be dreaming about what might or might not be, Clovis.* Rung by rusty rung, he ascended to a sub-basement level of the 'Mech bay. Crawling through shadowy access passages, Clovis headed deep into the facility the Kell Hounds had used as their temporary base.

Finally, in a water pipe tunnel just north of the east-west sewer line, he found what he had been seeking. A meter beyond the wall that separated Morgan Kell's private office from the room he used for staff meetings, Clovis felt a slender fiber-optic cable running along a waterpipe.

Bingo! Though I griped about spending five hours down in these stinking tunnels, now I'm glad Morgan wanted an independent visiphone line running out of his office. Groping around in his tool kit, Clovis located the small headset and cable tapper he'd used to check the connections when putting in the line.

He clipped the optical collar to the line and tightened it down until he heard a dial tone in his earpiece. On the alpha-numeric keypad dangling from the optical collar, he carefully typed in "COMSTAR," then adjusted the microphone before his mouth. He turned up its volume fairly high.

A gentle voice of indeterminant sex filled his ear. "ComStar, Lyons south. The Peace of Blake be with you."

Clovis kept his voice to a low whisper. "I have a message for Morgan Kell."

The ComStar technician's reply was firm but friendly. "Colonel Kell, in compliance with an order from Duke Aldo Lestrade, has left the world. I can put you in touch with his contact person here, a Clovis Holstein?"

"*I* am Clovis Holstein. I need to get a message to the Kell Hounds. New Freedom has been occupied by a company from the Third Dieron Regulars. I need to tell Morgan."

Clovis heard the gentle tapping of fingers on a keyboard. A computer beeped and the tech's voice again came on the line. "I do not have a current location for Morgan Kell."

Clovis thought for half a second. "They should be at Alphecca, at one of the jump points."

"That's not what my computer shows, Mr. Holstein."

Clovis frowned. The heat from the hot water pipe filled the narrow tunnel with a stifling warmth. Sweat poured from his forehead and stung his eyes. "All right, then they should be at Ryde."

The tech clucked lightly. "I show that they have not reported in to collect their messages. Do you want to send this message to Ryde?"

"Yes."

"Splendid." The click of computer keys again played through the line. "With our next transmission, the message should get there by the first of next week."

"You don't understand," Clovis whispered frantically. "This is an emergency. The message has to go out now."

"That will be expensive, Mr. Holstein. How will you pay for the priority transmission?"

"How am I going to..." Clovis growled with exasperation, then blurted, "Charge it to the Third Dieron Regulars."

"Very well. Initiating a call back on your line to get verification. Just a moment!"

"No!" Clovis heard a series of melodic notes, then a harsh ring from the room above him. A voice echoed in stereo from the earpiece and above him. *Moshi, moshi?*

Clovis ripped the optical collar from the phone line, then scurried on through the hot tunnel. *Here's one time my size is an advantage.* Above him, in the world of men, an alarm sounded and the pounding of heavy footsteps drummed over the floor.

Almost instantly, Clovis realized two things. *They will catch me. I've got to head away from the children.* Karla's smiling face came unbidden into his mind and softened his second realization. *When they catch me, they'll kill me. May my death keep you safe, Karla Bremen...*

A shaft of light stabbed down into the tunnel as someone ripped away one of the access panels to the crawlspace. Clovis filled his hand with the Foxfire and shielded his eyes against the light with his left hand. Two booted feet dropped down into the tunnel, then the legs attached to them bent as the Combine soldier sank to his knees.

Clovis pointed the gun at the man's stomach and pulled the trigger. Using the soldier's screaming as cover, Clovis cut into a cross passage. He traveled east along it, then headed back north at the next opportunity. He slid quickly through the tunnels and before he knew it, reached the outer wall and passed through it.

The dwarf cracked the external accessway's wooden doors and smiled. *Hot damn! Time didn't make any difference down in that hole, but here...* Outside night had fallen, and for the first time, Clovis dared hope he might make good his escape.

Cautiously, he pushed the door open enough for him to slip out. He pressed it down noiselessly, then hunkered down in the building's shadow. He scoured the surrounding landscape for any sign of movement, but saw nothing. *I wish they'd shut that damned alarm off. I'd prefer to trust my ears to my eyes in this darkness.*

Clovis set off toward the hills ringing New Freedom's north side. He moved a short distance, then dropped into a crouch and waited. When confident he had not been seen or heard, he moved again a short distance. His back pressed to the rough bark on an evergreen tree, Clovis allowed himself a smile. *Keep this up, and I'll hit the first hillside in no time.*

Swirling out of the blackness, an ISF commando dropped from above him. The warrior slapped the Foxfire from Clovis's hand, then drew his *katana* in a single deft motion. He pressed the sword's point against Clovis's throat. "Congratulations. By getting this far, you have eluded many who are your betters. I knew I would find you out here."

ISF. They're as bad as Loki. They killed so many people at our Styx base. Clovis glanced over toward the Foxfire.

The commando's low, mocking laugh stopped him. "You are mine now, little man. I'll take you back to our headquarters and we'll see what sort of treasures you hide in that dull package." He slid the sword back into its scabbard, but his harsh cackle sliced at Clovis's spirit.

Clovis shivered as his self-image collapsed in on itself. *I am done. They will break me and I will give up all I know. I have failed everyone...* The commando's ridicule cored through the last of the dwarf's self-respect. *I fooled myself into believing I was a man, but I should have known better. Blood will out...* Clovis nodded in submission to his captor.

Suddenly, the Combine guard's laughter died. Lit by the scarlet beam of a 'Mech's medium laser, he burst into flame.

14

Dan Allard growled a harsh message into his radio as he watched the ISF commando become a torch. "Better move in, Colonel. I just tipped our hand." Dan dropped his *Wolfhound* to one knee and used the 'Mech's steel left hand to scoop up Clovis. "I've got Clovis, but I've attracted some notice."

The flickering muzzle flashes from the heavy machine gun emplacement on the hangar's roof pinpointed the most obvious of the enemy oppositions. Dan's auxiliary monitor noted the impacts of heavy slugs against the *Wolfhound's* hand, but he knew nothing would get through to hurt Clovis. *As long as I don't clench my fist, friend, you're safe as a babe in his mother's arms.*

Dan swung the *Wolfhound's* right arm around and extended it toward the gunners. The arm had no hand, and from the speed of their reaction, the Combine soldiers did not take long to realize why that was. Dan guided the large laser's targeting crosshairs onto their position, then sent a bloody beam of coherent light pulsing into the machine gun nest.

Kilojoules of energy fused sandbags into glass with a gentle caress and liquefied the machine gun in an instant. The heat touched off a series of explosions as machine gun ammo cooked off. The gunners, who had jumped clear of their position, avoided the laser's fury, but could not escape the chaotic hail of bullets shooting from the gun emplacement.

A new element joined the wailing alarm that Clovis had caused to be sounded. A sharp keening that built to an ear-shattering crescendo, then dropped to an inaudible level, wove through the sirens. Dan narrowed his eyes and reopened his radio channel. "'Mech-raid siren just clicked on, Morgan. They know I'm here and they're scrambling." Dan looked up at the darkened airstrip beyond the 'Mech bay. "Looks like they're getting air cover up."

Two *Sholagar* light fighters moved down the runway. The disc-winged aircraft began to pick up speed when something burned its way onto Dan's holographic display from above. White lines stabbed down into the lead *Sholagar's* right wing and sliced through it like a table-saw. Half the wing dropped off to slide along the runway on a bed of red and orange sparks.

The damaged aerofighter, still getting full thrust from the engine mounted in its left wing, spun around and into the flight path of the second fighter. Without sufficient speed, the second pilot could not take off. He did get the nose of his ship up as he tried to pull away from his crippled wingman, but the tail of his *Sholagar* slammed into the deck and disintegrated. The second fighter came down on top of the first, and both exploded with the brilliance of a supernova.

Dan heard the voice of Major Seamus Fitzpatrick, commander of the regiment's air battalion, crackle through the static generated by the explosion. "Good shooting, Lieutenant Kirk. We'll keep them grounded, Colonel."

Morgan Kell's reply came back edged with anger and vibrating with emotion. "Seamus, nothing leaves here. Dan, is Clovis on line?"

Dan frowned, reacting to the sound of Morgan's voice. "No. I've not gotten him inside yet."

"Good." Morgan hesitated for a moment, choosing his words carefully. "Final orders, people. O'Cieran and his ground troops confirmed what we all feared. That dug-up spot we passed *is* a mass grave. No compromise—no 'Mech from this company leaves New Freedom operational."

Dan let Morgan's orders echo through his mind as he raised the *Wolfhound's* left hand to its left shoulder. He punched a couple of buttons on the command console near his right hand, and a hatch on the *Wolfhound's* neck opened. Dan glanced over at it as Clovis stepped through and pulled the hatch shut behind him.

Dan jerked a thumb at the area behind his command couch. "Get yourself a cooling vest from in there and a headset. You can jack into the comm-network." Clovis, pale and sweating, nodded wordlessly. He seemed so unlike himself. *Does he know about the others already?*

93

Dan wondered.

Clovis pulled the oversized cooling vest on as tightly as he could and snapped the power cord into a jack on the right side of the *Wolfhound*'s command couch. He settled the communications headset into place and plugged the jack into a socket beneath the command console. Adjusting the microphone, he smiled weakly. "Thanks for saving my worthless hide."

The traces of self-pity in Clovis's voice made Dan uneasy. *Hiding for two days in an overrun base must have done something to him.* Dan forced some levity into his own voice. "Hey, what are friends for? I'm just glad you lured him out of the tree." Dan's gaze flicked toward an area back to the right of the command couch. "We have company. Strap into that jumpseat, Clovis. The ride will get bumpy from here on."

A Kurita *Clint* stalked out from behind the 'Mech bay. It raised the pistol-like autocannon in its right hand, but before the pilot could pull the trigger, Dan hit two switches on the *Wolfhound* command console. Two spotlights mounted slightly below the *Wolfhound*'s head flashed to life, giving the Kurita pilot a good look at the 'Mech he faced.

Humanoid in body configuration, the *Wolfhound* scanned just like all other light 'Mechs on magscan or IR. Visually, however, the *Wolfhound* was a fearsome sight. The head had been designed to look like a wolf's, from jutting muzzle to high, pointed ears. Standing tall and lean, the fierce 'Mech might have been the avatar of some ancient war god.

Dan swung the *Wolfhound*'s large laser around and triggered it at the same moment the *Clint* pilot fired his autocannon. Shocked by the *Wolfhound*'s appearance, or by the fact that he'd never seen a 'Mech of that design before, the Kurita pilot's shot blasted wide to Dan's left, tearing great divots from the hillside behind him. The *Wolfhound*'s large laser burned through the armor over the *Clint*'s left breast. In a flash of incandescent fire, the laser's beam consumed one of the *Clint*'s medium lasers.

The *Clint* pilot corrected his aim and fired the autocannon a second time. Depleted uranium projectiles blasted armor from the *Wolfhound*'s left breast. The *Wolfhound* rocked back slightly as the slugs slammed into its chest, but none of them breached its armored skin. The *Clint*'s remaining medium laser, mounted in the center of its chest, slashed its ruby beam across the *Wolfhound*'s left thigh. Armor dropped away in molten ropes, but only revealed more armor plating beneath what the beam had destroyed.

Dan laughed aloud. "That's right, you bastard. This 'Mech is more than you can handle." Dropping the targeting crosshairs for all his weapons onto the *Clint's* outline, he glanced at Clovis. "It's gonna get hot!" He hit the triggers for everything.

One of the three medium lasers mounted on the *Wolfhound's* torso carved a jagged scar along the armor on the *Clint's* right flank, but that damage went virtually unnoticed by either shooter or target. The *Wolfhound's* large laser vaporized the armor on the *Clint's* right arm and melted the autocannon's muzzle. The medium laser in the center of the *Wolfhound's* chest sliced like a scalpel up through the myomer muscles controlling the arm, leaving their flayed ends dangling from the 'Mech's useless limb. The *Wolfhound's* third torso-mounted medium laser cored in through the *Clint's* armpit and melted more of the 'Mech's internal structure. Warped by the right arm's dead weight, the 'Mech's skeleton twisted toward the ground, pulling the *Clint* off balance.

Torrents of heat swirled through the *Wolfhound's* cockpit as if it were a blast furnace. The heat monitors spiked into the red zone, and the computer dropped 10 kph from the 'Mech's operational speed because of the heat buildup. Dan, afraid the cabin's heat might have overwhelmed Clovis, looked toward the dwarf just in time to see the small man mop his brow with his sleeve.

The *Clint's* pilot hit his 'Mech's jump jets to flee from his enemy, but the lifeless right arm whipped around as the 'Mech left the ground. The *Clint* pilot tried to compensate by boosting power to the jets on the right torso and leg, but the back-mounted ion jet ripped free of the 'Mech's damaged skeleton. As it skyrocketed upward, the *Clint* tipped back to the right, and driven by its jets, slammed into the ground. The 'Mech's head snapped off at the neck and bounced into a shallow gully.

Before the echoes of the *Clint's* crash-landing could die, another 'Mech stepped from the shelter of the hangar. Dan felt his mouth go dry as the humanoid war machine raised one of its double-barreled arms and pointed it toward him. "Allard here. I've got a *Rifleman* that wants my scalp!" he shouted into the radio.

Pivoting on his right foot, Dan jerked the *Wolfhound* around to protect the damage he'd already taken. He swung the large laser out toward the *Rifleman,* then cursed as the targeting crosshairs for his medium lasers lost their intensity. *Damn! Evading him puts the 'Mech outside my firing arc for the mediums*. Instead, Dan settled the large laser's crosshairs on the *Rifleman* and pulled the trigger.

The *Wolfhound's* heat monitors again spiked into the red as the heavy laser spat out its scarlet beam. The laser pared armor plates from the *Rifleman's* left flank but failed to fully penetrate the 'Mech's thick skin. Smoking armor plates littered the ground at its feet, but the damage did nothing to actually hurt the heavy 'Mech.

The *Rifleman*'s autocannon vomited out a salvo of shells amid a gout of flame, but the projectiles flew over the *Wolfhound*'s head. The large laser slung beneath the autocannon on that same arm drilled its infernal beam into the *Wolfhound*'s right leg. Armor boiled and evaporated beneath its hellish touch, but held and permitted no internal damage.

Despite the danger, Dan found himself smiling. *They sure built this baby for survival. But I'm done for if that* Rifleman *brings the other heavy laser to bear.*

Dan backed the *Wolfhound* further to the *Rifleman*'s left, but the 'Mech bay itself prevented him from moving far enough. The *Rifleman* pivoted on its left leg to face the *Wolfhound*. Both of its arms locked forward, then swung toward the *Wolfhound*.

"Hang on, Clovis!" Dan pushed off against the ground with the *Wolfhound*'s powerful legs. His move drove the *Wolfhound* back into the 'Mech bay, crushing bricks and shattering windows on the three-story building. Sparks flew as the 'Mech's flailing arms split electrical conduits on three levels, then fire geysered into the night sky as the transformer mounted on the roof exploded.

Dan rocked unsteadily in his command couch. His helmet ground down painfully onto his shoulders and he tasted blood from where he had bitten his lip. He glanced over at Clovis and saw his friend hanging half in and half out of the jump seat's safety harness. Blood ran from his nose, but his eyes still shone brightly.

Clovis righted himself and waved off Dan's concerned look. "Better than frying!"

Dan whipped Jeana's sash from where it was knotted on his upper right arm and tossed it to Clovis. "Tie yourself in tighter. Don't want you bouncing around in here." *It's kept me safe. Hope it does the same for you...*

Surprised by Dan's unorthodox maneuver, the *Rifleman*'s pilot could not shift his aim to pin the *Wolfhound* to the building. The heavy lasers burned their way into the structure a bit beyond the *Wolfhound*'s left shoulder, drilling through the place where the lighter 'Mech had just been. Dan expected to see the slashing beams of the medium lasers mounted in the *Rifleman*'s chest, but he heard the heavy thunder of the *Rifleman*'s autocannons instead.

Dan's fingers flashed over his command console keyboard, shifting his scanner from magscan to infrared. The *Rifleman*'s arms glowed bright yellow as the cooling coils labored furiously to dissipate

96

the heat buildup caused by the large lasers. "Hey, Clovis! We have him now. He's cooking himself. One shot!"

Morgan Kell's voice filled Dan's neurohelmet with an icy warning. "No, Dan. Stay where you are. This one is mine."

Off to his left, at the edge of his 'Mech's forward arc, Dan saw Morgan's *Archer* march from behind a hillside. The IR image flickered and faded, but the faint visual picture beneath it did not. As Dan shifted his scanners over to starlight and brought the *Archer* into clearer view, he killed his external radio link. "Look, Clovis. Morgan is doing it again. His 'Mech doesn't register on the scanners—only visual!"

The *Rifleman's* pilot seemed not to have noticed the lack of targeting image as he centered his guns on the *Archer*. Realizing that this 'Mech was a tougher nut to crack than the *Wolfhound*, the *Rifleman* cut loose with everything. The twin heavy lasers stabbed ruby beams at the *Archer* and the smaller medium lasers shot pulsed bolts in their wake. Spent shells spattered from the autocannon ejection ports as a hail of projectiles shot at the *Archer*.

The *Archer* neither twisted nor dodged to evade the *Rifleman's* onslaught. The large lasers flashed above the *Archer's* hunched shoulders, burning parallel lines up the hillside behind him. The medium laser bolts ignited a host of small fires on either side of Morgan's 'Mech, but none of the ruby light shafts struck the *Archer*. The *Rifleman's* autocannon bursts churned two tracks toward the waiting war machine, but they ended before they slammed into the *Archer*.

Dan's mouth went dry. *Oh my God! It's not just that a 'Mech can't target Morgan. It can't hit him! It's like he's a ghost. He's untouchable.* A shiver ran down Dan's spine. *He's invincible.*

The LRM launching pods on the *Archer's* shoulders clicked open with the finality of a pistol hammer being drawn back. Riding brilliant tails of flame, two-score missiles arced into the night. They slammed into the *Rifleman* with the force of a titanic hammer. Explosions blasted and tore armor in great jagged chunks from the *Rifleman's* chest, especially where the *Wolfhound's* laser had already melted armor on its left flank. Detonations within its cavernous breast caused the *Rifleman* to shudder, and the ghostly tendril of a plasma jet licking from the gaping hole in the *Rifleman's* chest hinted at the ruin of the 'Mech's internal structure.

"Close your eyes, Clovis! His reactor's been hit!" Dan raised a hand to shield his eyes, but he could not look away. *Get out! Punch out now! You can't save it!*

Armor plates buckled from internal pressure, plumping and

rounding the *Rifleman*'s angular torso as the runaway fusion reactor's heat touched off the autocannon ammo stored in its chest. A series of detonations blew armor away in small spots, and savagely harsh light stabbed out through the holes like sunlight shining through gaps in a thunderhead. More plasma tongues flicked through these wounds, then the *Rifleman* ripped in half across its waist. The torso shot into the heavens like a dark comet, then hung there motionless as the boiling plasma jet beneath it imploded.

The *Rifleman*'s torso, its lower edges still glowing molten red, finally upended and tumbled to the ground. It landed on its right shoulder, but autocannon ammo exploding in the firing mechanism flipped it over one last time. Though the 'Mech rested on its back with the cockpit apparently undamaged and pointing skyward, no pilot ejected.

Dan stepped the *Wolfhound* through the 'Mech bay wall. "Obliged, Colonel."

Morgan's voice had not fully lost its icy edge, but Dan heard a trace of compassion. "It had to be done, Captain. Let's move. We've lots more work if we're going to win the battle of New Freedom."

15

Daniel Allard closed his eyes and rolled his head in a slow circle. Pain stabbed like fingers of lightning through his neck and shoulders. *Even with the padding, the neurohelmet pounded my muscles into raw protoplasm.* He arched his back and heard a series of pops run up his spine. *I haven't been so sore since*—he swallowed sourly—*since the battle on Styx that cost Patrick Kell his life.*

Dan reopened his eyes and stared out the conference room's window toward the ruins of New Freedom. With roofs torn off and walls destroyed, the buildings the Kell Hounds had labored to build looked like twisted, diseased, defoliated metal trees. Oily black smoke still rose from some of the rubble piles to hang heavily in the limp, moist air.

Scattered throughout the area were the remains of two dozen 'Mechs. Most of the battered hulks lay in heaps on the ground while Techs, looking like ants in the distance, salvaged what they could from the carcasses. In some cases, like the *Rifleman* Morgan had killed, the 'Mech's legs stood tall and strong, but supported nothing.

Dan looked around at those assembled at the conference table. Conn O'Bannon, the stocky commander of the Second 'Mech Battalion, looked as though he'd not slept since the Kell Hounds landed two days before. His unit had met the Third Dieron Regulars First Battalion outside St. Johns. They broke the Regulars, but could not prevent two companies from retreating in good order to DropShips and leaving the world.

Across from him sat Salome Ward. Her command, the First 'Mech Battalion, overran the Regulars' command position near Montpelier. The enemy General, *Tai-sho* Sen Ti Ch'uan died in the assault, and his second in command, *Tai-sa* Hiro Akuta surrendered when he realized his DropShips had been cut off from his position. After being assured his men would not be mistreated, Akuta asked for and received permission to commit *seppuku*.

Major Seamus Fitzpatrick sat next to Salome and watched Techs explore the two *Sholagars'* melted wreckage for anything of possible value. Exhaustion bent him forward like a hunchback, and there were bags under his usually bright green eyes.

Unconsciously toying with the green sash, Dan shifted his gaze to Major Richard O'Cieran. *Damn. If the rest of us look tired, Rick looks dead.* The infantry leader cradled his gray-haired head in both hands and stared down at the table. *Digging down to confirm the site we found as a mass grave has taken it out of him. It's one thing to wage war on troops, but the wholesale slaughter of a town is unbelievable.*

Dan looked up as Morgan Kell entered the room, followed by Clovis and Cat Wilson. As they took up places at the table, Morgan moved to its head and leaned wearily against it. "Thank you for waiting. Tim Murphy just died from wounds he suffered here two nights ago. That puts our dead at seven, total casualties at thirty." Anger and frustration ran through Morgan's words. "Unacceptable, all of it."

Salome looked over at Morgan. "We've secured the planet. The two DropShips that got offworld will link up with their JumpShip in three days, if they continue at their current velocity. We've really no fear of a return engagement. Popping in so close to Lyons and using the moon to cover our approach surprised them. Are we going to pack up and still try to reach Ryde in time?"

Morgan shook his head. "We can't. On our original schedule, we had the *Cucamulus* waiting at Alphecca to transport us to Ryde. When we learned of the attack on Lyons and headed back, Janos Vandermeer brought the *Cu* insystem far enough to give us that tactical advantage. We've got ten days before the *Cu* can jump again, and then another ten days at Alphecca. We'll not make it in time."

Conn O'Bannon sank fingers back through his brown hair and frowned. "Perhaps Yorinaga Kurita will wait for us."

"No, Conn. I don't think so. He'll come insystem, perhaps land, and then will get out of there." Morgan lowered himself into a chair. "It doesn't really matter. We have to clean up this mess."

Dan sat up. "Am I missing something? I thought the world has been secured."

Morgan nodded. "It has. However, the whole reason for the execution of everyone in New Freedom raises new questions that have to be dealt with." Morgan looked toward Clovis. "Explain to them what you told me."

The haggard dwarf sighed heavily and rubbed a hand over his unshaven chin. "Despite Dan's valiant effort to destroy this building by backing his *Wolfhound* through it, he only managed to short out the entire electrical system and collapse the corridor leading to the computer center. This prevented the Combine staff from dumping the contents of their computers, as normal security procedure would dictate. With Cat's help, I've managed to bring the system back up and I've learned why..." Clovis stopped abruptly, choked up with emotion.

Morgan continued the narrative for him. "The ISF learned of New Freedom through normal channels and linked it with the group of people who had inhabited the Styx base two years ago. The ISF had always considered them a threat. Apparently, the ISF obtained information from agents in the Isle of Skye that suggested the Styx settlers were planning to have the Coordinator of the Draconis Combine assassinated. The Third Dieron Regulars were ordered to obliterate New Freedom."

Rick O'Cieran slammed his fist onto the table. "Jesus, Morgan! They bulldozed a trench and just shot people. Men, women...it didn't make any difference..." He glanced toward Clovis. "If you'd not gotten those children down to the shelter, they'd have shot them as well." He looked back toward the other officers. "Not everyone was dead when they filled the trench back in. Some people died trying to dig their way out..."

Silence filled the room. Dan swallowed hard as he remembered a young couple whose home he'd helped build. *They never imagined any future but that of growing old together. As a MechWarrior, I accept the risks of war, but those kids never had a part in any of that.*

Dan looked up. "We know that no one in New Freedom was plotting against the Combine's Coordinator. Hell, everyone here was a member of Heimdall. With their anti-Commonwealth history, I would have thought the Combine would have welcomed them as allies."

Morgan nodded. "That's probably one of the reasons that the ISF tolerated their presence in the Styx system. Unfortunately, the whole *Silver Eagle* affair changed the ISF's view. The Styx base cost them elite troops, 'Mechs, and ultimately, a chance to capture Melissa

101

Steiner." Morgan hesitated as everyone silently acknowledged the cost of that operation to the Kell Hounds: the loss of Patrick Kell and three other friends.

Dan shook his head. "What could make the ISF believe the Styx refugees had become assassins?"

Cat's deep voice carried finality with it. "Not what, but who..."

Morgan nodded. "Who, indeed. No doubt Duke Aldo Lestrade himself planted that little rumor in the ear of an ISF agent. He probably even pointed to our connection with New Freedom to suggest we were training commandos."

Salome shook her head, which spread her coppery locks over her shoulders. "I thought we decided before that Lestrade would not invite an assault on his own holding. It still makes no sense in my mind."

"Think of it in these terms, Salome," said Fitzpatrick. "Lestrade makes Lyons a nice target by planting this rumor. All he loses is a small settlement, whose destruction will hurt us, but costs him nothing. He knows the Combine can't hold the world, and he suspects that the Kuritans will pull their forces out the second the Commonwealth sends troops in."

Salome chewed her lower lip for a moment, then nodded. "Lestrade has an incursion into the Isle of Skye. He can complain all the more loudly about the Commonwealth's betrayal of his people." She paused as the logical extrapolation of this line of reasoning came to her. "Lestrade can even declare his holding neutral. This will keep Kurita out of it, allowing them to devote forces to other fronts."

Dan's mouth suddenly went dry. "The Isle of Skye going independent also cuts the Commonwealth off from the Federated Suns. Hanse will be forced to reopen the transit lanes, which means he'll be at war with a portion of his ally."

"It's worse than that," Cat said. "Civil Wars are unpopular. Katrina loses and someone else steps in. Melissa is tainted by her marriage, so that leaves Frederick Steiner."

Dan nodded. "Frederick is Lestrade's puppet. Fred takes over, and Lestrade returns to the fold. Fred ends the war with Kurita, and everyone is happy. Aldo pulls Fred's strings, and the Commonwealth goes to hell in a DropShip."

Morgan smiled cruelly. "That's what Lestrade must have planned, but we messed things up for him this time. He'll try again...I know it. I want everyone ready to move out within the week. Lestrade should be in his ancestral home on Summer. I want to bring it down around his ears. It's time to end his meddling for good."

Only one voice dissented from the quick shouts of agreement that

102

greeted Morgan's proposition.

"No!" Clovis stood on his chair, raising his head above the others at the table. "No. You cannot."

Morgan stiffened. "I appreciate your concern, Clovis, but I'm willing to risk any fallout from our strike against him."

Clovis shook his head. "I do not doubt your ability to handle both the military operation and the political turmoil your action would stir up, Morgan Kell. But I say you cannot kill Aldo Lestrade because I claim that right." Clovis held his head up high. "I demand to be the one who kills him."

Clovis looked around at the stunned mercenaries. "Do not think I speak purely from anger and grief at what has happened here." He swallowed past the thick lump in his throat. "It does play a part, of course. If you've ever had to tell a child his parents died for reasons he will never understand, you'll know what that does to you inside. Each time I said the words, anger and outrage were like daggers ripping at my soul. Revenge seems like just the salve to put everything right again."

The dwarf bowed his head, his carefully chosen words coming slowly. "I know that's what you're thinking because you've lost friends and lovers in the battle here. I think back to the celebration we had less than a month ago and how I'll never see some of those faces again. I want to pay someone back for that, but vengeance is not the reason I claim Aldo Lestrade as my own. The only way those wounds will heal is to rebuild New Freedom, and that I will do before I head out after the Demon of Summer."

Clovis paused and looked at every person in the room before continuing. "All my life I have known of his evil. My mother was once employed as a servant by Lestrade's family, and came to know Aldo Lestrade far better than she ever wished. During the same raid that killed Aldo's father and made him Duke twenty-four years ago, my mother fled Summer with the aid of a Heimdall cell. Within six months, I was born, and I've been with Heimdall ever since.

"Children can be cruel, and they were to me. My mother comforted me with stories of my father, who she said was a bold MechWarrior who would someday come and take us both away. I fantasized that my father would destroy all of my enemies for me, and I could endure anything while waiting for his return. Likewise, to make him proud, I learned all I could about lostech and drove myself to excel in things like computer programming because everyone else found it too hard."

Clovis shook his head. "Of course, there is no father of mythic proportions waiting to come for me. Instead, as I grew older, I heard uncharitable references to my mother as 'the Duke's whore.' Slowly, the truth began to dawn. One night, I finally confronted my mother. She admitted that she'd become pregnant by Aldo Lestrade. She'd been too terrified of him to deny his advances or to report that he'd gotten her with child. From that point, she forebade me to speak of this matter. Were she here instead of up on the *Bifrost,* I might not have said anything."

Clovis opened his hands. "You see. Aldo Lestrade is my father. He murdered his way to the throne of Summer, and his manipulation has destroyed my people, the people of New Freedom. In keeping with the precedent he himself set, it is my right to destroy my father, Aldo Lestrade." Clovis's handsome face hardened into a horrible mask. "Warriors kill warriors. Lestrades kill Lestrades. Leave him to me."

16

Justin Xiang looked on as Maximilian Liao smiled for the holovid camera. A smile crept across the Chancellor's face, sending a shiver down Justin's spine. *You'd never guess to look at him that a third of his realm has been conquered. That smile makes him look like a python studying a trapped rat.*

"*Zao*, citizens." Maximilian's expression softened, and his voice dropped to the calm, warm tone of a benevolent patriarch addressing his family. "It has been far too long since I last addressed you in this manner. Though piloting the ship of state is never an easy job, my people are ever in my thoughts. Indeed, these thoughts of you are what sustain me in this time of trial."

The Chancellor narrowed his dark eyes. "I am well aware of the hardships you have endured as this savage assault has nibbled away at our nation. I know that fear and doubt must touch you in many ways, yet I would not consider that treason. By no means—worrying about your family and your lives is logical. Only succumbing to that fear is treason, especially in light of what we have just accomplished."

Justin felt a hand at the small of his back push him forward as the Chancellor turned to face him and the camera panned to pull him into the picture. "This is my trusted and valued aide, Justin Xiang. He has just returned from an operation that took place deep within the Federated Suns. Braving untold dangers and even wounding, he managed to destroy a Davion *Centurion* and escape Prince Hanse Davion's wrath. More important, Justin Xiang and his team success-

105

fully stole from House Davion a sample of new technology that will turn the war around for us."

The Chancellor stood to tower above Justin. For the benefit of the camera, Maximilian extended his right hand and showed off a baton about a third of a meter long. Carved of ivory in a braided ribbon pattern, the baton bore the Liao crest in its center, and was inlaid with coral, malachite, and onyx bands at one end. The Chancellor handled it with extreme care and honor.

"Though an insufficient reward for the many duties you have performed for the Capellan Confederation, I present to you, Justin Xiang, the Baton of Illustrious Service." Maximilian smiled and handed the baton to Justin. "I hope your unflagging service to the land of your birth will continue forever."

Justin's metallic left hand closed on the prize. He bowed to the Chancellor, then straightened up, his facial expression serious. "Even death itself could not end my service to my nation."

The Chancellor bowed his head to Justin, then turned again to the camera. Justin retreated back to the wings, where Candace was waiting. He turned to watch the Chancellor continue his statement before the dozen members of the press corps in the audience would have their chance to ask questions, but Candace tugged on his right elbow.

"Justin, let's leave. Your part is done."

Justin frowned. "I should stay through the press conference."

"Why? You already know what the questions are. Didn't you help prepare them this afternoon?"

Justin smiled. "You win." He followed as she threaded her way through the people and equipment in the Palace's holovid studio. *The Baton of Illustrious Service this evening and being invested as Shonso of Teng tomorrow. There was a time when I used to imagine winning such honors, but they always came from Hanse Davion's hands. Now I get them for actions taken against the Federated Suns. How life changes things.*

Candace opened a doorway into one of the Palace's grand corridors. The exterior wall was made of glass that rose up three stories to provide a breathtaking view of the capital city below. Lights from a million houses burned like a mirror-image of the night sky above. The interior wall contained huge, framed rice-paper portraits of the royal family.

Though he had walked here hundreds of times before, it took a moment or two for Justin to identify the changes to the pictures. The portrait of Elizabeth Liao, Maximilian's wife, had been moved from his side and been replaced by Romano's picture. In addition, white ribbons hung from the frames of both her portrait and that of Liao's son Tormana.

Justin squeezed Candace's left hand lightly and pointed toward the paintings with his baton. "Why the mourning ribbons? Has there been some recent news about Tormana?"

Candace shrugged as they paused beneath her stepmother's portrait. "State militia found a body in a shallow grave near Dangao Lake. The victim's throat had been cut and the romanized letter A had been carved into her forehead—the cuts running deep enough to score the bone. Dental records have matched the body to Elizabeth, though my father has ordered that her death be listed officially as accidental drowning."

Justin nodded at the next picture in line. "And your brother?"

Candace stiffened as she looked at Tormana Liao's portrait. "Sources report that my brother was not among the prisoners taken when Davion overran Algol's defenses. Our agents there located his 'Mech, and there was blood in the cockpit. As nearly as we can determine, he escaped into the swamps and died there."

Justin slipped his arm around her shoulders. "I'm sorry, Candace. I know you two were close." He drew her closer. "I never met Tormana, but I'm sure I would have liked him."

Candace turned toward Justin and rested both her hands against his chest. "I thank you for your concern and your sympathy, but I doubt you would have liked Tormana. Unlike you or me, he became a MechWarrior because all the alternatives bored him even more. I think he even married his lowborn wife as much out of desire for scandal as for love."

She smiled weakly. "He was a useful ally in tormenting Romano when we were all children. My affection for him remains from those days." She looked into Justin's eyes. "You would find little in common with him, my love, and for that I am very thankful. Despite the vicious rumors Romano has spread, Tormana is not the sort of man I would wish to know on an intimate basis." She kissed his lips lightly. "But you are."

Justin enfolded Candace in a strong hug. "For that, my Duchess, I am most thankful." He released her. "Shall I assume, then, that I am being made *Shonso* of a world in your St. Ives Commonality so people will not be similarly outraged that you've bedded a lowborn citizen?"

Candace grinned. "A tad late for that now, isn't it, Citizen Xiang? Besides, your maternal grandfather served in the Ministry of Information Standards for years and was made a Lord before he died. You are hardly an ordinary citizen, Justin." She kissed his lips again. "How well I know that."

She patted him playfully on the right chest, then recoiled in horror when he winced. "Oh, Justin, I'm sorry."

Justin shook his head, giving the pain time to drain away. "No problem. Everything is fairly well healed. I react more from habit than actual pain." He paused and smiled as two Development Ministry officials walked past. "Let's find a more private place to talk."

"My sentiments exactly." Candace took his hand and led him down the passageway. "For the two days since your return, they've had you debriefed and tested by just about everyone in the Maskirovka. Tonight, I've arranged an intimate dinner for just the two of us."

Justin smiled. "And afterward?"

She smiled coyly. "And after that, I thought we could slip into something more comfortable, like my bed, and I could properly welcome you home."

Lying next to him in the bed, her head resting on his left shoulder, Candace brushed the fingertips of her left hand lightly across the patch of lighter colored flesh on the right side of Justin's chest. "Aside from the skin tone, I can't really tell that you've been hit."

Justin nodded and kissed the top of her head. "Thanks to Tsen Shang's foresight, we had a fully equipped biolab on the DropShip that remained with our JumpShip at Bethel. Though your father would not allow his top scientists to man the lab, those who did had enough knowledge to analyze the myomer fiber we stole. It's fortunate they also had the expertise and equipment to culture a skin graft to cover up my wound."

She shifted around so that her right forearm lay against his chest to support her chin. "The preliminary reports said you'd lost people and that the 'Mechs had been hit. I was worried."

Justin forced himself to smile. "Well, things might have been a bit worse for me if one of the JumpShips hadn't suffered a liquid helium leak. That meant its Kearny-Fuchida jump drive wouldn't work, so we had to recharge the JumpShip we were using. Because there was no transfer, and we had to wait ten days to recharge, the scientists had the time to make up the culture." He snorted a hoarse laugh. "That is, however, the last time I want research scientists to work on me. As one of them said, 'Citizen, if you were a rat, I could be sure this would work, but I cannot make a Human any promises.' Luckily, the Fourth Tau Ceti Rangers had a real doctor with them who supervised everything."

Candace smiled and kissed his chest. "I was so happy to hear you were alive that I almost took a shuttle out to meet your DropShip when you finally jumped into this system. I had no desire to lose my only ally against my sister."

Justin touched her cheek tenderly, wondering what Candace would say if she knew the truth, that it wasn't a Davion security officer who'd shot him but one of her own sister's agents. *Romano certainly took the news of Ling's death calmly. But then, she'd had a week of knowing I'd survived before I set foot on Sian.*

Candace traced a small circle on Justin's chest with her index finger. "Did you manage to deliver the present I left in the cockpit of your 'Mech?"

Justin nodded and gave her a squeeze with his left arm. "Unless my father's people have actually sunk to the level of incompetence claimed by our propaganda, they'll find it." Justin narrowed his brown eyes. "In fact, that's how I got shot—accomplishing that little feat. The guard shot Ling and then me before Alexi killed him."

Candace smiled contentedly. "Excellent." She reached up to caress the side of his face. "I shall have to remember to thank Alexi Malenkov for saving your life. What would be a suitable gift?"

Justin chuckled lightly. "Alexi is a man of simple tastes. Perhaps making him a Mandrinn on Warlock would suit him."

Candace's eyes became gray crescents. "Good idea, lover, but slightly off target. I shall make him a Mandrinn on Teng. He will become your vassal, to remind him that you are important to both of us. I believe Dao Shan Province is within your holding. I shall give it to him as a reward for his loyalty to you."

A light tapping sounded on the teakwood door. "Mistress?" asked a timid voice that Justin recognized as belonging to Candace's maid.

Candace looked toward the door. "I left orders that we were not to be disturbed, Li."

The nervous tremor in the servant's voice survived translation through the door. "I know, Mistress, but there are men here, and they have orders to bring Citizen Xiang to the Chancellor. I have told them you would not know where he might be…"

Candace swung her legs around over the edge of the bed and stood. "Tell them to wait in the outer chamber." She pulled on a silken yellow robe to cover her nakedness, but let it gap open as she leaned over to kiss Justin full on the mouth. "This had better be more than one of my sister's tantrums. If she has pulled us from my warm bed for no reason, I will personally supply reasons for white ribbons to decorate her portrait."

109

Justin felt a sinking sensation when the two Death Commandos escorted Candace and him toward the briefing room and not the Chancellor's throne room. *Something dire must have happened.*

The door of the chamber retracted into the ceiling, allowing Candace and Justin access to the black chamber. Behind them, the door descended again, sealing them within a nearly featureless ebon capsule. A holographic display table dominated the center of the room, and the Chancellor stood hunched over its far end. Midway along the left side, Tsen Shang feverishly entered data requests on a keyboard, then gave soft commands to Alexi on the other side of the table to repeat his calculations.

The Chancellor did not raise his head even though an image burned to life in the air before him. "You are certain, Citizen Xiang, that this new myomer fiber will make our 'Mechs strong?"

Justin nodded. "Yes, Celestial Supremacy, it will."

The holographic display taking shape above the table distracted Justin before he had a chance to notice the effect of his reply on Maximilian Liao. The image, which represented what had been the Capellan Confederation at the beginning of the Davion invasion, glowed with different colors. The renegade Tikonov Free Republic burned with a defiant blue, while a fierce red denoted the planets Davion troops now occupied. A rich green colored the space of still loyal and intact planets, but Justin noticed that a new fork of red stabbed into the Sarna Confederation.

Justin's mouth went dry. "The fifth wave…Davion's launched a fifth wave."

Tsen nodded his head wearily. "They hit Matsu, Zaurak, Menkib, New Macao, and Mandate—all defended by militia alone."

Justin narrowed his eyes. "Reinforced militia, or just the standard stuff?"

Alexi, peering closely at his data terminal, punched up a summary of the action. "Menkib, New Macao, and Mandate had all called up reserves, and they had supplies. Matsu had done no call-up. Zaurak had initiated some activity, but this is the season of storms in the northern hemisphere so we don't know how far they got in their efforts."

Justin nodded idly as he leaned forward to see. "What have we got to oppose them on Wei, Remshield, and Tsingtao?"

Tsen glanced at his data screen. "All three battalions of Sung's Cuirassiers were on Wei, but Davion dropped regiments in on them, as per past attacks. The other two worlds have single battalions defending them and are facing full regimental combat teams."

Tsen Shang shot a haunted glance at the holographic map as a dagger of red stabbed deep into the heart of the Sarna Commonality. "By the gods, they can't." He looked up at Justin, then over at Alexi. "Have you got confirmation?"

Alexi's head sank forward as he nodded. "I've got enough Jump- and DropShips for at least two RCTs."

Justin stared open-mouthed at the world now slowly burning red. *I don't believe it. They've actually done it!* "Sarna!" he said aloud.

Maximilian Liao's head came up as a deep, insane laugh echoed from his throat. "Sarna. They actually struck at Sarna."

The harsh sound of his laughter echoed in the room, and struck Justin with a momentary fear. *He's lost it. The Chancellor has finally lost it.* "Highness, this is their deepest and boldest stroke."

Liao's eyes narrowed until they were no more than black, reptilian slits. "Have you forgotten, Justin Xiang, that you yourself antici- pated this attack? McCarron's Armored Cavalry has not left Sarna. They will smash the invaders and then, with 'Mechs strengthened by the new myomer fibers, we will force the invaders from our domain." Liao smiled cruelly. "Hanse Davion does not realize it, but he has overextended himself. This attack is the beginning of the end for House Davion and its conquest of the Successor States!"

17

Captain Alanna Damu gritted her teeth and pushed her feet down against the foot pedals on her command couch. The gentle pressure ignited the *Victor*'s jump jets, slowing the assault 'Mech's rapid descent. She glanced at the altimeter readout on her auxiliary monitor. *Three, two, one...* A quick push on the pedals softened the impact, then she bent the *Victor*'s knees to absorb the shock of landing.

As her 'Mech hit, the landing did not jar Alanna as much as she'd expected, despite the speed. *Either I'm better at dropping than I remember, or...* She flicked a dark hand over the command console's keyboard, then snarled as the requested information flashed onto her auxiliary monitor. "Damn! The last thing I need is for my company to land in a goddamn marsh!"

The *Victor*'s sensors gave her full view of the wide, shallow valley that Invasion Command had designated Landing Zone Pulsar. Off to the west, on a slow rise, was an evergreen forest with trees so tall they dwarfed even the BattleMechs. The thick green growth broke against the rolling hills toward the north, where the Gray Mountains rose up to form the northern horizon. From their snowy heights flowed the broad, muddy river that had overflowed its banks to flood the valley. The mountains tapered off toward the east, but more hills in that direction restricted visibility as well. Only to the south, where the sluggish river escaped, was the landscape wide open.

Alanna frowned deeply. *Too much open ground. I wonder if*

112

Marshal Tamara Hasek picked this spot, or if the real power behind the throne chose this landing zone? She saw an *Orion* touch down amid the company's other 'Mechs and jettison its temporary rocket assembly. Opening a radio link, she contacted that 'Mech's pilot. "Look alive, Leftenant. This is an arcade shooting gallery if I ever saw one."

"Roger that, Captain. I bet old Heart-of-Stone closed his eyes and touched the map to plunk us here. Yuck! A swamp."

Alanna found herself smiling at Rex Archambauld's nickname for the Fifth Syrtis Fusiliers' "Combat" Commander. Tamara Hasek, the late Duke Michael's 70-year-old aunt, was listed as the unit's supreme commander and reportedly did take part in planning all the Fusiliers' activities. Day-to-day command, however, was handled by Duke Michael's crony, General Gordon Hartstone. Though a capable commander, his attitudes and manners did little to endear him to certain members of his command.

Rex knows he'll get another slug on his record for that remark when the battletapes are reviewed, but I suppose it won't make any difference to him. He's too good to be busted out of the service, and the AFFS knows it. I think they keep him a Leftenant just so he won't stir up trouble among the enlisted personnel. Alanna smiled. *I don't mind …Couldn't find a better second in command in the whole Army.*

Alanna switched her scanner over to magnetic resonance and scoured the hills to the north. "Rex, the hills north look clear. Let's get everyone out of this swamp and over onto the hill."

Rex's strong voice filled her neurohelmet. "Good idea. Do you want anyone to go over the top?"

Alanna chewed her lower lip for a second. "Yes. Get the company on the hill, then send Jack up in his *Ostroc*."

"Roger, out."

With a huge, sucking pop, Alanna worked the *Victor's* right foot free of the marsh. It left a hole the size of a luxury aircar behind that the swamp rapidly filled with brown, muddy water. Laboring mightily, she pulled the left leg free. *This could take forever!*

Suddenly, the computer painted a mass of highly metallic images on the edge of her holographic display. Like a swarm of bees, they headed down from the forest, speeding across the marsh. Alanna turned the *Victor's* head to center the approaching craft on the display, then flicked the sensor-feed back to visual. "Heads up, children. We have company."

Leftenant Opal Karsten snapped an order over the radio. "Fire Lance. Bogies, two-seven-oh degrees. Fire when ready!" After a pause, she asked hesitantly, "Cap, what the hell are those?"

Alanna's fingers flew over her keyboard. "The computer has no definite match, but profile and speed makes them Savannah Masters. Listed as experimental—a shipment of the hovercrafts was lost to Periphery pirates a year ago." Alanna narrowed her brown eyes as she studied the auxiliary information. "Hit what you shoot at. They're fast and nasty."

Knute King's voice, arrogant as ever, filled the combat channel with harsh laughter. "Bugs. Nothing more."

Alanna shivered with anger. On her screen, she watched the wedge-shaped hovercraft formation spread out as it came into range. Barely larger than a 'Mech's foot, each one-man hovercraft was little more than a fusion engine, some armor, a medium laser, and a huge fan. *Under normal circumstances, their attack would be suicidal, but with us stuck here and moving slow, we're sitting ducks!*

Alanna opened the radio channel. "All jumpers, blast off and move south two hundred meters. We'll bracket them. They're going to come at our backs. Make your shots count!"

The *Victor* blasted toward the sky. Feathering the left pedal, Alanna flared the left leg's jump jet and turned the 'Mech over so it stared down at the approaching hovercraft. Extending the 'Mech's left arm, she targeted a group of five coming in at Archambauld's mired *Orion. Too fast to track, she thought. Just have to trust to luck.* Without waiting for the computer lock she knew would never come, she tightened up on the trigger.

One of her two medium lasers hit a hovercraft. The beam sliced through armor on the Savannah Master's left side, dropping molten globules steaming into the marsh water. The craft skittered to the side as the pilot shied away from the intense heat, but it lost no speed. Firing in unison with the other four craft in its attack group, the pilot drilled his laser into Archambauld's *Orion*.

Four medium lasers hit the heavy 'Mech. Two lanced into its right flank, carving glowing red scars beneath its armpit. A third lopped a chunk of armor from the 'Mech's right arm and the last lanced into the *Orion's* right thigh. The beam played across the armor, vaporizing what it touched, but failed to pierce it fully.

The *Orion* let loose with everything it had except for its short-range missiles. The autocannon sprouting from the humanoid 'Mech's right hip fired high over its target, but the fifteen LRMs corkscrewing out from the launcher mounted in its left shoulder hit home. Explosions surrounded a hovercraft, lifting it from the water and pirouetting it through a firecloud. Visible for a half-second amid the smoke and

114

brilliant flames, the hovercraft disintegrated, showering the water with metal splinters.

Hovercraft swept in at Tom Clark's *Thunderbolt* from behind. Two of them hit with their medium lasers, but the damage they did was minor. As one swept past his position, Clark tagged it with a medium laser, blasting armor from its nose. Even more devastating, Nancy Campion's *Grasshopper* goosed one fleeing Savannah Master with a blast from her large laser. The beam ate through the small craft like swamp rot, filling the cockpit with fire and death.

The third group of hovercraft targeted Karsten's *Crusader*, slashing at the 'Mech's rear. One beam blasted armor over the *Crusader*'s spine. The other two beams that hit stabbed into the 'Mech's left flank and pierced its side. Steam and yellow-green fluid burst from the wound as the laser beams vaporized three heat sinks. Though Karsten unleashed two flights of LRMs and fired both medium lasers at the hovercraft, all five escaped unharmed.

Heart in her mouth, Alanna watched as Eric de Chanoui, anticipating the strike at his *Rifleman*'s rear, rotated the 'Mech's arms up and around to cover his rear arc. Mindless of the heat buildup it would cause, he blazed away with the large lasers and autocannon. *If he doesn't get them now, he's history!*

The *Rifleman*'s autocannon fired a salvo that hit one hovercraft on the nose. The shells blasted armor into jagged little chunks of ferroceramic alloy that careened off the craft's windscreen like hail. The impact slowed the hovercraft long enough for one of the *Rifleman*'s large lasers to sweep over it. The Savannah Master blurred in the ruby beam's grasp, then exploded in a rolling fireball that skipped like a stone across the water's tortured surface.

The other four hovercraft swept on through the fiery cloud that had been their group leader. Three of them hit with their lasers, and two cored through the *Rifleman*'s back armor. A series of explosions detonated within the *Rifleman*'s chest as the lasers destroyed the fusion engine's shielding and the incredible heat touched off the autocannon ammo stored next to it. As the fire built within the 'Mech, the angular outline of its torso softened and flames shot from the hole in its spine.

Seconds before a massive explosion tore the *Rifleman* apart, a gout of flame shot from the 'Mech's chest. De Chanoui's ejection seat shot straight up, then angled over toward the hills to the north. The 'Mech he left behind split down the middle as an argent spear of flame stabbed up toward the dawn sky. The 'Mech's arms flew off in two different directions while torso fragments peppered the water. The 'Mech's legs, untouched, but trailing smoke from where the torso had sat, remained stuck upright in the swamp.

Alanna saw another hovercraft explode as Eve Bors hit it with a burst from her *Ostsol*'s large laser. From her vantage point, Alanna could only see damage on the *Ostsol*'s right leg, but Eve quickly reported that the armor on her 'Mech's back was all but destroyed.

The hovercraft, which had attacked from the west, continued on toward the east. They followed the river as it curved north and quickly vanished behind the hills where de Chanoui had landed. Alanna frowned. *I don't like this at all. Those guys were too good to be Liao militia.*

Alanna radioed Rex Archambauld on their company's command frequency. "Rex, get the others on those hills. Keep alert. Use the jumpers to act as outriders. I'm going over to the Command Channel. I want air cover."

She hit two switches, expecting to hear the bored voice of a radio operator in the invasion's tactical center. Instead, a babble of voices and noise blasted through her neurohelmet. "We're taking heavy fire on Boomslang Ridge," she heard an excited voice report. The whine of an autocannon accompanied the transmission. "Get us some air support!"

"Negative, Deuce Battalion. Support allocations are only assigned on request of a commanding officer. My screen shows you're only a Captain. Where is Colonel Harkness?"

Irritation shot through the field commander's voice. "Harkness bought it when he marched his *Marauder* into a Liao militia ambush. They had inferno rockets and roasted him alive."

Alanna felt as if an icy dagger had been thrust into her stomach. *What a way to die!* Inferno rockets exploded just before they hit their targets, covering a 'Mech or building with a jellied fuel that burned like hell itself. The heat buildup was enough to render a 'Mech inoperable. Alanna shot a glance at her own heat monitors and felt a cold trickle of sweat run down her spine.

"If you don't get it, Taccom, I'm the only command officer left in the Second 'Mech Battalion. I guess that brevets me to Colonel, wouldn't you say?"

The command center's radio operator came back with nervousness twitching through his words. "I guess it would, Colonel Moultrie, but I still can't give you any air cover." The man's voice sank. "We don't have any more."

Alanna broke in before Moultrie could curse at the radioman at the tactical center. "Colonel, Captain Damu, First Battalion. You're east of our position. What's your opposition?"

Moultrie's voice lost its edge. "'Mechs and armor in the foothills. They're dug in, so we can't do anything. Can you swing over?"

Alanna summoned a tactical map of the area and thought she saw a way to hit Boomslang Ridge from the west. Before she could answer, however, Jack Cannon's *Ostroc* crested the hill directly north of the swamp. A light flashed on her command console, indicating a message coming in on the company frequency, then it died abruptly.

She looked up as the barrel-chested 'Mech staggered, then spun wildly. Armor flew in ragged sheets from its torso. Explosions from the SRM magazine began, shooting flame from the legion of holes opened in the 'Mech's chest. The *Ostroc* stumbled back down the hill, then exploded, blowing the upper half of the 'Mech's torso out into the middle of the swamp.

"Jesus, Mary, and Joseph! Colonel, we've just been hit by something!" Alanna hesitated, waiting for Moultrie's reply, but heard nothing. "Colonel Moultrie? Colonel?"

Rex Archambauld's voice broke into the radio frequency. "Cannon reported two Saladins were on the other side of the hill before they got him. He IDed them as part of McCarron's Armored Cavalry. We've got real opposition here, Cap. What the hell are we going to do?"

The panic in Rex's voice made Alanna get control of her own. *These people are my responsibility. I've got to get them out of this mess.* She swallowed past the lump in her throat before speaking. "Move everyone west, toward the forest."

Doubt bled into Rex's words. "Cap, that'll move us away from the concentration of our troops. We'll be on our own."

Alanna shook her head. *Can't have you going rogue on me, Rex.* "Leftenant, in case you've not noticed, we had opposition on what was supposed to be a milk run. We expected militia and we get trained mercs who've got a vendetta with us that runs deeper than a black hole. Command says our air cover's been swatted down and the Second Battalion's getting ripped to pieces on Boomslang Ridge. We're talking a bigtime snafu here. Some malfing idiot stuck our head in the *chiroptopard*'s mouth, and I'm not having anything to do with it."

Rex's voice came back strong and full of fire. "Roger, Captain. What do we do when we hit the forest?"

Alanna shuddered, the image of Colonel Harkness's death by inferno rocket flashing through her mind. "We torch the forest and try to stay one step ahead of the flames. With any luck, that'll flush our opposition and we can break out of what is obviously a very big trap." Her hands curled into claws. "And if we survive that, then we go looking for the idiot who got us into this situation and kill him!"

18

Myndo forced her fists open and held her head high. *I can feel their fear. They know the day of reckoning has come. They called the tune, and now they must pay the piper.* She smiled coldly. *This piper is more than ready to collect.*

The Primus looked at her with unconcealed rage in his dark eyes. "I believe we all know the reason Precentor Dieron has called us here for an emergency meeting." He inclined his head in her direction. "Precentor, I believe you have a motion to put forward?"

Myndo waited a second or two before killing her smile. "Hanse Davion's troops landed on Sarna yesterday morning. I demand, as we have agreed before, that we vote a complete and total Interdiction of service into and out of the Federated Suns—this to include information from Davion agents inside the Capellan Confederation or any other nation."

The Primus looked around at the other Precentors gathered in the wood-paneled, dome-shaped First Circuit chamber. "Is there any discussion?"

Precentor Tharkad nodded his gold-maned head. "My esteemed colleague from the Draconis Combine is correct that our threshold event has been reached, but the conquest of Sarna is not complete. I would suggest, therefore, that her motion is premature."

Myndo's eyes blazed. "You hypocritical fool! We agreed that an attack on Sarna would trigger Interdiction! I delayed calling for this

118

meeting until Davion's troops actually landed on Sarna because I expected you to balk before war was enjoined." She stabbed a finger toward her enemy. "How can you justify delaying a stroke that might save Sarna?"

Ulthan Everson rose to her challenge. "Have you forgotten, Myndo Waterly, that the holovid of a raid on our installation that you manufactured uses a location that appears to be the substation in the Weng-chu Prefecture of Sarna's Gold Coast? Davion's troops have not pacified that area yet. How can we base our Interdiction on so transparent a piece of fakery?"

Before Myndo could reply, Precentor Sian cut in. "I must agree with Precentor Tharkad. Despite earlier agreements, it would be an error to interdict right now. Davion's forces have taken a terrible beating on Sarna. Interdiction would prevent knowledge of their defeat spreading back through the Federated Suns. The bloodbath might be enough to kill support for the invasion all by itself."

The ghost of a grin twisting the Primus's lips made Myndo angry and then suddenly cold, with a clarity of vision she'd never experienced. Everything fell together. *Of course! We're so busy watching the Fox's hands that we ignore his true motives.* A small laugh escaped her.

The Primus stiffened. "Ridicule has no part in this place of reason, Precentor Dieron. Control yourself or be censured!"

Myndo bowed her head apologetically, then saw the other Precentors watching her as her head came up. *They've noticed the change. Now, while I have their attention, I must use what I have learned.*

She focused upon Villius Tejh. "Precentor Sian, why do you think Hanse Davion pursues this war?"

Tejh regarded her carefully, probing the expression on her face for the hint of a trap. "I am not fool enough to be taken in by his speeches about the threat Liao presents to the Federated Suns. The Prince must have realized, after Galahad 3026, that any assault by the Capellan Confederation would result in disaster for Maximilian Liao. Hanse Davion wishes to be the First Lord of a new Star League. He married into part of such a new government, and now he conquers yet another."

The Precentor of New Avalon shook his head. "With all due respect, Precentor Sian, I believe my own vantage point is better than yours. Quite simply, I believe the Prince has launched this war to capture major portions of Liao industry. Wars have repeatedly been fought for technology and the means to produce it. The NAIS is

119

learning much of the old ways and has even branched out into areas that the early technologists did not study. The Prince needs facilities to move these discoveries from the lab into the real world."

Ulthan Everson smiled broadly. "This has been my thought concerning his motive for war. His marriage with Melissa and the agreements made with the Archon before the wedding have linked the Lyran and Federal economies. The inclusion of Liao production facilities will expand both economies and enrich both realms."

The Primus looked at Myndo. His eyes narrowed as though his gaze could pierce her mask and penetrate her thoughts. Then he broke off and turned to Precentor Tharkad. "If this is true, Ulthan, why would Davion stab so deeply to take Sarna? It has no industry. If not for the history and symbolic power embodied by that world, it would be considered one of the poorest planets within the Capellan Confederation."

Everson nodded, but Myndo read the hesitation in his gesture as a portent of her coming victory. "You are quite correct, Primus, in noting the relative worthlessness of Sarna, but I believe Hanse Davion sees it as strategically important. Liao will realize he cannot afford to let the planet fall into Davion's hands. This is obvious because he garrisoned it with McCarron's Armored Cavalry."

Myndo sprung her trap slowly. "I would point out to my learned comrade from the Lyran Commonwealth that McCarron's Armored Cavalry was placed on Sarna by order of Justin Xiang, not Maximilian Liao. I would further suggest that had Xiang's return from Bethel not been delayed by a helium seal failure on a JumpShip, Maximilian Liao would have ordered him to redeploy the mercenaries."

Precentor Tharkad waved away her suggestion, distaste spreading over his florid features. "Nonsense. Liao knows of Sarna's importance. He's already lost the Commonality capital worlds of Tikonov and Liao. He cannot afford to lose another important planet."

"I see." Myndo let her words hang in the air as an indulgent smile slowly appeared on her face. "So you believe Hanse Davion's motives are political or economic? This could explain much, but not everything. There is a deeper motive behind the Prince's actions. One that *does* explain all."

The Primus's left hand nervously massaged the back of his right hand. "What is this motive, Precentor Dieron? Please, enlighten us..."

Myndo nodded. *Gladly. Primus.* "Let us examine the significant actions the Prince has taken, shall we? Start with his conflict with Duke Michael Hasek-Davion, who made an effort to depose and supplant Hanse immediately after former Prince Ian Davion's death.

Hanse won that covert little war by 3016, then systematically did all he could to break Duke Michael. Hanse forced Morgan Hasek-Davion to come to the court at New Avalon and neatly deprived Michael of his son's philosophical loyalty. Then, when Hanse and his watchdog, Quintus Allard, determined Michael was turning information over to Maximilian Liao, the Prince fed the Duke information that resulted in Michael's mortification and death."

Myndo opened her hands. "Shall we examine Hanse's hatred for Maximilian Liao? As we all know, and even discussed long ago, Hanse and Takashi Kurita seemed on a direct collision course until 3025. In the middle of the Galtor Campaign, however, Maximilian Liao almost succeeded in substituting a double in place of the real Hanse Davion. That plot failed ultimately, but Hanse has wanted to pay back Maximilian Liao ever since."

Precentor Sian scoffed aloud. "You are suggesting, then, that this whole war is because of a fit of pique on the part of Hanse Davion? Preposterous!"

Myndo eyed him sharply. "Is it? The Prince holds grudges and has a short fuse. Take the case of Justin Xiang, for example. The Prince was inclined to be merciful until Xiang insulted him publicly. The Prince exiled him, and when Xiang continued to prove a bother, Davion ordered him destroyed. He even sent the order out through Xiang's father!"

Myndo extended a hand to prevent Precentor Sian's riposte. "Another example is the Fifth Syrtis Fusiliers. Hanse knew that unit was unquestionably loyal to Duke Michael, and hostile to him. So what did he do? He lands it on a world he knows is defended by McCarron's Armored Cavalry. Yes, word of their presence did get through. My contacts have confirmed it, and I am sure Precentor New Avalon could do so as well. The other three regiments hitting Sarna were directed to locations where militia defended the world, but the Fusiliers were dropped—*at the Prince's own order*—right on top of the defenders. Furthermore, the Prince forbade General Hartstone to engage in "personal heroics," an admonishment that spurred Hartstone to send his troops in before the other Federated troops could land to support them.

"Hanse Davion purposely destroyed the Fusiliers. The Capellan March will back his call to avenge them, and the Fusiliers will no longer pose a threat to him."

Primus Julian Tiepolo rested his pointed chin on the thumb and forefinger of his right hand. "And striking at Sarna, for reasons already pointed out, is another stab at Maximilian Liao. Helping Pavel Ridzik and buying off the Northwind Highlanders are similar cuts at his foe."

Myndo watched as recognition seeped onto the other Precentors' faces. *They begin to understand.* She kept her voice soft, yet full of urgency. "That's right, my friends. The Word of Blake is full of directives on how we may blunt the advances and drives of nations and nationalism. Jerome Blake, in his wisdom, tells us how to manipulate economies and the demands of the populace for material goods. He points out to us the tools that can turn a minor, local protest into a cause that can unite worlds, and he has instructed us in ways to smother revolutions that work counter to our goal."

Her eyes glowed with the light of inspiration. "Jerome Blake foresaw everything we would face in pursuing the mission he laid out for us. He equipped us to deflect empires and turn nations in on themselves. He taught us to hobble that which did not conform to his ideals. He molded us in such a way that we are able to defeat all threats he foresaw, but Hanse Davion is outside anything in Jerome Blake's experience."

Precentor Tharkad bared his teeth as he hissed, "Blasphemy! You go too far, witch! Doubting the wisdom of Blake is sheer lunacy!"

Myndo smiled cruelly. "I am no initiate who must be inculcated with the mystical nonsense we use to cloak our motives and actions. Outside this room, we keep up the charade. But gathered here in council, we must base our discussions and decisions on what's real— the facts—not on the unrealistic fantasies of some other era. I do not doubt the wisdom of the Blessed Blake, for his words, as interpreted and modified through the years, have accurately predicted events. And Blake's foresight has often guided us in the correct course of action. In this instance, he simply did not envision someone with the audacity of a Hanse Davion, but that does not mean that *we* should be so blind or foolish.

"Let there be no question that Hanse Davion is not a threat that Jerome Blake or any Primus since his time saw coming. We must not blame Blake for this, nor let such a lack dim his brilliance in our eyes. In Blake's era, a time of Civil War, the closest thing to a Hanse Davion was General Aleksandr Kerensky. But Kerensky took his troops and fled beyond the Periphery to save them from more war. Jerome Blake must have imagined that any other such powerful man would do the same."

Deflated, Precentor Tharkad hung his head in defeat. "Your point is well-made and well-taken. No one could have imagined one man igniting a war to salve his own ego."

Myndo raised herself to full height. "This is the reason Hanse

Davion must be stopped now. We have seen his ability to carelessly discard a crack unit when its personnel are not loyal to him. We have seen his singleminded pursuit of one foe—first Kurita and then Liao. We know, just from his conduct of this war, that he will stop at nothing to destroy Maximilian Liao. We must interdict him now."

Precentor Sian, a gray pallor over his face, regarded Myndo darkly. "How will anything short of our intervention on behalf of House Liao stop Davion? The first part of his invasion was accomplished through sealed orders originating from New Avalon."

Precentor Dieron clasped her hands together. "Interdiction will slow his military advance because orders will not travel back and forth very quickly. In fact, for him to ensure any sort of timely communications, the Federated Suns will have to devote an inordinate number of JumpShips to these infernal 'command circuits' the Prince has devised. This will, in turn, totally disrupt the movement of goods within his realm. Let a mining colony run out of grain—grain that is more than plentiful on a world not fifteen light years away—and resistance will begin. We will not move messages in an official capacity, but will not hesitate to spread rumors of civil unrest to help make the home front a problem for the Prince."

The Primus stared blankly at the gold ComStar insignia worked into the polished floor. "If we interdict the Federated Suns, but keep our hands off the Lyran Commonwealth, the Lyrans will begin to question their link with Davion's pariah nation. Indeed, the evidence of a Davion attack on one of our facilities should disgust most people. The Interdiction will also cut off Davion funds from the liberation movements he's been sponsoring in the Free Worlds League. This might even permit House Marik to open a new front in support of their ally Liao and hurt the Prince's war effort."

Myndo abandoned all efforts to keep the pleasure from shining forth on her face. "We are agreed, then, that an Interdiction must be imposed immediately? For the good of mankind?"

The Primus nodded solemnly, but his tone was ironic and his flat, dark eyes twinkled with a rare show of humor. "For mankind, then, and the fulfillment of the Word of Blake."

Myndo glanced at the Primus and took secret delight at the fatigue revealed by his expression as the other Precentors unanimously agreed to impose an Interdiction on the Federated Suns. "It is decided, then. All ComStar traffic with the Federated Suns ends now. Blake's Will be done."

19

New Avalon
Crucis March, Federated Suns
1 June 3029

The image of Primus Julian Tiepolo's face faded from the holovision screen as the last of his message played out. Hanse Davion, standing at the head of the briefing table, used a remote control to shut off the viewer. *Each time I listen to that message, I get the feeling the Primus is a reluctant puppet. He jerks our strings, but who jerks his?*

The Prince stared at the four other people gathered around him. "Comments?"

Field Marshal Yvonne Davion, seated farthest from the Prince on the right side of the table, looked angry enough to spit fire. "Of course we didn't hit the substation their holovid shows us destroying. The 'Mechs that hit it have all the right insignia and serial numbers to be with the Fifth Syrtis Fusiliers, but that particular unit was engaged in burning down a forest at the time of the attack." The gray-haired woman looked at the others around the table. "I daresay that if we *had* hit that substation, no holovid camera operator would have escaped the perimeter with that recording."

Hanse smiled genuinely, then glanced at Quintus Allard. "Why did they decide to interdict us?"

Davion's Intelligence Chief leaned back in his chair. "ComStar is a pacifistic organization. They may see a refusal to move our messages as an act of civil disobedience."

The woman next to Quintus, a Marshal with the Third Crucis Lancers, shook her head in disagreement. "Were that their motivation,

124

they would have interdicted the Lyran Commonwealth."

Quintus smiled easily. "Quite true, Marshal Pedroza. That makes me think it's something else. To your knowledge, have our advances interfered with ComStar business?"

Jessie Pedroza smiled like a child caught stealing a piece of candy. "In keeping with security measures agreed upon before the start of the invasion, one of our first acts is to cut off normal civilian communications. We've not destroyed any ComStar equipment, but we have cordoned off some ComStar stations, restricting access to people we know are not Liao agents."

The fourth person seated at the table, Colonel Nicholas Furth, nodded quickly. "We saw the same thing in the Terran corridor when Kurita hit our worlds. Civilian authorities were prevented from using ComStar facilities to relay messages to our incoming troops."

The Prince raised one foot to the seat of his chair and leaned forward with his elbow on that knee. "We shall assume, then, that this is ComStar's opening gambit in some game they want to play. They may believe that limiting us is a way to pour oil on troubled waters, but that matters not at all to us. We are without ComStar's services as of now."

The Prince pointed to a metallic black box sitting on the table in front of him. A third of a meter long and wide, but only half as high, it was featureless except for the numberpad on its surface and a slot extending from side to side. "Marshal Pedroza...Colonel Furth, this is what we refer to as a Black Box, for rather obvious reasons. I cannot tell you exactly *what* it is because I do not fully understand its workings myself, but it has been the source of the 'faxes' you've received from messengers over the course of the war. This device, and the roughly four dozen others in use in the Federated Suns, will circumvent the most bothersome consequence of the Interdiction."

Both military men peered closely at the machine. The Prince lifted it up so they could see the slot on the bottom into which paper was fed, then turned it around to show the various power and computer jacks built into it. "What I can tell you about these boxes, gentlemen, is that they enable us to send and receive messages between stars. Messages travel much more slowly than the hyperpulse communications sent out through ComStar, but we can actually beat them on shorter distances because ComStar often batches messages for transmission. That was an economical feature that impressed the Lyrans who first examined these boxes."

Jessie Pedroza looked up. "How fast do messages travel?"

The Prince frowned momentarily. "We've run clocked messages

125

at roughly an hour per light year traveled. The biggest problem is that only simple data can be transmitted over this equipment. Text and crude graphics go out fine, but more complicated things like video or audio get garbled when sent."

The Prince drew in a deep breath. "Both of you have gotten the fax messages these machines transmit from our messengers. The messenger corps was set up by Quintus's MIIO, but we're moving the boxes out of the shadows and into your headquarters. This device is still codeword top secret, but you'll have direct access to it now that the Interdiction has been called.

"It is imperative that these devices not be captured, and that no word of their existence leak out. ComStar would see it as a direct threat to their power, and this Interdiction suggests any reaction from them would be hostile. Quintus's people will set up security for your comcenters, but in the event a headquarters is ever overrun, you must see to it that the Black Box is destroyed."

The Prince smiled, and looked up at Quintus Allard. "What does the Interdiction do to our intelligence efforts?"

The white-haired Minister frowned. "It hurts us badly. Our active agents are known to ComStar because they've been using ComStar to deliver messages to us. That flow of information will stop immediately. We can activate sleeper agents by jumping ships into a system and beaming a broadcast at a planet, and possibly gather intelligence by monitoring public broadcasts in a similar manner, but things will be dicey. The Confederation is such a repressed society that the only information in the media is information Liao wants out."

Yvonne reached across the table and patted Quintus's right arm. "What about our people in the Maskirovka? Can they issue orders to agents in our holdings that will tip us about upcoming things?"

Quintus shrugged. "That is possible, and something I'd expect of our more inventive operatives. Right now, though, I think the best we can hope for is some rerouting of important information in the Liao sphere so Max can make mistakes. If anything big comes up, like Liao's decision to kill Ridzik earlier this year, I'm confident Alexi will find a way to get the information to us. We'll get some warning."

The Minister's frown deepened. "What has me most worried is how the Interdiction will affect our communication with the subversive elements we've been fostering in the Free Worlds League. Right now their activities are keeping Janos Marik all tied up, but their supplies are bound to run out soon. Without ComStar to transfer money through, we can't support them. If they evaporate, House Marik will be free to enter the war."

The scowl on Jessie Pedroza's face told Hanse the Marshal had no desire to fight the Free Worlds League, too. "Thoughts, Marshal Pedroza?"

Pedroza stroked her chin. "If House Marik throws forces in at the old Tikonov-Sarna border, we could be in trouble. We've pacified those worlds, which means we've only garrisoned them with militia troops. In fact, on some planets, we're relying heavily on private minority militias to keep order. The Free Worlders could make some headway, which means I would have to pull line troops off the drive into that region. We'd lose the advantage we gained by not having to defend against Ridzik's troops because of our deal with him. Hell, he might even get greedy and liberate the half of Tikonov we've occupied to save it from House Marik."

Yvonne sat back, grinning broadly and her eyes sparkling with unholy lights. "If you please, my Prince, couldn't we urge Ridzik to lop off a chunk of the Free Worlds League to forge that link between the Lyran Commonwealth and the Federated Suns we'd discussed early on in the invasion? That would give him something to do with his troops, and it would give the Free Worlders someone to hate. If things went well, they might even kill him for us."

Hanse joined the general chuckling as the group considered her idea. *Very good, Yvonne. Whoever said, 'Just because there's snow on the roof doesn't mean a fire isn't burning in the cabin,' must have had you in mind. You and Quintus.*

"An excellent idea, Yvonne. My congratulations. Communicate the idea and some basic plans to Ardan Sortek immediately. I'm certain he'll enjoy passing them on to Pavel Ridzik." The Prince's remark triggered another round of chuckling as everyone assembled remembered the earlier holovid in which Ardan Sortek had expressed his true feelings for the ex-Liaoist Colonel, calling him "the Littlest Tsar."

Yvonne nodded curtly. "I'll send it out over the command circuit we've established to Tikonov immediately." A frown creased her brow for a moment, then she fixed Hanse with a steady stare. "I do think we should go ahead and requisition the JumpShips we have on reserve status. It will be clumsy, but it's important to establish and maintain communications between our soldiers and their families. It will be important for morale."

Hanse looked down as he considered the proposal. *If I strip more JumpShips from the commercial sector, trade will slow down. We can probably maintain traffic in essentials, but shipments of luxury goods will have to be cut back. Some people will hate that, but I suppose they'd hate not hearing from their loved ones more. The former will breed discontent, but the latter would create fear and resentment.*

The Prince brought his head up. "Quintus?"

The spymaster licked his lips. "I can have a report about a minimal maintenance network on your desk in twelve hours. We can move everything but exotics with this network, assuming the Kathil shipyards keep ships running and out of drydocks on schedule. I can have my people coordinate with Yvonne's subordinates to create a system that might allow some commercial movement of military correspondence, just to speed things up."

Marshal Pedroza cleared her throat. "I'd like to add that I support the Field Marshal's suggestion. Our warriors are living and dying at mail calls. On more than one occasion, I've had whole battalions volunteer for duty ferrying mail from a landing zone to the front."

"Very well," the Prince said. "Yvonne, get your people together with Quintus's and work this network out." He looked at his Intelligence Minister. "Tell the people in Ways and Means that if there's room for anything more than the basic necessities in the shipping schedule, priority goes to the lowest-priced luxury items—with emphasis on entertainment products, clothes, cosmetics, and other things people buy to make themselves happy. I don't want *one* Avanti air car coming in when something for *plenty* of people could be shipped instead."

Quintus grinned broadly. "As you direct, my Prince."

Now the most difficult part of this meeting. The Prince regarded both of the men nearest him. "You have heard, of course, of the disastrous assault made by the Fifth Syrtis Fusiliers on Sarna. It's true they landed on a position defended by McCarron's Armored Cavalry. The Fusiliers had not expected opposition, and as a result, got sliced up badly. As you have also heard, McCarron captured General Gordon Hartstone and I have refused to ransom him."

The Prince watched both men for reactions, but they kept them well hidden. "The Fifth Syrtis Fusiliers presented a problem for me, gentlemen. I had evidence implicating their general staff in a treasonous plot directed against me. I had hoped, after Michael Hasek-Davion's death, that all three of the Fusilier RCTs would return to the fold, as it were. But the Fifth did not mend its ways. General Hartstone demanded—not requested, *demanded*—a combat assignment that would avenge the Duke."

The Prince narrowed his ice-blue eyes. "I learned of a move within the Capellan March to support making Hartstone a warlord of sorts. Disguised as a patriotic movement within the March, it was nothing short of treason. I could not discharge the Fusiliers' leader because he would have bolted and taken most of his unit with him. Having no other reasonable choice, I gave him the combat assignment he wanted."

The Prince gestured at Quintus Allard. "We learned, after the JumpShips had headed out for Sarna, that McCarron's Armored Cavalry was on Sarna. Had Hartstone followed our original assault plan, we could have prevented the bloodbath. But Hartstone was looking too far ahead, imagining his glorious return to the Capellan March, and had boosted his DropShips in at 2.5Gs. That meant he arrived a full two days ahead of the mercenary regiments accompanying him."

Hanse Davion sighed heavily. "Their lead gave McCarron's Armored Cavalry two days to play with them. McCarron's people were dug in and threw everything they had at the Fusiliers. We recovered less than a battalion of 'Mechs, and only half of them operational. Losses of armor and infantry were even worse. For all intents and purposes, the Fifth Syrtis Fusiliers no long exists."

Silence settled over the meeting as the extent of carnage that could destroy a full Regimental Combat Team overwhelmed everyone in the room. Hanse felt anger burn his insides. *Damn you, Michael Hasek-Davion. Why did you force me to waste so many people? Was your hatred for me so deep? Was your dream of glory so blind?*

The Prince's voice came flat and controlled despite his internal rage. "Understand me, gentlemen, and make sure all the officers in your commands understand me. I cannot afford to have the Federated Suns divided against itself. There will be glory enough for all of us when this war is over. For now, we must stand together, or our enemies will exploit our weaknesses to pull us apart. With the Interdiction, we're half-blind, but we're not finished unless more people contemplate treason."

Hanse Davion leaned forward, letting his voice drop to a chilling whisper. "In short, gentlemen, I will reward those who serve me well, and discard those who work against me. We fight for the Federated Suns, and anyone who decides to work for himself should take a lesson from the Fifth Syrtis Fusiliers."

20

Leutnant Joachim Rhinestag swallowed hard as he keyed his radio mike and stared out from the massive gray dolmen. *Why me? Why do I always get the assignments that go to hell?* "Eagle One to Eagle's Nest."

A bored female voice replied to his signal slowly. "Go ahead, Eagle One. What have you got, Joachim?"

Joachim drew in a deep breath and fought against the nervousness tying his stomach into knots. "I found the place where those two *Overlord*s went to ground. I've got a reinforced company of Kurita 'Mechs about five hundred meters north of my current position. They look like mediums and heavies, with an *Orion* and two *Marauder*s being the top of the line for them. The unit insignia is a black tidal wave within a circle. The wave has stars and a little boat about to be smashed beneath its crest."

A new voice, one full of false courage, cut in on the frequency. "Eagle One, this is Komandant Wyler. What are your coordinates? We will send the militia out to deal with them."

Joachim's heart leaped to his throat. "No, sir. I mean, negative, Eagle's Nest." Joachim sneaked another peek at the nearly fifty 'Mechs moving round on the rubble-strewn plain below his position. "Sir, our militia would be eaten alive down there." He hesitated and swallowed hard. "I don't think they want trouble, sir."

"What! You're telling me a Kurita 'Mech company lands on Ryde

130

and doesn't want trouble? Have you been hit on the head, boy?"

Oh, God, now the Komandant thinks...Damn! I'm in deep trouble now. "Look, Komandant, they're out on Hanover Flats just moving rocks around."

Utter disbelief strung the Komandant's words together. "Moving rocks around? Are they creating a fortification?" The unspoken question in the Komandant's reply was "why?" Being a young planet, Ryde was prone to earthquakes and volcanic eruptions, which made construction a very fine art. Haphazard projects always came tumbling down.

Joachim passed his left hand over his mouth, wiping away the sweat on his upper lip. "No sir, not a fortification. I think they're building a replica of the battlefield on Mallory's World where the Kell Hounds and the Second Sword of Light fought thirteen years ago."

"What? How the hell would you conclude that?"

Jesus, Joachim, don't blow it now. "I read a book on that campaign, sir. Saw a map. From here, it looks the same. And...and I've monitored some of their radio chatter. I heard the phrase *'Kieru inu.'* That's Japanese for Kell Hound, sir. I got that from the book, too."

The Komandant's voice had gained an edge. "You read a book that's let you get into the mind of Kurita warriors. Is this what you want me to believe?" The Komandant paused for emphasis. "This from the junior officer who previously reported a mining site abandoned a century ago as a forward Kurita base?"

I'll never live that down! Joachim felt a bead of sweat course down his forehead and along his nose. "Sir, believe me, the weight of these 'Mechs is enough to destroy our militia a million times over. Were I asked, I'd devote myself to Civil Defense measures there in Heaven's Gate. They're minding their own business now, but if they wanted to take Ryde, you'd be telling me about them and not the other way around."

Joachim let the true depth of his fear flood his words, which seemed to have an effect on the Komandant. "Dammit, Rhinestag, when you get to my position, I hope like hell you have a recruit like yourself in your command. Keep an eye on them and report back if the situation changes. Eagle's Nest out."

Joachim closed his eyes. *Thank God.* "Roger, Eagle One out." The Steiner scout opened his eyes and looked up at the tall, bronze-haired MechWarrior standing over him. "How was that?"

Akira Brahe nodded slowly and returned his pistol to the holster on his right hip. "You did well, Joachim." He glanced toward where the rest of the *Genyosha* labored to transform the valley below into a replica of the Mallory's World battlefield where his father had last fought Morgan Kell.

"We will be finished soon, and you will be able to return to your home." Akira plucked a small holotape cassette from a pocket on his cooling vest. "Just before you leave, I will give you one of these with a message on it. When you get back to Heaven's Gate, you will give it over to ComStar for transmission to the Kell Hounds. You will not view it, nor turn it over to anyone else. *Wakarimasu-ka?*"

Joachim nodded.

Akira smiled. "Good. And don't look so dour, Leutnant Rhinestag. If you'd not been here to carry our message back, we would have had to raid Heaven's Gate. The citizens will never know it, but you saved their lives…"

21

Tharkad
District of Donegal, Lyran Commonwealth
20 June 3029

Jeana forced a smile as she sat on the edge of her bed and watched Misha feed the holodisk into the viewer. "No, Misha. I don't mind previewing our next warvid release. I should, after all, know what we're telling our people." *How can I tell you I've seen it twice already and nearly died both times when they showed Dan's* Wolfhound *getting hit?*

Misha brushed her long black hair back from the collar of her red gown. "Ever since your mother mentioned my theories to Simon Johnson, he's had me previewing these newsreels to see what intelligence we let slip. I'd rather not watch it now, but he wants my 'imprimatur' on it before you and I head up to the Winter Palace for the week." She punched a button on the viewer's remote control, filling the room with a martial soundtrack before pictures actually appeared on the screen. "Johnson hopes he can show a copy of this to the officers from the Federated Suns when they meet with him and your mother this afternoon. I guess, from his urgency, they were not expected. With the Interdiction, all planning is probably going to hell. Anyway, Johnson's waiting for me to call with approval so he can pick it up on the way down to his meeting."

Jeana nodded woodenly as the commentator's deep voice replaced the fading music. "Combine troops landed on Lyons in force in a daring strike behind the front. They hoped their assault on an unprotected world would extinguish our will to fight, but they couldn't

133

have been more wrong. They landed without opposition, but soon found themselves engaged in a battle to the death with the famous mercenaries, the Kell Hounds."

Battle footage, cut together from the sensor output of both Kell Hound and captured Combine 'Mechs, flashed across the screen. Jeana and Misha watched as the red and black 'Mechs of the Kell Hounds regiment advanced through the smoking ruin of what had once been New Freedom. "Though the town has been swept clean of opposition, the Kell Hounds are still vigilant. The night before, however, the Combine MechWarriors made the battle for this small outpost a thing of history."

Jeana stiffened as the exchange between Dan's *Wolfhound* and the Kurita *Clint* filled the screen. Autocannon slugs blasted a line of craters into the *Wolfhound*'s chest while a medium laser slashed into the 'Mech's left thigh. The *Wolfhound* reacted with the impact, then the scene shifted for a pilot's-eye view of Dan's crippling counterattack. "Outraged by the Kurita strike on this innocent village, Captain Daniel Allard fights back, regardless of the weight difference he surrenders to this enemy 'Mech."

Before the program could move on to Morgan's exchange with the *Rifleman*—the part Jeana hated most because of Dan's brush with disaster—a gentle knocking at the door saved her. "Yes?"

Misha killed the holovid as Melissa's chambermaid spoke through the door. "Highness, a Captain John Bailey of the Davion Light Guards has requested a word with you."

At the mention of Andrew Redburn's unit, Misha's face brightened. Jeana stood up and adjusted the silver belt on her navy blue jumpsuit. Misha smoothed the wrinkles in her long skirt, then both of them glanced at their reflections in the mirror and giggled.

Jeana moved to the door. "We'll see him in the parlor."

She waited long enough for her servant to usher the visitor into the parlor room of her suite. Allowing Misha to precede her into the rectangular room, she nodded to dismiss the maid. Extending her hand, Jeana crossed the white carpet to greet her guest. "Captain Bailey, I am glad to meet you."

The Davion Captain, resplendent in his maroon uniform, clicked together the heels of his cavalry boots and executed a respectful bow. He took her hand and kissed it lightly. "It is the honor of my life to meet you, Highness." Blue eyes flashed up from a handsome face, trying to communicate a message that Jeana could not fathom.

She withdrew her hand from his warm grasp and turned to introduce Misha. "This is my best friend, Misha Auburn."

The Captain smiled as he took Misha's hand. "The historian's daughter. The pleasure is all mine."

Something's not right here. Jeana saw a look of consternation flicker over Misha's face. *What is it?*

Misha smiled politely. "You must be newly assigned to the Light Guards, Captain."

Bailey frowned, his bushy black eyebrows furrowing into a sharp wedge. "I have been with the Guards for three years, Ms. Auburn."

Misha blinked twice, pointed to the campaign ribbons on his jacket's left breast. "Then why is it you don't wear the blue and green ribbon for the St. Andre strike?"

That's it! Even as Bailey covered his surprise with a pleasant grin, Jeana swept forward. She smashed her left knee into the soldier's groin, lifting him off the floor. She tangled her fingers in his curly black hair, and as he doubled over, she brought his head down to greet her knee as it rose again.

"Melissa!" Misha stared at her in horror.

Jeana ignored the outburst as she stripped the gun from the unconscious warrior. *Good. Mauser and Gray M-27 needle pistol.* She snapped the breech open and saw a virgin block of ballistic polymer in the chamber. *Enough plastic there for a nice long battle.*

Misha grabbed her shoulder. "Melissa, what are you doing? You're scaring me."

Jeana looked up, then pointed to the man's boots. "No spurs. He's not wearing any spurs…"

Misha's mouth hung open. "He's not a MechWarrior from the Federated Suns…I should have seen that…"

Jeana nodded curtly. "You *did* see something. You noticed the campaign ribbons." *I should have caught the heel click. We all learned it at Sanglamore because it pleased Duke Lestrade.* Jeana tore the soldier's jacket open and pulled up his shirt. She shook her head.

Wrapped around his waist, the man wore a long, slender strip of green silk. She pointed to it for Misha's benefit. "Sanglamore Sash. The idiot wanted to pass as Davion, but he couldn't be without his sash." Jeana unknotted it and pulled it free. "Help me roll him over, and pull off his boots."

Misha moved slowly, as if in a trance, as she followed Jeana's orders. "Slangmore…that means he's from Skye."

Jeana grimaced as she wrapped the sash around the man's throat, then used it to bind his wrists together. "And that means the other visitors from the Federated Suns are impostors as well. He was probably going to hold Melissa here as a hostage. The Duke must be

135

trying to kill the Archon yet again."

Misha stood and walked toward the visiphone. "I'll call Simon Johnson."

"No!"

Jeana's command stopped Misha dead in her tracks. "Why not? Your mother is meeting with the fake envoy right now. She's in danger."

Jeana stood, hefting the pistol in her right hand. "If we set off an alarm, they'll kill her for sure. I would guess they're waiting for Johnson to show up so they can kill him, too. If he dies, Lyran security falls apart, making a coup very easy. Lestrade is playing to win this one." She looked up at Misha. "Where are they meeting?"

Misha shrugged. "Your mother's office, I assume."

"Dammit, that's no good. One way in, one way out."

Misha frowned. "What about the passageway behind the book-case?"

Jeana's heart leaped to her throat. *My briefings mentioned Melissa's knowledge of the secret passages in the palace, but we never had time for her to show me more than a few meters of any of them. Hell, she grew up here—as did Misha—I'd never know them as well as either one of them did. And Melissa said she'd forgotten most of what she knew.* "Misha, show me the way."

Misha grinned. "You know the way. You used to sneak in there all the time to listen to your tutors tell your mother what they thought of you."

Jeana hesitated, then added more authority to her voice. "Misha, this is no time for games. Show me the way."

Misha's face darkened. "You're acting strange, Melissa. Maybe all this is a figment of your imagination. I'm going to call Simon…"

Misha's voice faded as Jeana lifted the pistol and clicked the safety off. "You'll do no such thing. The Archon's life is at stake here, Misha, and I will kill you to save her."

Misha's expression changed from confusion to horror. "Melissa, you need help…"

Jeana shook her head. *God, she's terrified and I can't get her to help me. I have to tell her.* "Listen, Misha, I'm not Melissa. My name is Jeana Clay, and I am Melissa's double. She's off with Hanse Davion."

Misha stared at her, her brown eyes brimming with tears and utter disbelief. "No, that's impossible. I would have known."

Jeana stared at Misha intently. "Think, Misha, think. Don't go to pieces on me now. What is the most important factor in Melissa's marriage to Hanse Davion? What do they need to stabilize things?"

"I don't know."

"Think, Misha. Think about all the history you've learned from your father. Use your head. What do they need?"

Misha looked down as concentration drew her brows together. "An heir. A child would unite both nations."

Jeana smiled. "Dead on. The Archon needed Melissa here to prevent her opposition from saying she'd sold her daughter to Hanse Davion. Melissa needs to be with Hanse so they can conceive a child. I'm here so she can be in two places at one time." She lowered the gun. "Now, take me to the office and pray we're in time."

Misha crossed to the fireplace in the back corner of the room. She pushed her fingers into the mouth of an ornamental lion's-head carved from the marble mantelpiece and pressed down. Jeana heard a click, then the fireplace slid away from the wall. Behind it, a narrow opening revealed walls of rough bricks and mortar.

Misha looked at her. "You'll have to go ahead because there's no place where you can pass me. The corridor goes along the wall for five meters, then we hit a circular stairway that will take us down to the main level where the office is located. At the base of the stairs, keep to the left, take the second right and the first left after that. The bookcase is at the far end of the office, facing the Archon's desk. The catch is above the opening."

Jeana nodded and entered the dark tunnel. A musty odor hung in the air and small clouds of dust rose with each step. Jeana felt cobwebs brush against her face and hands during the trek. As she walked, she trailed the fingers of her left hand along the wall, letting the cold, rough texture anchor her in reality.

So many games, so many lies. When this is over, Misha will feel like such a fool for having been deceived by me. She'll be offended that Melissa wouldn't trust her. Worse yet, she'll have to lie to her father and not reveal any of this to him.

She came to the spiral stairs and began her slow, careful descent. Fear fluttered through her stomach, but then died quickly. She found herself smiling almost the way she did back when her father was still alive. *This is it, isn't it? This is what you felt when you went to defend Katrina Steiner so many years ago on Poulsbo, isn't it, father? This is how it feels to know that what you're doing is right, no matter what the cost…*

Jeana reached out again with her left hand to touch the wall when she stepped off the stairs. Remembering that she had to take the second right turn, she shifted the gun to her left hand. Her heart pounded in her ears as she moved along the pitch-black passage. At the turn, she shifted the gun back to her good hand, charged it, then stopped as she reached the office's secret entrance.

She hit the catch and stepped through the moment the bookcase slid forward enough for her to squeeze past it. The Archon, a shocked look on her face, rose immediately. "Melissa! What a pleasant surprise." The surprise and anger arcing through her gray eyes demanded an explanation.

Jeana raised the needle pistol as the Archon's two guests rose from their chairs. "*Exitus acta probat,* as the Duke was fond of saying. It's over. Bailey spoiled your plans."

When the two Davion impostors heard her utter Sanglamore's unofficial motto, they reacted. The shorter one moved to Jeana's right, clawing for the gun at his belt, while the taller one moved to the left. *Dammit! Split shot.* Jeana saw the smaller man flick a glance at the Archon, forcing her decision. *You're it!*

Dropping into a combat stance, she pulled the trigger twice. The first cloud of needles shredded the uniform over the assassin's heart. The impact half-spun him, making her second shot slam home into his left shoulder. Already dead, he flopped to the floor.

Jeana pivoted slightly, swinging the gun into line with the other man. He brought his pistol up as she triggered her third shot. She saw it paint his throat and chin with scarlet, then stroked the trigger one more time. Before she could see whether or not that shot had hit, something huge and heavy kicked her in the chest. Stars exploded before her eyes as Jeana flew back and struck her head on the bookshelf.

A wave of blackness stole her sight, then she found herself slumped on the floor. She saw her gun lying centimeters from her right hand, but her body refused her order to grab it. As if to mock her effort, she rolled onto her back and lost sight of the gun.

Jeana tried to swallow, but couldn't. *Must have been hit...hit hard.* She felt a trickle of blood pool in the hollow of her throat. *Shouldn't there be more pain?*

The Archon knelt beside Jeana and made the Sign of the Cross. Reaching out with her right hand, Katrina Steiner closed Jeana's unseeing eyes. The Archon's lower lip trembled as she fought back tears. *First your father, and now you. Your family served the Commonwealth more bravely and selflessly than I or it deserves.*

Katrina looked up as Misha stepped through the passageway and uttered a small cry. She knelt at Jeana's head and lifted it into her lap. "Archon, is she...?"

Katrina nodded. She studied Misha's face and the conflicting emotions playing across it. "You know, don't you, that she's not Melissa!"

Misha stroked Jeana's hair. "I never would have guessed. Telling me was the only way she could get me to tell her how to get through the passageway. She knew you were in danger....She said the impostors were from Skye."

The Archon's nostrils flared for a moment. "Yes, they reacted when she quoted them something she'd learned at Sanglamore."

Misha looked up at Katrina. "What are we going to do?"

The Archon stood slowly. "You and Melissa are to be staying at the Winter Palace for a while, correct?"

Misha nodded. "A week."

Katrina thought for a moment, absentmindedly chewing on her left thumbnail. "Your stay there will be extended. Simon Johnson will seal the palace so that no one can see you or Melissa." She smiled wryly. "And then I'll have a special mission for you."

Misha stroked Jeana's hair. "What do you want me to do?"

The Archon peered down at her. "I cannot have you here where you father can ferret out what has happened. Not yet, at least. I have to send you away." Katrina nodded resolutely. "Yes, you'll go to the Federated Suns, and you will escort my daughter back home."

22

The bright vermilion and gold bursts of fireworks in the sky and the sound of cheering from the palace courtyard did nothing to lighten Romano Liao's foul mood. The rocket fire burned red highlights into her hair, but as the shadows fell in an explosion's wake, her mood likewise darkened and deepened. *Fools,* she thought, looking down at the people gathered in the courtyard. *You celebrate one minor victory as if we had won the war. Damn me to the Nine Hells, but you act as though McCarron's Armored Cavalry actually saved Sarna from conquest! They didn't. They just destroyed a Davion regiment. What about the other forty still breathing down on us?*

Romano turned abruptly and stalked back in from her balcony. In a pout, she dropped into the chair set before her vanity. Picking up a platinum-handled brush, she idly worked it through her hair, then spun and hurled it against the wall. "You're all idiots! You're celebrating a delay of the inevitable. We must take action to capitalize on the opportunity we now have."

Romano frowned at her own reflection, then forcibly relaxed her fierce expression before it could set wrinkles at the corners of her eyes. *They're celebrating the Interdiction as much as McCarron's destruction of the Fifth Syrtis Fusiliers. You'd celebrate it, too, if Justin Xiang hadn't embraced it as an omen of disaster for House Davion.*

Her green eyes flashed like an angry cat's as she thought about her sister's paramour. *You chose incorrectly there, didn't you, Romano?*

You thought, with Tsen Shang's war experience on the Marik frontier, that he'd share your hatred of the Free Worlds League. You thought you'd have a powerful ally in a full-blooded Capellan citizen. You thought a man raised in the Federated Suns would be too soft to establish a power base. And you thought wrong. Blood will out!

Romano let a sly grin tickle the corners of her mouth. *What sort of a game is Xiang working? Does he know you sent Ling to kill him? Ling did shoot him, of that I'm certain, but did he tell Justin who gave the order? If so, why has Justin withheld the information from Candace? Is Xiang playing with her the same way Tsen Shang has become my plaything?*

She closed her eyes and summoned up one of her more disturbing but favorite fantasies. Justin Xiang came to her, his rage and contempt at her attempt to kill his father changed now into passion. They made frenzied love and she thrilled to the cold caress of his steel hand...

The staccato string of explosions that mark the end of the fireworks display snapped her out of the phantom encounter with her sister's lover. *With him as my right hand, no one could stand before me. With him to oppose me and back my sister, I will never gain the throne I so rightly deserve. Can I co-opt him, or will I have to eliminate him as I have eliminated other threats to the Capellan state?*

The image of her dead step-mother lying half-decomposed in the morgue came to her, then was overlaid by another image. It was her step-mother and Colonel Pavel Ridzik rutting together like animals in a bungalow on Terra. She'd not seen it, but she'd heard about it from Tsen Shang. *Alexi Malenkov reported it to Justin and Tsen while we were all at the wedding of Hanse and Melissa. Ridzik and Elizabeth weren't even cautious enough to make sure someone did not follow them to their tryst.*

A sneer contorted Romano's beautiful features as she thought of Ridzik. *You are a contemptible bastard, Ridzik. How could I ever have considered you as a consort to solidify my power base? You toady up to Hanse Davion so he doesn't snap up your precious Tikonov, then you decide to go off on a little crusade of your own. You strike out at the Free Worlds League instead of helping your master subjugate your old homeland. Are we so meager a threat as far as you are concerned?*

Romano licked her lips. *Yes, it's time to clean up some loose ends before I make my next move. You, Pavel Ridzik, have arrogantly dismissed the Capellan Confederation. My father tried to have you killed before, but he failed. I'll not have the sins of my father visited upon me. It is time for you die.* Romano laughed softly as she wove together the final threads in a plot he could never escape.

BOOK III
DUTY

Never mind your happiness; do your duty.
—Will Durant

23

Riva Allard ran fingers back through her short black hair, then stretched. *Something is definitely odd about this exam.* She narrowed her blue eyes and read aloud the answer to a question about artificial stimulation of involuntary muscles from the viewer screen. "Though the technology of using electrical impulses to stimulate voluntary muscles and transform their tissue to resemble that of involuntary muscles has been available since the late twentieth century, the biomechanics of the change was not fully understood until 2947. Use of the transformation process information has made the manufacture of myomer muscles for internal organ transplant far more feasible." Nope, that answer was not like Bob Clark at all.

She looked over at her teaching assistant. "Julie, when we gave this exam in Biomech 104, the Thursday section, who was Clark sitting beside?"

Julie's brown eyes looked upward as she concentrated. "Linda Hoffmann, the transfer from the Lyran Commonwealth." She dug through a small pile of disks, plucking one from near the bottom of the stack. She tossed it across the narrow alley between their desks. "Here you go. She knows her stuff. I think I had her down for a 121 out of 128."

Riva deftly caught the disk and inserted it into the auxiliary disk drive. With a few quick keystrokes, she placed Hoffmann's answer for the question she'd been grading next to the answer offered by Bob

Clark. "Deja vu! It appears Mr. Clark liberally copied from Ms. Hoffmann." She turned in her chair to face Julie. "Give me a good reason I shouldn't flunk him right into some front-line unit…"

Julie glanced down then up again with a sheepish look. "You should have seen him in the lab. He was in my section and really knew his stuff. He's a natural with the equipment, Riva. He did all the neural suturing for the myomer transplant on that dog earlier in the trimester…" She hesitated, searching for a word. "I guess I can only describe his performance as intuitive because he knew from the readouts others were giving him what needed to be done and what doublechecked. He also knew when one of the monitors had wandered out of calibration just from the data he was hearing."

Riva nodded slowly. *I know he's good with the tools and can get the work done, but his performance has dropped off from where he started at the beginning of May.* "Do you have any idea what the problem is? His performance has deteriorated badly. He's still got the final exam, but even if he aced it and maxed your mark for his lab work, he'd still be looking at a 2.4 for the course. With those grades, he'll get chucked to a front-line unit faster than a shipment of coffee runs out these days."

Julie nodded, then sighed heavily. "I think things went to hell when he heard about the Fifth Syrtis Fusiliers' getting hammered on Sarna. He's got a brother…Tom…who was in that unit. He's not heard from him since the attack a month and a half ago. Not knowing is killing him…"

Riva glanced at the picture of her brother Dan sitting on her desk. *Bob Clark's not alone in worrying about loved ones in this war, but we all have to persevere. He doesn't know what happened to his brother, and I get to see holovids of mine getting shot up!*

She looked back at Julie. "All right. We'll play it this way. Tell him he's got five days to get me a 20k report on how he knew the monitor was out of whack during the operation, and the logical consequences of the problem. I also want a covering letter stating that his concern for his brother was what distracted him during the exam." *I'll see if I can talk to my father and find out if Tom Clark is O.K., or what the story is. Bob Clark will be more valuable here learning how to patch people up from the war than he will be dying to get some Liao soldier a medal.*

Riva jotted down a note about speaking to her father, then looked up and smiled as Kym Sorenson entered the office and perched herself on the corner of her own desk. The pretty blond woman leaned back against the wall and closed her eyes for a moment. Riva smiled sympathetically. "Bad down in the wards, huh?"

Kym nodded, her eyes still closed. "We got a new load of casualties from the front. Over a dozen are from Sarna, late of the Fifth Syrtis Fusiliers. For them, being shipped to New Avalon is something worse than being sent to hell." Her blue eyes came slowly open. "But I think I might have two subjects who'd be willing to take a chance on your program."

Kym glanced at her small compad. "One was looking forward to a career playing Zero-G soccer. His legs got badly burned when his *Warhammer* tangled with two *Marauders*, and so the doctors don't think they've got enough neural tissue to make fully articulated limbs work. The other was a pianist who lost her left hand. She's got an allergy that makes her a poor candidate for a cybernetic hand, and she doesn't believe a metal hand would give her the feel she needs to play anyway."

Riva smiled. "Good. Dr. Banzai wants to tour the wards on Friday. I'll give him their names and case histories tomorrow. Anybody else look promising?"

Kym sighed heavily. "Not really. Only the usual clowns who claimed they needed 'special stimulation' and they'd be fine. I took their names for Julie…"

Julie blushed and all three women laughed aloud. Riva shut down her computer and stacked the disks it spat out at her on the left side of her desk. "Nearly quitting time. What are we going to do tonight?"

Julie shrugged expressively. "I'm not going to go watch *The Immortal Warrior, Part 47* again. I don't mind looking at his body when they have him running around with no shirt on, but if I see him use a photon sword to cauterize that needler wound on his stomach again, I'll throw up."

Riva laughed lightly. "Second that motion. Every time I see the finale where he drives a Saladin Hovertank into that *Phoenix Hawk* Land-Air 'Mech, I don't know whether to laugh or cry. I also like the scenes where they didn't get around to covering the Kurita insignia with Liao insignia…You can't tell what front they're supposed to be fighting on."

Kym affected an air of wounded artistic pride. "Don't you two get it? This is an allegory for man's struggle against ignorance." She shook her head, letting golden curls ripple down over her shoulders. "I'm with Julie—oiled pecs are fine for a while, but the rest of that film is creative graveyard."

"Graveyard, that's what New Avalon's been like since the Interdiction." Riva ticked items off on her fingers as she spoke. "We all knew publicly broadcast holovid programs were insipid, but now we're limited to those produced here on New Avalon. The difference between yogurt and New Avalon is that yogurt has culture—all we've got is diplomats, soldiers on leave, and aging holovid stars who can't get offworld because they've not got priority."

Julie shook her head. "You're setting your sights too high, Riva. I'd gladly settle for something more than surly service and bland food in a restaurant."

Kym nodded enthusiastically. "I understand the need for rationing, but some of the chefs are hoarding spices as if they're worth their weight in gold."

"Hey, on the black market, the spices *are* worth their weight in gold." Riva locked her hands into talons and lightly clawed the surface of her desk. "I'd kill right now for a bottle of Tharkad Nicht-lager or Timbiqui dark."

"All right, then, I'll find you a target." Morgan Hasek-Davion filled the office doorway for a moment, then he stepped into the room and kissed Kym. He nodded to Riva and winked at Julie, which set her to blushing again.

Riva smiled happily. "To what do we owe the honor of this visit, Highness?" *He's looking better than he has since learning of his father's death, but he's still not his old self. Kym says he wants a command so bad he can taste it. It shows, too. He normally visits the wards on Thursday...I wonder if he heard we got some people from his father's old unit?*

Morgan returned her smile, slipping an arm around Kym's slender waist. "I came looking for some women who have dutifully put up with the deprivations this war has brought on all of us." He paused and glanced at Julie. "Last year, I had a complete set of the new Sherlock Holmes holovid series sent to Melissa Steiner-Davion. In return, on a diplomatic ship that arrived today, I got a shipment of a number of luxury items from the Commonwealth."

Riva shot a sidelong glance toward Julie. *Kym is aware Melissa is here on New Avalon, and I know it because I was Melissa's companion while she traveled incognito to New Avalon after the wedding. But I think Morgan's story is good enough to withstand scrutiny.*

Kym gave Morgan a playful punch in the shoulder. "Well, don't keep us in suspense, you fiend! What did she send to you?"

Morgan smiled like a predator. His long, reddish-blond hair fell over his shoulders like a lion's mane. "Well, soon-to-be Doctor Allard, they will probably put a kilo or two on her willowy figure because I've got three cases of Timbiqui dark that need a home. And Julie, well, there's a pile of new *Immortal Warrior* holodisks and a box of that white chocolate from Vorzel just waiting to be adopted."

Julie dramatically pressed the back of her right hand to her forehead. "It would be a strain, but I think I could handle accepting such into my home."

Morgan roared with laughter, then hugged Kym roughly to himself. "As for you, my love, the Archon-Designate had her seamstress make two gowns that she guarantees will turn the fashion world on its head and a round of that cheese from Nekkar that you fancied so much at the wedding."

Kym's smile faded into a mock pout. "If I eat the cheese, I'll not be able to fit into the gowns."

Riva shook her head. "No, Kym, you keep forgetting. If the food is a gift, it has no calories."

"Ah, how right you are." Kym kissed Morgan on the cheek. "I also understand that food consumed at a party won't fatten you up, either. I suggest we get together tonight to watch the holovids and sample the Lyran Commonwealth's largess. My place, in two hours?"

"I'll get the stuff over there," Morgan said, "but I'll beg off." He hesitated. "There's some work I want to do this evening."

Riva caught the loss of enthusiasm in Morgan's voice, and the quick flash of worry in Kym's eyes, but Julie missed them entirely. The teaching assistant smiled happily as she asked, "What did you get, Highness, if I may be so bold."

"A few things. Some programs and a case of Cuchulain Irish whisky from Arc-Royal."

Kym turned Morgan's face toward her with her right hand. "Are those the Nagelring programs you hoped would come?"

Morgan nodded. "I just want to check and make sure they survived the trip."

Riva kept her thoughts from her face. *I know Kym's been worried about how hard Morgan pushes himself. Morgan wants to prove he could be useful in the field so the Prince will give him a unit to command, but he just doesn't realize the risk that would be for the Prince. If Liao captured Morgan before Melissa gives the Prince an heir, Liao could use Morgan as a bargaining tool to stop the war or cause the Capellan March troops to go neutral to save Morgan's life. Studying for the Nagelring exams and maxing them isn't going to change that one whit.*

Kym looked up into Morgan's green eyes. "If that's all, why not check them on the computer at my apartment, *then* join our little party.

Please, Morgan? It will be good for you to relax."

Morgan was about to refuse, then let her concern melt his resolution. "I surrender," he said with a grin, "but I need three hours to play with the programs before we start. Agreed?"

Riva smiled slyly as an idea popped into her head. "How about four hours?" She waved a hand at her desk. "You can start working with them here because it will take us four hours to organize the party ...a real party."

The others looked at her with puzzled expressions, then Kym seemed to guess what Riva had in mind. "We're not talking about having a party at my apartment anymore, are we?"

Riva shook her head. "You said that being shipped to New Avalon to recover was like hell for many of the soldiers down in the wards. I think we should take the gifts Melissa sent and hold the world premiere of *Immortal Warrior, Part 48* right here in the hospital auditorium. It will be fun for the patients, and the publicity, along with the largess from Melissa, will help quiet some of the Prince's critics."

Pleasure shone in Morgan's eyes. "I like it. If we can't be out on the front, the least we can do is show our appreciation to those who are doing the fighting." He glanced at the computer on Riva's desk, then gave a slight shake of the head. "No time for playing games. We've only got four hours to organize that party."

Solaris VII (The Game World)
Rahneshire, Lyran Commonwealth
20 July 3029

Fuh Teng smiled courteously enough as Mandrinn Zhelang Qua stepped past Carrie, the buxom blond waitress holding open the curtain into the small alcove in Valhalla. Teng winked at Carrie, then killed his smile as he read the displeasure on the Liao official's face. *I'd best watch myself here. He's not in a good mood.*

Teng stood at the end of a rough-hewn table. Across from him, built into the alcove's wall, a holovid monitor displayed a closed-circuit feed of a fight from the Factory battlesite. He bowed respectfully. "It is an honor for a member of the Capellan Ministry of the Military to visit me, especially here in Valhalla." Teng glanced at the man's threadbare clothing, then smiled politely. "I can appreciate the danger of your mission...traveling here to enemy territory."

The tall, slender Minister bowed to Fuh Teng, but the stiffness and shallowness of the act revealed his anger and contempt for his host, despite the eloquent words he mouthed. "It is a distinct honor to meet you, Citizen Teng. Your success, and the successes of those you sponsor in the games here on Solaris, have reached the ears of the Chancellor himself. In his name, and that of your friend, Justin Xiang, I bring greetings."

Teng smiled at the mention of Justin's name. *Two and a half years ago, Justin cold-cocked me and took my place in a fight that probably would have ended with my death. But he was just a vagabond then, a wandering MechWarrior who had been disgraced. Who would have*

151

imagined he could rise so high in so short a time? "Any friend of Justin's is a friend of mine. This alcove is his actually, inherited from a legendary fighter—Gray Noton. Please, be seated."

The Mandrinn slipped past the monitor and onto the bench facing the alcove's drawn black curtain. "I am certain you know this is more than just a casual visit, Citizen Teng."

Teng nodded his head. "Would you like tea before we begin? I've finally gotten Carrie trained to make it perfectly. It's a blend from Hsien." Teng kept the smile from his face as the Mandrinn visibly struggled over whether or not to accept the offer. *I know he hungers for Hsien tea—it was always the best in the Confederation. But Hsien was one of the worlds to join Ridzik's Tikonov Free Republic. Round one of our game and the point goes to...*

Qua shivered as he nodded assent. Teng, smiling broadly enough to bring a blush to Qua's sallow face, turned to the waitress. "Carrie, be a dear and make us some tea. Use the Hsien stock—our visitor is important." Teng looked up at Maximilian Liao's messenger. "And bring us some of the *kincha* fruit. That new shipment can't be all used up yet, can it?"

Carrie smiled warmly at the smaller man. "As you desire, Master Teng." She bowed and withdrew, allowing the alcove drapery to slide shut.

Fuh Teng let the Liao Minister see him flip a switch on the arm of his chair. "That should deal with unwanted eavesdroppers. The tea will be here in a moment. Now, what can I do for you?"

Qua folded his hands and settled them in his lap as he composed himself. "Over the last two years, you have put together a stable of MechWarriors that is the envy of the Successor States..."

Teng nodded. "We have had our share of success in the arenas here in Solaris City. Justin has graciously let me reinvest his portion of the profits to expand our training program. This ensures us a steady stream of winners."

The Minister politely waited for an opening. "Yes, I knew it was your hand in managing things that made the program prosper. The Chancellor wishes you to know that your victories have inspired and heartened many of your fellow citizens. As you know, many believe the battles on Solaris are a window onto the military future of the Successor States."

Teng leaned back in his high-backed chair. "As within, so without, as we say here on Solaris."

Qua nodded curtly, obviously annoyed by the interruption. "Quaintly put. Your grasp of tactics is revealed in the training you give

152

your fighters. We believe this training is the edge that allows your fighters to defeat the Davion warriors on a regular basis."

The return of Carrie stopped the Minister's speech. She set small cerulean cups before each man, then poured the steaming, green-gray tea up to brim of each. She set the teapot on the table, handle toward Teng, and centered the bowl of *kincha* between the two men.

Qua glanced at the bowl of plum-sized fruit and frowned. A thick, golden brown skin protected the *kincha*'s sweet flesh. He looked up, then jerked back as Teng shook a razor-edged stiletto from the sleeve of his black and silver silk jacket.

Teng bowed his head when he saw the Mandrinn's reaction. "Forgive me, excellency. I did not mean to startle you." He looked toward the curtain warding them from the other revelers in Valhalla. "This place, as you know, is in the heart of the Silesia sector of the City. I would never be molested here in Valhalla, but the same cannot be said for the streets between here and my home in Cathay. Solaris is something of a lawless world and—" he proffered the knife hilt-first—"a tungsten lawyer is most useful in negotiating differences of opinion."

Qua took the weapon in trembling fingers and used it to slice through the *kincha* rind. He cut a small sliver from the fruit and closed his eyes as he touched it to his tongue. An expression of pure delight relaxed his features.

Teng smiled. *Kincha* had become little more than a memory for many after the Free Worlds League took Shuen Wan, the only place where the fruit could be grown. Ever since Maximilian Liao had lost the world, he had considered consuming the fruit equivalent to treason. Teng was surprised that Qua took the liberty.

The ex-MechWarrior sipped his tea as Qua lovingly pared the *kincha* down to its pit. "Minister, am I to assume from your remarks that you, or the Chancellor, would like me to instruct Capellan troops in the ways of defeating the Davion hordes?"

Qua's eyes snapped open, then darted around the alcove as he reoriented himself. "Ah, well, Citizen Teng, this is certainly a subject that has been discussed in the highest Maskirovka councils, but no conclusion has been reached."

Teng smiled to himself. *That I believe. Justin wants me right here making bundles of money for him.* "Then what is it that you want?"

The Mandrinn smiled as politely as he could manage. "The Chancellor asks that you turn all the MechWarriors in your stable over to us to fight in the war. You realize, I am sure, what it would mean for the war effort. Here on Solaris, you are fortunate that the war does not touch you."

Teng narrowed his brown eyes. "I beg to differ with you, Mandrinn. The war does touch us here. Since hostilities began, the number of championship-caliber fighters on Solaris has dropped by 50 percent. That's part of the reason the Teng/Xiang stable has done so well. All our competition is off dying out of sight of the holovid cameras."

Qua blinked his eyes and stared at Teng with the look of disbelief that only a bureaucrat can master. "I don't understand. What are you telling me? Don't you know how much the war with the Federated Suns is hurting you? Don't you want to see the war end?"

Teng laughed aloud, slapping the table hard enough to make the *kincha* bowl bounce a few centimeters into the air. "Oh, by all the gods, I do want the war to end. Do you realize that my revenues have dropped by 30 percent since the war began? I'd worked a deal for distribution in the Draconis Combine, but now the damned Dragons won't allow the broadcast of fights in which MechWarriors from House Davion, Steiner, or Kurita fight—and no one wants to watch fights between just Capellans and Leaguers. I just got a call from the current champion's manager. He said my bond of 50,000 C-bills would be forfeit if I didn't find Don Gilmore a suitable challenge within a month, but I've got no one capable of fighting him right now. And this damned Interdiction by ComStar just knocked my best market out of the picture. I've not got the numbers for June yet, but I'm betting my books will be hemorrhaging C-bills when I do. And now you want me to give you my warriors? Are you mad?"

Qua's face drained of blood, making him paler even than the meat of the *kincha*. His mouth hung agape, then his jaw closed and his black eyes became slits. "Need I remind you, Fuh Teng, that you are a Maskirovka operative. I have rank on you, and I could order you to turn those fighters over to me."

Fuh Teng stiffened. "Order me?" He folded his hands on the table, rubbing his thumbs together in irritation. "Have you not heard a word I've said, or haven't I made myself clear? Wake up, Mandrinn! The war is over. It's old news. This is the game world, and those of us who make our living here are used to picking winners and losers. Your side is definitely a loser."

Teng hit a switch at his end of the table and gave an order to the computer controlling the holovid display. "Patch in the political map of the Capellan Confederation, with the projections for the next wave of the Davion invasion."

At his command, the screen blanked, then flashed up a map of the Capellan Confederation. Each of the Davion invasion waves was overlaid in different shades of blue. The symbols designating several worlds in the Sarna Commonality flashed, indicating the local odds-makers' belief that they were next on the path to war.

Qua stared at the map like a teetotaler watching a beer-blast erupting in his own home. "This...this..." he sputtered, pointing a shaky finger at the screen. "This is treason!"

Fuh Teng shook his head slowly. "No, it's reality. The odds-makers say the next Davion wave will come early in September, but my money is on August 15th to the 20th. Got two to one odds on that bet." Teng pointed to the Liao world closest to the center of the map. "Not only do I have money on how quickly Palos will fall, but I've arranged to have three cases of Palos champagne shipped here through the Davion/Steiner military liaison office."

Qua slumped forward on the table. Teng patted the Mandrinn's left arm with his right hand. "Listen, old boy. I can fix it up for you here. You're a smart man. Forget your mission—the whole game will be up by the new year. I have a place for you here, in my organization."

Qua batted Teng's hand away. Turning toward the battle-promoter, his anger melted the mask of diplomacy he'd worn. "You pig! You filthy, gutter-dwelling pig! You'd put your personal profits and well-being above that of the Capellan Confederation." He picked up the knife Teng had given him earlier. "I'll kill you if you don't give me those fighters."

Teng drew back, then let a smile play across his lips. "This is your last chance to accept my offer, Mandrinn Qua. Refuse at your own peril."

Qua smiled with open joy. "I spit on your offer." He inched his way forward along the bench. "I will enjoy this."

Teng spun quickly from his chair toward the curtained alcove opening. Qua lunged at him, but missed and lay sprawled out over the table. The curtain slid aside and two men stood on either side of Fuh Teng with guns drawn and pointed at the Mandrinn.

On Fuh Teng's right, the taller one grinned. "Lyran Intelligence Corps, Mandrinn. You're under arrest for an attempt to coerce treason from a Lyran citizen, assault with intent to kill, and violation of a dozen immigration laws."

"You see," Fuh Teng said as the knife slipped from Qua's fingers and clattered against the floor. "I told you the war was over." Qua glared up at him venomously, and Teng added, "By the way, this was only business. The odds were six to one against you being angry enough to try to cut me, but I had confidence in you." He shrugged. "Remember, as within, so without. The Capellan Confederation is finished."

155

25

New Avalon
Crucis March, Federated Suns
20 July 3029

Hanse Davion looked up from his desk as Quintus Allard entered his office. Seeing the confident smile on his Intelligence Minister's face, he took heart in it. "I think this is the first time I've seen you wear a grin since this war began." The Prince came from behind his desk and waved Quintus to a brown leather chair as he seated himself on the padded arm of another.

The white-haired spymaster dropped into the chair and looked up at the Prince. "I think this is the first time operations have gone as well as we could have hoped."

Hanse smiled. *After Misha's arrival yesterday, and the news of the assassination attempt on the Archon, good news is something I could use.* "Well, don't keep it to yourself."

Quintus nodded, then looked at his compad. "First of all, Alexi Malenkov managed to get a short message out through Liao operatives to one of our people on Solaris. Though the message took seven weeks to arrive here, the DropShip that brought Ms. Auburn also brought word that the holodisk we recovered from Bethel actually did come from Candace Liao. Malenkov confirmed that Justin left it behind— or he assumes that because the dead Maskirovka agent worked for Romano Liao."

Hanse rubbed his chin, considering this news. *Internecine battling can do little to help the Liao war effort.* "Do you think Romano knows her sister has sent us what could be considered a friendly communication? Her agent could have been an attempt to steal it away and use it against Candace."

Quintus shook his head. "As we know from Romano's past actions, she never worries about needing proof of guilt before she acts. You will recall the terrorist attack on Kittery that she sponsored, and the attempt her assassin made on my life at your wedding. We even believe that Elizabeth Liao's absence of late may mean that she has run afoul of Romano. That one is very like her father—too much so for my peace of mind. She's as unstable and explosive as nitroglycerine."

"I understand that, Quintus, but I wonder if she's strong enough to oust Candace from her position as Heir Apparent?" The Prince slid from the chair's arm onto the seat. "Was the agent at Bethel there to kill Justin because of something he did to Romano, or was Romano trying to kick away Candace's support structure?"

Allard shrugged heavily. "I am not certain because I don't think Romano views problems that way. She strikes out at people without considering the consequences. It is similar to Maximilian Liao's attempt to substitute a double to take your place. If not for Ardan Sortek, he would have succeeded. But if he had guessed what his failure would mean, Liao would never have tried in the first place."

Remembering that plot and all the horror it had cost him and Ardan, Hanse felt an old but persistent fury. *Liao's plan was all but perfect. Had Maximilian's inside people been able to discredit or dishonor Ardan, the Federated Suns would have been his in one subtle move. Fortunately, Ardan was able to prove I was the real Hanse Davion.* The Prince forced himself to smile briefly. "I wonder, Quintus …Is Max capable of imagining himself a failure? It's hard to believe he would have backed away from so perfect a plan to eliminate me, no matter what the risks."

"You may be right, my Prince, but not every Liao family member is so irrational. His son, Tormana, has taken well to life here as a prisoner of war on New Avalon, and Candace's warm message to you suggests that she sees the phosphors glowing on a monitor." Quintus tapped a button on his compad. "In fact, Data Interp suggests that Candace has allowed St. Ives province to be denuded of JumpShips so we won't strike at it. She's gambling that an unspoken, unilateral agreement not to attack the Federated Suns will earn equal consideration on your part."

Hanse closed his eyes in thought. *If we need not fear a strike from the St. Ives Commonality, I can move the troops stationed on Kittery to help with the main body of the invasion.* When he opened his eyes, the Prince smiled like a fox watching a hen house. "Yes, I think her

157

gesture has earned such consideration. Let us move the Kittery forces up to help with the sixth wave of the invasion. Will they make it in time?"

Quintus nodded. "They will. The betting on Solaris still favors a strike after the start of September. If we go off in mid-August, we'll steal a march on anyone expecting us to hit later."

The Prince stretched. "Anything else?"

Quintus nodded. "We got the first report on Ridzik's strikes into the Free Worlds League. His troops struck deep into Marik territory and knocked the Leaguers back pretty hard. I think they'll counterstrike at Talitha, but Ridzik will see that attack coming and parry it. The Lyran Commonwealth came down on the coreward worlds behind Ridzik's lines and mopped up easily."

The Prince interlaced his fingers nervously. "Will there be trouble on any of the worlds where Melissa will be traveling?"

Quintus hesitated, and Hanse instantly realized he was about to rehash an old argument. "No, Highness, I do not expect trouble at the worlds in the occupied territory or in the Tikonov Free Republic. Still, I do not think it wise to return your wife to the Lyran Commonwealth on a command circuit that uses inhabited worlds in enemy territory."

The Prince's expression darkened. "What would you have me do, Quintus? I refuse to send her back through uninhabited solar systems. If a single JumpShip has a helium failure, she'll be stuck there—and with this damned Interdiction, I'd never know about it. No. She must go through inhabited worlds so repairs could take place in case of an accident."

Quintus rubbed his fingertips against his temples. "Highness, I understand your concern about helium failures, and I respect that concern. What I fear—treachery on Ridzik's part—could be avoided by sending Melissa back through the Terran Corridor."

Hanse shook his head sharply. "And risk another Kurita incursion? Last January, they almost cut us off on that frontier. We know all their strength is not committed to the battle with Wolf's Dragoons in the Galedon district, nor is it involved in driving back Lyran troops. Need I remind you that Melissa and her JumpShip were abducted from Fomalhaut two years ago?"

The Prince glared defiantly at the spymaster. "Ardan will order Ridzik to clear his troops from the systems through which Melissa will travel, and we'll be done with the problem. Kurita will not strike into Tikonov, and Liao cannot strike there."

Quintus stood abruptly. "Listen to yourself, Highness! If it were anyone else, you'd be thinking more rationally. Nothing happened to

Misha Auburn on her journey here through the Terran Corridor. That way is safe—safer, to my mind, than the path you have selected."

Hanse drew in a deep breath and forced his anger to dissipate. *How do I explain my sense of doom whenever he mentions Melissa traveling through the Terran corridor? I know his objections are valid, and I should heed his advice, but I can't. I know, somehow, that if Melissa travels through the Corridor, I will never see her alive again.*

Hanse exhaled slowly. "Quintus, old friend, please try to understand. I know what you are saying, and I hear the wisdom of your words." Hanse opened and closed his hands as if unable to grasp what he really wanted to say. "Trust me. Do what I have asked. The decision is made, and to change it now would invite disaster."

The plea in the Prince's voice touched something within his Minister. Quintus capitulated with a weary nod. "The orders went out for Ardan to relay to Ridzik yesterday, so it would be difficult to change things now." He gave the Prince a reassuring smile. "I do trust you and your judgment, sire. But I must make sure, for the sake of the nation, that you do as well."

The Prince stood and offered Quintus his hand. Gripping the older man's hand tightly, he pumped his arm firmly. "I doubt I will ever be able to repay you for the sacrifices and services performed by the Allard family, but I want you to know they do not go unappreciated. You give me a luxury only the leader of a great state can truly cherish —someone whom I can trust implicitly."

Quintus lifted his head high. "And you, Highness, have given the same gift to me." Quintus broke his grip with the Prince. "By the way, on a totally different subject, your decision to funnel the liquor and foodstuffs that arrived from the Lyran Commonwealth into a random distribution network has done wonders for morale here on New Avalon. People are already referring to it as the Lyran Lottery, and voter registration has climbed sharply over the last two days so more people will be eligible for the drawings."

The Prince clapped his hands. "Excellent! I'd hoped for good results from that move. Two things I do not want on New Avalon are charges of elitism among the nobility, and a thriving black market in consumer goods. That's why I was so glad to hear of your daughter and Morgan organizing an impromptu party for the folks at the hospital."

Quintus smiled proudly. "Riva was pleased that all the media attention for the party has resulted in an upturn in volunteers at the hospital. I guess it takes some exposure to let people know others have suffered far worse in the war than they have." Quintus ran his fingers through his white hair. "The newsvid coverage of the event made many people realize how many wounded warriors at the NAIS are far from their homes and that their loneliness is sometimes worse than their wounds."

Hanse tapped his left index finger against his chin as he thought. "Good point. I think we should encourage more contact between the citizenry and the warriors at the NAIS Medical Center. We need to show that the people on New Avalon are concerned for the sons and daughters of people from the frontiers." He fixed Quintus with his gaze. "Even though Michael is gone, those who backed him still might be encouraged to stir up trouble now that the war has become more difficult and costly."

The Minister of Intelligence, Information, and Operations bowed his head. "Consider it done, sire. We've struck the head from the snake. Now we'll make sure its thrashing does no harm."

26

Blue-white moonlight fell across Melissa's face as she slept. Standing in the shadowed doorway to their bedroom, Hanse watched the slow, rhythmic rise and fall of her chest and smiled. *Sleep well, Melissa, for tomorrow a DropShip will carry you away from me again.*

With that thought, a sadness bubbled up inside of him. He recognized it instantly and grappled with it like a physical foe that he could break and conquer. The emotion evaded the logical traps he set for it, then spread like a fog throughout his body, bringing with it fatigue.

Hanse stepped into the room, and turning away from the bed, slowly unbuttoned his uniform jacket. He was sad that she had to leave, yet felt guilty over the deception that had kept her here— a virtual prisoner on a world he hoped she would come to know and love as he did.

"Hanse, what's wrong?" she whispered.

He composed his face in a smile and turned slowly to face her. "Nothing, dearest."

Sitting up in bed, with the moonlight glinting in gold highlights from her hair and electric blue from her silken nightgown, Melissa looked like a goddess. She draped her arms casually around her knees, but the look in her gray eyes pierced his soul. "Please, tell me. I know it's no catastrophe because you're here, and not in your 'den' dealing with it. That means it's something inside you…something you cannot share with your advisors." She held out a hand to him. "That means it is something you *must* share with me."

Hanse walked around the end of the bed and sat on its edge facing her. He took her hands in his, then swallowed hard. "I'm sorry for how you've been treated here, and I'm incredibly reluctant to see you go."

Melissa gave his fingers a squeeze. "What are you talking about, Hanse? I'm very happy here…"

The Prince touched the fingertips of his right hand to her lips. "Don't say that to make me happy, because I know it's not true." He stood up and looked out through the gauzy curtain over the window. "I saw your face light up when Misha stepped off the *Caracol*. In that instant, you were the happiest you've been since we married."

Her denial came quickly, but lacked just enough emphasis to convince the Prince it was the complete truth. "That's not true, Hanse."

The Prince smiled, clasping his hands behind his back. "Ah, but it is, Melissa. You're a social creature. I've watched you charm all those who have met you, and I've watched you deftly deflect Morgan Hasek-Davion's thoughts away from his desire for a command time and time again." He turned toward her. "I've kept you in a gilded cage and denied you the freedom to be yourself. We did not even travel here together, you and I, from the wedding. Had I the chance to do it again, it would be different."

Melissa stared toward the darkness at the end of the bed. "Who is to say I would want it any different?"

Hanse frowned sharply. "What?"

Melissa glanced at the place where he had been sitting and waited until he seated himself again before continuing. "Yes, my husband, I cannot deny the times when I wished we could have traveled together to New Avalon, or that I ache to appear at your side at some important function here in Avalon City, but the lack of all that does not really make me unhappy."

She gathered up his hands in hers. "Being here, being with you is important to me. The elaborate dramas we've had to create so that we could be together reflect the depth of our feelings for one another. Were I nothing more than the means to securing an alliance, I would still be in the Commonwealth now—possibly shot dead in Jeana's place—and a mistress would be here with you instead."

The Prince slowly shook his head. "At least a mistress would have free passage within my palace and my world. You've only been permitted visits by people who can meet the highly restrictive requirements of security."

"Hanse, I cannot say that it hasn't been difficult, but you grossly overestimate the problem." When she smiled, joy woke somewhere in Hanse's heavy heart. "The people I've been allowed to meet have given me an insight into you and the realm I'm now part of. Riva Allard, for example, is a brilliant young woman full of life and the desire to make things better. Though I don't understand half the things she talks about in connection with the New Avalon Institute of Science and her doctoral work there, I do sense her buoyant optimism. The conformity demanded of those in the Draconis Combine, or the rampant paranoia of the Capellan Confederation would probably have broken her spirit by now. Even in my own Lyran Commonwealth, her work would be scrapped if her studies did not show a profit potential."

Melissa laughed lightly. "And it meant a great deal to me that you brought your old friend Kincaid Fessul here to meet me. I felt as though his approval of me meant more to you than all the advisors who ever said our marriage was the politically brilliant move. I was so nervous, then he cracked a grin and we started talking as if we'd known each other forever."

Hanse nodded as a smile spread across his face. "Kin may be only a fisherman, but he's uncommonly wise. I was overjoyed when you two hit it off so famously."

Melissa drew Hanse's right hand forward and kissed its palm. "Through him, through Riva and Morgan and Kym, I have seen your realm. I see why they love you and why they are willing to serve you despite personal disappointments. Morgan Hasek-Davion may want a 'Mech command in the field with every cell in his body, but he'd never dream of disobeying your orders that keep him here. That sort of loyalty can only be earned, never bought or coerced or compelled. Your ability to inspire it is your greatest gift and the secret heart of the Federated Suns."

Hanse felt a tightening in his throat as her words touched him deeply. He caressed the shadowed side of her face with his right hand. "Thank you for speaking these things, but I don't know if I'm worthy of such words."

"Hush." Her command came softly but with a strength that demanded immediate compliance. "You doubt your worthiness because of what you have been forced to do. You knew that forbidding General Hartstone to land his Fifth Syrtis Fusiliers before the mercenary regiments joined in the Sarna attack would goad him into an act of self-destruction, and I watched you agonize over that decision for a week. Even though you knew he was fanatically loyal to Duke Michael's memory and that removing him from command could have ignited a revolt in the Capellan March, you still fought within yourself over the problem. You knew the handful of MechWarriors who did not share Hartstone's politics would suffer right along with the majority who did, and that almost stayed your hand."

Her gray eyes reflected the silver moonlight as her voice dropped to a whisper. "What you don't acknowledge, my love, is that yours was not a decision that condemned those people to death. They would have died in any event—fighting in the Confederation, or leading a rebellion against you. You sought a way to save those who did not deserve death, and the very act of searching proves your sincerity and integrity."

Hanse chewed on his lower lip, then nodded wearily. "Perhaps you are correct, but I cannot allow myself to accept your assessment fully, nor be completely comfortable with the troublesome decisions I make. If I did, I might stop searching beyond the easy answers."

Melissa smiled at him. "Have no fear, my husband. In the most unlikely event you were to become complacent, I will always be there to remind you of who and what you truly are." She chuckled warmly. "And if I cannot manage it, I am certain Kincaid Fessul will be more than equal to the task."

Hanse joined her in laughter, then a wave of guilt overcame the happy sense of well-being. Letting her laughter die, Melissa noticed the change immediately and looked at the Prince with new concern.

Hanse slid forward on the edge of the bed and hugged his wife close. "Melissa, you are far more than I ever imagined, and you mean more to me than you can ever know." Hands on her shoulders, he held her at arm's-length to look at her. "I do have one regret, Melissa Arthur Steiner. In all the preparations and negotiations, in all the ceremony and politics, in the holodisk messages and your visit, I never actually asked you to marry me."

Melissa smiled gently, cupping his jaw gently in her hands. "Why stand on tradition, Hanse Adriaan Davion?"

Hanse dropped to one knee beside the bed, clasping her left hand in both of his. "Melissa Steiner, will you consent to be my wife, the keeper of my conscience and mother to my heirs?"

An expression of overwhelming happiness lit her face. "With all my heart and soul."

Hanse stood, sweeping her into his arms, and kissed her deeply. Melissa clung to Hanse, fiercely returning the kiss. The scent of her skin and hair was a delicate perfume that he would forever link with what had become the happiest moment of his life.

Melissa looked up and smiled as Hanse gently laid her on the bed. "It strikes me, husband mine, that I have already wed you, and I accept responsibility for your conscience." She slid over toward the center of the bed. "That means the only part of your proposal I have not

164

fulfilled is becoming mother to your heirs. As I am leaving tomorrow, I would suggest we take the rest of this night to see what we can do about fulfilling that third promise."

Hanse nodded, his smile broadening. *Those who imagined that our wedding was merely the forging of a political alliance will be sorely disappointed. From this union will spring nothing less than a dynasty.*

27

Colonel Pavel Ridzik, Supreme Lord of the Tikonov Free Republic, stroked his reddish beard as he struggled to keep his temper in check. He glared at the tall, handsome, dark-haired man he'd lately come to think of as his "keeper."

"But General Sortek," he said, forcing lightness into his tone, "it is totally impractical for me to shift my ships from their ward stations at the jump points of Acamar, Terra Firma, Carver, and Pollux. Their removal from that last site I consider especially risky because of the potential for a Marik counterstrike."

Ardan Sortek smiled in a manner Ridzik found decidedly patronizing. "I understand your apprehension, Colonel, but perhaps I did not make myself clear. *I* make requests of you. Prince Hanse Davion gives *orders*. His orders are, quite simply, for those jump points to be cleared of troops. He gives no reason, and he only expects compliance."

Ridzik leaned back in his red leather chair and steepled his fingers. *I am not so stupid as to believe that, Sortek. I have seen the change in your demeanor since you received that message from the Federated Suns. You have been edgy and worried. I know what goes on in your head, and I use it in our little game here.*

Ridzik lifted his eyes. "Your Prince demanded that I strike out at the Free Worlds League, and I have done so. My troops have done remarkably well, but that is because they are fighting for me and a free Tikonov. Your Prince promised that the occupied portions of the

166

Tikonov Commonality would be returned to my rule if I complied with his orders. I have done so, yet they remain under martial law and your thumb."

Ardan laughed and shook his head in mocking disbelief. "Again you try to link two distinct and separate issues. You already have administrative control of half the worlds we took. We maintain garrisons on those worlds so you will not have to waste your precious troops on little rebellions. Our presence there makes your government all the more welcome, and you know it."

Hanse Davion's liaison pointed toward the huge map hanging on Ridzik's wall. "Furthermore, my dear Colonel, we have made no demands on or claims to the worlds you have conquered in this campaign of yours. I think we have more than held up our side of the bargain."

Ridzik slammed his fist onto the top of his heavy wood desk. "You know as well as I that we're not talking about control of a dozen minor worlds. We're talking about *the* world. How can my Tikonov Free Republic have any standing and validity when you still hold the jewel of my realm? Tikonov has ever been the centerpiece of the Commonality, yet you deny it to me. If Hanse Davion wants these worlds cleared, I want Tikonov!"

Ardan flushed red with fury. "You are in no place to make demands, Colonel. My Prince denies you Tikonov, but he could deny you things that will hurt more." Ardan waved a hand that took in Ridzik's sumptuous office and the gilt framing that surrounded the mythical scenes painted on the walls and ceiling. "My Prince could pull the plug on the billion C-bills he infuses into your economy on a weekly basis. Or perhaps you would prefer our munitions shipments to stop?"

Ridzik felt a pain in his chest as Sortek threatened the pull-out of Federated Suns economic and military aid. He raised his hands and forced a smile to his lips. "Now, General Sortek, there is no need for "

Ardan cut him off with a sharp wave of a hand. "Yes there is, Colonel Ridzik. I told Hanse that it would come down to this one day, that I was not a diplomat who could stroke you with one hand while pushing you around with the other. I say what I mean and I can't stand dancing around points and sensibilities." He skewered Ridzik with a hot stare. "You and I are military men. We don't need the deceptions and false courtesies required by diplomats."

Ridzik's nostrils flared as his voice dropped to a rime-touched whisper. "Indeed, Colonel." The red-haired man spread his arms expansively. "Please, speak your mind. I am certain I will find your

167

opinion of me enlightening."

"I hope like hell you do, Colonel." Muscles bunched at Ardan's jaws. "You've been acting like a puffed-up dictator who believes he's the major partner in this little alliance. Well, I hate to burst your bubble, but that's just not true. I'll not deny—hell, I'll be the first to agree—that you've got a good military mind, a great one even. Still, as Frederick Steiner of the Lyran Commonwealth shows, that does not mean you are a political genius."

Ardan smiled as Ridzik's hands curled into fists. "Sure, get angry, but realize a few basic facts first. You know your worlds cannot hold us off if we decide to take them. You know you've got no basis to make demands on Hanse Davion, and no real reason to expect him to dance to the tune you call. Most important, you know you're a puppet and it's about time you remember who pulls your strings."

How dare you! Ridzik's dark eyes flashed with unbridled fury. *Do you imagine your status as Davion's watchdog will protect you so far from home? This* is *hostile territory, Sortek. Many strange things can happen here.*

Ridzik forced his anger down. "Very well, General Sortek. You have made your point. I shall acquiesce to Prince Hanse Davion's order and clear those worlds." He hesitated, groping for the right words. "As well I appreciate your frankness. Now I know where I truly stand, and I shall take steps to be sure I do not make attempts to slip my leash again."

Ardan Sortek bowed his head, then turned crisply on his heel and left the room. Ridzik fondled a crystal paperweight as Sortek departed, but resisted the temptation to hurl it in his enemy's direction. Instead, he set it down deliberately, then rose from his chair and paced his office.

Yes, General, you have told me precisely where I stand. In doing so, you narrow my choice of actions until there is but one. Ridzik paused at the map on the wall and studied the string of four worlds Hanse Davion had ordered cleared of defenders' ships at the jump points. *They make such a pretty line across my territory, linking a path from Tharkad to New Avalon. Now who might be making use of that little route?*

Ridzik laughed aloud to himself. "Are you that much of a sentimental fool, Hanse Davion? Do you so desire to have your wife with you on your first anniversary that you will place my star systems at risk to have her by your side? People do such foolish things when they're in love. That's why I've avoided such entanglements."

Ridzik tapped the small dot representing Terra Firma on the map.

The ambush will have to be here. We will ensure a helium failure on the JumpShip waiting to carry Melissa toward her beloved. We will divert her ship to the planet...No, it would be better to transfer her to one of my ships at the jump point. The diplomats traveling with her will not want to risk an affront to my dignity by refusing my offer of aid. Then I will have her, and I will treat her very nicely. Once Hanse gives me what I want, once he returns to me what is rightfully mine, I will return his wife to him.

Ridzik spun as someone knocked lightly on his door. "Yes, what is it?"

A Corporal opened the door to hand the Colonel a slender box tied with a string. "We've scanned it, sir. Nothing dangerous. It came to you, marked 'Personal.'"

Ridzik smiled and quickly read the soldier's name tag. "Thank you, Borosky." He accepted the slim parcel, but waited until the door had closed before he took the box to his desk and sat down. He smiled to himself as a giddy excitement bubbled up inside him. He had always loved surprises. Feeling like a child at Christmas, he slipped the string from the box and opened it.

His heart leaped to his throat. *Oh, I must have been a very good boy this year.* Lying on a bed of cotton was a pale green sheet of note paper that reflected rainbow lights from its glazed surface. Grasping it by the corners, he lifted it from the box. He recognized the handwriting immediately, and the shock of it made the presence of a hotel room magkey also in the box insignificant.

The *verigraphed* note trembled in his hands. Barely able to believe it, he read, "I have escaped him and now I will be with you for all time." Though he did not need verification, he let light play across the surface of the holographic seals encasing and fused with the paper. The beautiful, smiling face of a young woman with long black hair looked back at him.

Ridzik sank back in his chair. *Incredible! This is perfect!* He smiled like a cat with a belly full of milk. *Elizabeth Jordan Liao leaves her husband and joins forces with me. That gives me even more political pull in Davion's occupied areas. I could easily force more concessions from him because Elizabeth's influence could make holding his worlds a nightmare.*

Suspicion ripped a gash through his happiness, but he shook it off. *The* verigraph *proves she wrote the note. The holographic image is seared into the paper's coating while being processed. Prying the layers apart to substitute messages destroys the original. You cannot forge one of these.* He glanced at the image again. *No matter how good a dummy or double, the* verigraph *would show it up to be false. I know those lips and that throat too well to be deceived. She is here. I will make her my consort, in one deft stroke stabbing deep into Maximilian's heart and causing Prince Hanse Davion serious consternation. Then I will kill Davion's friend and kidnap his wife.*

Ridzik picked up the magkey and instantly recognized the hotel's logo. *Elizabeth, you always did have extravagant tastes.* He smiled and slipped the keycard into the inside pocket of his jacket. *First one conquest, then another. It is a pity, Ardan Sortek, that you will not be around to watch the finale of this puppet's revenge.*

Having changed from his uniform into civilian clothes, Ridzik stood in front of the Hotel Percheron. Even the drizzling could not dampen his spirits. He recalled their last time together, on Terra during Hanse and Melissa's wedding celebration, and his grin widened. *If tonight is but half as passionate, it will be a very warm welcome.*

Always conscious of security, Ridzik had managed to learn that the key belonged to Room 1145. The guest registered to that room was a Ms. Beth Geordana. Not only was it a close match to her maiden name, but Ridzik recalled that she once mentioned, during a tender interlude, that she had covertly written poetry under that name.

Ridzik moved toward the hotel's side entrance, avoiding the bright lights of the main entryway. She had told him that the State Poetry Review had rejected her poems as being too forced and commercial. When they had further suggested she write for greeting cards, Elizabeth had these editors sent to Brazen Heart. "My dear Pavel, it was the best thing I could have done for them," she'd said. He recalled how the flickering firelight had caressed her throat as she explained her logic. "How could they possibly release their artistic potential without having suffered in their lives?"

Ridzik knew better than to love a woman like that, for an emotional tie with her would hobble him. He did not deny the sexual attraction, and there might even be some affection for one another, but it was their lust for power that drove them together. *She will discard me as soon as she has what she wants from me, and I her. I will just have to make sure I strike first.*

The room clerk needed no prompting to remember Ms. Geordana. He described her as being tall and slender, with an arrestingly beautiful face and long, silken red hair. Ridzik smiled because he knew she'd colored her hair to match the shade of his as a sign to him.

He entered the hotel unnoticed among a group of guests, then joined them in the elevator. He ignored their chatter, thankful that the eleventh floor came before he lost control and shot one man for seditious talk. Ridzik let the doors snap shut behind him, then forced his anger away. *You cannot let that idiot spoil your evening. Find him tomorrow and have him killed, but tonight is for you and Elizabeth.*

He rapped gently on the door, then slipped the magkey into the door's slot. As he waited for the lock to open, he suddenly recalled his first visit to a bordello when he was a raw recruit bound for the Academy. *I was a gawky kid then, nervous and more afraid of the woman than I was of the ridicule I'd get from my comrades if I did not go through with it.* He forced himself to smile confidently. *That was long ago, the end of an era in my life.*

The lock clicked open and he slipped into the nearly dark room. Candles, three on each of the twinned bedside tables, illuminated the wide canopied bed in their wavering glow. She stood beyond it, silhouetted in the moonlight before the window. The white light shone through her diaphanous gown, tantalizing and teasing him with an erotic outline of her slender body. Her hair, red only on the edges where the moon touched it, formed a black veil against her back.

Ridzik swallowed hard. He felt his desire for her stirring, and for a fleeting moment, he wondered if so noble a woman might not make him a suitable consort for life. He closed the door, then removed his coat and tossed it onto a chair. "I have come, Elizabeth."

She turned from the window, filling her right hand with the dart pistol that had been hidden on the sill. Before Ridzik could react, she raised it and fired one hissed shot. Ridzik felt something sharp sting him, then looked down at the silver syringe cartridge sticking in the upper left portion of his chest.

Before he could frame a question in his mind and give it voice, his legs collapsed. He landed on the floor with a heavy thump, overturning the chair where he'd laid his coat. He tried to scramble to his feet, but his body refused to take orders. *What is happening to me?*

The woman tangled her fingers in his hair and tipped back his head. She lay on the bed, hanging over the edge just enough to reach his head and let him see her ample cleavage. Her red hair flowed down toward the carpeted floor, veiling her face in shadow. "Well, if it isn't my old friend, Pavel Ridzik."

With her left hand, she pulled off her wig. The candles provided just enough pale light for Ridzik to recognize her. His jaw trembled as he tried to speak, but her predatory grin stole any desire to make himself heard. "Yes, Pavel, I am the one they sent to kill you six months ago. You escaped the bomb I left for you, which reflected

171

badly upon me. I had to leave the service and start freelancing." She pursed her lips and shook her head. "That's such a nasty life for a nice girl like me. Wouldn't you agree."

She moved Ridzik's head up and down to make it nod in agreement. "Fortunately, my current employer is a woman with exquisite taste and the unusual ability of knowing what she wants and how to get it. In this case, she wants you dead."

"The drug I hit you with," she continued with clinical detachment, "has knocked your voluntary muscles out of whack. It's nice because it goes away without a trace after a dozen hours or so—not that you'll care. Even so, it should deaden the pain a bit."

She released his head, then slid from the bed and lifted him up. She pulled him onto the bed, rolled him onto his back, and crossed his forearms over his heart. She nodded and winked at him.

"Let's see, what else did Lady Romano want me to tell you?" She looked toward the ceiling, then smiled. "She said you would want to know that Elizabeth did make the *verigraph* herself. No one can forge them, you know. At least not in the Capellan Confederation, though there are rumors of a process in the Federated Suns. But that's news that doesn't concern you. In any event, Romano said that Lady Elizabeth created the *verigraph* after Romano promised to ship her off to you if Elizabeth would renounce all ties and claims to the throne. Then, of course, Romano had her killed."

Ridzik felt a thickness in his throat. *No! This is impossible! This cannot be happening. I am Pavel Ridzik!*

The assassin smiled down at him as she filled a syringe with a clear liquid. "I do want you to know that, under normal circumstances, I would not use this on a person of your stature in the Successor States, but Lady Romano was rather specific. In fact, giving you as much of the dart juice as I did would have displeased her because it will numb you somewhat."

She shook her head as she felt for his carotid artery. "They made this stuff in the Draconis Combine, to be used on traitors to the state. It supposedly attacks only neurons, nibbling them away like a slow acid bath."

Ridzik dimly felt the sting as she plunged the needle into his neck. "They say it will kill you in just five hours, Colonel, but the agony will make it feel like five centuries." She smiled sweetly, then bent down and kissed him full on the mouth.

She caressed the side of his face, igniting fire in all his nerves. "Sorry, Colonel, to leave you this way, but I have a reputation to maintain, and you've been living on borrowed time ever since you escaped my bomb." She straightened up, then winked at him. "They say that if you're lucky, you can swallow your tongue before the pain becomes too great."

Her mocking laughter and the click of the door shutting behind her were the last sounds, save his own sobs, that Pavel Ridzik ever heard.

28

Moore
Dieron Military District, Draconis Combine
1 August 3029

Chu-i Jinjiro Thorsen pressed his thick glasses back onto his nose, but otherwise dared not stir in the corner of the briefing room. *Why did* Tai-sa *Sanada bring me to this meeting? This is not the place for my sort.* He knew his lighter skin and blue eyes marked him as a half-caste from the Rasalhague District, giving the great and powerful people in the room yet one more reason to look down upon him.

Jinjiro looked over at the those seated at the table. *Generals and Warlords all. While at the Sun Zhang Academy, I and my fellows dreamed of taking their places one day. Never, ever, did I imagine actually meeting them. Especially not the Coordinator's son.*

Theodore Kurita stood tall and slender at the head of the table. The other officers were well-groomed and dressed in freshly laundered and pressed uniforms, but Theodore wore his black hair long and unkempt, as if the war had given him no time to mind his personal appearance. Neither did his black jumpsuit bear medals or insignia denoting unit or rank. It had only been zipped halfway up the front, giving those assembled a view of his cooling vest and the shoulder padding for his neurohelmet. A heavy pistol hung from his right hip.

Jinjiro smiled to himself. *How ironic that the* Tai-sa *only told me at the last minute of the request for my presence at the meeting. I had no time to change after morning exercises.* Jinjiro resisted the temptation to lower the zipper on his jumpsuit to the same height as Theodore's.

Theodore punched some orders into the keyboard at his position. A holographic map of the Lyran/Combine border burned to life above the center of the table. It slowly rotated so each person in the room could see it plainly, then locked in place facing Theodore.

Jinjiro studied the map intently, though he knew each world, each battle, each defeat by heart. *We have lost greatly in the Rasalhague District—even my homeworld of Gunzburg is now behind enemy lines. Steiner's initial thrust into the Dieron District destroyed Theodore's Eleventh Legion of Vega.* Through the glowing map, Jinjiro's gaze focused on the nearly healed scar running from the center of Theodore's forehead to the outside edge of his left eyebrow. *He barely escaped with his life, but managed to rally forces enough to blunt the Steiner advance. All that he has accomplished—and yet with so little support from Luthien—is incredible.*

Theodore leaned forward heavily on the table. "It is clear, gentlemen, that the Dieron Military District's defenses have succeeded in stopping the Steiner offensive and have even won back most of the worlds we have lost."

Jinjiro felt pride flutter in his heart as Theodore praised efforts of which he'd been a part, but that hopefulness died instantly as Theodore's look and voice became filled with anger. "Warriors are not defenders. We are meant to attack the enemy on his territory, not wait to dispute his right to our worlds."

Tai-sho Palmer Conti cleared his voice. "I hear and understand what you say, but we have been given little in the way of offensive assignments, Highness."

Theodore's cold smile snapped up Conti's look of smug self-confidence. "And you've made damned little of those opportunities, haven't you? Yes, you hit the Davion world of Northwind at the beginning of the year and destroyed the Fifth Deneb Light Cavalry, but you no longer hold that world, do you?"

The dark-haired *Tai-sho* stiffened. "There was no way we could anticipate the arrival of Davion reinforcements."

Theodore looked at the other officers at the table. "I seem to recall your Fifth Sword of Light had no trouble dealing with the first wave of Davion reinforcements. You broke Team Banzai easily enough." His eyes narrowed. "But then you had help from the *Genyosha*, didn't you?"

Conti's brown eyes flashed with anger. "Their aid was nothing. It was insignificant. And they left before the second wave of Davion forces arrived. That second wave brought four regiments of the Northwind Highlanders down upon us. We were lucky to withdraw in good order and save some of our strength."

Theodore Kurita laughed heartily, and Jinjiro saw Conti recoil from the ridicule as if physically assaulted by the sounds. "Palmer, tell me no stories about the battle prowess of old Liao units. It does you no credit. Yes, you saved the Fifth Sword, sparing my father undue embarrassment, but you sacrificed a battalion of the Thirty-sixth Dieron Regulars to do it." Kurita glanced at the dark-skinned officer across from Conti. "I'm sure *Tai-Sho* Hadji Rajpuman welcomed the opportunity to cover your retreat. Had you been less concerned about preserving your honor, you would have seen the way to preserve his forces as well."

Palmer Conti stiffened, a beet-red flush creeping up beyond the collar of his dress jacket. "There was no other way, Kurita-*sama*. I did what I had to do to salvage a flawed bit of strategy. We were attacking at the behest of Maximilian Liao," he said scornfully. "A questionable thing to do."

Theodore shook his head, and Jinjiro saw anger and pity wash over the Prince's face. "There are times, Palmer, when I wonder how you have risen to the position you now hold. Then I remember most clearly. Had you chosen to pull back to the Granite Fang mountain range instead of retreating, you could have covered for the Regulars. No unit, not even a Liao unit, would have been foolish enough to pursue a Sword of Light regiment through that twisted maze of canyons."

Theodore narrowed his eyes. "In fact, using that strategy, you could have launched out from the Condor Pass on the north side of Kuroiyama and hit the Highlanders hard."

Jinjiro saw Conti's eyes glaze over as he considered Theodore's suggestion. The flash of pain over his face told Jinjiro that Conti had seen the wisdom of the strategy. Instantly, the *Tai-sho* regained his composure, and Jinjiro knew that Conti would deny that the plan could have worked. *That marks Conti as more concerned for himself and his future than for the well-being of the Dragon. The brilliance of a Theodore Kurita is lost on such officers, to our detriment.* Jinjiro felt bile rise in his throat and glanced at his own commander. *It is a pity that there are so many Contis in the Dragon's service.*

Conti opened his mouth to say something, but Theodore cut him off with a sharp wave of his hand. He looked up at Jinjiro Thorsen. "Many of you are probably wondering why I have included a *Chu-i* at a meeting of such important military leaders."

The Coordinator's son paused long enough for that question to impress itself on those who had not even deigned to notice the inferior officer seated against the wall. Jinjiro blushed as two Generals studied him critically, and his *Tai-sa* glowered at him. Jinjiro swallowed hard. *What have I done? I must have been a murdering Lyran pirate in a past life...*

Theodore waved Jinjiro to his feet. "Look at him, gentlemen. He comes to this meeting dressed for combat. He has not forgotten what war is about. This man is prepared to fight, whenever, wherever we demand it." Kurita shrugged almost helplessly. "However, looks can be deceiving."

Jinjiro's heart sank as Theodore's gaze settled on the weak-chinned profile of *Tai-sa* Sanada. *I am here because Sanada reported my insubordination. They will make an example of me. I am doomed.* Jinjiro fought to hide his fear as Theodore unsnapped his holster.

"In combat on La Blon, *Chu-i* Jinjiro Thorsen ordered his medium lance to advance into a city apparently abandoned by the Lyran forces. This contradicted an order given by *Tai-sa* Sanada here. Sanada, who was bringing up his command lance, planned to take the city himself." Theodore smiled pleasantly. "He intended to claim it for his battalion."

Theodore drew the pistol and charged it. "Jinjiro, it is reported, had a 'feeling' that something was wrong and entered the city. He claims he just wanted to scout it, and planned to be back out by the time *Tai-sa* Sanada arrived. Unfortunately for him, Lyran commandos ambushed his command with SRMs and inferno rockets. Though his lance's 'Mechs were covered with fire from the infernos, they managed to evacuate the city, and infantry was brought up to clear the resistance."

Theodore brought the pistol up and Jinjiro found himself staring down its barrel. "For this act of insubordination, *Tai-sa* Sanada has ordered a court-martial and reduction in rank for this officer."

Jinjiro breathed in deeply and found a well of calm deep inside himself. *When I became a warrior, I accepted that death in service to the Coordinator would be my lot in life. If it is to come this way, it is not to be fought.* Jinjiro glanced at Sanada, seated at the end of the table, and smiled. *Insubordinate or not, I saved your life, you old fool. No one else will ever do that for you.*

Theodore turned and shot *Tai-sa* Sanada through the head. Jinjiro jumped with surprise, but unlike the others in the room, he did not stare at the fallen body. Instead, he watched the silvery cartridge from the pistol dance and spin across the black table-top. As his head came up, his eyes met Theodore Kurita's hooded gaze. *He knows. He knows I was prepared to die to satisfy the vanity of an officer. What he almost took away, I now pledge to his service.*

Theodore let the echoes of the gunshot fade completely before he spoke. "*Tai-sa* Sanada was a fool. His objective—to win personal glory by taking that city—was at odds with the army's objective of total victory. Of what use are battle victories when we lose the war? None, of course, but it is only individuals like *Chu-i* Thorsen here who understand this."

Kurita looked toward the holographic map. "My father has lost sight of this objective. He is obsessed with avenging the loss of honor he suffered in dealing with Wolf's Dragoons. His few competent staff officers are tripping over themselves to recoup our losses in the Rasalhague District. No one bothers with the Dieron Military District because there we have lost the least amount of territory to our enemies."

Palmer Conti leaned forward and studied the map. "It is as you say. You call us here to a meeting that will get us killed if your father ever hears of it, so you must have something in mind. What do you propose to do?"

Theodore smiled easily. Pressing a button, he illuminated a world behind the Lyran lines. "Dromini VI, gentlemen, is an agricultural world of little military import. The largely Buddhist population has given the occupying force little or no trouble, and so the LCAF has only a militia unit garrisoning the world.

"Their sense of security is false. I already have a *Nekekami* strike team on the world, and they will slaughter the militia in three days. I also have the coordinates of a pirate jump point out beyond the sixth planet that will allow us transit to and from that world quickly. Because the *Nekekami* have already broken the militia's security, no one will know this peaceful world has become an armed camp."

Hitting another button flashed a red circle to life around Dromini VI. The circle captured seven worlds in the Isle of Skye and five occupied worlds in its radius. "These worlds are one jump out from Dromini. Once our JumpShips recharge, we can strike into the heart of the Isle of Skye."

Jinjiro studied the map closely. *So simple a plan, yet so devastating. It will put us in position to strike beyond Lyran hard points, forcing them to withdraw troops so they can protect all their holdings, not just key worlds. In this way, they will equalize their forces and make it easier for us to concentrate our own forces to defeat them. It turns the war into a guessing game we can win.*

Conti pointed at the Lyran world of Lyons. "I assume you want to hit these worlds to force the Isle of Skye to pull out of the

178

Commonwealth and declare itself neutral. The Third Dieron Regulars tried that and died on Lyons."

Theodore nodded slightly at the Fifth Sword's commander. "You are correct that I want to force the Isle of Skye out of the Commonwealth. Duke Lestrade graciously denuded his holding of troops, inviting us in so we could supply him the excuse he needed to withdraw, but that plan died with the Third Dieron Regulars. Still, the Isle of Skye is definitely understaffed and I mean to force the Isle of Skye out of the Commonwealth because I own it! Seven worlds, gentlemen, there for the taking. Then we leap deeper and deeper into the Commonwealth, cutting the invaders off from their own lines of supply."

Jinjiro swallowed hard. *He means to do more than force the Lyrans back across their side of the border. He wants to take worlds from them to increase the Dragon's realm. This will be such a severe blow to House Steiner that they will be forced out of the war, giving us the chance to fall upon House Davion with a vengeance.*

Tai-sho Rajpuman looked up at Theodore. "What of the mercenaries that destroyed the Third Dieron Regulars on Lyons?"

The Coordinator's son smiled, then hit a button on the table. Off to his right, facing Palmer Conti, a wall panel slid silently into the ceiling. Theodore turned to the gray-haired officer standing in the doorway. "What of the Kell Hounds?"

Yorinaga Kurita did not smile. "They are of no concern. By the time your attacks take place, the Kell Hounds will be nothing more than a memory."

Theodore nodded solemnly. "The *Genyosha* will meet and battle the Kell Hounds on Nusakan in October…"

Conti snorted derisively, "That means we'll be fighting them in November."

Yorinaga regarded Conti with a fierce stare that sent shivers up and down Jinjiro's spine. "The *Tai-sho* would be wise to remember that the *Genyosha* kept Team Banzai's Blue Blazer battalion from overrunning his command post on Northwind."

Conti regarded Yorinaga like a cobra watching a mongoose. "True, but you lost your base to a raid by Morgan Kell…"

Pounding his fist into the table, Theodore cut off discussion. "Enough, Conti. This is shameful. If you resent Yorinaga on a personal basis, settle your differences with him outside this room. His *Genyosha* is a superior fighting force, and all of us in this room know it. By the same token, we know my father has abandoned it in much the same way he has forgotten the whole Dieron Military District. The *Ge-*

179

nyosha are an elite unit, but they get no supplies. This holds true for the entire district. My father is not giving us the materials, support, or respect we are due."

Theodore pointed to the star map. "My plan will enable us to beg, borrow, and steal the supplies we need to sustain a campaign of conquest. The *Genyosha* will be our first unit going into the Isle of Skye, and they will destroy the Kell Hounds. Yorinaga has earned the glory and the right, and he shall have it."

Palmer Conti's face darkened, and Jinjiro sensed wheels turning within wheels in his mind. The Kurita *Tai-sho* looked up. "Will not the strike at Nusakan tip our hand?"

Theodore chuckled slightly. "No. The Archon has given her blessing to this battle between the Kell Hounds and the *Genyosha*. She is enough of a warrior that she will not move troops into that area for fear of dishonoring Morgan Kell. What few troops remain in the Isle of Skye will not be anticipating an attack, and we will catch them unprepared."

Theodore watched as Conti reluctantly nodded his agreement. "That settles it, then," said Kurita. "By the new year, we will rule the Isle of Skye. If he's lucky, I will let Aldo Lestrade live long enough to see how brilliant his plan truly was."

29

Moore
Dieron Military District, Draconis Combine
1 August 3029

Tai-i Jinjiro Thorsen moaned as Caterina Enritsu, the concubine Theodore Kurita had presented him in reward for his service, massaged the *ciotat*-scented oil deeper into the muscles of his right thigh. He raised his head to look at her, but without his glasses, she appeared as a blur of golden hair and lightly bronzed skin. He reached out, brushing his fingertips against her shoulder, and she kissed his hand.

"So, Thorsen-*sama*, you must be a very important man. It is not often the Coordinator's son sends his personal aide to demand special treatment for a patron."

Jinjiro nodded, then let his head sink back down on the futon. Caterina slid her hands up his body, sending a thrill through him, then started to massage his left shoulder. "No, Caterina *san*, I am not that important." *I wish I were, then I could afford your services, and you would admit me into that closed circle of important clients you keep. Your importance is far greater than mine.*

She laughed lightly and melodiously. "I think you are being modest, Jinjiro. You must have done something to deserve a promotion from *Chu-i* to *Tai-i* today."

Jinjiro tried again to focus on her face. *Is she teasing me?* "How did you know I was promoted just today?"

She winked at him and urged him to sit up. As he raised himself up on his elbows, she moved around behind him. With her hands on his shoulders, she gently pressed him back down so his head rested in

181

her lap. "A guess, nothing more. You started to introduce yourself as a Lieutenant as if you were used to that title. As Theodore Kurita arranged for me to be your hostess and—just between us—called to make sure I would be especially good to you, I assumed the promotion had taken place today."

Jinjiro's eyes grew wide with amazement. *She knows the Coordinator's son, and he asked her to take special care of me!* Warm fire ignited in his belly as she rubbed her hands over his chest and down his abdomen. "You are correct. After a big meeting, Theodore Kurita himself announced my promotion."

Jinjiro expected her to comment, but Caterina said nothing. She reached for a cup of *sake* on the low table beside the futon and brought it to his lips. Jinjiro sipped some of the rice liquor, then lay his head back down against her thighs. "What is wrong?"

Caterina shook her head briefly, then forced a smile onto her face. "Nothing, really." She paused, set the cup down, and then began to massage his temples. "It is just that I hear so often about meetings and more meetings. Moore is within striking distance of the front and I fear our warriors will be in their meetings when the Lyrans come to conquer us."

Jinjiro felt the shudder throughout her body. "No, no, you do not understand. This was not a meeting like those you describe." Jinjiro smiled as she brought the *sake* cup to his lips again. He swallowed more of the liquor and felt the glow in his belly slowly spread up to his head. "You need not fear the Lyrans much longer."

Her fingers shifted down to knead the muscles in the back of his neck. "I think you say this to humor your little *mekake*, Jinjiro-*sama*, but you need not fear. I will not let my personal anxieties spoil this night for you. I appreciate your effort, but it is not necessary to lie to me."

Jinjiro shook his head. "An officer would not lie. This is the truth." A voice inside him warned against saying anything more, but a giddy feeling overrode his caution. *She knows the Coordinator's son.* "Within two months, you will find yourself deep behind the lines."

Caterina smiled lustily down at him. "Perhaps, Jinjiro, perhaps." She shifted around, gently lowering his head to the quilted mattress, and stretched her naked body down next to his. "Then again, I might just follow a considerate, ambitious officer like you as far as you care to take me."

Caterina Enritsu looked down at the lean, sleeping form of Jinjiro Thorsen. *Sleep well, lover, for it would not do for you to notice my absence.* She glanced at her chronometer, then pulled on a dark sweater. She felt uneasy about leaving in the middle of a performance, but knew the drug she'd slipped into the *sake* would keep Jinjiro safely unconscious for the short time she was gone.

Indeed, the drug had worked perfectly. It loosened Jinjiro's tongue enough that he'd easily revealed the information she wanted. *I knew from the first look at that innocent face and those thick glasses, that an appeal to his protectiveness would work. I wish I could wait until tomorrow to deliver this information, but it's too vital. The LIC needs it now. I have to risk it.*

She crossed back to the sleeping MechWarrior and kissed him on the forehead. *When I get back, I'll give you something to remember that will blur anything and everything else about this evening in your memory.* She smiled to herself. *After all, all that I've done so far has been to thank you in the name of Theodore Kurita. When I return, though, I will show you the full depth of the Lyran Intelligence Corps' gratitude.*

30

Justin realized something was very wrong when he noticed members of the House Imarra battalions standing guard on either side of the briefing chamber's portal. *Where the hell are the Death Commandos? Who authorized a shift of duty for them?* Remembering the urgent sound in Candace's voice and the worried look on her face on the visiphone's view screen, Justin answered his own question. *Romano. She has to be the source of this trouble. I hope she's done nothing I can't fix.*

The two hulking guards did not look at Justin as the chamber door rose into the ceiling, but they moved instantly to block Alexi Malenkov's passage. Seeing their movement out the corner of his eye, Justin spun and batted the nearest guard's hand away from Alexi's shoulder. "Let him go."

The Imarra warrior glanced over his shoulder as Romano framed herself in the doorway. "Malenkov is not allowed in here. I do not trust him." She held her head high, and her green eyes blazed with defiance. Her black trousers and green tunic had been cut in a military style, but the way she let the blouse gap open to reveal tantalizing glimpses of her breasts mocked the crisp correctness of the guards' uniforms.

Justin stared at her implacably. *Warlord or seductress, Romano? Which will it be today?* "I do not care if you trust him or not. I do." Justin let his voice drop so that only Romano could hear his words. "If not for him, Ling would have had me."

184

Justin's revelation smashed Romano's haughty facade like a sledgehammer hitting bone china. He guided Alexi through the door, then entered the chamber himself. Romano nodded reluctant permission to the guards, then turned away from the door. Despite the blow, Justin noticed that her color and confidence returned as she moved toward the head of the table and drew closer to both Maximilian Liao and Tsen Shang.

Justin glanced at Candace, reassuring her with a smile. Her expression lightened somewhat, but she looked anxiously at her father and the holographic map suspended above the holotable. *What is going on here? Candace looks as though she's been through a month-long campaign. Max seems enthused and Tsen is beaming like a child who's won a contest.*

The Chancellor folded his arms across his chest. "Please, *Shonso* Xiang, do not feel slighted that this is the first time that I discuss this matter with you. I know you have many worries concerning the refit of the House Imarra regiment with the new myomer muscles. I wanted this to be a surprise."

Justin nodded. "I am honored by your concern, Supreme Counselor." *A surprise! What now?*

Maximilian smiled at Romano. "Romano, who has been as concerned as you about the recent Davion advances, has worked with Tsen Shang to come up with a way to break the back of the invasion. The Interdiction has already slowed our enemies. This will stop them dead in their tracks and even force them to retreat."

Justin shifted his gaze to Tsen Shang and appraised him openly. The tall, slender analyst's smile nearly died under Justin's gaze, but a squeeze on his arm from Romano buoyed his spirits. Justin noted this new fire in Shang with a mix of amusement and fear. *He's abandoned himself to her. That will make him either useless or very dangerous.*

"What have you got, Tsen?" Justin asked.

Smiling at Romano, Tsen disengaged his arm from hers and moved to the table. He hit a few keys, commanding the computer to redraw the map. It formed itself into the strategic display Justin had become all too used to seeing of late: red worlds denoted those taken by the Federated Suns, and green stood for those still loyal to the Chancellor. The Tikonov Free Republic, governed by a Davion-backed military council since Ridzik's death, had been colored in with blue.

Tsen pointed his right hand toward a world in the Capellan March of the Federated Suns. Red highlights sparkled from diamond chips mounted along the long fingernails of his last three fingers. "This is the key to the Davion war effort. If we cripple this world, we will hamstring Hanse Davion's invasion."

Justin peered closely at the map, then felt his heart rise to his throat. *Kathil!* Justin's head came up. "You can't hit the shipyards at Kathil."

Tsen's grin faltered momentarily, then Romano slid her left hand along over his right shoulder as she advanced to the table. "His plan is brilliant, Justin Xiang!" The map's reflected light bathed her face in blood. "You're just jealous because Tsen Shang found the one assault that will stop our enemies while you were out hunting down a measly scientific base."

Justin stared at her, his mouth hanging open in disbelief. "You can't hit Kathil. That world is one of a dozen planets in all the Successor States that has factories capable of repairing damage to or building new JumpShips." He looked over at Shang. "Those JumpShips are the apex of *lostech*. We don't know how to build them anymore. We don't know what makes them work. But we do know how to keep the factories running to turn them out. If you destroy those orbiting factories and drydocks, you will cripple the Federated Suns all right, and the future of mankind along with it!"

Romano sneered. "That hardly sounds like the Justin Xiang who hates Hanse Davion enough to mount hunting expeditions into Federated Suns territory."

"Romano," Candace broke in sharply, "you have forever been too stupid to look five minutes into the future. Hanse Davion did restore production of the yards just for this war, but destroy the factories capable of creating and repairing JumpShips and you doom mankind. The JumpShips we have now will eventually wear out and fail. When the last of them does, we will be forced to remain on our worlds forever. Trade between our diverse colonies—trade that makes life in the Successor States possible—will wither and die!"

"Stop!" Maximilian Liao's voice, again filled with the strength of command it had lacked so often since the invasion, cut off his daughters' bickering instantly. Candace stared savagely at her sister, but Romano smiled and turned to her father.

The Chancellor nodded appreciatively toward Justin. "Once again, I find your concern and insight a blaze that marks the boundary between suitable action and recklessness." He rested a hand on Tsen's shoulder. "However, in all fairness to Tsen Shang, he anticipated that objection and has worked around it."

Justin bowed respectfully to the Chancellor and Tsen Shang. "Forgive my presumption, Citizen Shang."

Tsen curtly returned the bow, then poked several more keys on the table's keypad. Portions of a holographic promotional video created by Kearny-Fuchida Yare Industries flashed up to replace the map. Shot from a small shuttle, the footage showed close-ups of an orbiting factory. Tsen froze the image when the factory's bank of microwave collector dishes came into view.

"I realized we did not want to destroy the factories for a number of reasons, the primary being that we might want to use them ourselves when we return to take the world." Pointing to the microwave dishes, the analyst smiled easily. "Because the Kearny-Fuchida drive components are not shielded during the manufacturing process, radiation outputs from fusion and fission engines can damage them. For this reason, power is sent from Kathil up to the orbiting factories in the form of microwave beams."

Tsen moved the vid ahead to a point where it showed one of the large generating stations on the planet's surface. A grove of smaller dishes moved along, tracking a factory until its orbit took it over the horizon, or just into another power district. "While KF drives might be lostech, geothermal generating stations are not. If we hit the generators and destroy them, the shipyards will be out of business."

Justin frowned. *He has a good point there. A chain is only as strong as its weakest link, and those stations are a very weak link.* "The generating stations can be rebuilt."

Tsen smiled, then looked beyond Justin. "True, but as the figures Alexi ran for me point out, one station would take over seventy billion C-bills and two years to build. Davion could do it faster, but…"

Justin nodded. "…But he'd be unable to continue financing his war."

Romano smiled sweetly in victory. "And he would face opposition at home. More and more JumpShips would have to be pulled from his consumer economy to move troops. The product shortages caused by the war's hunger for JumpShips have already caused him some problems. He would have to withdraw his troops to bases he can support with fewer ships."

Justin turned to Alexi. "Comments?"

Alexi moved forward enough to use the keyboard on that side of the table. He punched in a request for data, shifting the display to a tactical readout on Kathil. Tsen Shang smiled broadly and Justin realized the grin came easily because spies reported Davion had only a half-strength militia unit garrisoning the world.

Color drained from Alexi's face. "My God, has the Fox been so stupid as to leave this world naked?"

Romano looked down at Alexi. "Would you have expected

anything less arrogant from him? He imagines us broken and defeated. He will pay for that."

Tsen shot Romano a quick smile, then met Justin's hawk-gaze. "JumpShip circuits rotate troops out of Kathil on a regular basis, but a circuit got disrupted right after Ridzik's death. It will be another six weeks before troops arrive on Kathil."

Justin studied the readout again. "Can you get there in time?"

Romano usurped Tsen's answer. "We've shifted and extended the command circuit you used to return from Bethel. Our troops land during the first week in September."

Anticipating Justin's needs, Alexi hit a button that summoned the strategic map to the screen again. Justin mentally counted the number of jumps required for the trip. *Seven jumps, with a week out of this system and a week heading to the target planet. It can be done.*

Justin nodded. "You can use the House Imarra troops, if you wish. Their 'Mechs are all refitted."

Romano laughed aloud. "No. They will remain here. Our troops have already left."

Alexi looked at Justin. "That's why the Death Commandos aren't around."

Justin straightened up. "Just one battalion? Is that enough?"

Tsen shook his head. "The Death Commandos and the Fourth Tau Ceti Rangers headed out this morning at 2.5 Gs to the nadir jump point. That gives us two battalions to face the militia, or whatever rotates in, if the schedule is repaired somehow. Our people will travel in complete radio silence—not even ComStar will know of this mission until it is over. Davion's only ever had a battalion on station there anyway. Like you," Shang sneered, "he could never believe anyone would attack the world."

Tsen allowed himself a loud laugh. "Even if he knew of the assault—which is impossible because ComStar is not passing information from Davion spies—he doesn't have any troops in a position to do anything about it."

The Chancellor looked over at Justin. "Well, *Shonso* Xiang, are you surprised?"

Justin breathed in deeply, using the time to sort out his emotions. He smiled slowly, but let it widen into a grin. "Surprised, yes." He stabbed his right hand through the holographic map, offering it to Tsen Shang. "Your plan is flawless."

Taking Tsen's hand, Justin shook it heartily. "Yes, Tsen, with the success of your assault, we will finally be in a position to take back what Hanse Davion has stolen from us."

Justin looked up from his desk as Alexi Malenkov came through the door. "Good, Alexi. I'm glad you could get here so quickly."

The tall blond man smiled. "I came as soon as I heard you needed me." Concern knitted his pale brows together. "What is it?"

Justin waved Alexi to a chair, then walked around and sat on the front corner of his desk. "I want to ask your advice about something, and I want you to be perfectly honest with me." The smaller man shrugged uneasily. "Seeing Tsen's plan, and knowing how near the end is for Hanse Davion, it got me to thinking about a lot of things."

Justin smiled grimly. "As you know, I have suffered gross humiliation at the hands of Hanse Davion and my father. Hanse engineered a sham trial that stripped me of my rank, my name, and my honor. My father testified against me — his own flesh and blood—in that trial, then later assigned one of his spies to seduce me and watch me on Solaris. Then Hanse Davion offered a warrior a world and a 'Mech regiment of his own if he would kill me. And then the wedding…" Justin shook his head. "He declared war on us at his own wedding, making us the laughingstock of the Successor States!"

Alexi jumped when Justin's steel fist slammed down onto the corner of his desk and snapped a triangle of wood off. "Easy, Justin," he said. "We'll have the Fox soon enough."

Justin's dark eyes smoldered. "Not soon enough for me." He forced his expression to lighten. "But then, I don't think there ever was a time that *would* have been soon enough, if you follow me?"

Alexi nodded. "I understand some of what you feel. With Tikonov gone, I can never go home again." Alexi smiled ruefully. "Hanse Davion has orphaned us both."

"Yes. He's caused us much pain—pain I wish to return as soon as possible." Justin reached back and plucked an unsealed envelope from his blotter. "I have created a *verigraph* I want to send to my father. In it, I tell him much of what I've wanted to say since he betrayed me. In very indirect terms, it will let him know that his downfall, and that of his Prince, is in the offing. I imagine they will believe I am boasting about the information we stole from Bethel, but when the raid hits Kathil, they will realize what I really meant."

Alexi winced. "That's shoving the dagger in and twisting it— which is nothing less than they deserve." His eyebrows sunk into a frown. "I think it would be a great idea to send it, but ComStar won't carry it though to your father because of the Interdiction, will they?"

Justin shrugged. "I spoke with an aide to Villius Tejh, the

Precentor here on Sian, and he said it might be possible. I transferred an ungodly amount of money from my Solaris accounts to ComStar, and he said that increased my chances. But he thought the First Circuit might have to discuss it first."

Justin looked Alexi straight in the eyes. "Do you think I should indulge myself in this personal bit of revenge?"

Alexi thought for half a second, then nodded. "Go ahead. Do it. I won't tell anyone if you don't."

"Deal." Justin extended the envelope to Alexi. "Can you take it to the ComStar station for me? I've told them I was sending it along in your custody. Candace is still upset about today, and she's flown out to the Summer Palace." Justin glanced at his chronometer. "I've promised to meet her there, and I'm already late."

Alexi took the envelope. "They know I'm coming with it?"

Justin nodded. "It has all been arranged." He crossed his fingers and held up his right hand. "With any luck at all, my revenge begins now."

31

Myndo Waterly's laughter echoed lightly through the First Circuit chamber. She shook her head slowly as she stared at the small, dark-haired Precentor from Sian. "Did you honestly expect us to allow that message to pass through here without a fight, Villius? Justin Xiang's request should be refused for no other reason than he has tried to send a message to someone in an Interdicted place." She waved Villius's request away like a queen shooing a beggar. "Give him back his money, and tell him no."

Precentor Sian spitted her with a hellish stare, then shook his head in disbelief. "I would have thought you would be the last to oppose me on this subject, Precentor Dieron. You have read the text of this message, and you know that Xiang is full of himself as a result of the successful strike into the heart of the Capellan March. This message is nothing more than bragging about the effort and a hint at future problems for the Federated Suns. This should cause Hanse Davion and Quintus Allard some discomfiture—something I thought you would welcome."

Myndo looked around at the other Precentors' faces. *They all wonder at this change on my part. Are they stupid, or are they just so used to opposing me that no argument I make seems logical to them?* "You are correct, on a basic level, Precentor Sian. However, my desire to see Hanse Davion twist slowly in the wind does not blind me to the obvious problems with this missive. It is bound for an Interdicted

191

nation-state."

Precentor Tharkad brushed his left hand through his blond hair. "You know as well as I that we can vote to make an exception." He glanced at the other Precentors. "In fact, as I recall, we need only a two-thirds majority to allow this message to pass. Your argument over the *verigraph*'s legality is invalid."

She bowed her head. "I understand our regulations, Precentor Tharkad, but I appreciate your reminder. I would like to point out that the message was given to our station chief by an Interdicted agent. Alexi Malenkov is a Davion agent. The *verigraph* passed from him to us. It is tainted and, therefore, cannot be delivered."

The flesh around the Primus's eyes tightened. "Do not play these childish games, Precentor Dieron. The message came from Xiang."

"Oh?" Myndo met the Primus's hard stare openly. "And if I were to send a child to a store to purchase wine in my name, do you think the shopkeeper would oblige him? No. Of course not." She turned toward the other Precentors. "We have no way of knowing if that message came from Xiang, or if it really is being sent by Alexi Malenkov to his master on New Avalon."

"This is outrageous!" Precentor Sian appealed to the Primus. "Honorable One, please remind Precentor Dieron that we are dealing with reality here, not some fantasy world. Justin Xiang created a *verigraph*, not a holovid, not a written message. He spoke with my aide via visiphone, and our trace verified the call. He said he was sending Alexi Malenkov down with a *verigraph*."

Before the Primus could grant Villius Tejh's request, Myndo spoke in a loud and clear voice. "Do not make your case on the basis of lies, Precentor Sian." Her accusation shocked the other Precentors, but she paid them no attention. "The transcript of the conversation, as you provided it, proves you incorrect. In the conversation, Xiang says, 'I've already sent Alexi Malenkov down with the *verigraph*. He should be there in half an hour.'"

Huthrin Vandel frowned deeply. "What earthly difference does that make? The important thing is that Xiang told our people Alexi Malenkov was carrying the message for him."

Myndo opened her hands. "That statement makes *all* the difference, Precentor New Avalon. The transcript marks the time of that line in the conversation as occurring at 6:30 P.M., standard time. That means Malenkov should have arrived at our station at 7:00 or 7:15, at the latest. He arrived at 9:00 P.M. What was he doing for that hour and three-quarters?"

The Primus tucked his hands into the sleeves of his tan robe. "You

192

cannot mean to suggest Alexi Malenkov forged a new *verigraph*, can you?" The look of contempt on his face matched the derision in his voice.

"It is not impossible." She realized the second she'd spoken that the Primus had provoked a thoughtless outburst, and she rushed to shore it up. "There are rumors that say the NAIS has successfully managed to dissect *verigraph*s and put them back together."

The Precentor of New Avalon laughed heartily. "You must forgive me, but that is utterly ridiculous. The New Avalon Institute of Science has developed no such technology recently, and even if they had, it would make no difference. There is no way they could have gotten so complicated a device to an agent in the field, especially not to a mole like Alexi Malenkov."

Myndo fixed him with a razored stare. "I was unaware we had agents in the NAIS that could confirm or deny this wild assertion of yours, Precentor. Are you certain you wish to live or die on that pronouncement?"

Vandel pulled himself up to his full height. "I think, Precentor Dieron, that you grossly overstate the case. I stand by my explanation because I know it to be fact." His voice ripped back at her. "You, on the other hand, argue vapor and fairy tales."

Myndo started to reply, but the Primus raised his hand to stop her. "We know well your opinions on this subject, Precentor Dieron. Precentor Sian, do you think there was a chance that Malenkov could have forged or tampered with Xiang's *verigraph* to communicate information to the Federated Suns?"

"Forgery, no. There is no way he could have forged a message. This is, after all, a *verigraph*." The small man hesitated as he pondered the second half of the question. "As for tampering with it, that could be possible. My people reported he was nervous, but we assumed that was because he is a Davion agent. Face it. Having us refuse to take the message from him because of his true allegiance could have destroyed him."

The Primus smiled easily, his sallow flesh gathering in flat wrinkles around the corners of his mouth. "Then the solution is simple. Duplicate the *verigraph* and send the duplicate. If Malenkov did something to it—like injecting a chemical dye that would react to another chemical—our scanning and duplication process will not pick it up. A duplicate should take care of your concerns, shouldn't it, Precentor Dieron?"

"Should it?" Myndo balled her fists in frustration. "We don't know the genesis of this message. What if Malenkov suggested it to

Xiang? What if he advised Xiang on the wording? What if he did forge a new message?"

The Primus smiled deprecatingly. "What if Malenkov had General Kerensky return and bring him a Star League-vintage *verigraph* forging machine?"

Myndo fumed inwardly. *You bastard! You back them just to take a cut at me. Very well. You've out-maneuvered me this time, but not again.* "I acquiesce, Primus, and bow to your superior wisdom. You are correct. This message can do no harm—unless, of course, Malenkov did manage the impossible. As impossible as someone smuggling weapons on to our island at last year's wedding, perhaps?"

Her reminder of the previous summer's security fiasco stung all present, but Myndo realized that it also galvanized their opposition to her. She did not allow defeat to show on her face, however. *I will remember this, all of you. If the impossible has occurred, I will not let up until it has destroyed every one of you.*

32

The fear that had coiled like a snake about to strike now sunk its fangs into Hanse Davion. "Say that again, Quintus. They're going to hit Kathil?"

The spymaster nodded grimly. Color had drained from his face, leaving it half a shade darker than his white hair. The *verigraph* he held in his hand trembled, as did the older man's lower lip. "He buried it well inside this note. This one paragraph is not remarkable in context, but it contains all the key words. 'A bird without wings cannot fly, but what need have we of clipping wings if we scale the cliff and fire the nest? Before this is ended, Father, I wish I could see your face one more time. We have come far, you and I, and are now just opposite sides of the same coin.'" The old man looked up from the message in his hand. "It sounds so like Justin."

Hanse sank back into his leather chair. "Kathil. Has Max gone completely over the edge? If he destroys the factories at Kathil, he'll be strangling mankind's travel between the stars."

Quintus looked up. "Forgive me, Highness, but the codeword for factories did not appear in the message. A reference to eggs would have indicated an involvement with the factories. I have to interpret 'fire the nest' to mean they will hit the generators or subassembly facilities on the world itself. That would slow us down without destroying a most precious resource." Hanse frowned deeply. "What could they use to hit Kathil?"

An angry, anxious expression congealed on Quintus's face. "I have to believe they'll use the best they have left. I know where McCarron's Armored Cavalry is, so it's not going to be them. The units will probably come from Sian, and that would have to mean House Imarra troops or the Death Commandos."

Hanse slammed his right fist against the top of his desk. "And we still only have militia protecting the world?"

Quintus nodded ruefully. "If Liao has been able to set up a command circuit directed at Kathil, they could be there next week. Our own force scheduled to show up there is without transport. Ever since we stripped some ships off to our rotation circuits to carry Melissa back to the Commonwealth, we've got nothing close enough to get them there.

Hanse sat and stared at his balled fists, letting the silence hang heavily in the air. *The ambitions of a petty Lyran noble makes him do one thing, and that creates the potential for disaster here in the Federated Suns. The desire for little personal victories inspires this raid on Kathil, but it also got ComStar to pass this important message on to us, without realizing its importance.*

Hanse swallowed hard. "Well, my friend, we'd best find any troops in the area that we can deliver posthaste. And we better pray they can stop Liao's raiders, because otherwise we'll lose everything we've won this past year and then some."

Rays from the setting sun lanced through the tall windows of Hanse Davion's office, stretching the Prince's shadow so it touched the doors to his office. The Prince, his face shadowed, looked up as Quintus Allard escorted Kym Sorenson into the room. "Thank you for coming on such short notice, Lady Sorenson."

She curtsied, then blushed. Her long blond hair was gathered back, and she wore faded trousers and an oversized shirt emblazoned with the crest of the Davion Heavy Guards. "Forgive my appearance, Highness. I came as soon as the Minister called me, I…"

Hanse forced a smile and raised a hand to forestall her explanation. "No need to apologize. This is a situation that calls for a swift response, not protocol or ceremony." Hanse hesitated for a moment, searching through the different ways he had thought to ask his question. He rejected all his previous ideas and waved her toward a chair. "Please, Kym, be seated."

She stiffened. "Highness, if this is about Morgan, I think I should remain standing." She tugged nervously on the ends of her shirt, pulling it tight at the shoulders.

Realizing the reason for her anxiety, the Prince said quickly, "Nothing has happened to Morgan, Kym. He's fine." The Prince looked beyond her toward the closed doors and Quintus Allard. "In fact, he's waiting to speak with me as soon as I have spoken with you, though he does not know you are here."

Relief flooded her pretty face, bringing back animation and color. "Thank you, Highness."

Don't thank me yet. Your feelings for him are obvious. How have they affected your mission? "There is no easy way for me to ask you this, Kym, so forgive my clumsy approach." He looked into her blue eyes. "Can Morgan be trusted with troops in the Capellan March?"

It pleased the Prince that she met his gaze without flinching. "Highness, if you have another subject who is more loyal and trustworthy than Morgan Hasek-Davion, you are unique and blessed among the rulers of the Successor States." Kym stopped as emotion choked her, and she turned slightly away.

Hanse granted her the time to recover. Wiping away tears with the sleeve of her shirt, she turned back. "Forgive me."

"Nothing to forgive, Kym."

She smiled weakly, took in a deep breath and calmed herself. "In my opinion, Prince Hanse, you have nothing to fear from entrusting troops to Morgan."

Hanse narrowed his eyes. "He's not had contacts with dissidents in the Capellan March? He's not anxious to take his father's place as their leader? The death of the Fifth Syrtis Fusiliers affected him deeply…"

Anger flashed through Kym's eyes, but she stopped herself before letting it form into words. "Highness, you have no idea the conflicts Morgan has fought within himself over the years. His father's death hurt him deeply. The loss saddened him because he loved his father, and also because he realized his father was foolish and disloyal. Ultimately, Morgan accepted responsibility for his father's death because he believed he had not worked hard enough to bring the two of you back together."

Hanse shook his head. "There is no way he could have healed that rift."

"I know that," Kym said, "but Morgan doesn't see it that way. He's constantly struggling to atone for his father's mistakes and to prove himself worthy of the honor of being named your heir. The destruction of the Fifth Syrtis hurt him because it was another link lost with his father. More importantly, though, he knew that had he been commanding that force, he would have crushed McCarron's Armored Cavalry. It tore him up to think an idiot like Hartstone would embarrass you so."

Kym half-turned so she could see both men. "You have asked if Morgan has communicated with Capellan March dissidents. He has." She ignored the shocked looks on the two man's faces. "He's told them to go to hell. After his father's death, Count Anton Vitios pledged his personal support to Morgan. Morgan's reply was short and succinct: 'The Capellan March is now and forever shall be a loyal part of the Federated Suns. If you want to shed your blood on the altar of separatism, you'll find my hand on the knife.'"

Hanse saw the smile on Quintus Allard's face and it mirrored his own. "Your words, your tone, your eyes all tell me that what you say is the truth." Hanse's smile grew as he felt a heavy weight falling away from his heart. "I've always hoped what you've said about Morgan was true, but I feared he might be his father's son in more than blood." Hanse crossed to Kym and rested his hands on her shoulders. "Thank you. I owe you a debt I can never repay you."

Her gaze searched his face for a moment. "There is something you can do for me."

"Name it."

Kym glanced at Quintus. "I will continue to work for you in the NAIS until the war is ended. After that, I will terminate my service with the MIIO." She looked up into Hanse's ice blue eyes. "Never tell Morgan I spied on him for you. I love him too much to see him hurt that way."

Hanse smiled and enfolded her in a hug. "Neither one of us wants him hurt, Kym. Your secret is safe."

Pulling back, she smiled, then glanced down as tears rolled from her eyes. "When does he ship out?"

So quick, so smart. Your departure from the MIIO will be a great loss. Hanse brushed her tears away. "You'll have tonight…Some of it, at least." He put an arm over her shoulders and gave her a squeeze as he directed her to the side door of his office. "From here, you can leave the Palace without Morgan seeing you."

Kym opened the door, then turned to the Prince again. "Morgan will do whatever you ask of him, or die trying. I hope this is worth it."

Hanse nodded solemnly. "It is. If he falls, the Federated Suns falls with him."

Hanse Davion accepted Morgan Hasek-Davion's proffered hand gladly. He met and matched his nephew's firm grip and pumped his arm strongly. He sensed in Morgan the ability and strength to crush his hand, but felt no concern. *From what Kym just said, Morgan would strike off the offending limb before harming me.*

Hanse waved Morgan to a chair. "Please, Morgan, be seated. I must speak with you about something urgent."

Morgan sat down, his long red-gold hair falling over the shoulders of his olive-drab jumpsuit. The fabric pulled taut over his massive chest, revealing the outline of a cooling vest underneath. He did not relax, but sat forward on the edge of the chair, following Hanse's pacing with restless green eyes.

Feet shoulder width apart, Hanse clasped his hands at the small of his back, then turned to face Morgan. "I have a confession to make to you. Sixteen years ago, my brother Ian died in a war with House Kurita. Perhaps he was foolish to place himself in such jeopardy, but that was his right as the Prince of the Federated Suns. Right or wrong, his action left him vulnerable, and when he died, it placed me on the throne…"

Morgan shook his head almost imperceptibly. "You don't have to do this, Hanse."

Yes I do, Morgan. As much for me as for you. As Hanse forced himself to smile, Morgan settled back in his chair. Hanse glanced at

Quintus and bade him sit as well.

"Before that, I had never given much thought to ruling the Federated Suns because I was not raised for that job. I studied to be a military man, and I discovered, soon enough, that tactics and strategy mean little in the political arena. My brother's last heartbeat moved me from the world of battles waged in the open to a realm where you often don't see the attack until it's too late."

The Prince smiled at his nephew. "I never much liked your father, but I respected the hell out of his ability to create alliances and form power coalitions. When he and I struggled over who would actually sit on Ian's throne, I think my lack of guile threw him off. He spent so much time and energy looking for my hidden attacks that he let my frontal assaults weaken him. The only political lesson I had ever learned was that you can't fight a dead man, so I used the image of my brother's trust in me to keep a Davion on the throne.

"Over the years, I've learned more about politics, and the paranoia that made your father vulnerable began to infect me, too. I looked at you and took all the myriad signs of your loyalty and friendship for a facade hiding a possible plot for my downfall. I should have realized sooner, much sooner, that in you I was seeing the image of myself before Ian's death. I'm sorry it took so long for me to see."

Morgan looked down at his hands. "All I've ever wanted was to be a friend you could trust."

Hanse swallowed against the lump in his throat. "I know. For the record, I realize now that it wasn't my fear of your following in your father's footsteps that prevented me from giving you a combat assignment in this war. Nor was I afraid of what might happen were you captured or killed by Liao forces." He looked into Morgan's eyes. "The truth is, I couldn't bear the idea of losing such a close friend."

Morgan frowned. "How can you call me that when you said you were afraid of my disloyalty."

Quintus laid his hand on Morgan's shoulder. "Being afraid of fire doesn't mean you never strike a match. You just don't strike one in a place where the fire can get out of control. Hanse knew, deep down, that you could be trusted. He just had to be sure others could not twist you and use you against him."

Hanse nodded in agreement. "Now, however, a situation has come up that requires handling by a tactical genius. It is of vital importance. I will not repeat Ian's mistake. Besides, I'm not certain my skill could bring us a victory. You're the only one I can trust with it."

Morgan nodded once. "Give me a bucket of water and I'll storm the gates of Hell for you."

200

Hanse smiled uneasily. "Would that this mission were so easy." He plucked a folder from his desk and handed it to Morgan. As the younger man scanned the material, Hanse continued speaking.

"Liao has a minimum of one elite battalion—most probably his Death Commandos—heading in to Kathil. We believe they're going to destroy the generating facilities on the ground. On the planet, we have a very green militia unit. The only other forces I can give you are a reinforced 'Mech company and the tailings from the Fifth Syrtis Fusiliers. We've nothing else in range that can get there in time."

Morgan looked up anxiously. "If they cripple Kathil, we'll have no way to repair JumpShips, nor will we be able to build new ones to replace those that can't be fixed. Our troops will have to pull back, our supply routes become more chancy, and our reaction time to enemy raids goes to hell."

Hanse sat back on the edge of his desk. "Now you know why you've got to stop the assault. The Death Commandos are suicide troops. They'll keep coming until you blow them to pieces. They might have some help—in which case, things are going to get really nasty."

Morgan snapped the folder shut. He stood and saluted Hanse Davion. "I'll stop them. If it takes every man and every 'Mech I have, I'll stop them."

Hanse returned the salute. "You'll have to do better than that."

Morgan frowned in confusion. "Pardon?"

"We learned of this attack because of a risky move by an agent inside the Maskirovka." Hanse looked his nephew straight in the eye. "After the defense of Kathil, whatever you have left in the way of men and machines must go to Sian to bring him back home."

34

Katrina Steiner stood before her throne as Frederick Steiner entered the hall. The tap of his heels against the polished marble floor sounded a rhythmic tattoo, faltering only when Frederick noticed Ryan Steiner standing in the throne's shadow. The Archon saw Frederick's valiant struggle to keep the surprise from his face, and she savored it. *Yes, you idiot. You are undone.*

Frederick, resplendent in the gray uniform of the Tenth Lyran Guards, came to a halt at the base of the throne. He clicked his heels and bowed to the Archon, but she did not offer him her hand. He straightened up stiffly. "You have summoned me, Archon?"

The Archon looked down at him. "So I have."

Frederick squirmed uneasily beneath her cold stare. His right hand almost rose to massage the scar at his temple, but he caught himself. "What is it, Katrina?" Frederick transmuted some of his fear into irritation. "There's a war on out there, and it's time for my troops to rotate back to the front. What do you want?"

The Archon smiled cruelly as she seated herself on the tall throne. Above and behind her, the two *Griffin* BattleMechs belonging to her Household Guard seemed to stare down at Frederick like executioners. "What do I want, Frederick?" She leaned forward. "If I had my way, I'd have your head on a platter!"

Frederick drew back a step. "What are you talking about?"

Katrina waved his question aside. "You moron! It's bad enough

202

that you plot little treasons with Aldo Lestrade, but now you actively join him in this latest of his plots! Until now, I'd always assumed the attempts on my life were the work of Lestrade, and Lestrade alone." She turned to Ryan. "Now he brings me a holodisk you sent to Alessandro demanding his support in the situation resulting from my downfall. How could you have been so blatantly stupid?"

Frederick's mouth dropped open. "Aldo has tried to have you killed? I knew there had been attempts, but I assumed they were made by dissidents, by Heimdall…or by House Kurita. I…"

The pained look of betrayal in his eyes touched something in Katrina. *Frederick has always been hostile and malicious, but I've overlooked many things because of his loyalty to the Commonwealth and his general lack of imagination. Am I wrong in supposing he was desperate enough to sanction this latest attempt?*

"Frederick, two months ago, assassins nearly murdered me and Simon Johnson. If not for a member of Heimdall, you'd be sitting in my place now. Are you telling me this was not the incident you hinted at in the holodisk sent to Alessandro?"

All color had drained from Frederick's face, but fire still burned his eyes. He glanced hatefully at Ryan, then looked at the Archon. "I swear on my honor as an officer in the LCAF that I knew nothing of any attempt to kill you. Depose you, yes. I've wanted to do that ever since you usurped the throne. But I wanted to defeat you in a political battle, not destroy you like a thief fighting over the swag from a job."

Katrina's nostrils flared. "Your honor as an officer in the LCAF means nothing, Frederick, but the desire for an open battle is you, through and through." The Archon leaned back in her throne, resting her elbows on the arms and steepling her fingers. "What incident did you refer to in your message?"

Frederick stiffened as though prepared to deny her that information, but Katrina never gave him the chance to offer honor as a defense. "Face it, Frederick. Aldo Lestrade betrayed you a hundred times over. I know he is behind this—he's pulled your strings like a master puppeteer. What did he use to seduce you into cooperating this time?"

Frederick's resolve broke. "He planned, after any hostile action by the Combine forces, to declare the Isle of Skye independent. He would restrict trade, cutting you off from the Federated Suns." His eyes full of a plea for understanding, Frederick looked up at Katrina. "I would negotiate a settlement between the two of you. I would be seen as a leader and—" he glared at Ryan—"with Alessandro's support, I could force you to abdicate. Or at least share power with me in some coalition."

Katrina glanced at Ryan, despising the smirk on the young man's lips. *Just as he told me, though that plan was obvious from the political situation and the holodisk. Obvious enough for even Frederick to plumb its depths and decide it might work.* Katrina felt a cold chill. *Yes, with the people's irritation over the war's stalemate and my daughter's marriage, it probably would have worked.*

She nodded solemnly. "The Kell Hounds defeating the Third Dieron Regulars put a crimp in that plan. Lestrade could not claim I had neglected him when the Hounds defended his world for him, could he?"

Frederick stared down at his boots. "No. He said the plan had just been delayed, not permanently stopped." His head came up. "You've seen that he's kept the Isle of Skye defended as lightly as possible, with the exception of Summer. He's still afraid of a raid there, though I think he fears the Kell Hounds more than he does the Dragon."

Katrina let her hands drop to her lap. "It is well that he does. The Kell Hounds have business of their own to attend to, and after that, I am not certain I can restrain them from taking Summer apart." *Indeed, if Yorinaga Kurita had not sent Morgan a message setting up a battle on the desert world of Nusakan IV in two months, Morgan might have already killed Lestrade.*

Frederick Steiner tore the epaulets from his uniform and tossed them at the Archon's feet. "I resign from the Tenth Lyran Guards. They're the best troops an officer could ever hope to lead." He looked into Katrina's eyes, letting the barest hint of a smile lift the corners of his mouth. "But you know that. You commanded them before becoming Archon. They're still the best. I will not have their reputation soiled when you try me for treason and have me executed."

Katrina looked down at the shoulder-boards, momentarily entranced by the light flashing from the silver double diamonds on each one. *I wish it were that simple.* She nudged them back in his direction with the toe of her boot.

"Believe me, Frederick, I wish I could accept your offer. Had I a choice, I'd have you shot and Aldo Lestrade hung from the highest Triad tower. As it is, that's impossible. I cannot have you killed, nor can I accept your resignation."

Frederick's white brows met as a puzzlement made deep wrinkles in his forehead. "I do not understand."

Katrina moistened her lips with the tip of her tongue. "In leaving the Isle of Skye open for attack, Aldo Lestrade has made his holding very attractive to the Draconis Combine. True, they did try a raid that would give him the excuse to pull out, but that plan came from Luthien.

A new, more deadly plan has been drafted by Theodore Kurita. In short, he plans a major offensive based from the world of Dromini VI. The offensive is to begin in late October and will stab deep into the Isle of Skye."

Frederick closed his eyes as he summoned up a mental map of the region. "That puts a half-dozen worlds in jeopardy, and makes many more vulnerable to second- and third-stage jumps." His eyes opened. "With our forces strung out through the Rasalhague District and fighting along the Marik border, we don't have time to get troops and supplies to Skye to stop their offensive."

"Not unless we want to let our front collapse like a house of cards," Katrina said. "I could pump troops into the Skye worlds, but they'd not have the needed support or supplies. Given another month, I could do it, and another month is what I mean to have."

She leaned forward, all Archon-to-subject protocol abandoned. Speaking as one MechWarrior to another, she quickly outlined her only hope. "Theodore Kurita has already hit Dromini VI with commando attacks that have eliminated the world's militia. He'll begin filtering troops and supplies onto the planet over the next two months. Then, late in November, he'll head out. The JumpShips are using a pirate point less than three hundred thousand kilometers from the world to keep the evidence of activity to a minimum. The only hope we have of delaying the invasion is to prevent sufficient troops and supplies from being gathered. I need to hit Theodore's supply base."

Frederick nodded slowly, rubbing his hand over his chin. "An elite unit could do it. We could destroy the stores, but it would be a suicide mission."

Katrina met his unwavering stare. "Dying a hero is a much better way to be remembered in history than being executed for treason."

Frederick raised himself up to full height. "Promise me that a JumpShip will wait for any of my men who do somehow survive to make it back." He narrowed his eyes as she hesitated. "You need not fear, Katrina, that I will be among them."

The Archon stood and offered him her hand. "It shall be done."

Frederick kissed her hand, then took one last look at the throne room he had yearned to call his own. He bowed and turned to leave, but stopped to stare coldly at the other Steiner in the room. "What you have seen here, Ryan Steiner, is what happens when you lose to a gracious victor. I hope, when your time comes, that your defeat will serve the Commonwealth as well as mine."

BOOK IV
HONOR

*It is better to deserve honors and not have them
than to have them and not deserve them.*
—Mark Twain

New Avalon
Crucis March, Federated Suns
15 August 3029

The frustrated look on Riva Allard's face melted as Kym Sorenson entered the office. "Kym, can I use you as a character reference?"

Kym set a small stack of disks down on her desk, then turned to look suspiciously at Riva. "What do you need references for?" She grinned and dropped her voice to a conspiratorial whisper. "You're not going to take that job with Biotron Industries, are you?"

Riva glanced at the data terminal on her desk. "No, no. Nothing like that. I just need to get an increase in my security clearance to be able to look at that Star League library memory core. The MIIO investigators have to hear it from you that I'm not going to sell what I learn to the Draconis Combine."

Kym raised an eyebrow. "You tend to eat lots of *sushi* when we order lunch out..."

Riva's shoulders slumped. "Don't even joke about that, Kym. This Star League library data is the hottest find in the past two hundred years. A mercenary company, the Gray Death Legion, apparently recovered it from an old Star League depot in the Free Worlds League two years ago. Copies have been slowly working their way through the Successor States and finally made it here to the NAIS."

Kym shrugged nonchalantly. "Probably just a romantic literature storehouse."

Riva shook her head resolutely. "That's not the word down in Advanced Research. They think it's chock-full of technical data on

209

scientific discoveries and experiments. I've even heard a rumor that it has 750 kilobytes on Kearny-Fuchida drive theory alone." She smiled hopefully. "It could have all sorts of stuff that would help with my doctoral thesis."

"Hmmm, that's interesting." Kym pulled out her chair to sit down at her desk. "Why do you need to fill out a security report form? I mean, with your father being the Minister, can't he just clear you?"

Riva looked down. "Look, with Justin going over to the Maskirovka, I'm considered a worse risk than a Kurita prisoner of war." She tugged the sleeves of her blue sweater up to her elbows, then held her hands out, wrists next to each other. "Maybe I should just have them cuff me and cart me off to detention."

"Can't let that happen," Kim said mock-seriously. "Prison grays are just not your color." She laughed as Riva smiled. "Sure, put me down. Have you asked Dr. Banzai for a recommendation yet?"

Riva hesitated. "I was going to wait…"

"For what? He's agreed to teach next trimester, and he's expressed interest in your thesis." Kym looked mystified. "There are times I don't understand you at all, Riva Allard. Dr. Banzai has been nothing but helpful and encouraging with your studies, yet you shy away from him as though he's got the plague."

Riva stood and came around to the side of Kym's desk. Leaning heavily against the wall, she crossed her arms. "I find him scary, Kym. He's so brilliant he makes me feel like a child again. And he knows all sorts of diverse things. I never know when he's going to offer a non sequitur that will throw me for a loop."

Kym sat back in her chair, light flashing from the silver neckpiece she wore. "For example?"

Riva shrugged, wracking her brain for an example, then a spark flashed through her eyes. "Well, he was in a coma when they brought him from Northwind to the NAIS. I assisted with the myomer quadricep replacement on his left thigh. When he came out of it, I went up to see him. He took one look at my name tag and said, 'Don't worry about your brother Dan. He's in a good machine.'"

"What!" Kym's blue eyes grew wide with amazement. "He told you about your brother's 'Mech?"

Riva nodded in exasperation. "His mind works so fast. He placed me as Quintus Allard's daughter, knew Quintus had a son Dan who was with the Kell Hounds, and he knew Morgan Kell had given my brother a *Wolfhound*." Riva opened her hands and shrugged. "That's the simplest of his deductive chains, and the only one I understand fully. Banzai has done everything, from fighting in 'Mechs to helping heal those who've been hurt by the wars. He's just a bit scary."

Kym nodded thoughtfully. "I know how you feel." She smiled weakly as she remembered. "I recall Morgan watching news reports about the war and predicting how things would work out in any particular battle. At first, I thought he already knew the outcome, and accused him of tricking me. He denied it and took me by the hand to his computer. He quickly ran up a simulation of the battle in question and showed how it would go. At the same time, he noted what variations he would have thrown at the Liao commanders. Whenever the computer ran his variants, the battle always turned out worse for Liao than it did in real life."

Riva reached out and squeezed Kym's shoulder. "Have you heard from him since he left?"

Kym's hand strayed to the neckpiece. "Yes and no." She forced herself to smile bravely. "Morgan told me he'd be running under complete silence for this mission, so 'no news is good news.' On the other hand, he had this neckpiece delivered to me yesterday. It's the ceremonial gorget he wore at the Prince's wedding."

Riva kept a reassuring smile on her lips as her mind raced. *Morgan must be mixed up in whatever has my father worried. Morgan leaves the morning after my father gets as jumpy as a cat at the dog pound. Something big is going on. I know it.* She glanced out the window toward the darkening evening sky. *I'm just glad it's out there. The last thing I want to see is the war coming to New Avalon...*

36

ComStar Primus Julian Tiepolo half-closed his eyes as Precentor Myndo Waterly stepped to the center of the circle. She planted her feet defiantly in the middle of the gold ComStar insignia worked into the floor. The wood-paneled chamber's recessed lights flashed from her long, golden hair and burned highlights into her scarlet robe. The look in her dark eyes pierced his heart like a dagger.

"I, Myndo Waterly, Precentor Dieron for these past ten years, call for a Vote of Expulsion against you, Primus."

So this is it, eh, Myndo? You believe you have me? Tiepolo folded his hands into the voluminous sleeves of his tan robe, relishing the roughness of the simple woolen fabric. "Such a call need not be seconded, Precentor Dieron."

The Primus looked around at the other Precentors and read shock on half their faces. *You've not laid enough groundwork, Myndo. You always were overconfident.* He nodded patronizingly. "I see that no one challenges your right to speak first on this subject."

Myndo's eager smile irritated the Primus, but he set it aside as she began to speak. "I realize, fellow Precentors, that my action may seem rash, ill-mannered, and poorly timed. We are, I acknowledge, in the midst of a great crisis, yet I feel that unless ComStar gets a new pilot at the helm, we will no longer be the flagship of human destiny."

The Primus watched her move elegantly within the circle of podia. *You always were an excellent orator, Myndo. I saw that long*

212

ago, which is why I made you my protegé. Not only did you understand the Word of Blake, but you expressed it so eloquently. If only you had accepted the true wisdom I tried to share with you. Instead of embracing the new philosophy and greatness, you have consigned yourself to fight a reactionary war. It will destroy you.

Myndo gestured toward the Primus. "This man, and Adrienne Sims before him, represent a rogue twist in the philosophy of ComStar. His actions are a perversion of the Word of Blake, yet his mastery of that sacred document has allowed him to quote it to justify his position and to punish opposition. This renegade school of thought will destroy us if we do not root it out now."

She drew her outflung hands back to her chest, then let them drop to her sides as she looked down contritely. "We all remember the changes Adrienne Sims made in the service. She created the Explorer Corps of ComStar, which has made discoveries of incalculable worth in recovering technology from the Star League era and before. We cannot doubt the usefulness of this service, or its vital part in bringing us closer to our destiny."

The Primus curled his hands into fists to stop their trembling. *Is this part of it, Myndo? I once predicted great things for you, even that you would one day become Primus. How your eyes lit up at my confidence…But not now, not this way.* A slow burning began in his chest. *Damn, my ulcer is coming back.*

Myndo glanced at the Primus like a wolf watching a sheep pen. "Had Julian Tiepolo remained as nothing but a caretaker for his predecessor's programs, ComStar would have been blessed with his election. His thirty-year reign would have been heralded as an age of unprecedented stability during which we could have gained more information and strength. Unfortunately, Julian Tiepolo began to think of his place in our history, and after twenty years, moved to create fame for himself.

"He gambled. He looked at the Word of Blake and read only of the good times in which ComStar would share technology with a united Humanity. He thought that he could unite the Successor States quickly and be the Primus who finally led mankind out of the dark ages. Wanting to be a new Prometheus, he attempted to accomplish in a decade what it will take centuries to bring about."

The flesh around the Primus's eyes tightened at the jolt of pain her words gave him. *Excellent use of a mythical reference! Yes, I would be the light-bringer, but I am not so guileless as to proceed in the manner you suggest. Yes, I combine our foes, but only to more easily direct them at each other.* A trickle of sweat rolled down his right temple.

Quickly, Precentor, finish your speech so I may pull it apart!

Myndo opened her hands wide as though to embrace the whole chamber. "We all know the list of things Julian Tiepolo has tried to do in the last ten years, and many of you have been present when I opposed his wild machinations in this very chamber. I steadfastly fought against the alliance between the Lyran Commonwealth and Federated Suns. The Primus believed that uniting these two nations would spur the fall of the other states. That was his reason for forcing me to negotiate a treaty between Houses Kurita, Marik, and Liao. It may appear that he created two strong foes out of five smaller enemies—a formula to bring about the destruction we have long awaited—it did nothing of the sort."

Myndo lifted her chin. "All this time, I was seeing the true danger within the Successor States: Prince Hanse Davion. Other short-sighted rulers before him believed they could force their enemies to elect them as new First Lord of a new Star League, but this man is different. Someone like Maximilian Liao dreamed of being elevated by his peers and given free rein to create a new League. He imagined that he could reform, in months or years, what centuries of war and hatred had torn asunder.

"Hanse Davion suffers no such illusion. He does not seek personal glory and gain. What he plans is the founding of a dynasty. Already he has united the two economically strongest realms with his marriage to Melissa Steiner. His armies have gobbled up the most productive parts of the Capellan Confederation, and our Interdiction has not slowed those troops in any measurable way. It is as though Hanse Davion knows our true purpose and uses that knowledge against us."

A wave of heat passed over the Primus, beading sweat on his shaven head. The burning in his chest increased and with it, so did his fury at Precentor Dieron. *Full retribution...is that what you want, Myndo? Did it so pain you ten years ago when I did not take you as my consort? I refused to take you to my bed because it would have forced me to choose between you and my great mission as Primus and guide of ComStar. You would have seduced me with your physical charms and then, intellectually, accomplished the same thing. We would have still reached this place, you and I, because I would not have moved quickly or ruthlessly enough for you. You have never understood how this office hobbles even the boldest of those who attain it.*

Myndo ticked off points on her fingers as her voice rose to fill the chamber. "The Primus failed when he said there would be no change in the Liao-Davion border in our lifetime. He failed to maintain security during the Davion-Steiner wedding. Jaime Wolf appeared with two swords. Three ComStar ROM agents died. A Liao assassin made an attempt on the life of Quintus Allard. When I pressed for an Interdiction of House Liao for this violation, the Primus blocked it. When I asked for an Interdiction of House Davion to cut off their invasion in the early stages, again he blocked it. Now that Ardan Sortek has stepped in to run the Tikonov Free Republic until 'free' elections can be held, the Primus will not allow us to interdict Tikonov, which is no more than a Davion puppet-state!"

Her hands tightened into fists. "Every time I suggest action that could slow the unification that is anathema to our goals, Primus Julian Tiepolo opposes me and puts into place a program that assists our enemies. He is a heretic! We must remove him before he has a chance to block our response to a most serious situation."

The Primus's left arm jerked slightly as a sharp pain jolted from shoulder to fist. *What is she talking about? These cryptic references will be the death of me.* He pulled his right hand from his left sleeve and rubbed it against his chest. *Damn. Why does my ulcer have to flare up now?* For a moment, his attention wandered to the trivial thought of another year of bland food and foul concoctions.

Myndo's face hardened with contempt. "We all recall the gross failure of the Primus's personal aide, Precentor Emilio Rachan. Under the Primus's watchful eye, Rachan tried to carve himself a little kingdom and compromised security by allying with renegade Marik lords. Rachan located but failed to recover a Star League library memory core. In fact, he allowed it to fall into the hands of civilians who have treated it as a storehouse of *lostech*."

Her arctic gaze swept around the room. "For two years, we have hunted down every copy of the core we could find. To destroy these cores, we sponsored terrorism and let the blame fall to Davion or Kurita. Until now, we have kept the information in the copies from reaching people skilled enough to realize what they have. But that is no longer true because the New Avalon Institute of Science now has a copy of the core!"

More pain wracked the Primus's chest, again clawing down his left arm. *No, that's not possible! She must be lying. How could Myndo have such information? We have no ROM agents in the NAIS….If it is true…By the Blood of Blake, we are undone!*

Myndo smiled cruelly at her shocked compatriots. "Yes, the core has reached the NAIS. Their experts are studying it, but their enthusiasm has let hints of their great find leak through the security net. How do I know?" Her eyes glowed with triumph. "I have placed an agent in the area and she managed to seduce the son of the military research

215

chief. He told her just enough to communicate to me what is really happening in the NAIS."

Myndo turned and pointed at the Primus. "We must take action... action that this man will not sanction. Otherwise, this core will provide the NAIS with data that will allow them to take quantum leaps in technology. We must strike and destroy the NAIS!"

No! Such a naked display of power is impossible! Julian Tiepolo glowered at Myndo and opened his mouth to bellow at her, but no words escaped his throat. A bolt of pain exploded in his chest and engulfed his left arm in agony. The world swam out of focus as it spun away.

He tore at his chest with his right hand and collapsed in a heap. His breath, coming in ragged gasps, stoked the fire in his chest.

Myndo watched the paramedics wheel Julian Tiepolo away to the infirmary. As the chamber's door slid shut behind them, she faced her peers. "We must vote."

Still pale, Precentor Tharkad stared at her, unbelieving. "I, for one, will not sanction removing the Primus's title and office while he lies fighting for his life!"

Even before the others could voice agreement, Myndo cut them off. "Not that, you fool! Do you think me so heartless and cruel that I would take that from him? I may have opposed him, but I would not strip him of his dignity on his deathbed." She shook her head slowly. "No, I would not do that. Still, we must vote on whether or not to take action against the NAIS."

Villius Tejh watched her with the eyes of an eagle. "We cannot openly strike at the school."

Myndo laughed, wondering what sort of a fool he took her for. "Point well taken. "Since our impersonation of a Davion unit was so successful in creating the holovid for the Federated Suns Interdiction, I have prepared a 'Mech battalion that in every detail matches that of the Liao Death Commandos. As far as anyone will know, Liao has launched an attack on the NAIS."

Precentor Tharkad rubbed his chin. "When?"

"They can be there in three weeks," she said. "Infantry will scour the research center to recover information that we do not have while the 'Mech battalion destroys whatever we don't need. Finally, they raze the whole research facility to cover our tracks."

Slowly, Precentor Tharkad raised his hand to signal agreement. Following his lead, in fits and starts, the other Precentors also voted in favor of the attack. Savoring her victory, Myndo made the vote unanimous by being the last one to raise her hand.

She smiled at her fellows, knowing herself the strongest among them. *Thus begins a new age for ComStar. The Word of Blake be done!*

37

Kathil
Capellan March, Federated Suns
29 August 3029

Captain Andrew Redburn hunched his neck into his shoulders as cold, hard rain slashed at his face. *This Fredek Vebber may think Kathil is his own fief, but he's wearing on me.* The MechWarrior shot a glance at Morgan Hasek-Davion, admiring the look of calm nobility on the other man's face. *His ability to stay cool even under less-than-ideal conditions is why he and not you is in charge of this operation, Andy.*

The main doors to Kearny-Fuchida Yare Industries sprang open, releasing a flood of harsh white lights that blinded the quartet of officers walking toward the building. The lights, mounted on holovid cameras, reduced Fredek Vebber to a corpulent silhouette. Andrew smiled despite the lash of windblown rain. *Vebber's not a complete fool. He, at least, is out of this downpour.*

The crowd melted back as Morgan Hasek-Davion passed through the door. Tall, with broad shoulders and a narrow waist, Morgan moved with a grace that was almost feline. Without looking back, he continued far enough into the lobby for his compatriots to follow, then slid back the hood and doffed his rain-cloak.

Andrew read Morgan's tension in the way his hands curled into fists and the intentness with which he studied those around him. *I remember when we first met at Warrior's Hall, pitted against one another in a plebe boxing tournament. When he looked at me just that way, I knew I was done for. Two minutes later, I was kissing canvas. I hope you're up to it, Mr. Vebber.*

Vebber stepped forward as KFYI staffers whisked away the MechWarriors' sopping raingear. He offered Morgan his hand, making sure to hold the pose long enough for the holovid cameras to shoot everything they needed for a promotional film.

The two men contrasted with one another in almost every way. Younger, healthier, and more physically imposing, Morgan bore himself with a strength Vebber would have lacked even in his youth. Morgan's black fatigues and the pistol riding in a hip holster also marked him as a military man, but it was more than that. *Morgan is so vital and powerful,* Andy thought. *He is the predator and Vebber the prey.*

Fredek Vebber, swathed in a gray business suit, looked old, soft, and heavy. "It is an honor, Highness, to have you tour our facilities," he said. "I am Fredek Vebber and at your service."

Morgan let a thin smile form on his lips, but his green eyes gave Vebber no quarter. "We found the visit to your antenna facility most instructive."

Andrew shared a smile with the other two officers who had accompanied Morgan to the microwave antenna dish plantation. "Instructive" had not been one of the words that came to mind while they stood out in the rain looking at those dishes.

Morgan turned to introduce his entourage. "Mr. Vebber, these are my staff officers." He smiled genuinely as he gestured to the Mech-Warriors. "This is Captain Andrew Redburn."

Vebber pasted a smile on his face that almost fell off when Andrew half-crushed the plant owner's fleshy hand in a solid grip. "I've heard of you, Captain. You're a hero—this is a thrill for me."

Andrew nodded politely. "Indeed. I'll not soon forget our meeting."

Vebber pried his hand free as Morgan introduced the beautiful black-skinned officer standing next to Andy. "This is Captain Alanna Damu." Vebber took her hand and would have kissed it, but Alanna shifted her palm around for a more appropriate greeting. Her ebon eyes flashed with irritation, prompting Vebber to nod silently and move to the last officer.

Vebber smiled warmly as he shook hands with Colonel Geraldo de Velez. "Highness, I know Gerry. I've known him since he was a kid. We sponsored his childhood soccer team." Vebber winked at the Prince. "Yare always takes great care of its employees and their little ones."

"I am certain, Mr. Vebber, that Colonel de Velez was chosen to command the Kathil militia's third battalion because of his maturity and skill at tactics." Morgan's voice took on a sharp edge. "He is young, it's true, but woe to any who mistake him for a child."

Vebber straightened his double-breasted gray coat. "I see." He waved them forward toward a long corridor. "Please, let me conduct you on the tour."

Morgan nodded slowly. "Do proceed, sir. We have come a long way for this." He glanced back at his aides, silently communicating his intentions to them. Andrew nodded understanding. *Morgan wants to be in and out. We only want one thing from a visit to Yare, and now we'll get it.* Andrew smiled as one of the cameramen moved ahead to catch the party as it turned a corner. *This is one vid no one is ever going to see.*

Ahead, Vebber's tenor voice filled the corridor. "This is only a small part of KF Yare Industries, but the most important part. You saw the KF drive manufacturing plant in orbit as you came insystem, and you saw one of our many energy broadcast stations this morning. What you didn't see were the numerous smaller factories circling this world at high speed. With the computers here in our command center, we track all of them and supply their energy needs by beaming microwaves up to them."

Vebber pushed open a door and waved his guests into the dark, cavernous command center. In the backlight from hundreds of display terminals, Andrew saw a legion of technicians moving around the room. He whistled involuntarily. "This looks like the cockpit on a JumpShip, only a hundred times larger."

Vebber smiled and pointed down over rows and rows of technicians seated at command modules. They sat facing a wall on which was projected a map of the whole planet, with the trajectories of various satellite factories plotted over it in glowing detail. "On that map, we track all factories, communication satellites, and incoming ships. We know where everything is at any time."

Morgan moved to the nearest station, smiling down at the friendly-looking man at the post. "From here, you track factories and feed them power?"

Vebber nodded, patting his hair into place. "We make sure each plant gets the power it needs. This requires delicate work as it passes from energy zone to energy zone. We power down one feed at a rate inverse to the powering up of the next feed so there's not an overload."

Andrew frowned. "Why track satellites? They all have their own reactors on board, don't they?"

Vebber smiled condescendingly but massaged his right hand nervously. "True, Captain. They do not require our power. If, however, they got caught in one of our energy feeds, well,"—he made his hands fly away from each other in a mock explosion—"our insurance carriers would be upset with us."

Morgan turned toward Vebber. "Your equipment is good enough to track a satellite? I mean, you could hit it with a microwave beam if you wanted to?"

Vebber glowed under Morgan's attention. "Yes, Highness. Easily. In fact, our equipment is good enough to hit a dinner plate up to 400,000 kilometers away with no focal distortion or waver."

Morgan smiled. "Then you could hit a DropShip running into the atmosphere on a raid."

Vebber stiffened. "No, Highness. That could never happen."

Morgan raised an eyebrow. "Even if I wanted it to happen, Mr. Vebber?"

The plant owner shook his head. "No, Highness. I would not permit it."

Morgan smiled slowly and cruelly. "Even if I gave you an order, Mr. Vebber?"

Vebber's jowls trembled as he shook his head. "No, Highness. This is a privately held firm, and you cannot give orders here."

Morgan's smile died, replaced by a darkening look of anger. "If I order it, Mr. Vebber, you will do it!" Morgan pointed back at the map. "If Liao invaders are burning their way into this atmosphere, you will do it!"

Vebber's jaw dropped and, for a moment, Andrew thought the administrator had seen the light. The hope died at Vebber's derisive reply. "You're not Hanse Davion, and you're certainly not your father. I take no orders from you."

Morgan looked down at the man sitting at the command station. "What's your name?"

Swiveling his chair about to face Vebber, the operator adjusted his glasses. "Lyekiz, Highness. Tim Lyekiz."

Morgan unholstered his pistol and charged it with a metallic snap. "You could use your station here to hit a Liao ship coming insystem, right?"

Lyekiz nodded.

Morgan looked up at Vebber. "And you'd do it if I told you to, right?"

"Yes, sir."

Morgan raised the gun and aimed at Vebber. "Then we have no need for Mr. Vebber, do we?"

Lyekiz grinned. "No, sir."

Vebber's eyes popped wide open as he stared down the bore of Morgan's pistol. Sweat beaded on his brow, then coursed down his face. Strands of hair splayed down over his forehead as Vebber's mouth opened and closed like a fish trying to breathe air. For a moment, Vebber looked as though he might faint, then some color returned to his ashen face and a low, slightly mad laughter rolled from his throat.

"Oh, Highness, I misunderstood." He glanced back at Andrew, eyes begging for someone to confirm the lie he was about to tell. "I thought you meant one of *our* DropShips. Rainstorms always affect my hearing...you know, *Liao...our*—the words sound so similar. I thought you were testing my loyalty to the Prince, Highness."

While Vebber was pleading for his life, Andrew noticed that the expressions on the faces of a number of the operators showed hope that Morgan would pull the trigger. *Hell, it looks like a Maskirovka hit team could get directions to Vebber's office from just about anyone in this company.*

Morgan held the gun on Vebber, letting the man blubber on until he realized no one believed his outlandish story. "I understand your confusion, Mr. Vebber," Morgan said, pointing the pistol toward the ceiling. "You were correct that I am not Prince Hanse Davion, nor am I my father. I was sent here to do a job. No one and nothing will stop me."

With those words still echoing through the command center, Morgan Hasek-Davion turned on his heel and left to accomplish more important work.

Though the Kathil Militia Reserve auditorium was less than half-full, Andrew felt as though it were packed to bursting. *It's the anticipation and fear. It radiates off all these MechWarriors like heat from a BattleMech.* Seated in the front row, Andrew felt the pressure increase as Morgan Hasek-Davion stepped behind the podium to address the crowd.

Morgan's green eyes swept over the assembled MechWarriors. Hanse Davion's heir nodded slightly, his smile commmunicating his approval to those gathered in the room. He glanced at the sheaf of notes on the podium, then set them aside. When Morgan looked up, his red hair framed his head like a mane. He gripped the edges of the podium with strong hands and leaned forward to speak. "This is a meeting that historians without number will study and remember. We are the metal to be heated in the crucible of battle and shaped into something incredible—or destroyed on a cold anvil named Kathil. Our old lives end here and now, shed like a snake sloughs its skin, to give birth to a legend."

Morgan straightened up, head high. "Many of you may believe that glory and fame can only be won on the front with the Capellan Confederation. You may be thinking that your failures in that theatre are the reason you've been transferred to a backwater like Kathil. You wonder if this is a kind of punishment, as history marches past you, leaving you in the dust of obscurity. This, my friends, is an error of the greatest magnitude because everything, *everything,* in this war hinges upon what we do here on Kathil."

Morgan opened his hands to encompass his whole audience. "We know from impeccable sources that Maximilian Liao has sent a force to destroy this world. Liao, like an animal blinded by mortal pain, is striking out in desperation. He does not realize that in hitting Kathil, he will repeat the gross errors of the First Succession War.

"That war, as everyone knows, resulted in destruction so wide-spread that mankind has not yet recovered from it. Kathil, this jewel of *lostech,* is a prime example of the pitiful consequences of such intemperate assaults. One of the jewels of the Star League because of its JumpShip production, the planet was nearly destroyed by successive Liao attacks. Only with great effort and expense has the Federated Suns been able to enhance production in the past few years. Orbiting overhead are factories that produce JumpShips, yet nowhere within the Succession States do we have the knowledge of how and why JumpShips work. We are children assembling kits, with no idea how to improve the parts we use. Because of the First Succession War and the slaughter of the intelligentsia that accompanied it, mankind has been in decline for 250 years."

Andrew nodded his agreement with Morgan's words. *It's true. I've seen specs for my new 'Mech, and I've seen the same data for a Star League model of my* Marauder. *Even after 300 years, one of those antique* Marauders *would make mine look sick.*

Morgan paused long enough for his words to sink in. "I cannot tell you much about the troops we'll be fighting because we only have our intelligence service's best guess on what to expect. I do know it will be at least one full battalion, and probably two. I expect over half the troops to be elite MechWarriors. Their aim will be to destroy the four major geothermal generating stations on Kathil. Our job is to stop them."

The flame-haired MechWarrior pointed toward the section of seats occupied by Redburn's Delta Company. "With us, in this effort, we have Captain Andrew Redburn and his Delta Company. These double-dozen MechWarriors have already fought enough battles to end every war, defeating their opposition every time. They are specialists in close-assault tactics, and while they normally use light 'Mechs, some will be piloting heavier 'Mechs for our operation."

Over to the right, Morgan pointed to a small knot of fifteen MechWarriors seated near Captain Alanna Damu. "This is the Omega Company of the Fifth Syrtis Fusiliers. They are battle-hardened veterans who have the knowledge and skill to match the best of our Capellan enemies. They know how to fight hard, and they know that sometimes the battle is not over until you're dead."

With both hands, he indicated the MechWarriors gathered in the center section of the auditorium. Though they sat up tall and proud, Andrew noticed how young they all seemed. The fire in their eyes reminded him of the expressions his Delta Company had worn when he'd first gathered them together, years ago, into the First Kittery Training Battalion. *It comes full circle. My former trainees will be teaching these kids to survive.*

Morgan's strong voice filled the hall. "And we have you, Kathil Militia, Third Battalion. Yes, I know most of you were called up when the other battalions left to garrison worlds in the conquered territories, and that because of munitions shortages, your training to date has consisted mostly of computer-adjudicated mock battles."

Morgan gave them a look of dead-seriousness. "By order of Prince Hanse Davion, you are all now part of a new Federated Suns regiment. Officially, we are the First Kathil Uhlans, but I have named us the Lions of Davion. We will have two battalions. Captain Damu is now breveted to Major and will command the Alpha Battalion. It will consist of her Omega Company and the first two companies of the Kathil militia. Brevet-Major Redburn will command the Delta Battalion, which will consist of his Delta Company and the remaining company of Kathil Militia." Morgan looked toward Colonel de Velez. "Colonel de Velez will be my aide and will assist me with his knowledge of Kathil so that we can effectively destroy the force Liao throws at us."

Shocked by his sudden promotion, Andrew barely felt Robert Craon's congratulatory slap on the back. *Major...me? In charge of a battalion of half-trained MechWarriors and a bunch of local kids who want to be MechWarriors?* Andrew blinked his eyes several times and looked up toward Morgan. *Do you really know what you are doing?*

Morgan waited for the crowd to quiet before speaking again. "I know what many of you are thinking. Some may resent being split up from your fellows, and others may dislike having to wet-nurse your new partners through their first battle. You wonder how a ragtag band of half-trained and tired MechWarriors can hope to oppose an elite Liao force."

As Morgan spoke, he ticked off each description on the fingers of his left hand, then curled the fingers into a fist. "We will do it because we will become a unit. We will think as one, and we will use each other's strengths to fill in the cracks." He pointed at Andrew's people. "Delta Company here understands the weaknesses of various 'Mech designs, and they know how to exploit them. They have mastered the techniques of hitting without getting hit back. They know the importance of working together, and through such cooperation, they have become a unit Capellan mothers name when they wish to frighten bad children."

Morgan turned to face the remnants of the Fifth Syrtis Fusiliers. "You are all that's left of the best fighting unit the Capellan March ever had. Through audacity, quick thinking, and foresight, you escaped the careful trap laid down by McCarron's Armored Cavalry. You took risks no one could ever have anticipated. In so doing, you saved yourselves and others. You are survivors, and we need that quality in the Lions."

Lastly, Morgan looked at the militia. "You we need most of all. You have the enthusiasm that has turned to cynicism for some of us over the years. You don't see things as impossible because there's so much you've yet to try. Besides that, you all know this world better than we could ever hope to. You know the places where the maps are wrong, and you know details about things that no gazetteer could ever tell us. Most important, you have a love for this world that can become contagious. It will keep us going when all might seem lost, and it could give us the edge we need to destroy the invaders."

Morgan wet his lips. "As your commander, I promise you one thing. I may have to give you assignments that could kill you, but I will never issue you a suicidal order. I will never abandon you to the enemy. The Lions will be one force, one power. Together, we will prevail."

Morgan again hunched forward over the podium. "Mark me, gentlemen and ladies. We will win because we *must* win. Liao's forces are coming here to claim victory for themselves. We will battle against a wanton carnage that could suck mankind down into another Dark Age. We cannot allow it. We *will* not allow it. Ours will be a victory for all mankind, a beacon of hope for the future."

38

Nusakan
Isle of Skye, Lyran Commonwealth
3 September 3029

Daniel Allard's smile died as he passed through the circular doorway into Morgan Kell's office. The pain and sorrow on Morgan's face filled him with cold dread. "What's happened, Colonel?" Dan knotted the Sanglamore sash off over his left ear. "They caught me right before I went out on patrol saying you had a message from the Archon…"

Morgan Kell looked down helplessly at his hands. "The message was sent before we left Lyons for our wait here on Nusakan. ComStar sent it to New Freedom. It was broken down there, re-encrypted and sent here." His head came up, and he pointed to a chair in front of his desk. "Have a seat, Dan. You'll want to hear this sitting down."

Dan crossed the plaster-walled room to sit in an old log chair. *News from the Federated Suns would come through the Archon because of the Interdiction. What's happened to my family?* Clad only a cooling vest and shorts, Dan gripped the chair's rough-hewn arms.

Morgan said nothing, but reached out and touched the controls on a holovid viewer. The dark screen brightened to show the Archon sitting on her throne. Barely visible behind her, and then lost as soon as the camera zoomed in on her handsome face were the legs of the two *Griffin* BattleMechs that flanked her throne. Katrina stared into the camera, the power and compassion in her gray eyes flowing from the holovid screen into Dan's heart.

Katrina swallowed hard before she began. "I extend to you, Captain Allard, the greetings of the Lyran Commonwealth. With all

226

the gratitude I owe you for past services, I consider this message loathsome and unfortunately cruel. It's a duty I would avoid, but it's best you hear it from me than from anyone else."

She drew in a deep breath. "On the 20th of June, three assassins disguised as members of the AFFS gained access to the Triad. Their papers were in order, and two of them were escorted to my private office. I was chatting amicably with them while we waited for Simon Johnson, head of the LIC and your father's counterpart in my realm. The third individual paid a social call on my daughter."

Dan felt as though his mind and body went numb except for one thought, *Jeana, my Jeana, is Melissa's double. That assassin went to see Jeana!*

The Archon nodded, as though anticipating Dan's thoughts even as she had recorded the message. "Jeana recognized the assassin as an impostor and dealt with him. She appropriated his pistol, and by traversing a series of hidden passageways in the Triad, entered my office through a secret door. She confronted the other two assassins and killed them before they could do me any harm."

The Archon paused for a moment, biting back tears. "She died without pain, but not before knowing she had succeeded in eliminating the threat to my life. For obvious reasons of security, her mortal remains were cremated. Her ashes have been interred in the Steiner crypt beneath the Triad. If you wish, the crypt will be open to you at any time."

Katrina Steiner looked out of the monitor and gave Dan a brave smile. "In the time she was here, Jeana and I became close friends. She spoke of you often and was overjoyed that her gift had indeed kept you safe. Never doubt that she loved you, Captain Allard, and know that she lives on in our hearts."

The screen faded to black and left Dan with a hollow pit in his chest. His throat ached because of the emotions beginning to choke him, yet his feelings did not flood over him. They were there, waiting, just waiting, like thunderstorms on the horizon.

Dan looked over at Morgan. "I felt I'd known her all my life, yet I knew nothing about her. That she was"—he hesitated at the word—"'safe' on Tharkad made things easier for me. I knew we'd be apart and that I'd not hear from her, so I just walled off the worry and pain of separation." He shrugged helplessly. "Now I want to feel something, but it's empty….just a void in me."

He pulled the green silken sash from his head and picked at the knot. "I never even knew her full name."

Morgan hesitated, then began to speak quietly. "Her name was

Jeana Clay. She was born in 3002 on Poulsbo, where she lived with her father and mother. Her father died in 3005 in a raid on the Bangor military facility there, enabling Katrina Steiner, Arthur Luvon, and me to escape from the Loki agents Alessandro had sent to kill us."

Stunned, Dan looked up at his commanding officer. "How do you…? Why didn't you tell me before?" Anger flashed through him, but ultimately proved as elusive as the other emotions he'd sought to capture. A realization formed itself into one word and he repeated that word in a hushed voice. "Heimdall."

Morgan nodded. "Jeana and her family were Heimdall. I don't believe Clay was her original surname—I only knew her father as Grison. After our return to the Lyran Commonwealth, Arthur Luvon created and had placed into the LIC computers a whole series of new identities for the families and survivors of the Poulsbo Heimdall cell that helped us. In fact, it was through a scholarship created by Arthur that Jeana went to Sanglamore."

Dan sank back into the chair and pressed the palms of his hands against his eyes. "All this sleight of hand. Melissa's double is a woman who belongs to an opposition movement. Duke Aldo Lestrade's son belongs to the same group, and his father does the best he can to cause a whole Heimdall settlement on New Freedom to be destroyed. Secret files in the LIC computer." His hands fell away from his eyes. "Simon Johnson would go mad if he knew about this."

Morgan shook his head slowly. "I don't think so." He stood and came around to sit on the front of his desk. "Simon Johnson is the one who put Jeana's new identity in the computer, and her connection with Heimdall is the reason Johnson selected her to be Melissa's double."

In shock, Dan's jaw dropped. "Simon Johnson, the head of the LIC, is a member of Heimdall?"

Morgan smiled wryly. "Recall that we are a group formed from the *loyal* opposition. We knew it would be useful for us to have people inside the Lyran Intelligence Corps. Especially after Poulsbo, I must that admit Arthur, Patrick, and I used to laugh about Alessandro's elevation of Simon. The idea of Alessandro relying on a member of Heimdall to help identify Heimdall cells and destroy them is gratifying."

Dan nodded weakly. You didn't tell me about Jeana because I'm not Heimdall?" Unspoken was Dan's sense of betrayal, but it was expressed in his tone.

Morgan reached out and squeezed Dan's forearm. "You may never have been formally inducted into Heimdall, but you might as well be a member. Regardless, I would have told you that much about her if I'd known it earlier. I didn't get that information until this message came in. Clovis appended the data."

Dan gave Morgan a feeble smile. "Thank you." He looked down at the knotted sash and used it to focus himself. His voice flattened out, barely more than a hoarse whisper. "Do they know who did it…who sent the assassins?"

Morgan drew in a deep breath, then narrowed his dark eyes. "He left no real evidence, and the man Jeana disabled gave up no information. But Katrina knows the plot originated in the Isle of Skye."

Dan unknotted the sash, then wound the loose ends around each fist until he held the cloth taut between them. "Aldo Lestrade." Staring at the garrote, Dan's blue eyes narrowed with rage. "He's been calling a lot of tunes lately. Once we've dealt with the *Genyosha*, it'll be time for him to pay the piper."

The fury in Morgan's voice matched the anger in Dan's. "I agree."

Dan looked up. "I'll send a message to Clovis. I won't deny him the right to kill the Duke, but I want Clovis to know he'll not travel alone to do the job."

Morgan frowned. "Remember that I said the holovid had gone to Lyons first? Clovis saw it, then forwarded it to us." Morgan sighed deeply. "I already sent such a message via ComStar to Clovis, but only got a reply from Karla Bremen. Clovis is gone."

Godspeed, my friend. Dan let the garrote sag, then snapped it taut again with a crack. *I place my vengeance in your hands.*

Kathil
Capellan March, Federated Suns
7 September 3029

The spherical *Union* Class DropShip, boldly emblazoned with the death's-head insignia of the Liao Death Commandos, flew through the night sky with the ease of a condor gliding lazily on updrafts. As it slowed to hover, the guns retracted against the terrible heat of atmospheric entry popped out and searched the ground for any sign of the enemy. When the gunners found no targets, the ship began a slow descent.

Only five hundred meters above ground, the DropShip shuddered and drifted sideways. Blue sparks arced from laser mounts and PPCs. One LRM pod sprayed its missiles into the air while another belched a great gout of black smoke. The landing jets all pulsed out flame in a haphazard pattern, tipping the vessel right and then left. The ship righted itself and began to fight against Kathil's gravity, then the ion jets quit altogether.

The DropShip hit the ground hard, sending tremors out that Andrew Redburn could feel even in the cockpit of his *Marauder*. The ship's starboard hull crumpled, then an explosion in an LRM magazine blasted the ship up again. The volcanic detonations continued, spinning and bouncing the DropShip across the dark landing zone. The ship convulsed violently as it landed heavily on the port side, then a blazing red-yellow fireball blew the DropShip apart.

Pieces of hull split open like a *naranji* rind. Full-sized Battle-Mechs rocketed out of the broken sphere, spinning wildly out of

230

control. Andrew watched a *Marauder* whose arms flailed madly against the air as its cylindrical body wheeled over and over again. The heavy 'Mech landed on its feet, but the birdlike legs snapped at the knee. The *Marauder*'s body broke in half. The cockpit section tumbled across the landscape while the fusion engine in the torso exploded, spitting armor and parts carelessly over the landscape.

Hand trembling, Andrew punched up the communications link that ran through a landline to Morgan's headquarters. "Delta Lion to Pride. The microwaves got the first DropShip, but I make two more coming in low and hot." Andrew hesitated, searching for words to describe the carnage in the landing zone. "Pride, no one survived the landing. That shouldn't have happened to anyone."

Morgan's voice, tinged with regret, filled Andrew's neurohelmet. "I agree. If I thought they would have given our new people some quarter, I might have had a choice. Alpha reports having a battalion of Fourth Tau Ceti Rangers heading for the Median Power Company plant. Two *Union*s landing in your area means we'll have two companies of Death Commandos targeting Yare."

Andrew nodded mechanically. "Roger, Pride. We'll stop what we can." Andrew severed the landline with his commander. *I hope like hell we don't let much through. Those retired MechWarriors you've gathered as your staff might be all heart, Morgan, but their fighting days were over a long time ago. As good as you are, Morgan Hasek Davion, you cannot defend that generating station by yourself.*

Andrew punched up a magnified view of the two *Union* Class DropShips that had settled onto the landing zone. The flames from the burning first ship flickered yellow highlights onto the other two ships' pitted armor. They also provided enough light to reveal the 'Mechs marching from the DropShips' bellies onto the hellground, filling Andrew's guts with ice.

The Death Commandos moved from their DropShips swiftly. Instead of lining up in formation, as some units might have, they spread out to make themselves harder to hit. None of them stopped to check on the condition of their fallen comrades, but instead they used debris and broken 'Mechs as cover. Their scouts moved forward with great caution, searching out any sign of enemy 'Mechs.

Andrew swallowed hard. *These guys really* are *as hot as their reputation. I guess we'll just have to be better than ours.* Seeing a lance of scout 'Mechs move beyond the blast perimeter and onto the edge of the landing zone, he punched a button on his command console. His auxiliary monitor redrew the map of the landing zone, adding two rings of polka-dots around the whole area. The scout lance's 'Mechs appeared as golden triangles in the dark area between the two rings.

The lead scout 'Mech, a *Raven*, crossed into the outer circle of dots. Its right foot came down on the ground, then shot back up as the mine beneath it erupted. An argent column of flame ripped the *Raven*'s foot clean off, spinning the leggy 'Mech back into the safe zone. It squatted, listing badly to the right, but the pilot did not leave his 'Mech. The other scouts, after a short discussion with their commander, carefully began to retrace their steps back toward the DropShips.

Ten meters into the interior ring, the lead *Ostscout* hit another mine. The explosion blasted up into both of the humanoid 'Mech's legs. Armor sowed shrapnel all over the landing zone as the discharge blew the 'Mech's legs out from under it. The *Ostscout* landed on its back, then rolled, detonating another mine beneath its chest. The second mine ripped a huge hole in the 'Mech's left flank.

Andrew smiled as the 'Mech's faceplate exploded outward. The pilot flew from the damaged 'Mech in his command couch. The gyrostabilizers trimmed the seat's flight, and the pilot directed it back toward the DropShips. *First blood goes to the Lions. It'll take them forever to get out of this trap, and we can pick their sappers off with LRM fire from Demon and Archer lances.*

Almost before Andrew had a chance to grin in smug satisfaction, the Death Commandos sprang into action, showing just how nasty a force they really were. Both DropShips launched flight after flight of LRMs in a computer-projected pattern that ate its way out through both rings. The missiles and their explosions detonated all the mines for a hundred meters. Fiery blasts shot flares into the darkness and sprayed dirt everywhere. Thunder rattled the *Marauder* as lights flashed from each succeeding barrage.

Andrew punched a button on his command console. "Heads up, Demon and Archer lances. They'll be coming through fast. Fire and move, fire and move. Fox and Cat, be ready to move. The rest of you, stay alert. Our first position won't hold long." Andrew glanced down at the list of 'Mechs and styles his computer could identify. *Hell, we'll be lucky if it just slows them down.*

Through the smoke and dust poured the Death Commandos. The wounded *Raven* and the other two 'Mechs in its lance came into view first. They moved into the line of buildings in the factory town surrounding Yare Industries as the first volley of LRM from Archer and Demon lances hit them.

So many missiles blasted into the *Raven* that it appeared to have burst into flames spontaneously. The *Wasp* on its right reeled under the pummeling barrage. The humanoid 'Mech, stripped naked of armor by missiles, collapsed into a two-story-tall adobe building. The lance's remaining 'Mech, a *Stinger*, started to jet off, but a flight of missiles peppered its head, crushing the cockpit completely. The 'Mech crashed to the ground, blocking one of the town's narrow streets with its corpse.

Suddenly a half-dozen Death Commando 'Mechs ignited their jump jets. The humanoid BattleMechs arced overhead, converging on the locations from which the LRMs had been fired. The scarlet shafts of medium-laser fire wove a deadly energy network above the low hill toward which the Liao 'Mechs flew. The beams sliced armor from the incoming 'Mechs, but stopped none of their advances.

As the Liao 'Mechs sank from sight, Andrew growled out orders through the radio. "Cat lance, hit them now. Archer, Demon, get out of there if you can and fall back to second position. Bullseye and Fox, it's our turn. Craon, hold your company until we need it." Andrew glanced at the tactical display that showed some of his *Valkyries* jetting away from the assault site, then he turned his attention back to the action in his area.

The main body of the Death Commandos moved through the town along the main road toward Yare. They proceeded as swiftly as possible, clearly uneasy about the shadowed sidestreets and darkened buildings surrounding them. Two *Centurions* scouted ahead, while two *Vindicators* secured the streets intersecting their line of march.

They never imagined anything by way of an organized defense, and no militia in its right mind would fight them in a city—placing its own homes at risk. As the last 'Mech, a *Rifleman*, shuffled past the tin-walled warehouse where Andrew's *Marauder* was hidden, Andrew severed the connection with the visual sensor pod mounted on the building's roof. He leaned his heavy 'Mech against the warehouse's corrugated wall, and amid a shriek of metal and the loud snap of wooden wall studs, he burst into the street behind the *Rifleman*.

Andrew shoved both of the *Marauder*'s arms at the *Rifleman*, stabbing his thumbs down on the firing buttons. Twin bolts of azure lightning knifed through the enemy 'Mech's back, slashing armor into ribbons. Half-melted armor chunks fell to the ground while blue fire raced through the *Rifleman*'s body. Autocannon armor started a staccato series of explosions that blew both arms off the 'Mech, sending them spinning off through buildings and houses. Freed of the electromagnetic fields holding it captive, the miniature sun powering the fusion reactor melted its way free of the engine housing and rose like ball lightning up through the 'Mech's head. It exploded free of the war machine, lighting the landscape like noon, then imploded, bring-

233

ing darkness again.

Missiles and lasers, PPCs and autocannons all fired from within the darkness toward the street and back out again as Bullseye and Fox lances joined Redburn in his ambush. From his left, Andrew saw SRMs fly in from the squat, birdlike *Jenner*s that made up Bullseye lance, and they were followed up by skilled laser fire from the same 'Mechs. From the right flank, two *Jenner*s in Fox lance struck. The two *Panther*s that completed that lance's complement of 'Mechs unleashed PPC blasts at the most heavily armored of the Liao invaders, then launched volleys of SRMs to capitalize on the damage their particle beams had done.

Fire turned the night into day as chaos reigned. Andrew traded PPC blasts with a *Vindicator*. The Liao attack buckled armor plates on his *Marauder*'s right arm, but failed to damage the PPC mechanism. Almost as though the PPC pod had merely absorbed the energy, it spat the cerulean bolt back at the *Vindicator*, tearing a hideous scar through the armor over the other 'Mech's heart. The medium laser on the same arm flayed armor from the Liao 'Mech's left flank, while the other arm's medium laser sliced through the armor on the *Vindicator*'s right hip.

The *Vindicator*'s pilot shifted his 'Mech back toward the left to protect his wounded flank. The PPC mounted as its right forearm vomited out another jagged lightning spear, again blasting armor from the *Marauder*'s right arm. Andrew watched as the computer redrew the 'Mech's right arm with only a minimal amount of armor. *Next hit wastes that arm. Best use it now!*

Andrew dropped the gold targeting crosshairs onto the image of his enemy and again fired with one PPC and two medium lasers to avoid a heat buildup. As though the 'Mech realized the threat the *Vindicator* represented, the *Marauder* vented its fury on the *Vindicator*'s right arm. The blue PPC beam arced its way up and down the limb, blasting layer after layer of glowing ferro-ceramic armor off into the night. The right-arm laser sliced along the Liao PPC's barrel, splitting the last of the armor, then skewering a heat sink in a spray of green-yellow coolant. The left-arm laser pulsed into the *Vindicator*'s shoulder. Corded myomer muscle snapped, torn fibers flailing wildly, as the beam slashed through it. The laser tracked up into the joint, melting titanium bones. With a thundercrack and flash of bloody light, the *Vindicator*'s right arm cartwheeled off into the darkness.

The *Vindicator*'s neutralization gave Andrew a moment to survey the battlefield. At least two of Fox lance's *Jenner*s were down and burning, but a Liao *Scorpion* had lost its two front legs. On the left,

Andrew couldn't see Bullseye lance, but the continued fire coming from and heading back to their position told him that at least some of them still lived. Up on the hill, where Cat lance would have jumped the Liao 'Mechs sent to root out the *Valkyries*, Andrew saw two burning buildings and the stuttered flash of autocannons, but could not make order out of the chaos up there.

Despite the damage taken in the ambush, the Death Commandos continued to push their way up the hill toward Yare Industries. *They've stripped off their medium 'Mechs to tie us up while most of their heavies head toward the target. I don't want to, but I'll have to commit my reserves.* Andrew punched a button on his command console. "Now, Craon, bring Gorgon, Hellion, and Jackal lances in. We have to stop them now!"

Craon led the three Kathil Militia lances out from hiding to cut across the Liao line of march. Gorgon lance, composed of four *UrbanMechs*, fired their autocannons in unison on the *Ostsol* leading the Liao advance. Armor exploded from the 'Mech's torso, blasted away by twin sprays of depleted uranium projectiles. One hail of shells ripped off the *Ostsol*'s right arm, half twisting the heavy 'Mech around with the ferocity of the attack. The fourth 'Mech's fire blasted armor from the *Ostsol*'s left leg, yet the *Ostsol* did not go down, despite heavy damage.

The *Ostsol* concentrated its return fire on one of the *UrbanMechs*. Two large laser beams shot from the *Ostsol*'s chest, impaling the smaller 'Mech. Armor evaporated under the laser's hellish caress, then internal structures, half-melted, exploded outward in a gout of black smoke. The smaller 'Mech staggered back, sagging into a building, more of its guts running in molten streams down its torso than actually remained in place.

Hellion lance, a matched quartet of *Javelins*, launched flights of SRMs at the Liao *Marauder* following the *Ostsol*. Half the missiles corkscrewing in on their target blossomed into fiery clouds of napalm that covered and clung to the *Marauder* like a burning skin. The other missiles exploded after impact, ripping away chunks of the 'Mech's armored flesh, but they neither hurt nor slowed the birdlike 'Mech.

Andrew's mouth went dry. *They mixed their SRM loads…they're carrying inferno rockets! Are they crazy? That's like strapping plastique to yourself.* Even as the thought came to him, Andrew found himself grimly pleased with their action. *At least they hit the right 'Mech—damned* Marauders *run hot anyway…*

The *Marauder* pilot had already picked out his targets and fired both PPCs before he knew what he was facing. The blue fire from his

235

right claw hit one *Jenner* dead-center, stripping the armor from its chest as though it were a paper label. That *Jenner* staggered, but remained upright. The other PPC bolt flayed the armor from its target's left flank, spinning the second *Jenner* away and into a small house.

The heat buildup from firing both PPCs and the inferno rockets ignited the autocannon ammo stored in the *Marauder*. A series of explosions bulged the armor on the 'Mech's left side, then burst outward in a jet of silver flame. The blast spun the *Marauder* around, tossing it through a building like a ragdoll. Its flaming corpse ignited yet another fire in Yare's corporate township.

Jackal lance moved its four *Commando*s up to block the roadway, but the next Liao 'Mech scornfully ignored their threat. Heedless of the damage done as their SRM volleys peppered its hide, the hunched-over *Cataphract* raced forward, battering the two central *Commando*s aside and bursting free of the Davion lines. Behind it followed an entire heavy lance.

Craon stepped his *Hunchback* into the breach and let fly with the shoulder-mounted autocannon. The heavy gun vomited a stream of metal that blasted armor from the *Cataphract*'s left leg, but failed to cripple or stop the 'Mech's headlong charge. Swatting the *Hunchback* aside, the *Cataphract* continued its race to the top of the hill. The blow crushed the *Hunchback*'s cockpit.

"No! Robert!" A burning rushed up from Andrew's stomach to his throat as he saw the *Hunchback* crumple. He raised both of the *Marauder*'s arms, directing them toward the *Cataphract*'s back, but the Liao 'Mech slipped over the horizon before the computer would give him a lock.

Andrew slapped a button on his command console, opening a channel to all Davion defenders. "They're through our lines. Move it if you're able and harass them. They can't get to the plant! Morgan, do you copy?"

Andrew looked up as four strobing explosions lit the horizon. For half a second, he thought the *Cataphract* had managed to destroy the generating station, but then he saw the 'Mech appear again at the top of the hill. Staggering backward, then twisting around like a drunken sailor, the *Cataphract* careened down the street it had conquered just moments before. As it rolled down the hill, bits and pieces of it littered the ground behind. Finally, the 'Mech came to rest against Craon's *Hunchback*.

Over the open radio channel, a militiaman's hushed voice filled Andrew's neurohelmet. "Whatever the hell it was that did that, I hope it's on our side."

40

Curtains of oily smoke twisted and parted enough to let the flames glint from the 'Mech's skullface. The tall, broad-shouldered BattleMech looked to Andrew for all the world like the Grim Reaper himself had ascended from Hell to gather souls.

The autocannon muzzle over the *Atlas's* right hip swiveled down, targeting an advancing Liao *Warhammer*. Flame flashed from the gun as it sent a sizzling stream of metal at its victim. The projectiles tracked up the 'Mech's right arm like a tailor slicing open a seam. The armor protecting the *Warhammer's* arm dropped away in a tattered ribbon.

The Liao *Warhammer* triggered both its PPCs. Twin azure bolts raked their needle-sharp tendrils over the *Atlas's* broad chest, clawing away sheets of ceramic armor. One bolt lingered for half a second on a spot over the *Atlas's* heart, exploiting a weakness. The giant 'Mech staggered, but never even came close to toppling.

Andrew smiled openly. "Thank God you showed up, Morgan. Hellion lance, flame that *Warhammer*! Demon and Archer lances, walk your LRMs down the main street. Cat lance, if you're done, get down here. Gorgon, Jackal, Fox, and Bullseye, targets of opportunity! This ends now!"

Andrew marched his *Marauder* forward. A Liao *Centurion*, fire trailing from the muzzle of its right-arm autocannon, reeled beneath the impact of an SRM volley. It staggered right into Andrew's sights, so he dropped the crosshairs onto it, flashing the PPC in his right arm

237

to life. The blue particle beam stabbed deep into the 'Mech's right elbow, vaporizing the last of the protective armor, then melted the joint. The pilot, suddenly aware of Andrew's *Marauder*, lurched his 'Mech off into a sidestreet.

As ordered, Demon and Archer lances launched volley after volley of LRMs onto the main street, concentrating on the knot of Liao 'Mechs toward the middle. A birdlike *Catapult* sent two LRM volleys arcing back toward its tormentors, but that did nothing to squelch the long-range fire. In fact, the next barrage wreathed the *Catapult* in fire, crushing its armor and dropping it to the ground.

Hellion lance turned the *Warhammer* into a torch, but lost one of its 'Mechs in a fireball as a Liao *Thunderbolt* blasted it with laser fire. In turn, Gorgon lance's *UrbanMech*s ripped the *Thunderbolt*'s armor to shreds with autocannon fire. Morgan's *Atlas* finished the *Warhammer* with another autocannon burst, knocking the 'Mech over.

The *Ostsol* broke toward the right, dashing down a darkened side street. From the flaming battle higher up on the hill, a 'Mech arced into the sky, then descended on the larger 'Mech. In the firelight, Andrew recognized the humanoid machine as a *Hatchetman*. *At least one person from Cat Lance is alive!*

The *Hatchetman* landed, then wrapped both hands around the hilt of the warclub that gave the 'Mech its name. Despite the damage taken when the *Ostsol* triggered its two rear-arc lasers, the *Hatchetman* raised the hatchet and brought it down on the *Ostsol*'s head. The titanium blade sheathed a depleted uranium core and sliced through the *Ostsol*'s cockpit like a sharp knife. The *Ostsol*'s momentum slammed it into a low building, tripped it, and dumped its corpse on a row of tract housing.

Realizing the battle was lost, the remaining Liao *Cataphract* threw itself into Jackal lance. It battered the smaller *Commando*s with its arms, knocking them aside, then tried to stomp them into scrap metal. Despite the terrifying sight of this gargantuan war machine clubbing them, the militia pilots released flights of SRMs, blasting armor from the *Cataphract*'s thick hide. They fought their way free of its embrace, retreated far enough to give them range for their missiles, then let fly again.

The *Cataphract* was lunging forward to trap one of the *Commando*s when autocannon fire goosed it. The *UrbanMech* that the *Ostsol* had all but destroyed had no mobility, but its gun still worked and the *Cataphract* had obligingly impaled itself on the pilot's sights. The autocannon shells stripped all the armor from the *Cataphract*'s rear. The tremor-filled sidestep in the Liao 'Mech's advance suggested to

Andrew that one of the large 'Mech's gyros had been blown to bits in the attack.

Morgan's *Atlas* blazed away with its autocannon, capitalizing on the work already done by the *UrbanMech*. As the *Atlas*'s salvo blew everything inside the *Cataphract* to titanium dust, Andrew turned both his PPCs on the Liao *Thunderbolt*. Waves of heat washed over him as the twin particle beams blasted away sheets of armor from the *Thunderbolt*'s chest and flank.

The *Thunderbolt* turned to face its attacker, but before it could bring up the large laser on its right arm, several LRM flights pummeled it. The missiles shaved layer after layer of armor from the Liao war machine. The blasts rent gaping holes in armor, exposing titanium skeletons and purple myomer muscles to the withering autocannon fire from Gorgon lance. Thigh muscles exploded into gobs of pseudo-flesh. Top-heavy, the 'Mech fell over backward.

Streams of tracers from autocannons and the red flash of lasers swept over the battlefield. Flights of LRMs sowed more fire along the main street, filling the township with thunder and debris. Fires burned hot and high into the night sky.

Slowly, gradually, the weapons-fire died as the defenders realized that no Liao 'Mechs were firing back. Andrew looked out over the battlefield at the twisted hulks of metal and melted shards of armor. Occasionally, a round of autocannon ammo would cook off, exploding with a pop and scattering more armor chaff around. Aside from that and the flames, nothing else moved on the main street.

Andrew looked up at Craon's fallen *Hunchback. We've won, but what a price we paid for victory!* Then he looked toward the *Atlas* standing tall on top of the hill. *It's just like Morgan said. We had no choice.*

Andrew slumped in the doorway to Morgan's makeshift office. "Redburn reporting, sir."

Morgan Hasek-Davion waved Andrew into the room and to a chair between Gerry de Velez and Alanna Damu. Concern creased his brow. "How's Craon?"

Andrew sighed heavily. "We got him out of the *Hunchback*, but he was in pretty bad shape." Andrew shook his head. "The doctors think he'll live—most of him at least. Left arm, both legs. He'll never pilot a 'Mech again."

Suddenly, unbidden and unwelcome, thoughts of Justin Xiang came into Andrew's mind. *We all thought he was done, too, when his*

239

left forearm got shot off. The Federated Suns gave him a new arm, then he betrayed us. Justin must have had something to do with this assault—he's the one who got Craon so ripped up. What a waste! Andrew's fist slammed down on the arm of the chair.

Morgan's head came up. "What?"

Andrew shivered. "Sorry. I was just remembering how the NAIS fixed Justin Xiang up with an arm that let him pilot a 'Mech." He looked up hopefully at Morgan. "You don't suppose they could do that for Craon, do you?"

Morgan shook his head. "I don't know, but I've already made arrangements for him to be transferred there as soon as he has been stabilized." Morgan glanced down at a sheet of paper on his desk. "Andy, what's the status of First Battalion?"

Andrew leaned back in the chair. "Out of thirty-nine 'Mechs, I've got eighteen operational. I lost four pilots—including Craon. De Molay died when his *Jenner* exploded. The other two casualties were kids in the militia." Andrew looked helplessly at his hands. "I never even learned their names."

De Velez cleared his throat. "Todd Aiken and Barbara Hardy."

Andrew patted de Velez on the arm. "Thanks." He glanced over at Alanna. "How did your people fare?"

Alanna's voice was low and quiet. "The Fourth Tau Ceti Rangers were not as tough as the Death Commandos. I lost a dozen 'Mechs, mostly lights in the militia. Unfortunately, I also lost eight pilots, including two who survived Sarna. The Rangers hit my right flank hard, causing most of the damage. We stopped their advance, then rolled up their left flank, forcing them back into the minefield we'd laid out."

Morgan smiled broadly. "A half-dozen of the Rangers surrendered, and the crews of their *Union* Class DropShips turned them over to us in return for repatriation in Tikonov. I told them we'd do that if they'd perform one service for us."

Andrew frowned as a reckless light began to shine in Morgan's eyes. "What…? What is it?"

Morgan leaned back in his chair, steepling his fingers. "We learned of this assault because one of our agents in the Liao capital managed to get word of it out to us. His life will be in jeopardy when Maximilian Liao learns the raid failed. The second half of our mission is to go to Sian and pull this agent out."

Andrew looked at Morgan as though he'd gone mad. "We've got little more than a battalion here, Highness. We won't stand a chance in hell of raiding the Liao homeworld. They'll blast us even before we get into the atmosphere. It can't be done."

Morgan, his red-gold hair falling down over the shoulders of his black jumpsuit, disagreed with a shake of the head. "I have some equipment being transferred over from my DropShip to one of the Liao craft. We'll head back in their DropShips, repairing our 'Mechs as we go. We'll even use their command circuit to make the trip. They'll know the mission was a bust on Sian—I'm sure ComStar will report such to Liao—but they'll welcome us with open arms."

Andrew frowned. "Max Liao's more likely to blow us up because we failed to destroy Kathil. How do you expect to make him welcome us home?"

A bit of the predator seeped into Morgan's smile. "The same way we'll convince the JumpShip captains to carry us along the route. We'll tell them we're the Fourth Tau Ceti Rangers and that on Kathil we managed to capture Hanse Davion's heir—Morgan Hasek-Davion."

41

New Avalon
Crucis March, Federated Suns
10 September 3029

Pushing herself away from the data terminal, Riva Allard yawned and stretched. *My eyes are killing me.* She glanced at her chronometer. *Oh, God, three-thirty in the morning already. I thought time was supposed to fly when you were having fun, not sorting through all this library data. If I go home to sleep, I'll only get a couple of hours before I have to head back to teach that early class.*

"Bet you could use some of this coffee."

Riva whirled at the sound of a voice behind her. Kym Sorenson, a large, steaming cup of coffee in either hand, smiled at Riva. Gratefully accepting one of the plasterine mugs, Riva breathed in the rich aroma. "This is great, Kym. If I didn't owe you a favor, I do now. And if you owe me any, forget them."

Kym grinned. "Sorry to startle you."

Riva shrugged and sipped some of the hot brew. As a scientist, she knew the coffee had not yet achieved a physical effect on her, but Riva felt the warm liquid revitalizing her tired body. "At this hour, anything will make you jumpy. The guards are supposed to keep everyone out of this area. I think there are some experiments over in Lab 13J that could be fairly destructive if they were let loose."

Kym nodded distractedly as she looked around the lab. Four rows of slate-topped lab tables ran the length of the room. On the far wall, over a sink, a peg-rack had been filled with test tubes and beakers. Workbenches with countless devices, from scanning positron micro-

242

scopes to bipolar spectral digitizers, lined the long wall facing her and took up space on the exterior wall as well. Strange symbols and equations written in various colors of chalk covered the blackboard over toward the right. "So this is Dr. Banzai's home away from home, eh? Almost looks normal." She glanced down at a watermelon clamped in a tensometer. "Why is this watermelon…?"

Riva shook her head. "Don't ask. Some of his aides told me that to touch the watermelon was trouble. The doctor has lots of things going on here that can get someone hurt if they don't know what they're for. So I just confine myself to this data terminal and my little workbench over in the corner." She picked up her coffee cup and took another sip. "So, what prompts this mission of mercy?"

Kym shrugged nonchalantly, but Riva saw the haunted look in her eyes anyway. *It's been a month since Morgan left, and she's not heard anything. I know she doesn't get along with her family…That's got to leave her feeling incredibly alone.*

"I couldn't sleep and I saw the lab lights from my apartment…" Kym hesitated as if remembering an evening spent more pleasantly. "I just hate sitting around waiting to hear that something has happened to Morgan." She looked into Riva's blue eyes. "You've got brothers in the military…How can you stand it?"

Riva winced helplessly. "First off, I'm not as attached to my brothers as you are to Morgan. Uh, that sounds bad, doesn't it? I'm not close in the same sense…" As Riva struggled for words, a thrumming, loud vibration began to shake the building. The test tubes in the drying rack rattled against the pegs.

Anger flashed over Riva's face. She shouted to be heard over the roar. "Another of those damned freighters bringing broken 'Mechs from the front for the guys in the weapons lab to analyze." She crossed to the window beside Kym and looked out as the DropShip's ion engines lit up the large commons area between the civilian research center and the military academy portion of the school. "What does that idiot think he's doing? He's supposed to land on the other side of the campus."

Hovering twenty meters above the ground, the *Overlord* Class DropShip opened its drop pod doors. BattleMechs, tall and dark and emblazoned with the Liao Death Commando insignia, dropped to the ground. Bile bubbled up in Riva's throat, but before she could turn and say anything to Kym, an explosion on the roof of the research center knocked her down.

"What in hell?" Riva shook her head to clear it. *The NAIS is under attack by Liao! That's impossible.*

243

Riva tried to get up from the floor, but Kym pressed her back down with her left hand. Kym's right hand pulled up her own trouser leg to reveal a Foxfire needle pistol strapped to her ankle. She drew it and snapped the action back to fill the breech with ballistic plastic needles.

She looked down at Riva. "Stay here. I'll check things out."

Riva shook her head. "No way. I go with you."

Kym narrowed her eyes, giving Riva a cold blue stare. "Riva, I have training in things like this." She hesitated, then smiled weakly. "I work for your father. I'm one of his operatives."

Riva smiled and slid over on her belly to her knapsack. "I know. The second you were assigned to my project as an aide, I knew you were MIIO." She reached into her knapsack and withdrew a Meridian-Nagant Pulsar laser pistol. "I spotted you because I'm my father's daughter—it's in the blood. Anyone in my family would have made you. My father makes me carry this in case there's trouble."

She dialed the pulse duration regulator down to make the pulses last longer when she shot the pistol. "If the guys outside left guys on the roof, this'll burn through any armor they might be wearing." Riva looked up at Kym hopefully. "Partners?"

Kym looked reluctant, but agreed when she heard the heavy thump of commandos dropping through the roof to the level above the lab. She nodded, then led Riva back to the corner of the room. "What are they after?"

Riva shrugged. "They're Liao. They just want to trash the place."

Kym shook her head. "Think, Riva. If they wanted to destroy the NAIS, they would have dropped the 'Mechs onto the roof and let them blast their way through the building."

Riva shot a quick glance at her data terminal. "The library core…Hell, the memory core for the whole NAIS!"

"Where?"

Riva pointed toward the floor. "The basement."

Gunfire erupted in the hallway outside the lab as security guards heading up met commandos on their way down. The door to the lab disintegrated in a cloud of glass shards and wooden splinters as the body of one guard flew through it. Bullets ripped an uneven line across the chalkboard as a Death Commando fired blindly into the room before entering.

Just as the Commando framed himself in the doorway, both Kym and Riva popped up from their hiding place. Kym triggered two bursts of needles. One glanced from the warrior's plasteel breastplate, but the second burst through the opening at his armpit. As he spun with the impact, Riva's laser pulsed a stream of ruby-red energy darts at him. Two ricocheted from the breastplate, but one of those hit the warrior under the jaw. The third bolt burned through the center of his chestplate, knocking him back into the hallway.

Another Death Commando tossed a spherical object into the room. Kym tackled Riva, knocking her back toward the wall as the plastic ball bounced once, then exploded in a flash of red fire and white smoke. The concussion grenade blew the lab's windows out and sent Riva's terminal sparking to the ground.

Riva felt the explosion like a punch in her stomach and a club against her head. Sharp pain shot from her ears inward, then an incessant ringing filled them. Her lungs burned as she fought to breathe, but she could only gasp like a fish out of water. Blood slowly leaked from her nose and tasted salty against her lips. Slumped against the wall, with Kym lying unconscious—*or dead*—across her legs and her pistol blown just out of reach, Riva fought against panic.

A Death Commando strode into the room through the smoke and stood above them. "Women! I should have known." He shook his head slowly, his helmet's mirrored faceplate and computer-modulated voice utterly devoid of emotion. "Henderson always said dames would be his death."

Riva lunged for her laser pistol, closing her right hand around its cool, plastic grip. She brought it up, but faster than she would have thought possible, the Death Commando swept forward. Using the muzzle of his autorifle, he batted the pistol out of line with his body even as her finger tightened on the trigger.

The bolt of coherent light sizzled through the air and struck the end of Banzai's watermelon. The beam burned through the green rind in a nano-second, then instantly converted the fruit's water-filled pulp to steam. The melon exploded with a muffled thump, spraying organic shrapnel all over the office. The melon's structural integrity destroyed, the tensometer's top plate slammed down, liquefying the rest of the melon and grinding it into the metal plate below. Suddenly, equipment on the far wall started a hideous wailing and a tape of Dr. Banzai's voice filled the room.

The Death Commando spun. The autorifle in his right hand lipped flame as he sprayed a full clip over the equipment making noise. Sparks flew from the machines as the bullets savaged them. Ejected shells flew in an arc from the rifle, then stopped when the breech snapped open, demanding again to be fed.

As the Death Commando dropped the spent clip and reached down to pull a fresh one from his belt, Riva tracked her pistol back in line with the Death Commando. Her finger tightened on the trigger as he filled her sights. The first bolt hit him on the inside the right thigh, blasting him back against a lab table. The second and third pulses of coherent light burned through his armor chestplate like an arc-welder's torch through cheap tin. The Liao Commando jerked convulsively, then pitched over dead.

Riva stared at his unmoving body and started to tremble. Lost in a maelstrom of fear, anger and revulsion, her thoughts ran wild. *You're in danger, Riva, Think! Think! Concentrate on something! You've got to get yourself and Kym out of here!*

She heard Dr. Banzai's voice, strong and even, repeating the same message over and over again. Grabbing at the sound, she used it to fight her way back to sanity. What he was saying didn't matter at all, only that he sounded calm and normal in a situation that was anything but.

Riva rolled Kym over onto her back, then checked her for pulse and respiration. *She's just unconscious, bleeding from the nose and ears.* She grabbed Kym by the armpits and dragged her deeper into the room. Armed with both the Foxfire and the laser, Riva crept back to the dead Commando and stripped him of weapons and ammo. She intended to return to Kym, but bright lights and the whine of autocannon from outside brought her to the window. She stared out at the battle unfolding below and shook her head. "No, Doctor. I think you're wrong."

Banzai's taped voice again repeated its loop. "This was just an experiment. The watermelon was unimportant except that it shows that you should not touch something you do not understand. This was just an experiment, but next time you could ruin something real."

Riva narrowed her eyes. "No, Dr. Banzai, this time it's very real. It looks like the war has come to New Avalon."

42

Angry, Hanse Davion sat upright in bed. He glanced at the darkened screen of his holovid viewer, but forced himself to leave the remote control where it sat on his nightstand. *No, Hanse, you'll not watch that editorial again. No matter how often you view it, the words will not change. New Avalon Broadcasting has every right to say whatever they wanted—that's part of the game. I just received news that the sixth wave seized planets between the front and Sarna. The editorial ignored this success, but that's part of the game, too.*

Though he was alone in his bedchamber, the Prince answered himself aloud. "It may be part of the game, dammit, but this is nothing short of a personal vendetta…" He threw back the bedclothes, and clad only in MechWarrior shorts, slid from bed. "I refuse Karl Green's request to have his son posted in a non-combat area, which the boy didn't want anyway, and now Green uses his broadcasting company to attack the war as senseless aggression."

The Prince stared out through the curtains of his bedroom window at the lights of the New Avalon Institute of Science. *Face it, Hanse, you resented his painting you as a man who has torn children from their mothers and husbands from their wives in a mad quest for power. He suggests that you are incapable of sympathizing with the common folk in your realm….that you are an emotionless dictator….*

The Prince turned and stared back at his empty bed. *Would he understand that I, too, have felt the separation and loss caused by the*

247

*war. Would he believe that my one choice was to fight Liao in his own
realm or to fight him in mine?*

Hanse's internal voice answered him. *For a man like that, all
explanations are just lies covering other lies. He'd find some deeper,
more sinister motives for your actions. You only tell him what you want
him to know, and he digs for more. It's part of the game, and the key
is not showing him how much his attacks annoy you.*

Hanse rubbed the unshaven stubble on his chin. "But do the
people—*my* people—believe him? And does he tell more of the truth
than I allow myself to see? When I first came to the throne, I saw
myself as a caretaker of my brother's realm, but that time is long gone.
Have I become some kind of dictator out for personal gain?"

A DropShip burning low through the sky near the NAIS drew the
Prince's attention. He smiled. "As long as DropShips keep bringing in
Liao 'Mech salvage, Green will probably not have too much support.
True patriots never listen to complaints about a victorious war."

As the DropShip slowed, then sank toward the ground, something nagged at the back of Hanse's mind. *Is there a shipment coming
in today?* He crossed to his desk and used the visiphone to reach New
Avalon's Spaceport Control.

The clerk stationed at the phone jerked alert and smiled at the
Prince. "Highness, what can I do for you?"

Hanse returned the young man's smile. "The DropShip that came
in on an NAIS vector...what is it?"

The clerk's face drained of color. He turned, and in his nervousness, forgot to mute the speaker. "Henry, we're done. That DropShip
woke up the Prince. Waddyamean, what Prince? *The* Prince, you idiot!
What was that ship's name?"

Henry, out of sight, yelled an answer to the question. Hanse heard
it before the clerk could relay the message and his blood went cold. He
stared into the visiphone. "Get tactical command and have them put
aerofighters in the air. That ship's not the *Camelot!*"

The clerk's jaw dropped open. "How...?"

"Never mind how I know." Hanse said sharply. "Just do it!" He
snapped off the connection, then whirled toward the door. *That ship's
an impostor. It can't be the* Camelot, *but only a handful of people know
that right now the* Camelot *is carrying my wife back to Tharkad.*

Hanse burst from his suite, startling the two guards at his door to
attention. Barefoot, he sped past them and down long marble corridors
he'd not run through since the nearly forgotten era of games with his
brother Ian. At the end of one corridor, he slapped the button to
summon the elevator, but then dashed away impatiently and flew

down the stairs. Three flights later, deep in the ground beneath the Palace, he reached his goal.

Chest heaving with excitement and exertion, the Prince flicked on the lights in the 'Mech bay. The cavernous room, bereft of the battalion of 'Mechs belonging to the Heavy Guards, dwarfed the sole 'Mech inhabiting it. Tall and humanoid, with a massive, pistol-like PPC in its left hand, the 'Mech looked down on him the way he imagined a warhorse might have regarded the knight who rode it.

Hanse was smiling as he sprinted across the open bay toward the rope ladder hanging down from the 'Mech's cockpit to the floor. *It's been a long time...far too long.* He eagerly scrambled up the *Battle-Master*'s broad chest. *They've brought the war to me because they've forgotten. They've forgotten that before I became Prince of the Federated Suns, a command couch was my throne, a neurohelmet was my crown, and the battlefield my domain. After tonight, no one will ever forget that again.*

The *BattleMaster*'s long-legged gait ate up the five kilometers between the Palace and the NAIS campus like a cheetah chasing an antelope. Hitting top speed, Hanse sped his 'Mech through the Davion Peace Park, leaving two-decimeter-deep footprints behind him. Aware of his surroundings in the vaguest way, he avoided the monuments scattered throughout the park only because of the damage a collision might do to his 'Mech. Gone was the Prince who had presided over the tearful dedications of these memorials; the 'Mech's cockpit held a man whose sole concern was tactics and strategies of combat.

The flames billowing from the NAIS dormitories silhouetted most of the Death Commando 'Mechs and threatened to burn out his infrared display. Without conscious thought, Hanse shifted the scanning mode over to normal light as he barreled into the fray. The PPC in the *BattleMaster*'s left fist cored the aft armor on a *Panther*, spitting armor-shards and melted parts out in its backwash. The *Panther* pitched forward, then exploded when the fusion engine consumed its SRM magazine.

A *Marauder* turned around to face him. It stabbed one massive arm in his direction, but Hanse angrily batted it aside with the *BattleMaster*'s right hand. The *Marauder*'s PPC blasted into a small guard house, its cerulean thunderstrike blowing the building into brick dust and fiery splinters. The Liao 'Mech, having missed its first strike, pivoted to bring its other arm into play.

Sitting tight in the *BattleMaster*'s cockpit, Hanse Davion shook his head. *No way do you get behind me!* He leaned his 'Mech into the *Marauder*, jamming into the thorax with his shoulder. The ungainly Liao 'Mech tottered, then landed on its back, clawing at the sky like an overturned turtle.

Seeing movement on the 360-degree display, Hanse swung back to the left. His PPC pistol-whipped the humanoid *Griffin* that had been coming at his unprotected back. The massive weapon exploded as it smashed into the *Griffin's* face. The *Griffin* spun away, smoke billowing from the shattered cockpit, and collapsed much as its Human analog would have.

Alerted by frantic calls from the *Marauder*, the other Death Commandos turned from their wanton destruction to face the Assault 'Mech in their midst. Hanse cursed them silently. *Damn! There are so many of them!* Grim determination filled him, and outrage burned in his veins. *To hell with the odds and the numbers. They've attacked my home. If I'm to die in this war, let it be here.*

Hanse dropped his targeting crosshairs onto one *Locust* and fired all four of his forward lasers. The four beams focused on the birdlike 'Mech's chest, slicing it open like a surgeon's scalpel. The beams lanced through the fusion engine, letting superheated plasma leak from the 'Mech's heart like puss from a boil. In a flash of heat and brilliant light, the *Locust* vanished.

Hanse ducked his ponderous war machine to the right as the enemy returned fire. He ignored the shafts of coherent light that melted scars across the *BattleMaster's* broad chest as he discarded the shattered remains of his PPC. He barely felt the shower of short- and long-range missiles peppering the 'Mech's flesh, pockmarking it with craters. For all the thunder of explosions and the rainbow of lights that made up the Liao counterattack, none of it breached his defenses.

The *BattleMaster* reached out for and grabbed the right arm of the downed *Marauder*. Hanse set his 'Mech's right leg against the *Marauder's* torso, crushing armor and warping the other 'Mech's skeleton. With a heave of myomer muscles, the *BattleMaster* ripped the *Marauder's* arm free. Sparks shot from the ruined shoulder, the metal and armor screaming as though the *Marauder* were alive and protesting its maiming. Like Beowulf raising Grendel's severed arm, Hanse Davion brandished the limb triumphantly at his foes.

Except for those moments that burned into his consciousness from stroboscopic explosions or the harsh glare of a PPC's azure fury, the scene was a blur for Hanse. The *BattleMaster* lunged forward like a bear into a pack of wolves. A *Stinger* ignited its jump jets in an effort to escape him. It rose too slowly on twin columns of ion flame, so the

BattleMaster's shoulder hit it at the knees. Upended, the light 'Mech slammed headfirst into the ground behind the Prince of the Federated Suns, crushing the cockpit and killing the pilot instantly.

Charging into their midst, Hanse turned the Death Commandos into their own worst enemies. In such close confines, a missed shot almost invariably hit a comrade, and in a few cases, enemy pilots actually squared off against one another. Lasers shot through the chaotic fray, vaporizing armor of friend and foe alike. Only Hanse, fighting alone, could strike without fear of damaging an ally.

Twisting and turning with an agility that only a master MechWarrior could wring from his machine, Hanse repeatedly presented himself as a target, only to fade before an assault. Wielding the *Marauder*'s arm like a club, he laid about with it mercilessly. An overhand blow crumpled the right side of a *Centurion*, spinning it into the arms of a *Crusader*. Whirling, letting the blow's momentum carry him full circle, Hanse brought the arm up, catching a *Cicada* beneath its chin and dropping it onto its back.

The *BattleMaster*'s canopy shattered as an SRM burst against it. Hanse felt the stinging fire of shrapnel as pieces of the polarized glass sliced into his left arm. A trickle of blood slicked the command couch's left arm. Hanse narrowed his eyes and tightened his grip on the left joystick control. *There it is, Mr. Green. I bleed for the Federated Suns. Is it not my right to demand the same from my people?*

Hanse lashed out with the club, bringing it down like a fly swatter on the Liao *Scorpion* off to his right. The blow flattened the quadruped 'Mech, crushing its missile launcher and splaying its four legs out in different directions. Missiles damaged in the magazine began to explode, jetting the canister into the sky.

Horrified, Hanse stared down as fire spread through the *Scorpion*'s boxy body. *Punch out! Punch out!* His heart leapt as the cockpit canopy sailed into the night, but instead of a command couch rising up on escape jets, an incandescent flamespear shot out through the cockpit opening. It imploded, leaving only a thick, oily, black column of smoke to mark the pilot's passing.

Hanse looked up and saw explosions from behind the Death Commandos pressing toward him. He saw Liao BattleMechs turn away from him to face this new threat. Relief flooded through him, but he suppressed it. *The battle's not over until it's over*. Searing another Liao 'Mech with his lasers, Hanse Davion fought on.

251

Hanse frowned as the doctor buckled the sling's crossband snugly around his bare chest. "Doctor, you yourself said the glass did not damage my muscles. You've stitched the cuts, packed them in salve, and wound enough gauze up and down my arm for it to be mummified." Hanse winced slightly as a tongue of pain lanced down from his shoulder. "It does not hurt, and I do not need a sling. The sling suggests I suffered much more of an injury than I did."

Doctor James Thompson pushed his long, slender fingers back through his sandy hair. "No disrespect meant, sir," he began forcefully, "but I'll tell you again what I told you before. While you and the Hong Kong Cavaliers were out there repulsing those 'Mechs, Death Commando infantry ran riot through the research and medical centers." Thompson pointed to a ragged line of bullet holes running along the wall behind the Prince. "They damaged diagnostic equipment I would have liked to use on you to make sure everything is all right. Furthermore, I've got Team Banzai pilots stacked up like cordwood out there, so I don't need static from a surly patient who's more in need of a seamstress than a doctor. Got it, Highness?"

Hanse saw the doctor's concern that he might have spoken out of turn, but the man's greater concern for his other patients swallowed it. *By rights, in a battlezone, I wouldn't have been seen for days with these minor wounds. He's doing his job.* Hanse nodded and extended his right hand to Thompson. "You are correct, of course, Doctor. I apologize."

The anger in Thompson's look melted. He shook the Prince's hand, then loosened the sling's strap. "You can raise your arms victoriously for the holovids once, then get someone to strap you back into this thing. I don't want stitches ripping out, because I don't want you back here before I've dealt with the others."

Hanse slid from the examination table. "Once only." He reached out as Thompson turned away. "And, Doctor, thank you."

Thompson smiled, nodding once, then left the emergency room through a door marked "Surgery." Hanse slung his bloodied cooling vest over his right shoulder, then marched into the hospital corridor. At the far end, behind two closed doors set with large glass panels, he saw a throng of reporters and cameramen. Halfway down the corridor, seated on a couch until they saw him emerge through the alcove's curtained opening, three men waited to greet the Prince.

Quintus Allard hung back as the other two men approached Hanse Davion. The Prince read their haggard faces like advertising broadsheets. *They're worried and frustrated because of the injuries their men and women suffered fighting against the Death Comman-*

252

*dos. How ironic that Team Banzai came to New Avalon to recover from the devastation of Northwind only to find the front had followed them here. But if they'd not been there...*He shuddered at the thought.

The Prince warmly accepted Dr. Banzai's extended hand. "I cannot tell you how grateful I am for your efforts. You saved my life and at incredible cost to yourself and your people."

A distant look filled Banzai's blue eyes. "We fought to preserve the NAIS, and almost failed. The work done here—both in recovering old lost knowledge and in pioneering new research—is all that will keep man from blasting himself back into the Stone Age." Banzai looked down and broke his grip with the Prince. "Maximilian Liao obviously does not realize this. If he did, he'd never have launched such a relentless attack. Preserving mankind's future was a goal worthy of the sacrifice you and the others made."

The Prince's eyes narrowed. "Don't let yourself fall into the trap that snaps up battle survivors—especially those who survive a savage action like the one we just went through. You'll go crazy if you assume you weren't injured or killed because you didn't do your utmost. There's no way out of that trap. Acknowledge that you were good enough to survive and that you did your part. We did, after all, defeat them."

Banzai's nod of resignation, and the grim expression on his aide Tommy Lester's face, brought back to Hanse the last moments of the battle. Less than a dozen 'Mechs stood tattered and half-broken over a cratered hellzone. His own *BattleMaster*, missing its right arm and standing on an armorless left leg with its knee joint fused, was one of the more operational 'Mechs in that group. Hundreds of little fires burned in the hulks of dead and destroyed 'Mechs. A few pilots—all of them mercenaries—limped between the shattered bodies and debris that marked all that remained of the invading force. *It was bad...*

None of the Liao pilots even attempted to escape their machines. They fought to the end, even when we'd blown off their legs and destroyed all their weapons. They made us kill them, each and every one. I've never faced such fierce and tough opposition.

Hanse turned to Tommy. "How are your people?"

The blond MechWarrior let his expression lighten just a bit. "Those who got out are in good shape. Sprains and cuts mostly. Reno's got compound fractures of both legs, but I've been told he'll recover without any problems. Rawhide will probably lose a lung, but his prognosis is good, too." He looked back up the hallway. "We're waiting for him to come out of surgery now."

Hanse nodded. "Let me know if you need anything, anything at all. And let me know how Rawhide does." After shaking the hands of both men, he slipped past them and fell into step with Quintus Allard. "How's your daughter?"

The elder Allard smiled slightly. "Fine, really. She's angry at being held for observation. They only convinced her to stay by promising to notify her the second Kym woke up."

A pang of regret shot through Hanse. "How is she?"

Quintus's smile faded slightly. "Still unconscious, but all the signs are good." The Minister of Intelligence, Information, and Operations glanced back over his shoulder at Dr. Banzai. "When Banzai came in off the battlefield, they wouldn't let him work on his own people because the doctors thought he'd be too emotionally attached to function objectively. He immediately took charge of Kym's care, and she's already begun to respond to treatment. She won't remember the events that put her out, but she should be fine."

Before they could reach the doors and the waiting press of reporters, Hanse reached out and stopped Quintus. Turning his back to the throng, the Prince spoke in a low, urgent tone. "What happened? How the hell did that ship have the proper clearance codes to get a landing vector at the NAIS?"

Quintus shook his head. "I haven't tracked that down yet, but I would guess we had some sloppy security in the occupied territories. Most of the worlds we've captured are taking to pacification, but there are still Liao loyalists operating on them. If they heard something…"

"Were we wrong, Quintus? Did the message refer to this strike at the NAIS as opposed to a strike at Kathil?"

Shielded by the Prince's body from the cameras' prying eyes, Quintus shrugged. "I don't believe so. We got a faxed message this morning from Morgan reporting that a contingent of Liao DropShips had arrived insystem and were burning toward Kathil. We won't know for a couple of days yet what happened, but the tone of the message was confident."

Hanse drew in a deep breath. "At least we know he didn't have to face Death Commandos."

"But that's a minor consolation, I think."

Hanse nodded agreement. *We stopped you here, Maximilian Liao, and I know Morgan stopped you on Kathil. That's it…That was your last gasp. Within three months, you and your mad recklessness will be behind us forever.*

Composing his expression, Hanse Davion turned to face the questions and the cameras of the media.

43

Dromini VI
Kessel Prefecture, Dieron Military District,
Draconis Combine
15 September 3029

Duke Frederick Steiner winced in pain as the Draconian guard grabbed a handful of white hair and forced his head up. On his knees, with his hands and wrists bound together in a peculiar, cross-shaped set of shackles, Steiner stared up at his captor, but his blue eyes did not admit defeat. *You have me in body, but never in soul.*

Clad in a gray *shitagi* and traditional black *zubon*, Theodore Kurita frowned at the guard. He shook his head as he rested his right hand on the pistol holstered at his right hip. "*Iie.* Do not treat the Duke so. His surrender brings no dishonor on him."

The guard released the Duke's hair, and Frederick slumped back down onto his haunches. "Thank you, Prince Theodore." Frederick's head rose slowly, as did the emotion in his voice. "I would not have imagined that your code of *Bushido* would see anything but gross cowardice in my action."

Theodore did not answer Frederick directly. Addressing the guard, he ordered Frederick's right hand freed, then dismissed the soldier. Theodore turned from the Duke. Staring out the plate-glass wall at the city of Kanashimi, he granted the other man a moment of privacy to stretch and unknot the muscles of that arm. "We have most of the fires under control now."

Frederick took some comfort in that, though he kept his face blank of any emotion. *Six hours after the fight is over and the fires still*

255

burn. Good. That means this mission may actually have accomplished something positive. "You will forgive me if I take little joy in that news. I would much prefer to hear that the fires are utterly out of control."

The younger MechWarrior turned from the window, his expression bemused. "I would expect no less from you, Duke Frederick. I would probably feel the same way in your position because we seem to be much alike. I always imagined that we would face off with one another, but that the circumstances and timing would be far different."

The note of regret in Theodore's voice confused Frederick. "You and I are both MechWarriors, Prince Theodore, but there the similarity ends. With our vocations, was this not the only sort of meeting we could have? Perhaps we could have fought on the battlefield, but I see no other conflict being waged between us."

Theodore crossed to the sideboard and splashed some *sake* into a pair of small bowls. "Well, Frederick, as we are both MechWarriors, there should be no titles between us." The tall, slender Prince brought one bowl of the rice liquor toward Frederick, but set it on the floor where the Lyran captive would have to shuffle forward to get it. Then he drew back beyond Frederick's possible striking range.

Frederick bowed his head in Theodore's direction. He appreciated the gesture indicating he might be dangerous despite being hobbled. Frederick worked his way forward and lifted the bowl. "How *did* you see us battling, Theodore?"

The Coordinator's heir smiled emotionlessly. "I had imagined you and I waging war as the heads of our respective nations." His eyes half shut. "I had expected by now for you to have supplanted that woman..."

Frederick spat to the side in disgust. "As I have lately discovered, I would have been a puppet controlled by Aldo Lestrade were I on the throne. I feel no honor in making such an admission, but this is not the time for self-deception. Only through Aldo would I have outsmarted Katrina Steiner, but the sword that cleared my path to the throne would have become the dagger pressed to my throat."

Theodore sipped his *sake*. "Of this I am aware." He smiled, but his eyes focused distantly. "I had standing orders with some of the *Nekekami* to kill Lestrade as soon as he had succeeded in his plan to make you Archon."

The sharp-tasting liquid burned a path through Frederick's chest and warmed his stomach. "A puppet with no puppetmaster would not be difficult to deal with."

Theodore set his bowl down on the sideboard to free his hands.

"You grossly undervalue your abilities as a military leader. With you on the throne, the Lyran Commonwealth and the Draconis Combine could have joined in a glorious war. You would have learned that I ordered Lestrade's death, and you would have sent the forces of Skye against me. It would have been spectacular…a straight contest of military power—the ultimate fulfillment of *Bushido* for all involved."

Frederick laughed derisively. "Easy for you to wish for such a battle with me in chains and you the victor."

Theodore turned, waving a hand at the window wall and the thin trails of gray smoke rising from half a dozen locations. "In some ways, this actually increases my estimation of you. You brought a crack regiment in to destroy the supplies for an invasion, knowing you would be facing at least three times your number in defenders."

Theodore turned, his eyes ablaze. "Through your leadership, your MechWarriors sublimated their own dreams of personal glory. They fought as whole units—almost like hive minds—in their relentless drive to reach their targets. When one fell, another moved to take its place in line. Those who were damaged fought on beyond all reason, forcing my people to destroy them before they could pursue the bulk of your strike force. Many of the companies actually reached their targets and caused great destruction before we stopped them. It was magnificent."

Frederick narrowed his eyes. "But then I spoiled it by surrendering?"

Theodore waved away Frederick's inquiry. "No, not at all. You exacted a promise from the Archon to leave one JumpShip behind to carry away the survivors, but you assured her that you would not be among them. You negotiated a deal with me to let some of your people live, trading yourself for them. You must recall that *Bushido* demands not only perfection in the arts of war, but perfection in the art of being a warrior. Compassion and concern for your people is very much a part of that, and as such, does you no dishonor."

Frederick kept his face impassive. *Were you in my shoes, you would ask to commit* seppuku *to cleanse your family's name of shame. This mission was my act of atonement. Now, having survived this long, I do not wish to be dead. Does this invalidate what I tried to do?* "My people are being sent offworld?"

"Yes. About two hours ago, your JumpShip moved from the pirate point and began heading in for a rendezvous. The DropShip left an hour ago and should link up in a day or two." The Prince frowned slightly. "I hate to tell you that your assault, brave as it was, did not succeed in destroying enough supplies to stop my plan. With the

JumpShips already insystem, I have enough transport to bring in the supplies needed for the invasion. Conti and the Fifth Sword arrive next week, and with them come more supplies. You have cost me, at best, a week. I am sorry."

Frederick shook his head. "Not as sorry as I am."

"Spoken like a warrior." Theodore retrieved and raised his bowl in Frederick's direction. "A toast, Frederick. To what could have been—a return to the honorable ways of the warrior."

As the Lyran JumpShip *Tyr* moved from its position amid the seven Combine JumpShips still recharging at a pirate jump point off Dromini VI, it jettisoned all the refuse produced during its wait. Waste water crystallized instantly into glittering ice fangs, while more solid garbage and scraps spun away from the ship and slowly fell toward the Kurita fleet and the planet rotating below them.

Hidden in silvery bags emblazoned with the yellow and black tags used to denote biohazards, fourteen Lyran Intelligence Corps Loki operatives floated toward the enemy JumpShips. Each agent gently guided his bag toward his target ship using specially modified jump infantry flight packs to accomplish the job. Though sent in pairs to the target ships, their assignments had been drawn by lot and created by a computer program that randomized among the optimal assaults needed to cripple a JumpShip. Neither agent knew who else was being sent to the same ship. That meant he could not give his compatriot away in the highly unlikely event he was taken alive.

Raised from birth to be a Loki agent, James felt his heart pounding as the *Monolith* Class JumpShip *Samayou Hito* filled the tiny viewport of his EVA bag. Long and silver, the twin-domed sensor pods at the head of the craft looked like giant, composite eyes, accentuating the vessel's wasplike appearance. Mobile arms attached to the trio of docking collars evenly spaced along the body of the ship were locked down in their stowed position, but James angled his amoeboid craft toward the arm directly amidships nonetheless. Splayed out in absolute rainbow brilliance, the doughnut-shaped solar collector hung from the ship's stern, soaking in the energy needed to recharge the JumpShip's fragile Kearny-Fuchida drives.

After an hour of casual movement through space, James reached the JumpShip's central docking arms. From afar, they had looked much like the mechanical arms used by mining robots in hostile atmospheres. Up close, the Loki agent saw their true size. Each of the twin fingers was a cylinder six meters in diameter that ended in a docking collar. By extending the arms, the JumpShip could link up with six DropShips. In addition, the three docking collars on the JumpShip's hull meant it could accommodate a total of nine Drop-Ships. This capacity left no doubt in James's mind about why the *Monolith* Class JumpShip was most highly prized in the Successor States, and why the successful completion of his mission was of the utmost importance.

He guided his bag into the gaping maw of one finger, then sliced the bag's silvery flesh open with a vibroblade. Stepping free, he wadded up its thin skin and stuffed it into a thigh pocket of the gray fatigues he wore over the skin-tight vacuum suit. For a moment, it pleased him that the Draconis Combine saw fit to give their astechs such utilitarian garb, but he shut away that tiny emotion as he had been taught. Like a mantra, he murmured, "Reason is the engine that drives us, and passion for success is the only fuel we feed it. Clear mind, clean victory."

He worked his way through the shaft by feel. A hundred meters into it, he reached the large, iris-type hatchway, shut now to keep the ship's atmosphere inside. Off to the left, he found the slender doorway that admitted the astechs who traveled out to monitor docking operations. The mission had gone well so far, but he felt a pang of regret. Because one Kurita JumpShip had moved off toward a rendezvous of its own and out of range of the operation, the Loki teams' mission could not be 100 percent successful.

James shook off his disappointment and set to work. From his left-thigh pocket, he pulled a thin packet of mylar fabric. He unfolded it into an oval just slightly larger than the astech hatchway, then carefully pulled away a protective strip from around the adhesive-treated edge and pressed the canopy against the hull. He checked the seal, carefully twisting himself around to keep from rupturing the membrane that trapped him between it and the hatchway.

Confident he'd gotten a good seal, James opened an oxygen canister on his belt. The hissing sound grew as released gas filled the cocoon. When the digital readout on his bracer reported one atmosphere worth of pressure, he shut off the oxygen and turned his attention to the hatch's lock mechanism.

The Loki agent pulled a silver cylinder from his breast pocket and shoved it into the round keyhole. He pressed a button on it and watched a red light pulse as the skeleton key played out one digital combination of codes after another. Finally, a green light shone on the key and was quickly mirrored by the atmospheric pressure sensor on the lockplate. Satisfied that pressure had been equalized on both sides of the hatch, he opened it with a click.

James slipped through the hatchway quickly and shut it behind him. He doffed the jetpack and mirrored helmet he'd worn during his trip over. In the muted yellow glow of the docking arm's safety lights, he caught a reflection of his own face. His right hand rose involuntarily to touch the corner of his eye. Despite having worn this surgically altered face for a month, he was still not used to the almond eyes, black hair, and bronzed skin.

It never occurred to him that he would have preferred to die wearing his own face. As an orphan raised by and for Loki, his conception of self had been inexorably linked with the fate of the Lyran Commonwealth. He thought of himself as nothing more than a white blood cell whose mission was to do whatever was necessary to protect the health of the state. His success—and he harbored no doubts of it—would save the Commonwealth. That he would have to die to succeed meant nothing because the Commonwealth had given him everything. How could he refuse to return to it all that he was?

Stripping off his gloves and discarding them, James pushed off the hull and floated through the arm toward the second atmospheric bulkhead. Reaching it, he again used his key to open the small hatch built into the giant airlock's bulkhead. Slipping through that hatch, James closed it, then straightened up. He made sure his uniform hung right, then surveyed the interior of the ship's drive section.

Like a long, slender balloon twisted into sausage-like segments, seven helium tanks surrounded the length of the Kearny-Fuchida drive. This discovery caused James a moment of annoyance because intelligence had reported that the *Samayou Hito* had not been refitted with sequenced tanks but still had one long, all-encompassing helium system. As his mission called for him to blow the helium tanks— crippling the JumpShip without destroying the irreplaceable K-F drive—this refitting made things difficult.

Operating on the principle that people do not question those who know what they are doing, he kicked off the hull and floated directly toward and under the nearest helium tank. He located the welded seam running the length of the tank and pulled a lump of gray explosive from the tool pouch on his belt. Into the center of it, he pressed a titanium shoe. Taking special care that the hollowed bottom of the shoe was filled with plastique, he molded the whole packet of explosive to the tank's steel flesh. Then he drew a small digital triggering device from his left breast pocket and pressed it into the gray lump. He set the timer for a hour and locked it so it could only be overridden by the control module built into his belt buckle.

James completed the same operation with three more tanks before they found him. A guard demanded that he come out from beneath the tank and present his identification papers. In reply, James set the timer on the lump of explosive in his hand to eight seconds, wadded it all up into a ball, and bounced it off the hull toward the guard.

The explosion sent a sharp shockwave through the zero-gravity atmosphere, slamming James down into the hull. Through the red haze and scraps of cloth that had been the guard, James saw two more security officers right themselves and dive toward him.

James smiled and slapped his belt buckle. Explosions filled the engine chamber with fire and whirling shards of hot metal. Thick gouts of white fog flooded the atmosphere as liquid helium gushed through the gaping holes in the tanks. The Kurita astechs and guards screamed as an icy wave swept over them and immortalized the terrors of their last moments.

James, whose frozen body fragmented when the wave carried it against the hull, could not have imagined dying happier, no matter whose face he wore.

Theodore Kurita lowered his *sake* bowl. "You know, Frederick, my only regret in this assault of yours is that it came after the *Genyosha* had left the world. I'm sure you noticed their DropShips leaving the system as you burned in. I would have loved to see Yorinaga Kurita duel with you."

Frederick smiled slightly. "It would have not been much of a fight, and you know that as well as I do. From what I understand of reports concerning the January action on Northwind, Yorinaga Kurita has only one target in mind. I doubt you could have ordered him to fight against me, just as you could not order him to avoid combat with Morgan Kell."

Thinking of Morgan Kell, Frederick knew he had to respect the man, as much as he hated him for his steadfast support of Katrina. *Something inside drives him and gives him an edge I will never know. On Mallory's World, he traded his life for the lives of his people, much as I have done here. The difference is that he survived. To willingly embrace death and survive gave him a strength I would have loved to touch just once in my life.*

Theodore nodded as though agreeing with Frederick's comment, but the buzzing from the visiphone unit on the sideboard cut off further conversation. Theodore raised an earpiece to the side of his head and turned the phone so Frederick could not see the picture.

Even without hearing what the caller told the Prince, the questions Theodore barked and the rage turning his face scarlet told Frederick all he needed to know. Something had gone wrong, very wrong. *Whatever it is, I'm glad I was here to see it,* he thought.

Theodore swept the visiphone from the sideboard, sending it crashing to the floor amid *sake* bowls and crystal decanters of other potables. He whirled, his eyes molten with fury, stabbing his left index finger out toward the captive Lyran noble. "You bastard! How could you sit here and listen to me prattle on about honor and agree with me when you were planning such treachery?!"

Frederick stiffened as Theodore drew his pistol. "I have no idea what you are talking about," he said, meeting Theodore's stare defiantly.

Theodore watched him for a second, then nodded. "No, you would not have resorted to such trickery. Your cousin sent Loki agents to cripple the JumpShips of my fleet. Four have blown helium tanks. Two have had their solar recharging exchanges destroyed, and the last has lost its station-keeping engine. That vessel is currently falling toward the sixth planet, though other ships should be able to stabilize its orbit." Theodore snorted with disgust. "What you fail to do honorably in combat, she accomplishes by trickery."

Frederick's stare, like the barrel of the gun in Theodore's hand, never wavered. "Get used to it, Theodore. It is the way of things. Politicians will forever betray warriors because what we observe as the conventions of war they exploit as our weakness." Frederick smiled, a sense of completion filling him as Theodore's finger tightened on the trigger.

44

With his chopsticks, Justin Xiang plucked one last piece of kung pao beef from the platter and popped it into his mouth. The tidbit crunched between his molars as the thick sauce added its spice. *I've stuffed myself, but this food is so good that my mouth hungers for more.*

He looked over at Alexi Malenkov as the slender analyst finished off the last of the tangerine beef. Alexi closed his eyes and chewed slowly, a smile growing on his face. He swallowed, then chased the meat down with some green tea. He looked at both Justin and Candace Liao. "Thank you for inviting me to dine this evening. Not only is the food superior, but this is probably the first chance I've had to sit down for a meal in the last two months."

Candace, pleased that Alexi had enjoyed the meal, bowed her head in his direction. "Under normal circumstances, Alexi, you would not be able to get a seat here in the Szechuan Inn. With good reason, as you have discovered. It is the most popular restaurant in the capital." She looked around at the utterly empty dining room. "The necessities of security are sometimes a blessing."

Justin nodded, recalling making the reservation for their dinner. *The owner only asked for an hour to clear out the customers, as if a visit by the heir to the Capellan throne was nothing out of the ordinary. When the sweeper team hit the building, the owner had his people feed all of them as well as us. If past practice remains true, he'll only bill us for what the three of us have eaten, and in return, I will tip*

263

generously.

Alexi stretched, plucking the napkin from his lap and setting it on the table. "I can understand your point of view, as it's nice to eat without having to listen to a howling child in the next booth or having somebody's cigar smoke ruin the meal. In some ways, though, I miss being able to watch people." Alexi smiled weakly. "I suppose it's because of the work I do, but I always like to imagine the secrets of the people around me."

A new voice injected itself into the coversation. Tsen Shang, flanked by two Maskirovka Security Officers, came around the corner from the kitchen and faced the open side of the horseshoe-shaped booth. Resplendent in a gold silk robe embroidered with red dragons, he folded his arms across his chest and hid his hands in the robe's voluminous sleeves. "It does not surprise me that you find secrets interesting, Citizen Malenkov."

Justin stiffened at Tsen's sinister tone. "What is it, Tsen?"

Shang's eyes narrowed to slits of shadow. "It, *Shonso* Xiang, is word of the task force sent to destroy Kathil. What is left of it arrived at Hexare and relayed a message through ComStar."

"What's left of it?" Justin asked uneasily. "They should have had no problem on Kathil. Your plan was flawless. What happened?"

Tsen paused for a second, as if weighing the surprise in Justin's voice. "The Death Commandos met resistance in the form of two hastily cobbled-together line units. The fighting was fierce, and the Commandos were destroyed. The Fourth Tau Ceti Rangers likewise failed in their mission to destroy the geothermal generators on Kathil, but they have redeemed themselves."

Candace's fist slammed into the table. "Enough riddles, Shang. Tell us what has happened."

Shang bowed his head in Candace's direction, but the gesture conveyed neither respect nor obedience. "As you wish, Duchess. The Fourth Tau Ceti Rangers managed to capture the enemy force's leader." Shang smiled broadly. "They are bringing us Morgan Hasek-Davion."

Justin's chopsticks clattered against his plate, and Alexi's face went ashen. Justin shook his head to clear it of shock, then smiled. "Morgan Hasek-Davion. Who would have imagined we would win such a valuable weapon to use against Hanse Davion?"

Shang unfolded his arms and inspected the long nails on the last three fingers of his right hand. Light glinted from the diamond chips encrusted there and shone dully from each nail's carbon fiber-reinforced razor edge. "Who, indeed? Certainly not the spy who communicated the information about the assault."

Even before Justin could demand information, Shang drew a folded sheet of paper from inside his robe and passed it to him. Justin unfolded it slowly, feeling the crisp bond paper stick to the fingers of his right hand. *I know that watermark. This is the special stock used by ComStar Precentors*. The letterhead inside confirmed the source of the missive. The message was short, but Justin read it over twice:

"Greetings, Chancellor Maximilian Liao. It is with deep regret that we at ComStar apologize for a violation of our own Interdiction against House Davion that may have caused you some inconvenience. Under false pretenses, a Davion agent managed to send a message to the Minister of Intelligence, Information, and Operations of the Federated Suns. We feel it might have compromised your operation on Kathil, and for this we are sorry. It will not happen again.

"The Peace of Blake be with you. Villius Tejh, Precentor Sian."

Justin returned the message to Shang, who accepted it, glanced at it once, then refolded it. He smiled. "I've checked the records. I know the identity of the spy in our midst."

Muscles bunched at Justin's jaws. "Do what you must, Citizen."

Shang turned to Alexi Malenkov. "I arrest you in the name of Chancellor Maximilian Liao for high treason and crimes against the state." The guards behind him drew their guns. "By order of the Chancellor, you are to be executed here and now for your crimes!"

BOOK V
COURAGE

One man with courage makes a majority.
—Andrew Jackson

45

Romano Liao forcibly resisted the delicious temptation to smile triumphantly as Justin Xiang was ushered into her father's presence by two Maskirovka Security Officers. Though he held his head high and was unbound, Romano sensed a change in him. Glancing at her lover, she did allow herself the hint of a grin. *Tsen senses it as well. Alexi's exposure as a spy has made Xiang vulnerable.*

She studied the fierce resolution on Xiang's face as he marched down the scarlet carpet to where Maximilian Liao sat on his throne. Sitting in the massive stone seat with its circular back carved into a representation of the universe with Sian dead-center, the Chancellor dwarfed the steel-handed Maskirovka agent.

When Xiang spoke, his voice was free of fear or apprehension. "You have summoned me, Celestial Wisdom?" Xiang glanced back over his shoulder, throwing the guards a withering stare. They withdrew to the side of the carpet.

Maximilian Liao, long and gangling like an ancient spider, stirred on his high throne. His long-fingered hands gripped the throne's arms, his knuckles bulging and becoming white. "I ordered Tsen Shang to arrest and execute Alexi Malenkov immediately. You countermanded that order! This is not the first time you have usurped my right to command my subjects to do my bidding, but by the gods, it will be the last! What possessed you to defy me?"

Romano saw conflicting emotions flash over Justin's face. *Do*

269

you acquiesce or do you meet your destruction head on? When she saw his chest expand and his eyes narrow, she thought, *Good. A battle.*

Justin answered coldly and calmly, but his tone was razor-sharp. "What possessed me last night was a desire to see the evidence against Alexi Malenkov myself. I have worked with him since joining your service two and a half years ago. I have counted on Malenkov to perform countless tasks for me, and not once has he or his work been deficient or suspect. My God! The man saved my life on Bethel. I hasten to add that Alexi Malenkov is a Mandrinn. By law, he cannot be executed without a trial. Furthermore, I am his overlord, with the right to appeal any such sentence of death to the Chancellor."

Xiang raised his metallic left hand to forestall the Chancellor's denial of that appeal. "As for times in the past when I have, as you claim, usurped your leadership prerogatives, it should be noted that my actions have paid off handsomely for us in the end. You will recall that I gave the order for McCarron's Armored Cavalry to take up a position on Sarna. There they broke the Fifth Syrtis Fusiliers, handing Hanse Davion his first and only major defeat in this war."

Seeing the fire in her father's eyes waver beneath the logic of Justin's argument, Romano moved to stoke the blaze. "You forget, Citizen Xiang, that Morgan Hasek-Davion has been captured. This is Hanse Davion's greatest defeat in the war."

Justin looked at her with eyes full of scorn. "Is it really, Lady Romano?" He bowed his head toward Tsen Shang. "I do not deny that his capture is a boon to our cause, but I know first-hand how valuable people are to Hanse Davion. The same hands that pinned the Diamond Sunburst to my chest for bravery under fire were the hands that stripped my rank from me. The voice that congratulated me in the name of the Federated Suns was the same voice that exiled me from my home! As far as Hanse Davion is concerned, Morgan may now be only a failure, the fruit of traitorous seed. For all we know, Hanse offered Morgan up to be well rid of him."

"Enough!" Maximilian Liao stood tall, pointed down at Justin with his right index finger. "You will not deflect me. You have seen the evidence against Malenkov. How can you still be against his immediate execution?"

Justin shook his head slightly. "Is it not obvious? Alexi Malenkov is a valuable tool. If we can turn him against his former masters, we can use him to destroy them..."

Tsen Shang laughed harshly. "Just as your captured technology has been used against Hanse Davion?"

"That is not my choice, Shang," Justin said bitterly. "House

270

Imarra's two battalions have both been refitted with the new myomer muscles. You have seen the reports…you know what those units can do. How is it that you, the master planner of our strategy, have not yet deployed the troops in places where they will be useful?"

Romano saw Xiang's remark hit home with Shang, and she spoke quickly to mitigate the damage. "House Imarra's 'Mech battalions remain here because I have demanded it. In the past, the Death Commandos were the unit who kept the Chancellor inviolate. Now this duty has fallen to House Imarra."

Justin turned to Maximilian Liao. "There, Highness, is much of your problem. How am I to act in your interests when your own daughter conspires to disrupt the most logical of plans? You have lauded her assassination of Pavel Ridzik, but never did she pause to consider the consequences of her action."

Romano frowned angrily. "I eliminated an enemy of the state!"

Justin nodded patronizingly. "Yes, you did. Unfortunately, that enemy of the state had just succeeded in taking a number of Marik worlds. This focused the attention of the Free Worlds League on him and his Tikonov Free Republic. But without the threat of a competent military leader on that front, House Marik is now licking its wounds and looking for easier fights. In the latest wave of Davion attack, seven of our worlds simply surrendered to the Federated Suns rather than suffer invasion from the Free Worlds League."

Justin raised his face to the Chancellor. "Face it. Janos Marik will come after us like a shark after blood if he thinks we can be chewed up. Alexi Malenkov and Morgan Hasek-Davion may be the tools we need to slow the Davion advance—perhaps even stop it cold which will give us the time to shift our forces around to face a Marik threat."

Anger and fear flared through Romano. Memories of her first lover and the report of his death at the hands of Marik troops on Altorra brought burning bile into her throat. *No. We will never allow the Free Worlds League to take any of our worlds. I will not allow it.*

With that one thought, she felt an electric jolt race through her body. *I will not allow it! I cannot permit my father's blind hatred of Hanse Davion to open the way for House Marik.* She appraised Justin with restless green eyes. *Likewise, I cannot let my animosity toward Justin Xiang color my evaluation of the wisdom of his words.* She smiled. *At least, not until I can afford to be rid of him.*

Romano, reaching out to take Tsen Shang's arm, forestalled her father's denial of Xiang's analysis. "How do you see Morgan and Alexi being used against Hanse Davion?" she asked Justin. Confusion arced through his eyes momentarily, which brought a smile to Romano's lips. She gave Tsen's arm a squeeze to reassure him.

Xiang bowed his head to her. "Hanse Davion's Achilles' heel is public opinion. The Prince has been forced to rationalize an excuse for launching his unprovoked assault upon us. Using rumor and innuendo, he has claimed that he struck to forestall an attack that he knew was coming from us. He has claimed to be liberating our people, and in that way, has gained a moral high ground for his war."

Justin pressed the fingertips of his hands together as he continued to speak. "We have had reports of unrest because of ComStar's Interdiction. Our agents have successfully spread rumors of disasters on the front that Davion has had a hard time countering. The destruction of the Fifth Syrtis Fusiliers did much to raise the level of discontent. The people were willing to accept his explanation of a pre-emptive strike while they were winning, but a stalemate or loss means warriors are dying for naught.

"I propose we do two things. The first is to put Alexi Malenkov on trial for espionage. We can point out how he worked in conjunction with Michael Hasek-Davion in planning the whole of Hanse Davion's treacherous war. We will have Alexi confirm that Hanse Davion sent Michael here, sacrificing him on Sian to eliminate a potential rival for power back home. In addition, we will welcome Morgan Hasek-Davion and treat him royally. Once the people of the Capellan March see how well we treat their nominal leader, they will begin to question the worth of Hanse Davion's war. We can get the Capellan March to withdraw support. If we can turn Morgan, we might even be able to incite a civil war within the Federated Suns."

Romano nodded slowly. "I see the merit in this plan, as I am sure you do, Father," she said, smiling up at him. "I believe it is worthy of consideration. We have Malenkov. We might as well get some use from him before we have him shot."

Maximilian hesitated, then slowly and thoughtfully sank back into his throne. His eyes focused distantly and his lower lip trembled. In an instant, he went from being the leader of a star-spanning realm disciplining an insubordinate vassal, to a man questioning his own judgment. He glanced down at Romano, uncertainty in his eyes, then nodded.

The sight of her father's transformation created a spark of regret in Romano, but her ambition smothered it before it could even begin to approximate sympathy. *Xiang's plan could well divide the Federated Suns against itself. It is curious that the same freedoms that make our enemy strong are the freedoms that make it open to such a covert assault.* She smiled at Justin. *Likewise, only such an open society*

272

could breed an agent with the skill to recognize and exploit such a weakness.

Romano licked her full lips. "Very well, let us prepare a welcome for Morgan Hasek-Davion and a trial for Alexi Malenkov. We will take the moral high ground away from Hanse Davion, then leave him to drown in his own plots and deceptions."

46

Andrew Redburn, lost in thought as he stared out the DropShip's viewport, nearly jumped out of his skin when Morgan Hasek-Davion slapped him heavily on the back. "Dammit, Morgan! Don't do that to me!"

The larger MechWarrior smiled warmly. "Sorry, Andy. I really didn't mean to startle you." He rested his huge right hand on Andrew's left shoulder. "You've been preoccupied ever since we jumped to Sian and started our trip insystem."

Andrew stared out at the second planet orbiting the star called Sian. Still two days out, despite arriving at a non-standard jump point and heading in at just over two gravities, the world was nothing more than a white ball in the distance. *You're down there, Justin. I can feel it. Have you figured out what we're doing or are we going to trick you this time?*

Andrew forced a smile. "Don't mind me, Highness. I'm not worried about the plan. It's flawless. They appear to believe wholeheartedly that we're remnants of the Fourth Tau Ceti Rangers returning in triumph with Prince Hanse's heir in tow." His smile grew a bit more genuine. "I can't wait to see the expression on Maximilian Liao's face when our DropShip opens up, and we drop out a battalion ready for a fight. The First Kathil Uhlans should build quite a reputation in this action."

Morgan chuckled softly. "Yes, I believe you are correct. Our

274

JumpShip will be recharging the KF drive from its ion engine in preparation for our return trip. All we have to do is find Hanse's agent and get him out."

Turning his back to the viewport, Andrew frowned. "I don't like not knowing who the agent is."

Morgan shrugged. "That can't be helped. We just have to listen for the countersign. He's got half an hour to make contact with us. If we knew who he was, it would be information that we could reveal if captured. We're to find the agent, give him the packet of stuff our Intelligence Liaison Officer issued yesterday, and then cover his back as he gets out."

Andrew nodded slowly. "What if they've already captured him and he misses the pickup?"

Morgan frowned. "In that case, I guess we'll just have take the Palace apart and find him." He narrowed his green eyes. "Somehow, Andy, I don't think that's what's been bothering you. I can read your uneasiness like a book. You're telegraphing like you telegraphed your punches in our first boxing match back at Warrior's Hall."

"That obvious, huh?" Andrew sighed heavily. "Somewhere down there on Sian, I'm going to run into Justin Xiang. I know that if I see him, I'll have to try to kill him." Andrew looked up at his friend. "I know he's the enemy, and my face still burns when I think of how easily he dealt with me on Bethel, but there's still part of me..."

Morgan held up a hand to stop Andrew. "I know exactly what you're saying. You're angry at him not so much because he's the enemy but because you feel he betrayed you. He taught you a great deal while you served under him in the Kittery training battalion, and you stuck by him during his treason trial. But then he tried to have you assassinated on Kittery, and he defeated you in a 'Mech battle on Bethel. Part of you wants to fight him and beat him, but part of you doesn't want to lose the friendship you felt for him."

Andrew saw sadness in Morgan's eyes. "Yes, that sums it up almost perfectly. How did you know?"

Morgan folded his arms across his broad chest and leaned back against the DropShip's hull. "When I was a boy, my father taught me to play chess. We'd play once a week or so, and those games became very important to me. No matter what problems my father had to deal with at court, he refused to miss our game. He always encouraged me and told me that when I could finally beat him, I would become a man. Yet, try as I might, I could not win and felt myself smaller in his eyes for my failure."

Morgan glanced away, focusing his malachite eyes beyond the

ship's metal shell. "Finally, when I turned fourteen, I took to studying chess. It became an avocation for me, and was sufficiently martial for my tutors to indulge my desires. During this time, my father was called to New Avalon, so we did not play for three months. But when he returned, the first thing we did was to face off across a chess board."

Morgan lapsed into silence for a moment as pain and confusion passed fleetingly over his face. "It was no contest, really. I had become very good in his absence, and I beat him even before I knew it. When I announced, 'Checkmate!' I expected congratulations from him, and to be seen in a new role as an adult."

Andrew moistened his lips with the tip of his tongue. "What happened?"

Morgan shook his head ruefully. "He swept the board and pieces from the table. He demanded to know who had conspired with me to humiliate him. He grabbed me and tried to look into my ears to see if I was wearing a radio earpiece because he couldn't believe he'd been bested by 'a half-grown whelp.'"

The Lion of Davion met Andrew's stare. "I've not played chess since because even the idea of a game reminds me of what that last match cost me in the loss of intimacy between me and my father. For years, I thought I'd done something wrong. I beat him, and he hated me for it. After a while, I realized this conflict would probably have developed one way or another, no matter what either of us would have chosen to do about it. My father had become a different person, and I had to deal with him on that basis."

Andrew thought for a moment, then nodded grimly. "What you're saying is that Justin's responsible for the changes in his life. I've got to make sure to keep the past in the past, because dwelling on it will get me killed in the here and now."

"Yeah," Morgan said with a grin. "That's what I'm saying. I don't know what sort of a reception we're going to get down there, but I don't want anyone thinking about anything other than the mission. We get our man and get out."

Andrew nodded. "Get our man and get out. Right." *That means, Justin Xiang, that I'm looking for someone different than everyone else. When I settle with you, I'll consider my mission accomplished.*

47

Clovis Holstein eased himself from the shadowed corner of Aldo
Lestrade's library and moved into the light as the Duke made his way
toward the crystal service on the sideboard. Clovis made no noise, but
the Duke, as though sensing the emotions raging in the dwarf's breast,
whirled unsteadily. Clovis stopped. "I have come for you, Duke Aldo
Lestrade."

Lestrade jammed both fists onto his hips and screwed his face
into a grimace that looked like the prelude to a furious outburst. Then
his eyebrows tipped up in a mocking expression. The short, squat
Duke threw back his head and laughed raucously. "Does Morgan Kell
hold me in such contempt that he sends you to kill me? Be off with you
before I find a stick and beat you to death as I would any other vermin."

"He doesn't even know I'm here," Clovis said. "If Morgan Kell
truly wished you dead, he'd have crushed you beneath the heel of his
Archer months ago. He would gladly have killed you for any of your
attempts against the life of the Archon. With Duke Frederick gone,
Morgan assumes you are no longer a threat."

Lestrade's jovial expression grew darker, and Clovis took secret
pleasure in the change. *Yes, Duke Lestrade. I know of Duke Frederick's
demise. I am privy to highly secret information. This makes me an
unknown quantity in your eyes, doesn't it? I am a mystery to be
unraveled before you destroy me.*

Lestrade frowned, then crossed to a massive wooden sideboard and poured himself a brandy. "Duke Frederick's loss is a blow to my plans, but it matters little. Alessandro Steiner is dying, and Ryan, his heir apparent, will still need a political mentor to wrest control from Melissa. It may take ten or twenty years, but I will be there to see my plans come to fruition."

Clovis unzipped the Kell Hound flight jacket he wore. "All your planning will be for naught," he said, a cruel smile tugging at his mouth. "The same raid that killed your father, the raid that took your left arm and destroyed your left hip, maimed you in another way. Reconstructive surgery is wonderful, but even the best in the Successor States could not give you back the ability to sire a dynasty, could it?"

Lestrade's face drained of color. He swirled the brandy in his snifter, then gulped down the amber liquid. It restored sanguinity to his cheeks, but the haunted look in his brown eyes remained. "How do you know that? Who are you?"

Clovis's laughter clearly irritated the Duke, so the dwarf lashed him with it mercilessly. "How did I know you were castrated in that raid? I've been in your castle for two days now, and I've sorted through every piece of data in your computer system. What other conclusion could I draw from the fact that one of the greatest womanizers in the Lyran Commonwealth has testosterone derms sent to him from a dozen different sources? You've never had an heir and never even been involved in a paternity suit. As I suggested before, reconstructive surgery can be wonderful, but some things it cannot rebuild."

Lestrade, slightly unsteady, eased himself into a green leather wingback chair. He stared at Clovis, appearing almost mesmerized. "You broke my security? The computer security system I created?"

Clovis nodded patronizingly. "I've a knack for that sort of thing. Some say I inherited it." The dwarf's smile grew as he looked around the dark, cavernous room filled from floor to ceiling with shelves of valuable, leather-bound books. "As for your other question, I am offended that you do not recognize me. I didn't think I had that much of my mother in me."

Lestrade squinted through the room's dim light at the dwarf. He pulled back for a second, then looked closely at his visitor again. Finally he settled back in his chair, an astonished smile spreading across his wide face. "My God, is it possible? I thought she died in the raid. Someone told me afterward that she'd been pregnant…I couldn't have cared before…." The Duke looked at the plastic left hand he wore as a result of the Kurita raid twenty-four years before. "Afterward, I would have given my *right* arm for her child. What was her name?"

Clovis threw back his long black hair with a proud shake of his head. "Danica. Her name is Danica Holstein. I am Clovis."

A chuckle began deep in Lestrade's barrel chest and grew to fill the room. "Clovis. That's a good name, a strong name. It means illustrious battler. Yes, yes…Clovis Lestrade." The Duke's eyes flashed with unadulterated joy. "Clovis Lestrade…That's as good a name as I would have chosen for you myself."

The dwarf rested his hands on his hips. "Now I have come for you."

Lestrade nodded enthusiastically. "Of course you have, my boy. You've come for what I can give you, what we can share. The Lyran Commonwealth is a ripe plum, just waiting to be plucked by someone with the courage and knowledge to take it." The Duke leaned forward, resting his elbows on his knees. "Of course you broke through my computer's security—by the gods, you've got to be brilliant. Now my people will have someone to lead them when I have passed on."

Clovis smiled easily. "I have people as well, father."

The Duke heard his words, but placed different emphasis on them. "Father," he said, musing over the sound of the word. "How often have I been jealous of other men who have children? There I was, a strategist without equal, a political leader who is a god in his own realm, yet I had no heir, no future on which to build. I would look at some halfwit peasant toiling on an agrocombine, with a dozen wailing brats surrounding him like a pack of mongrels. I could not understand my fate because I knew God had chosen me for great things."

Lestrade smiled at his son. "Now I see that it makes sense. It does not surprise me that you have followers of your own. That would only be natural. I can see it in you, the Lestrade fire. You can speak passionately and make people listen. You can inflame them and direct them. How many are your followers? What is your power base?"

Clovis's dark eyes hardened. "It was a small community on Lyons. It was called New Freedom and it died when you ordered the Kell Hounds to abandon the world."

The Duke frowned for a moment as the pain in Clovis's voice confused him, but his dreams of empire carried him away again. "It was too bad about that. But the important thing is that you survived." The horror of losing the son he'd not known sent a tremor through him. "Do you have a son? Am I a grandfather?"

Clovis shook his head. "Not yet."

The Duke laughed aloud. "But you will, Clovis. You will. I will arrange for you a marriage that will strengthen our ties with the Tamar Pact. When your son assumes the throne, he will rule a realm a third the size of the Lyran Commonwealth."

Clovis shook his head. "I'm afraid you don't understand why I am here. Just as you killed your father, I will kill you. First, I wanted you to know who I am, and that your foul line ends with you."

The joy on Lestrade's face melted into outrage, then changed to calculated pity. With his right hand, the Duke tugged on his artificial left hand, bending it all the way back against his forearm. At his wrist, the barrel of a laser pistol popped out and pointed directly at Clovis.

The Duke shook his head. "I am not as stupid as my father. I am never without a weapon."

Clovis laughed at him. "As I told you before, I've been in this castle for two days. I learned about your little trick from the computer and I drained the battery cell last night after you removed the arm to sleep."

Lestrade stabbed the laser at Clovis, but no beam shot from it to impale him. The Duke levered himself out of the chair and raised the plastic and steel limb. "It does not matter! You are nothing! I will crush you!" He took one step toward the dwarf, then clutched at his chest. The Duke sank heavily to his knees before pitching forward onto his face.

Clovis approached him, pleased to see his father's breath moistening the cold marble floor. "I'm a Lestrade, father. I've been here two days and you never saw me. I would have remained here a week or a month or a year if I had to."

Clovis lifted the Duke's head just enough so the man could see the sideboard. "Were I acting just for myself, or the people you caused to be murdered at New Freedom, I would have killed you cleanly. But in your attempt to kill the Archon, you had my best friend's lover killed. You gave Daniel Allard untold pain—pain he does not deserve—and for that, I decided to break you. The only reason you saw me tonight, *Father*, is because you were moving to drink from the brandy I poisoned when I first got here. I just wanted to see your face when you realized that you would die a complete and utter failure."

Clovis laid the Duke's head back down on the cold floor, then walked away, leaving Aldo Lestrade to die very, very much alone.

48

Chu-sa Akira Brahe left his company under the command of Jack Seaborg to pace his way through the *Genyosha* column. Pulling parallel to his father's *Warhammer*, he keyed up a radio link. "*Sumimasen, Tai-sa Yorinaga.* Please speak with me on our private channel."

His father's voice came after a moment's hesitation. "*Hai.*" After a short buzz of static, Yorinaga Kurita's voice again filled Akira's neurohelmet. "As you asked for this conference by addressing me by rank, I shall assume we will speak only of military matters?"

Akira winced at the anxiety mixed with an uncharacteristic eagerness in his father's voice. *What we are to face both worries and exhilarates him. The calm that seemed the core of his being erodes as he draws closer to his meeting with Morgan Kell.* He drew in a deep breath in a weak attempt to allay his own anxiety. "*Hai, sosen.* My primary concern is military, but it does not smother all else that I feel. But the Way of the Sword enables me to put aside personal concerns to consider the military necessities of a situation."

Yorinaga's laughter brought a smile to Akira's lips as the Mech-Warrior stepped his *Orion* around a wind-carved dolmen. "Well put, *Chu-sa* Brahe. I am rebuked for placing my personal concerns ahead of military ones, though, in actuality, I have not done so."

Akira frowned. A desert wind swirled red dust up into a bloody dervish that coated both lead 'Mechs with a layer of ochre. He glanced

281

at his heat monitor and noticed that because of the external temperature, his 'Mech's monitor lights were already creeping into the yellow cautionary zone.

"Forgive me, *Tai-sa,* if your statement confuses me. Ever since you learned that Palmer Conti—at loose ends because of the attack on Dromini VI—jumped his Fifth Sword of Light Regiment in here to destroy the Kell Hounds ahead of us, you have driven us hard in a race you knew we could not win. You've heard the reports of combat communications. You know they joined in battle twenty hours ago, and you know it will be over by the time we get there."

In the silence that greeted his words, Akira visualized his father slowly shaking his head. "*Chu-sa* Brahe, I think you have made an error. Do you mean to suggest that I have pushed the *Genyosha* across this sandstone and lava-rock desert because I fear Conti will kill Morgan Kell?"

Akira swallowed against the fear gnawing at his stomach. "I think you have become wrapped up in personal rivalries. You even ignored a priority transmission from the Coordinator himself, directing you to break off this personal vendetta."

The strength in Yorinaga's voice reassured his son that his father had not abandoned reason. "You will learn, Akira, that there are times when your masters do not know what is right and proper in the world. The message from the Coordinator had obviously been garbled in transmission, for he would never deny me this battle with Morgan Kell. As for my haste in reaching the Kell Hounds, it is not based on any fear that the Fifth Sword of Light will rob me of my battle, or out of a desire to kill Palmer Conti. He is insignificant, and his quarrel with me is a war waged on his side alone. Indeed, I hurry us along because I merely wish to save the Dragon the embarrassment of their total destruction at the hands of the Kell Hounds."

Anger flared up in Akira. "Why is it you concern yourself with the Coordinator's honor? He denied you release while you waited in exile, then promised you the Kell Hounds' destruction as part of the price for your cooperation and leadership in the *Genyosha*. He has vacillated in his treatment of us, supporting us one moment, then leaving us like orphans to be spat on by units like the Fifth Sword. Even this last message, the one you choose to see as garbled, is meant to deny you vindication. You guard his honor, yet he gives you nothing but shame."

The anger in Yorinaga's voice told Akira he had struck a nerve, but the reply cut off all chance of further discussion. "I guard his honor because he is the Dragon. That is enough. My life, and the life of every person in the Draconis Combine, is his to play with, to use or to warp in any way he sees fit. He is the Dragon, and I live to serve him."

Yorinaga's voice lost some of its intensity. "We will not speak of this again, my son, for some might consider the conversation treasonous. There is no more time. We have arrived and must, once again, become warriors and serve the Way of the Sword."

Akira shifted his radio back to the tactical frequency he shared with his company. "Jack, I'm back, but I'll stay up here. If we get hit, we'll form up as the left flank. Have *Korasu* lance keep their eyes open on our back-trail."

Seaborg replied quickly and positively as Akira brought his *Orion* around the last bend in the canyon they had traveled to the heart of Nusakan's equatorial desert. Opening out away and down from his position, framed by canyon walls that widened out and vanished at the horizon, Akira saw a flat scarlet plain dotted with purplish succulent plants sprouting golden spikes. In the center of the plains rose up one massive mesa, shaped by eons of harsh desert winds. Like lesser Acolytes surrounding a Precentor, smaller outcroppings of purplish lava-rock rose up from the desert floor to surround the centerpiece.

Dragon's Blood! It's incredible! Mechanically, Akira directed his 'Mech forward into the desert valley, seeing but disbelieving everything. *Can anything be left, or has my father been cheated after all?*

Beginning at the valley entrance, the shattered bodies of Battle-Mechs lay scattered about. At first, Akira saw them as toys smashed in anger by a child, but he rejected that analogy. *The destruction here is too complete. A child would have been careless in lashing out. This is deliberate.*

'Mechs from the Fifth Sword of Light lay staring up at Nusakan's twin suns, the desert heat rising in blurry waves from their shapes. All had gaping rents in their armor. Limbs, broken and maimed beyond recognition, covered the sandy surface chaotically. In several places, one or two legs stood as monuments to the 'Mechs they had carried into battle, though no sign of their torsos remained.

Mixed among them, but too few in number for Akira's ease of mind, were 'Mechs with the black legs and red body color scheme favored by the Kell Hounds. Those 'Mechs, though equally as dead as the Draconian machines around them, had not been as savaged in battle. With the exception of two 'Mechs whose heads had been crushed, the Kell Hound war machines were uniformly missing their faceplates. *All this carnage, yet the Kell Hound pilots still managed to escaped their doomed 'Mechs. They value their lives over their honor and their machines.*

A shiver ran down Akira's spine. *The Coordinator directed us to destroy all the mercenaries on Northwind because he claimed mercenaries had no honor. When I faced Team Banzai on Northwind, I saw mercenaries fighting to save people not even in their company. Here these 'dishonorable' Kell Hounds have managed to rip up one of our best units and still save their pilots. I fear we too often die for honor in our 'Mechs rather than fight as best we can and escape to fight again.*

Catching sight of movement in the distance, Akira added magnification to his forward sensor readout and directed his attention to the large mesa. Before it, in an arena-like, bowl-shaped depression, two 'Mechs squared off. At the north side of the arena were several ranks of 'Mechs with their backs to the large mesa. Akira recognize their colors as those of the Kell Hounds. Opposite them, in the black and gold of the Fifth Sword of Light, a half dozen Kurita Mechs also watched the battle in the pit.

The Kell Hound 'Mech, a humanoid *Cyclops*, looked tired and battered. Armor hung from it in broken sheets. Its left leg, which had been virtually stripped of armor, had been fused at the knee. Despite its injuries, however, the 'Mech triggered a staggering burst from the autocannon mounted at its right hip, then drove in at its foe.

The *Banshee* it faced took the hail of slugs in the chest and rocked backward. Armor, the first it had lost in battle, streaked away in smoking shards. The crater in the armor looked like a raw wound over the *Banshee's* heart, but still showed evidence of yet more armor between the hole and the 'Mech's insides.

A transmission from one of a half-dozen other Fifth Sword 'Mechs watching the battle from close up crackled through Akira's neurohelmet. "Praise be to the Dragon! You have come. Now we can complete the destruction of the mercenary dogs. Hurry! When *Tai-sho* Conti destroys this Bradley, the Kell Hounds will kill him."

Yorinaga's sharp reply came quickly. "*Iie.* It is an even battle. The mercenaries will respect it."

The name "Bradley" rang a bell in Akira's mind. *Bradley...Scott Bradley. He commanded the mercenaries on Northwind. Conti's Fifth Sword used us to destroy Bradley's command while Conti ripped up the Davion garrison, the Fifth Deneb Light Cavalry. Bradley wants to avenge the warriors who died there.* Akira's tawny eyes narrowed. *How is it that a mercenary whose 'Mech has obviously seen battle can demand satisfaction of the Fifth Sword's leader and not know honor?*

The *Cyclops's* rush forward seemed to surprise the *Banshee's* pilot. As the Combine 'Mech twisted to avoid the brunt of the charge, the *Cyclops*'s balled left fist smashed into the *Banshee*'s right shoulder. With a sound like a thundercrack, the mechanical fist pulverized ceramic armor plates into dust.

The *Banshee* brought its left fist round in a murderous hook, but the *Cyclops* leaned dangerously to the right, ducking beneath the blow. Bradley pushed off with his good right leg and twisted awkwardly around to slam his Mech's right fist into the *Banshee*'s spine. More armor evaporated into dust, opening a hole in the *Banshee*'s back.

Unbalanced by the missed punch and sped on by the blow to the *Banshee*'s spine, the ninety-five-ton 'Mech pitched forward. Conti, reacting quickly, reached out and grabbed the *Cyclops*'s damaged left leg as he fell. Rolling the *Banshee*, he snapped the limb clean off, dropping the *Cyclops* onto its back.

Gracelessly, Palmer Conti brought his 'Mech to its feet and raised the *Cyclops*'s leg in both arms like a club. Flat on its back, the *Cyclops* lifted both arms to protect its head. Conti's voice, full of victory, filled the radiowaves with a wide-beam broadcast. "That, Major Bradley," he boasted, "is why your people died on Northwind!"

A gout of red-gold flame erupted from the *Cyclops*'s autocannon muzzle. The stream of shells it spat out sliced into the *Banshee*'s right armpit like a chainsaw. Armor parted like tissue paper and rained down confetti-like over the arena. Myomer muscles snapped like rubber bands stressed beyond tolerance and the ferro-titanium ball-and-socket shoulder joint gave way. Still clutching the *Cyclops*'s leg in its fist, the *Banshee*'s arm sailed from the arena.

The impact of the autocannon's fire spun the *Banshee* to the right. The *Cyclops* lashed out with its leg, crushing armor on the *Banshee*'s left ankle and slamming that leg against the *Banshee*'s other leg. The *Banshee* flailed madly against the air in a vain attempt to regain its balance, then toppled slowly and inexorably onto its face.

The *Cyclops* flipped itself over onto its stomach, then dragged itself around to the *Banshee*. Resting its torso against the *Banshee*'s body to pin it to the ground, the *Cyclops* reached out with both hands. In one deft, savage motion, the *Cyclops* ripped the *Banshee*'s head from its shoulders and victoriously thrust it aloft in its right hand.

The *Banshee*'s faceplate exploded outward, dissolving into a blizzard of glittering glass fragments. Conti's command couch blew through the smoke and fire, then slowed as the gyrojet stabilizers ignited. The MechWarrior floated gently to the desert floor, freed himself from the safety straps, then gesticulated wildly toward the mesa and the mercenaries.

285

One of the Fifth Sword's 'Mechs moved forward, but a jagged bolt of PPC lightning from Yorinaga Kurita's 'Mech stopped it. "No more. Your fight is done."

An excited voice replied over the radio, "But *Tai-sho* Conti directs us to battle for the glory of the Dragon!"

"As he has done?" The biting edge in Yorinaga's voice mocked the warrior's devotion to Conti. "Stand aside, all of you. If you do not, I will order my *Genyosha* to destroy you."

After a moment's hesitation, the Fifth Sword's 'Mechs withdrew, opening a path from Yorinaga to the arena. The *Cyclops*, refusing aid, had dragged itself free of the pit. Several other Kell Hound 'Mechs moved into the depression and cleared away the *Banshee*'s headless corpse. Their task complete, they resumed their places among the mercenaries.

Morgan Kell's *Archer* stepped from amid the Kell Hounds and slowly stalked down into the arena. The valley's red dust covered it except where the flaming exhaust of launched missiles had burned the 'Mech's shoulders black. Though showing every sign of having engaged in combat, its armor was somehow undented, untouched. The *Archer* stopped at the north edge of the depression's floor and waited.

Akira watched his father's *Warhammer* advance like a man welcoming his destiny, but afraid he would fail in attaining it. *For thirteen years he has dreamed of this battle*. Akira looked over at his targeting crosshairs as he brushed them over both 'Mechs. His computer acknowledged neither of them.

As his father's *Warhammer* entered the arena, Akira suddenly remembered the chilling words once spoken to him by Jaime Wolf, one of the most feared MechWarriors in the Successor States. When Akira had asked Wolf to explain what his father and Morgan Kell had discussed cryptically at Hanse Davion's wedding, the mercenary had stared at him for a moment with his predator's-eyes. "It's simple, *Chusa* Brahe," Wolf said. "Morgan Kell and Yorinaga Kurita both know that the next time they meet in combat, they will kill one another."

49

Andrew Redburn adjusted the contrast on his *Marauder*'s auxiliary monitor. It carried a live feed from the Capellan State Broadcasting Facility's coverage of Morgan Hasek-Davion's arrival. A glance at his primary monitor showed him that the DropShip hung five kilometers above the planet's surface and was descending at a little less than a hundred kilometers per hour. Looking at the seconds tick on the digital display at the corner of the drop chart, Andrew opened a channel to his command. "Mark, three minutes thirty seconds to drop."

He heard the acknowledgements of his communication, mentally checking off each voice as it came through his neurohelmet, but his attention centered on the holovid feed from the ground. The camera panned over the reviewing stand and the dignitaries gathered to greet Hanse Davion's captive heir. Behind the stand, all shiny, tall, and proud, stood the 'Mechs of House Imarra's two battalions to welcome their esteemed visitor. *If Morgan's spy reports are true, they won't be much trouble.* Fluttering behind the stand were massive gold banners with the Hasek lion crest worked in red. Similarly designed pennants snapped in the breeze atop flagpoles.

The camera zoomed in as it made a pass across the nobles crowding the reviewing stand. It lingered for a few seconds on each face, waiting just long enough for technicians to display the Capellan pictographs for each person's name down the right side of the screen. When the image of the last man on the left materialized on the screen,

287

Andrew felt ice-water flush through his guts.

Good, Justin. You're here. That means the Capellans have been taken by surprise. Andrew ground his teeth together. *Had you been on your game, Xiang, you would have been waiting for me in your vaunted* Yen-lo-wang. *I guess that means I will just have to wait for you.*

Justin tugged at his black jacket's uncomfortably tight collar. "I hate this uniform. It makes me feel like a Jesuit."

Candace, standing beside him on the reviewing platform, patted his shoulder reassuringly. "You need only endure it a moment or two longer, my love." She smoothed out a wrinkle on the sleeve of her smoke-gray silk blouse. "I wish the ship would get down here so my sister will stop preening herself."

Justin glanced over at Romano. The low-cut backless red dress she wore seemed appropriate for the day's heat, but not the occasion of greeting Hanse Davion's heir. *If she means to catch Morgan's attention, she should have no problem. Maybe she's planning to seduce him and use him to lead the Capellan March into some crusade to recover what Hanse Davion has won away in this war?* Justin frowned. *Of course, that's what she's planning—the plan is simple, shallow, and centered around her. Tsen's not noticed because he's irritated by his inability to break Alexi and get him to talk.*

Candace pointed toward the sky. "There! It's coming in on final approach."

Maximilian Liao, dressed in a golden silk robe trimmed with black at the hem, neck, and sleeves, smiled and adjusted the black Mandarin's cap on his head. "Finally, to have a weapon against Hanse Davion—one that will cripple and kill him."

Justin nodded along with the Chancellor. *Having Morgan fall into our hands is indeed a blow to the Federated Suns.*

From his position at Liao's right, Tsen Shang spoke up loudly enough for the holovid microphones to hear. "Your words echo my own thoughts, Celestial Wisdom. This is a great day, indeed."

Justin looked up, his left hand shielding his eyes from the glare of the DropShip's landing rockets. Motion high up on the hull caught his attention, then gave him a jolt. *What in hell is going on?*

The DropShip's missile pods snapped open, freeing a cargo of missiles. They rocketed away on jets of yellow-white flame, arcing down toward the landing zone, but never reached the reviewing stand or the 'Mechs arrayed behind it. They exploded thunderously overhead, filling the air with a thick, blinding, green smoke.

288

The explosion's shockwave tossed Justin back off the reviewing stand. He landed hard on his right hip, but rolled up into a crouch. *We're under attack. That ship has to be crawling with Federated troops...*

The screams of the spectators replaced the explosion-born ringing in his ears, and Justin suddenly realized something was very wrong. *Candace! Where is she?* He stood and tried to see through the heavy smoke, but all he could make out were splotches of people running madly back and forth. "Candace!" he shouted. "Candace! Where are you?"

The gas burned his throat, coating his mouth and tongue with a slick, sour taste. He had to find her. Though Candace's disappearance pushed him toward panic, years of combat training overrode his emotions. *Stop it, Justin. Think clearly. If she's dead, she's dead. If she's alive, she'll head into the Palace. You know that's where you should be.*

Justin took off in a low sprint for the Palace 'Mech bay. He heard the hideous snapping and crackling of PPC discharges. As he dodged the advance of a Liao *Locust*, he heard the whine of an autocannon. The *Locust* exploded in an argent plasma ball, producing a shockwave that knocked him rolling to the 'Mech bay's personnel door. Shaking his head to clear it, Justin stood and opened the hangar door.

Morgan Hasek-Davion's voice echoed confidently through the radio speakers. "This is it, people. We drop at fifteen meters. It'll be confusing out there, so keep your heads on. Don't crush any civilians. You won't know the agent until you're given the countersign. Remember, it's 'Sic Semper Tyrannis.' That's old Terra Latin for 'Thus ever to tyrants.' You've all got it digitized into your computers to check in case you don't hear it right. It's more than just the countersign. It's our motto for this assault. Let's show this tyrant what the Lions of Davion are made of!"

The ground feed focused on the descending DropShip, then tightened in as the *Overlord* Class DropShip's LRM pods opened and launched scores of missiles. The missiles traveled only a short distance before they exploded, filling the air with a greasy green smoke. The live picture went black as the drop hatch below Andrew's *Marauder* opened up.

The heavy, birdlike 'Mech landed solidly on the ferrocrete. The ringing collision of feet on earth sent a shudder up through the 'Mech, but Andrew balanced himself and his war machine instantly. His right hand punched two buttons on his command console, shifting his sensors over to magscan. *That'll cut through this gas.*

The sensors painted him a picture of the action taking place within the verdant fog that drifted over the scene. The House Imarra 'Mechs, drawn as yellow skeletons on the display, had already begun to break ranks, but Andrew ignored them. Hitting another button on his console, he engaged a search routine he'd programmed into his battle computer earlier. The holographic images wavered, then a small circle surrounded what appeared to be an L-shaped metallic cylinder roughly 45 centimeters in length.

Andrew smiled. *Got you! Your metal arm gives you away.* Andrew's joy at having located Justin vanished along with the image his search program had created. *Gone. Ducked back into the Palace barracks. Going for his 'Mech, I bet. All the better.*

Swirling through the green mist, a Liao *Crusader* charged at Andrew. In an instant he dropped the *Marauder*'s targeting crosshairs on the humanoid 'Mech's outline, then triggered both PPCs. Dancing forks of blue lightning rippled up and down the *Crusader*'s right arm. Glowing gobs of molten armor dripped from the 'Mech like liquid glass. Exposed by the PPC assault, myomer muscles, blacker and heavier than those familiar to Andrew, contracted to bring the arm-mounted laser into play.

Suddenly, the muscles began to smolder. An oily vapor rose from them as the *Crusader*'s pilot struggled to make the limb respond, then the muscles burst into flame. Burning droplets of molten myomer splashed over the *Crusader*'s leg and streamed to the ferrocrete. The limb, engulfed in the fire of its own muscles, swung like a man hanging from a gibbet.

Andrew opened a radio frequency to Morgan. "It works. Exposed to the gas, the myomer they stole from Bethel ignites when they run power through it to make it contract!"

"Yes!" Morgan roared back triumphantly. "But take care anyway. Until the muscle hits this gas, it's very powerful."

As if he had overheard Morgan Hasek-Davion's warning, the *Crusader*'s pilot continued his rush forward, left arm raised to club Andrew's 'Mech. Andrew immediately dropped the *Marauder* under the blow, then lunged up and stabbed both arms into the *Crusader*'s midsection. The double-claw punch shattered the armor over the humanoid 'Mech's abdomen and lifted it three meters into the air.

The *Crusader* landed unsteadily on its feet and then, like a boxer with round heels, toppled ungracefully backward. Wary of the 'Mech's powerful legs, Andrew fired one PPC bolt into the ruin his punch had made of the *Crusader*'s stomach. The searing particle beam blasted away what little armor remained and exposed the Mech's inner workings to the battlefog.

As the pilot tried to force his 'Mech back upright, fire erupted in the *Crusader*'s belly, but Andrew ignored it. A Liao *Marauder* streaked past in front of him, its legs burning like torches. Finally, the last of the myomer melted away, sprawling the *Marauder* on its back. Sparks flew from beneath it as the 'Mech's armor ripped free on the ferrocrete deck.

Justin thrust the door shut behind him, then bent down to breathe the hangar's cleaner air. He wiped the tears from his eyes and inhaled deeply, soothing the burning in his chest and throat. *The gas isn't meant for anti-personnel use or it would have done more than make my eyes water and torch my throat. They only brought an* Overlord, *which means they've got a battalion at best. They aren't here for the duration, so this must be a pick-up or quick raid.* Then the truth dawned on him. *Only Hanse Davion would dare be so bold in an effort to recover an agent. If it's an agent Davion wants, it's an agent he'll get.*

Justin sprinted the length of a hallway, then shot down three flights of stairs. At the bottom, he hammered on the heavy security door until a slovenly guard opened it. "*Shonso* Xiang, what can I do for you?"

Justin brushed his way past the man into the small watch station. "There is an emergency. We need the prisoner. Tsen Shang sent me to get him." Justin studied the bank of holovid monitors lining the walls. Each revealed the interior of a high-security Maskirovka holding cell, but only one was occupied.

The guard frowned and glanced at the visiphone. "I've had no word."

Justin looked at him sternly. "I said *emergency*, you idiot. Do you want to explain the delay to Shang or the Chancellor?"

The guard shook his head. Pulling a magcard key from the wallet chained to his belt, he inserted it into the lockslot on the door. With a click, the mechanism opened and Justin wrenched the heavy door open. He dashed down the small corridor and stopped in front of Alexi's cell.

Justin waited for the guard to reach him. "Quick! Open it."

The little man's piggish eyes grew wide. "But Tsen Shang has taken the only keycard for this door…" Realizing what he'd said, the guard began to backpedal.

Dammit! Justin pounced on him like a leopard, carrying the man to the ground. Justin blocked a flailed punch with his right arm, then delivered a savage chop to the throat. The guard gurgled and died.

Justin crossed back to Alexi's cell. "Alexi, this is Justin. Stand away from the door."

Alexi's voice, weak and full of confusion, reached Justin through the door's narrow viewport. "What? Justin?"

"Stand back!"

Justin stripped the glove off his left hand and curled the middle and ring fingers into his palm. Grasping the artificial hand with his right, he pulled the hand out away from the wrist, twisted it ninety degrees to the left so the thumb was up, and pulled again. The whole hand turned back flat, then slid back along the top of his forearm. At the wrist, where the hand had been, the dungeon's dim light glinted from the muzzle of a laser weapon.

Justin snapped the index and little fingers of his left hand up to form a crude open sight for the weapon. He centered the door's lock between the two fingers, then tightened the muscles of his upper arm. A coruscating green beam of laser light stabbed deep into the door's lock. In seconds the mechanism boiled away to nothingness and the beam snapped off abruptly.

Justin frowned as smoke rose through from the cloth of his sleeve. *Damn. The lasing cell is gone. I'd hoped to coax more than three shots out of it.* He moved his left hand back down into place and flexed it. Mindless of the heat, he reached his left hand into the lockhole and pulled the door open.

Alexi Malenkov had backed himself into the corner of his cell like a wild animal. "It won't work, Justin. I know about friend/foe interrogation techniques. I don't care how elaborate your charade is, I won't tell you anything!"

The wildness in Alexi's blue eyes and the fear in his voice told Justin that his former aide was near the breaking point. Justin opened his hands. "Come with me, Alexi. Davion troops have landed and they'll rip this place apart looking for you. I'm going to give you up and defect at the same time. My position here is no longer tenable."

The hope that flashed in Alexi's eyes sank beneath utter disbelief. "No. It won't work. You'd never do that. You hate the Federated Suns more than Maximilian Liao himself."

Justin's face hardened. "Have it your way. I'm doing this for you, this once. I owe you. For Bethel."

The anger in Justin's voice shocked its way through Alexi's delirium. The Federated agent slumped forward and Justin caught him. "Can you walk, Alexi. Can you?"

Haggard and exhausted, Alexi nodded weakly. "Some. My feet hurt, but I'll manage." His right arm, which he'd draped over Justin's shoulders, tightened down around Justin's neck. "Never work, Justin!"

Justin, feeling the arm move, ducked his head out of the stranglehold and shoved Alexi across the hallway into the wall. Alexi rebounded, turning to face the Maskirovka agent, but Justin laid him out with a right hook to the jaw. Alexi slumped down over the body of the guard.

Andrew blasted an *Enforcer* that barred his way to the Palace 'Mech bay. The Liao 'Mech's autocannon blew a series of craters into the armor over the *Marauder's* right thigh while the large laser burned a scar across the heavy 'Mech's left arm. Andrew's assault, mixing the PPC and medium laser of his right arm with the torso-mounted autocannon's metal storm, stripped the armor off the *Enforcer's* right side.

Like a living creature suffering a stroke, the *Enforcer* shuddered when its right flank ignited. The torso muscles controlling movement of the right arm burned through in an instant, dropping the autocannon's muzzle toward the ground. At the same time, thigh muscle insertions in the abdomen melted away. Robbed of stability and mobility, the *Enforcer* crashed to the ground.

Three long strides deeper into the fog brought Andrew to the Palace 'Mech bay doors. He hammered both of the *Marauder's* arms in overhand blows against the doors. Amid the screams of torn metal hinges and snapping chains, half of the doors collapsed and green vapor drifted into the bay.

Andrew moved with it, and toward the back of the structure, he found what he was looking for. *Yen-lo-wang* stood silent and solitary guard beside the entrance to the Palace proper. Andrew smiled, raising the *Marauder's* arms in a silent challenge, then noticed that the 'Mech's canopy hung open and the pilot's ladder had been run out from the cockpit to the floor.

He walked the *Marauder* over beside the *Centurion*, then hunkered down. *If you aren't here now, you will be later. I can wait.* He nodded to himself as he watched the door into the Palace. *I can wait as long as it takes.*

293

Justin knelt by Alexi, pressing two fingers to either side of the man's Adam's apple to check his pulse. *Rapid and strong. Good.* Justin looked at the filthy prison clothes they'd given Alexi and at the burn marks on his toes from where they'd strapped electrodes during interrogation. *All that and you didn't break? Where the hell does my father find people like you?*

Justin hefted Alexi up onto his left shoulder and carried him from the security cell area. As he ascended the stairs from the depths of the dungeons, the sounds of fighting grew louder and the thick scent of burning myomer hung in the air. Panicked servants ran through the hallways and corridors, but no one so much as slowed when they saw Justin.

The Maskirovka man chewed his lower lip. *I have Alexi out of his cell. Now how do I get the both of us to the Feds?* An even larger problem loomed up in his mind. *And how the hell do I get out of here?*

He glanced down the corridor leading to the 'Mech bay. *With all the fighting going on outside,* Yen-lo-wang *seems to make sense. Everything I need's in there.* Smiling, Justin kicked open the door to the 'Mech bay and stepped through.

His smile died as the *Marauder* reared up on its feet and shoved both arms toward him. Andrew Redburn's voice, full of anger and ridicule, burst from the *Marauder*'s external speakers. "I knew you'd come here, Justin Xiang, and I've been waiting." Andrew's cruel laughter filled the bay. "Any last words before I blow you away?"

294

50

Daniel Allard tightbeamed a radio message to Morgan Kell as his *Archer* marched into the arena. "Colonel, don't! You don't have to do this. We're not back on Mallory's World. We can take them—even after fighting against the Fifth Sword, we outnumber them."

Morgan's deep voice came back strong and calm. "Thank you for that observation, Captain Allard. What you do not realize is that, in the end, it would come down to this fight between Yorinaga Kurita and me. It's better this way."

Dan frowned, but words failed him as Yorinaga's *Warhammer*, in its march to the arena, moved into Dan's sights. Automatically, Dan's right hand kept the crosshairs trained on the large, PPC-armed BattleMech, but his computer never even acknowledged the *Warhammer's* existence. *Just like Morgan on Mallory's World and just the way Yorinaga was when he killed Patrick Kell.*

Dan shifted his crosshairs over to Morgan's *Archer* and saw the instruments ignored him as well. *These two...the computer pays no more attention to them than it would to ghosts.* A sudden shiver ran down his spine. *Perhaps that's it. Maybe they should have died back on Mallory's World and the computers understood that. They've just been waiting for living folks to realize it as well.*

Morgan's voice filled Dan's neurohelmet, but he knew instantly that Morgan was not speaking for his benefit. "I am Morgan Kell. I apologize for missing our appointment on Ryde."

Yorinaga's reply came in precise, practiced English. "I am Yorinaga Kurita. I apologize for the intervention of these other warriors. Yorinaga hesitated for a moment, then continued. "If you require time to re-arm your 'Mech, we can temporarily postpone this battle."

"I thank you for your courtesy, but that is not necessary."

The echoes of Morgan's reply still ringing in his ears, Dan keyed up a radio frequency he knew Cat Wilson monitored. "Cat, I thought Morgan was out of missiles. Did you see him re-arm?"

Cat's bass voice contained a disquieting note of concern. "No."

Dan's mouth went dry. "What's going on?"

The doubtful tone of Cat's voice undercut the confidence of his words. "Morgan knows what he's doing. This is his fight."

Morgan's *Archer* executed a slight bow in Yorinaga's direction. "Thirteen years ago, in a battle between us, I discovered something within myself that could make me invincible. I spent the next twelve years in a monastery running away from it."

Yorinaga returned the bow with his *Warhammer*. "In that same battle I saw, in you, the seeds of invincibility. In exile in a Zen monastery, I spent the next eleven years remembering, studying, and working to gain your secret. Now I believe I share your gift, but the only way to test that belief is to defeat you."

Controlled fury poured through Morgan's voice. "You call it a gift, but that gift is a horrible and terrible burden. I stalked the battlefields on Lyons and here on Nusakan knowing none of those I faced could touch me. Look at this *Archer*! After a day in the heart of battle I am untouched! At the same time, there is not a 'Mech I targeted that did not go down. They were like children, like toys. They stood no chance."

Puzzlement underscored Yorinaga's reply. "And you consider this a burden? You are a warrior, as was your brother and as am I. Does not our vocation demand us to become as great as possible? Is that not what you see as the pinnacle of attainment? We honor those we destroy by giving them a warrior's death."

Morgan's voice was grim and flat. "Death honors no one, and if we fight, we will kill each other. You know that, as do I. I offer you this chance. Let us both be reasonable. Let us both walk away and return to exile."

"To do this would bring shame upon us both, Colonel Kell."

"I don't care about shame, *Tai-sa* Kurita." Morgan's voice faded to a whisper. "I will not kill you."

The *Warhammer* bowed again. "Then I must kill you."

Searing blue snakes of man-made lightning struck from the *War-*

hammer's forearm-mounted PPCs. One gnawed hunks of half-melted ceramic sheeting from the virgin armor on the *Archer*'s right arm. The second particle beam slashed like a swordcut across the *Archer*'s midsection, dropping a ribbon of molten armor to the ochre talus at the pit floor.

Morgan moved the *Archer* to the right, but failed to bring the 'Mech's arms up to use the medium lasers mounted therein. Dan marveled at the agility and grace of the maneuver, but Morgan's lack of offense confused him. *Hit him, Morgan. You picked Sword 'Mechs apart like a surgeon. Nail him!*

Yorinaga's right PPC lashed the *Archer* with another azure energy beam. It flayed armor from over the 'Mech's heart, blasting more shrapnel down into the debris that lined the arena. The *Warhammer*'s medium lasers likewise ripped armor from the 'Mech's body. Two parallel scars ran from the *Archer*'s right shoulder to its abdomen, blackened, melted armor puckering up on both sides of them.

A flight of SRMs leaped from the launching rack on the *Warhammer*'s right side. They peppered the *Archer* with a series of explosions that chipped armor away. One slammed into the *Archer*'s right shoulder, destroying Morgan's regimental identifier, but failed to pierce the *Archer*'s armored hide.

Morgan lunged the *Archer* forward, but Yorinaga danced the *Warhammer* backward, circling to his right. The *Warhammer*'s twin lasers stabbed out from its chest and lanced into the *Archer*. One melted a crater into the armor on the *Archer*'s left arm, while the other whittled away all but the last of the armor over the *Archer*'s heart.

Yorinaga swung both of his PPCs into line with the advancing *Archer*, triggering another pure energy assault. The cerulean beams vaporized all the remaining armor on the *Archer*'s right arm, then ate away the myomer muscles driving the heavy limb. Their vitality not yet spent, they reduced the *Archer*'s ferro-titanium arm bone to argent metallic mist and hurled the arm from the arena.

The *Archer*, just as it had done thirteen years before, stumbled and fell to its knees.

Dan's heart rose to his throat. *It's happening again, but Morgan's not fighting back. It's like he wants to die, to die the way he should have on Mallory's World!* Dan beamed an urgent message to the *Archer*. *"Dammit, Morgan! Do something! Do something or you're dead!"*

Morgan did not reply over the radio, but Dan knew he'd been heard when the *Archer*'s LRM launch pods snapped open on the humanoid 'Mech's shoulders.

Yorinaga let loose with every weapon on his 'Mech. Exploding missiles wreathed the *Archer* in flames and shrapnel. A cloud of PPC-spawned plasma rolled over the mercenary's 'Mech, boiling off armor in its hellish heat. The *Warhammer's* medium lasers raked like talons across the *Archer's* armored hulk, and its small lasers cored twin holes like a viper strike on their target's left leg. The Kuritan's chest-mounted chain gun vomited a dizzying hail of bullets into the maelstrom of destruction, blasting little bits of armor away with their metallic bites.

Dan slammed his fist against his command console. "Now, Morgan! Use the missiles!"

The *Archer* closed the empty missile launching pods and struggled to its feet. More gracefully and honorably than Dan could ever have imagined, the *Archer* executed a bow. After long moments of stunned horror, he finally looked away from the *Archer* toward its foe.

Smoke seeped from the shoulders, hips, and neck of the *Warhammer* in black plumes that rose straight through the still desert air to the heavens. The Kurita 'Mech tried to execute a bow in return, but the motion only produced more smoke and locked the *Warhammer* forward, with its head bowed.

Dan shifted his sensors over to infrared and shielded his eyes against the glare of the display. *In this heat, in the desert, Yorinaga burned his* Warhammer *up*. Dan glanced at Morgan's *Archer*, comparing its relatively cool maroon outline with the *Warhammer's* bright white silhouette. *Did Morgan expect this?*

The Kell Hound commander's voice crackled over the radio. "Forgive me for being such a coward, Yorinaga-*sama*. If we fought, I knew we would kill each other. I refuse to have your blood on my hands. I meant you no dishonor."

Yorinaga's reply, full of exhaustion yet somehow more serene now, sent a shiver down Dan's spine. "I see now what I should have seen so long ago: there is no shame in being unable to defeat a superior adversary. I was wrong to believe that to become invincible is the apex of the Way of the Sword. To do what you have done, to win while refusing to fight, this is the ultimate. My shame is that I failed to understand this reality before."

51

Sian
Sian Commonality, Capellan Confederation
24 October 3029

"Sic semper tyrannis."

The words hung heavily in the air between Justin and the *Marauder* like the green smoke wafting through the shattered doorway. Justin shifted his gaze from the bore of the PPC leveled at his head to the polarized canopy over the 'Mech's cockpit.

Andrew's hushed voice crackled through the *Marauder's* external speakers. "What the hell did you say?"

Weariness entered Justin's voice. "I said sic semper tyrannis."

The edge returned to Andrew's voice. "The guy on your shoulder, he's got to be our agent. How did you get the countersign out of him?"

Justin shook his head. "You're right. He is one of ours." Justin stared at the *Marauder's* dark cockpit. "You know me, Andy. If I'd wanted to fool you, I'd not have brought him along. Sic semper tyrannis—I want to go home."

"Jesus, Mary, and Joseph! It is you! You're it!" Andrew's voice echoed with joyous surprise and relief. "Thank God I didn't pull the trigger on you without wanting to rub your face in it first. Damn…"

Justin laughed aloud. "I'm glad it was you that found me. Anyone else and I'd be ion vapor right now." Justin motioned for Andrew to squat his 'Mech back down again. "This guy really is one of ours, and we're going to get him out, too. Crack your hatch and pull him aboard."

Andrew lowered the *Marauder* and opened the hatch in the top of the torso. He stepped down on the 'Mech's right arm and got his hands under Malenkov's armpits. With Justin's help, he pulled Alexi into the *Marauder* and strapped him into a jump seat behind the command couch.

Andrew handed Justin a canvas satchel. "Everybody got one of these. We were told to give it to our agent."

Justin smiled and slung it over his shoulder. "Yeah. It's got some things I can use if I have the time." Justin popped his head out of the hatch and looked around for Liao infantry. "Looks safe enough for now. Spread the word. Let them know I'll be coming out in *Yen-lo-wang.*"

Redburn glanced at his chronometer. "You've got ten minutes. We've been down for twenty. Our window is closing."

Justin winked at him. "Got it." The slender MechWarrior hoisted himself out of the *Marauder*, then looked back in. He extended his hand to Redburn, who shook it heartily. "Take good care of Alexi there. He saved my life, just like you did once. I owe him."

Redburn nodded solemnly. "Then I'm in his debt too for saving a friend of mine. Good luck."

Justin slid from the *Marauder*'s torso and ran back into the Capellan Chancellor's Palace. Racing through the corridors, he reached the Chancellor's throne room without incident. He cracked open the massive bronze doors just enough for him to slip into the room, then silently made his way down the length of red carpet and mounted the steps to the throne itself.

Justin smiled as he swung the satchel around and unfastened the velcro strips holding it shut. In addition to some standard medical gear, a Davion ID module for a 'Mech, and a replacement lasing cell for his arm, he found a holodisk with the Davion sunburst and sword crest. As he had been directed, Justin deposited the disk in the center of the throne's seat, then turned and descended the steps.

Her voice and the sound of a needle pistol being charged behind him, stopped Justin a half-dozen steps away from the throne. "Who are you, Justin Xiang, and why are you here?"

He turned slowly to face her, raising his weaponless hands. "Major Justin Allard, Armed Forces of the Federated Suns, currently on special assignment."

Candace moved forward into the muted half-light coming down from the lattice-worked balconies. The needle pistol in her right hand did not waver. "This special assignment…" Her voice trailed off as anger and other emotions strangled it to silence.

Justin raised his head. "To convince Maximilian Liao that House

Davion had perfected a new and improved myomer fiber and to get him to equip his 'Mechs with it."

Candace's gray eyes glittered coldly. "And becoming part of the crisis team?"

Justin shrugged. "I was to suggest the formation of such a thing because Alexi would have been a logical choice to work in it. I knew he was a Davion plant, but he did not know who or what I was. No one did except my father, the Prince, and Ardan Sortek. And Sortek only learned of it because he threatened to go public with his outrage over my trial."

"Why did you do it?"

Justin moistened his lips with the tip of his tongue. "Orders. I pledged my loyalty to Prince Hanse Davion, and this is what he asked me to do."

Her eyes narrowed to steel slivers. "And what about me? Was *I* something he asked you *do*?"

"No." Justin lowered his hands. "I wanted to—I really tried to—avoid you. I knew this would happen. I knew we would fall in love... And I do love you very, very much. You *must* believe me."

"What I believe, Justin Allard, is that you have proved yourself a very convincing liar in the past."

Justin nodded his head sadly. "Then I guess you have two choices. You can shoot me," he said, meeting her arctic stare, "or you can come with me."

Her finger tightened on the trigger and her gun lipped a long flame. The cloud of plastic needles it shot out passed wide of Justin, smashing Tsen Shang back into one of the bronze doors and chasing the two Maskirovka agents with him back out into corridor.

She triggered two more blasts at the door as Justin scrambled to cover behind the throne, then she ducked back as ruby laser bolts burned into the walls behind her. Kneeling down beside Justin, she gave him a quick smile, then poked her pistol back around the throne and fired another pair of shots.

"Damn this pistol." She stared at the gun as she moved the selector lever from single shot to three-shot burst. "Fine for shooting people, but the needles can't get through the bronze doors." She glanced over at Justin. "I'm sorry we're both going to die here, but I can't think of anyone else I'd rather spend the rest of my life with."

Justin returned her smile. "Keep them busy for a moment, if you really mean that 'rest of your life' remark."

As Candace triggered a burst that kept the guards back behind the doors, Justin ripped the left sleeve of his jacket open to the elbow. He

301

depressed a rectangular section on top of his blackened steel forearm, then flipped it up with his thumbnail when it clicked. He twisted his left arm, dropping the burned-out lasing cell to the throne room floor. He fished the replacement cell from his satchel and slid it into place. He snapped the coverplate back down, then worked his hand off and configured it for sighting.

Candace stared quizzically at his left hand's awkward position. "What in the name of…"

Justin smiled. "I'm double-jointed. Are they behind both doors?"

She nodded. "They're keeping their heads down. You can see where I've scraped some varnish from the doors."

"Got it. On three."

Candace counted off, then triggered a long burst from the right side of the throne. Justin popped out to the left and sliced the laser's green beam through both bronze doors about a meter above the floor. The clatter of metal hitting the ground drowned out the guards' dying screams.

Candace took Justin's right hand in her left as they sprinted past Tsen Shang and into the corridor outside the throne room. They raced through the hall of portraits and into the 'Mech bay. Candace strapped herself into the jump seat on the right side of the *Centurion*'s cockpit while Justin closed the canopy and went through the ignition sequence.

He pulled the Davion ID module from his satchel and inserted it into a slot beneath the command console. With it firmly in place, he flipped the 'Mech's radio over to Davion military frequencies. "Changeling to Davion Force Commander. I'm coming out of the 'Mech bay in a Solaris-style *Centurion*."

Justin recognized Morgan Hasek-Davion's voice. "Long way from home, aren't you, Changeling?"

Justin laughed and saw Candace, who had plugged an auxiliary headset into the jack near her head, smile widely. "Roger that, Commander." Justin guided the *Centurion* through the 'Mech bay and out through the opening Andrew had created earlier. The mist had all but dissipated, though the thick, black smoke produced by burning myomer had replaced it.

He saw an *Atlas* standing halfway between the 'Mech bay and the DropShip. The broken bodies of a half-dozen burning 'Mechs surrounded it, yet the damage done to the Atlas had barely scratched its armor. Though no moving Liao 'Mechs were visible on the field, the *Atlas* stood guard while the other Davion 'Mechs reboarded the DropShip.

Justin smiled to himself. *That has to be Morgan.* "Going my way?"

The *Atlas* waved him forward with its left hand. "Wouldn't think of leaving without you. Next stop: home."

52

Nusakan
Isle of Skye, Lyran Commonwealth
24 October 3029

From his position in the front rank of the Kell Hounds, Dan Allard marveled at the peace on Yorinaga Kurita's face. The Combine MechWarrior, flanked sides and back by a half-dozen of his *Genyosha*, walked around to the north side of the hastily erected platform where his son waited, and stepped up onto it. *He looks more like someone heading to some pleasant social occasion than to his own death.*

Walking to the platform's western edge, he removed the formal gray *shitagi* bearing the *Genyosha* crest on the sleeves, breasts, and back. He exchanged it for a *kimono* of purest white and slipped it over his bared torso. Yorinaga bowed his head to the man who assisted him in the change of clothing, then turned and crossed back to the center of the platform. There, where two white *tatami* mats had been laid out in a T pattern, Yorinaga knelt with his back to Akira Brahe and faced south.

Clad in the *Genyosha's* formal gray raiment, another assistant brought Yorinaga a tray bearing a *sake* flask and a small cup. Grasping the barrel of the flask in his left hand, Yorinaga poured the *sake* to the left, filling the cup in two motions. As he watched the Kurita warrior lift the cup to his lips, Dan recalled what he had been told of this portion of the ceremony. *He'll drain the cup in four swallows—two and two—because the Japanese word* shi *means both "four" and "death."*

Yorinaga replaced the empty cup, and the aide whisked it away

304

silently. He held his head high, then bared his chest and abdomen by stripping the *kimono* open in the front and bringing the neck of the garment to the middle of his back. He carefully folded the sleeves beneath his ankles so the *kimono* would prevent his body from falling backward in the moment of death.

The elder MechWarrior looked out over the assembly of mercenaries and Combine MechWarriors. "I thank you for honoring me with your presence today." With hands resting on his knees, he glanced to his left and nodded. *Tai-sho* Palmer Conti brought a white tray bearing a paper-wrapped knife onto the platform and set it down near Yorinaga's left hand. He bowed and withdrew.

Akira Brahe, acting as Yorinaga's *kaishaku*, readied himself for his part in the ritual suicide. Also wearing a white robe, Akira rose up from his seated position to his left knee. He slid a white-hilted *katana* from its scabbard and raised it high over his head in his right hand. His tawny eyes measured the distance from himself to the back of his father's neck, then his left hand closed on the hilt.

As assistant, Akira must strike off Yorinaga's head before Yorinaga can dishonor himself with any show of pain. Dan studied the fierce expression on Akira's face. *It's tearing him up, but he is determined not to dishonor his father.*

Sunlight glinted sharply from the bared tip of the seppuku knife as Yorinaga grasped it in his right hand. Razored edge to the right, he plunged the blade into his belly over his left hip and drew it across to the right. Then he twisted the blade and made a *jumonji* —a crosswise cut coming up. His body rock-still, his control unbroken, Yorinaga withdrew the gore-streaked knife and brought his right hand to rest on his knee again.

Akira's sword flashed down, severing his father's neck completely and ending the agonies Yorinaga never permitted to show on his face. The headless body wavered for a moment, then sagged forward.

Allard, Ward, Wilson, and the rest of the Kell Hounds watched the senseless and barbaric loss of life in horror. No matter how familiar they were with the *seppuku* ceremony, they could not reconcile it with their values.

From within the breast of his *kimono*, Akira drew a thickness of white rice paper, folded into a triangle. Using it, he grasped Yorinaga's head by the hair and raised it up. He showed it to *Chu-sa* Narimasa Asano, who nodded, confirming Yorinaga's death. Akira reverently lowered the head back beside the body, then used the paper to cleanse the blade.

Akira backed to his earlier position and slid the *katana* home into its white scabbard. He bowed in the direction of his father, and according to tradition, should have withdrawn as the attendants bore the body away. Instead, he stood and looked out over the assembled Combine soldiery.

The bronze-haired MechWarrior drew their immediate attention. "It is a minor comfort to me that, according to the laws and dictates of our nation, I am not legally the son of Yorinaga Kurita. This action I am about to undertake would bring shame upon him and his memory, which I would not do for anything. All of you who saw him here, saw how he faced death. You know this was a man who deserved more respect than what marked the later years of his life."

Beginning in a low whisper, his voice grew in intensity and vitality as he went on. "Yorinaga Kurita wanted only one thing: to account for what he saw as his personal shame for the last thirteen years. Two years ago, the Dragon, Takashi Kurita, offered him that release if he would create and train the *Genyosha*. He gave Yorinaga free rein to gather to himself the finest MechWarriors in the whole of the Combine, and through our training, he created an elite unit—one that surpasses even the vaunted Sword of Light regiments in skill and ability."

The scorn in Akira's voice as he mentioned the Sword of Light regiments stung Conti, but the younger MechWarrior never gave the *Tai-sho* the chance to respond. "What did we get in return? On Northwind, we are treated like *ronin* or bandits or, worse yet in the eyes of the Dragon, mercenaries. The *Genyosha*, the troops that prevented mercenaries from overrunning *Tai-sho* Conti's headquarters, we are commanded to execute prisoners like *ashigaru*. We are not green warriors who should be given such menial tasks. We are samurai! We deserve to be shown more honor."

Akira turned and thrust a finger at Palmer Conti. "This man brought his regiment here to steal the glory of destroying the Kell Hounds for himself. Look at him. Even now he schemes and plots. He will find a way to lay the blame for his command's destruction at the feet of my father. He will tell the Dragon that we arrived too late, or that we refused to attack or that his people died trying to save us from the Kell Hounds. No matter how feeble the fiction he creates, it will save him.

"It will save him because Takashi Kurita will believe anything. The Dragon is old and worried. His personal vendetta against Jaime Wolf prompted him to order all mercenaries to be killed on sight. As a pretext for this order, he reminds us that mercenaries fight for money and, therefore, have no honor. They cannot be true warriors because of this character flaw, and we should find them an affront to our sensibilities."

Akira looked over at Morgan Kell. "There is your honorless mercenary. My father slew Patrick Kell on Styx, but Morgan did not hate him for it. On Terra last year, Morgan Kell and Jaime Wolf, both gold-grubbing thugs in the eyes of the Dragon, joined with and helped my father win through a very dangerous situation—saving my life and probably his in the bargain. And then here, after a day's worth of battle in this desert, Morgan Kell honored my father's desire for a duel, yet refused to shame my father in it."

Akira raised his head high. "I find more honor in one mercenary colonel than I do in the Coordinator of the Draconis Combine. For this reason, I resign my position within the *Genyosha* and, if Morgan Kell will have me, I bind my personal honor to that of the Kell Hounds."

Chu-sa Narimasa Asano stood at his place on the platform's eastern edge. He bowed respectfully to Akira, then turned to face the *Genyosha*. "I have listened to Akira Brahe's words, and I find much truth in them. Yorinaga Kurita was the finest and most competent leader I have ever served within the Combine. The indignities heaped upon him, and upon the *Genyosha*, serve only to shame the Coordinator."

Asano glanced over at Morgan Kell. "This being said, and without any intention of dishonoring Colonel Kell or his valiant warriors, I cannot pledge allegiance to a mercenary company. I am certain the Coordinator's madness will pass, one way or another. The true Dragon, the Combine itself, will endure. Of the leaders in the Combine now, only one showed Yorinaga respect, and only that one leader treated the *Genyosha* like the elite organization it is."

The elder Combine MechWarrior looked out over his troops. "I bear no ill will to those among you who share Akira Brahe's feelings. If you wish to follow him to the Kell Hounds, or strike out on your own, you have my respect for your decision. I, however, am renouncing my service to Takashi Kurita and pledging myself to his heir, Theodore. The Kurita Prince is a warrior I can follow, and his destiny is one I wish to empower."

Perhaps a dozen *Genyosha* MechWarriors—most of them appearing to be from Rasalhague District—walked toward the platform. One by one, they executed two deep bows of respect, the first to *Chu-sa* Asano and the second—held a second or two longer than the first—to the bloodstained mat upon which Yorinaga had knelt. Then they passed to where Morgan Kell stood and bowed to him. Morgan returned the bows, then welcomed each warrior with a hearty handshake.

Akira turned to face Narimasa Asano. "Thank you, *Chu-sa*, for your wisdom. I do not look forward to the next time the Kell Hounds meet the *Genyosha*."

"Nor do I." Asano smiled warmly at Akira. "You are every bit your father's son. Never forget that." He bowed deeply, then straightened and walked from the platform.

Having returned his bow, Akira likewise stepped from the stage. He bowed again toward where his father had died, then turned and walked to Morgan Kell. "I would be grateful if you could find a place in your command for a humble MechWarrior."

Morgan offered him his hand. "Your request honors us. Welcome to the Kell Hounds."

53

Justin looked up from the front row of the audience in Avalon City's Notre Dame Cathedral as Prince Hanse Davion took his place at the podium. His heart pounded heavily in his chest, and Justin thought to himself that it hadn't beat this hard when he used to wait for a fight on Solaris to begin. Smiling at his nervousness, he reached out with his right hand and covered Candace's left.

The Prince nodded his thanks to Cardinal Maraschal. "Thank you for that invocation, Cardinal." He faced the packed crowd in the cathedral, then adjusted the podium light to shine more directly on the text of his speech. Taking a deep breath, he began.

"The war means different things to different people. To soldiers in the front lines, war is long periods of utter boredom punctuated by moments of unrelenting terror. Machines the size of buildings stalk over the surface of a world destroying anything that opposes them. The weapons they use are hellishly powerful; the scars they leave on people, places, and things never heal.

"Those left behind at home face a different challenge. Their terror, while more subtle, is equally uncompromising. Is the next visiphone call going to tell you your husband has been killed? When you scan your electronic mail, or get a message from ComStar, will you learn that your son or daughter is being shipped home in an urn? Or worse yet, will that soldier at your doorstep tell you that your grandson is missing, but the AFFS is doing everything they can to find him?"

As the Prince's strong voice filled the church, Justin glanced over at Candace and then beyond at her brother Tormana's smiling face. *We both thought he'd been killed in the first waves of the war. I've never seen Candace as happy as she was when the Prince reunited them.*

Hanse Davion continued eloquently. "Despite these burdens borne by those on the front or at home, we can take comfort in one thing. At all times we know who we are and what we are a part of. We are not ashamed of letting this pride show through because it reinforces our confidence and belief in our society. It confirms the correctness of our mission and gives all of our efforts meaning. Seeing this confidence and pride reflected back from the others around us is the ultimate reward and sustains us even in the darkest times."

Hanse shifted the top sheet of his text to the bottom of the pile. "This is not true of a third class of individual working in our war effort. These people have to subsume what and who they are to fulfill their role in the war. For some, this means they must forge a whole new identity to perform their duties. For others, the job is to become more than they ever wanted to be. The stress of leading such a dual life would tear anyone apart at the best of times, but in a time of war, the pressure can be lethal."

Hanse looked up at his audience. "This evening, we are gathered here to honor four individuals whose singular and collective contributions to the war defy quantification, but cannot be overstated. The first of these individuals is Alex Mallory."

Far to Justin's right, Alex stood. The slender, blond man adjusted his black tuxedo jacket, then leaned occasionally on a black cane as he walked to the front of the cathedral's altar. Unable to genuflect, he crossed himself, and strode proudly to the Prince's side.

The Prince opened a box on the podium and drew from it a black medal encrusted with diamonds arrayed like the sunburst of the Federated Suns. "Known as Alexi Malenkov in the Capellan Confederation, Alex Mallory became a trusted member of the Maskirovka. At great risk to himself, he managed to send enormous amounts of intelligence back to the Federated Suns. It was through his efforts that we were able to thwart Maximilian Liao's first assassination attempt on the late Colonel Pavel Ridzik. Out of gratitude, Colonel Ridzik concluded a peace with us that saved countless lives on the Tikonov front. Later, when discovered by the enemy, Alex endured torture without surrendering one piece of information about himself or his confederates."

The Prince pinned the medal to Alex's jacket pocket. "In recognition of your efforts, I award you the Diamond Sunburst for service and devotion to the Federated Suns." Hanse offered Alex his hand, and the two men shook hands warmly. Alex, smiling, withdrew to a chair back behind the Prince and sat.

Hanse Davion looked at and invited the next recipient onto the altar. When Andrew Redburn, dressed in the black and gold dress uniform that the First Kathil Uhlans had adopted, reached him, the Prince smiled broadly. "All too rare in the services, but in excellent company here tonight, is a warrior who does not ask, "Why?" when given an order. This man, Major Andrew Redburn, led his troops on a half-dozen of the most dangerous missions this conflict has yet offered us. He never begged off an assignment. He just went out and did what had to be done. In addition, he was able to set aside his own personal feelings and hatreds to accomplish the most dangerous mission of all: the recovery of two agents—one of whom was Mr. Mallory—from the capital of the Capellan Confederation."

The Prince opened another slim medal-case on the podium. The light glinted sharply from the gold sunburst disk that formed the back of the medal. Superimposed over it was a platinum sword driven into an anvil. The Prince pinned it high on the black breast of the Uhlan uniform, right beside the Golden Sunburst Andrew had won two years before.

"For your service to the Federated Suns, I am proud to award you our highest medal: the Medal Excalibur. From this time forward, you will be known as a Knight of the Realm, and you will be granted a parcel of land on your homeworld of Firgrove."

Andrew, beaming broadly, shook the Prince's hand, then retreated to stand beside Alex.

The Prince let a smile light his face. "The third individual I would honor here tonight has requested, repeatedly, that I should not reward him. Though I appreciate and respect his request, I cannot grant it. To do so would be to deny him the long overdue praise and thanks for invaluable services he has performed."

Hanse looked down into the front row. "Morgan Hasek-Davion, please come forward."

Tall and strong, Morgan unfolded himself from the front pew. His red hair rode down over the shoulders of his Uhlan dress jacket, almost totally obscuring the golden epaulets. He glanced back once at Kym Sorenson, then mounted the steps to the altar. He genuflected crisply, then joined his uncle beside the podium.

Hanse looked from his nephew to the audience. "When we learned of a planned Liao strike at Kathil, a strike that would have crippled our JumpShip repair and construction capability for years, I needed a commander I could trust to stop the assault. I only had a handful of veteran troops to give him, and very little time for him to organize a defense. Morgan willingly accepted this assignment, and in the course of a week, managed to do just what had been asked of him."

Hanse glanced over at Morgan, then shook his head slowly. "And then, so he could get to Sian quickly and rescue the agent who had communicated news of the assault to us, he put himself at great risk. Using captured Liao DropShips, he convinced a succession of Jump-Ship captains that his force was the remnant of the Kathil strike force, and that they were returning with Morgan Hasek-Davion as a captive! Unmindful of his personal jeopardy, he led his people into the capital of the Capellan Confederation and made sure that everyone, including our agents, were on board his DropShip and accounted for before he left the field of combat."

Hanse slipped an envelope from his dress jacket. "Moreover, Morgan endured untold frustration before he was given the assignment on Kathil. Because of his position as my heir, I refused his repeated requests for combat duty." The Prince smiled broadly. "And, in fact, had he let *me* know about his plot for reaching Sian quickly, I probably would have denied him that as well."

Hanse handed Morgan the envelope, and with a nod of head, bade him open it. "As you would refuse any reward I would offer you—though you *will* be inducted into the Order of Davion at the end of the year—I give you this."

Morgan tore open the envelope and unfolded the yellow half-sheet. His green eyes scanned the message printed on it quickly. His smile grew as he read it through again and then threw back his head in a deep, hearty laugh. He grasped his uncle by both shoulders. "Is it true? Really, Hanse?"

The Prince nodded his head, then enfolded Morgan in a hug. They separated, and Morgan threw him a salute that the Prince answered sharply. A broad grin on his face, Hanse turned to the crowd while Morgan took his place with the other two award recipients. "That envelope contained a message communicated to me through the Lyran ambassador. It seems that during her covert visit here last June and July, my wife managed to conceive a child."

Thunderous applause erupted spontaneously from the crowd. Justin felt his heart leap. *Hanse will have an heir!* He glanced back over his shoulder at where his father sat and threw him a wink. Quintus Allard acknowledged it with a nod and a pleased smile.

The Prince waited for the applause to begin to die, then raised his right hand to put it to rest. "As joyous news as that is, and as much as I dearly look forward to welcoming another Davion into the Successor

States, I have one more person I wish to acknowledge here tonight. In a way, this is a birth of sorts, or a rebirth, and could only be described as the product of a fiercely difficult labor."

Hanse Davion swallowed hard. "Over four years ago, we began an effort to groom an agent we could use to leak information, believable information, to Liao forces. His work, which was slow and meticulous, had begun to pay off. He had established a series of contacts with Liao agents on Kittery and appeared to the enemy to be a potential defector. Unfortunately, three years ago, he suffered a maiming injury in a Liao ambush, and investigators looking into the incident unraveled the network of contacts he had created."

The Prince looked out at Quintus Allard. "At that time, only the agent, the Minister of Intelligence, Information, and Operations, and I knew of the preparations that had been made. Because information about our agent's treasonous activities had already begun to leak out, we were faced with a choice between abandoning the operation, or using this hostile information to make him even more attractive to the Capellan Confederation."

The Prince motioned to Justin. "Please, come up here."

Murmurs swept back through the crowd as Justin stood. He looked out at the people arrayed behind him and felt their confusion. *The last they knew, I was someone to be reviled. I was the half-breed who reverted to his baser nature. I was safe to hate, yet now I am honored.* He smiled weakly while making his way to the altar. *I don't doubt it confuses them...It confuses me.* He genuflected, then crossed to where the Prince waited.

"Justin Allard himself made the decision to continue with the operation. He knew, because of the evidence against him and how we would be forced to arrange things, that he would be degraded, ridiculed, and hated. He knew that, because only his father and I were privy to the truth, he could expect no help from anyone he had called friend in the past. He knew, because we had given him the identities of various agents in the places we expected him to end up, that he would have to destroy himself if captured. He knew, if he died at any point in the operation, his name would never be cleared and he would join the ranks of Judas and Stefan the Usurper in the annals of history's great betrayors."

The Prince looked out over the crowd. "Through his efforts, we were able to locate and plug a serious breach in our security. Through his efforts, House Liao wasted valuable time and resources on a research and development project that caused serious harm to their war effort. Because of him, we learned of the planned raid on Kathil.

Because of him and his influence, the St. Ives Commonality has seceded from the Capellan Confederation and entered into an alliance with the Federated Suns.

"The last time most of you remember seeing the two of us in the same place, I stripped him of his rank, his honor, and his name. For all of the services he has rendered the Federated Suns, I would gladly return those three things, but it is for yet another action that I chose to do so. When he sent us the message warning us about the Kathil raid, he asked to be withdrawn from Sian. When Morgan arrived with his DropShip, all Justin had to do was identify himself and he would have been taken away to safety. Instead of doing that, he entered the dungeons beneath the Liao Palace and rescued Alex Mallory. For this act of selfless bravery, I welcome you, Major Justin Xiang Allard, back home to the Federated Suns."

Justin met Hanse's strong grip with one of his own and shook the Prince's hand heartily. "You don't know how good those words sound coming from your throat."

Hanse smiled warmly. "You don't know how many times I feared I would never get a chance to say them." The Prince broke their grip and drew a medal identical to the one awarded Andrew Redburn from the small box. "Though wholly insufficient, I award you the Medal Excalibur as a token of this nation's gratitude for you, and at the ceremonies at the end of this year, you will be inducted into the Order of Davion along with Morgan."

Justin waited for the Prince to pin the medal on the breast of his jacket, then shook his hand again. Retreating to join the others, he congratulated them on their awards, then turned back to listen to the Prince complete his speech.

"Our war with the Capellan Confederation is all but complete. Our conquest has not been total, but then that was never our intention. Our goal all along has had two parts. The first was to eliminate the Capellan Confederation's ability to create the materials they need to wage war against us. Aside from a few minor facilities in the Sian Commonality, this has been successful.

"The second half of our objective was to free a people that has been oppressed for far too long. This is not a task that can be accomplished in months or even years. Our success in this area will be measured in generations, but I am confident it will be success we can measure."

Hanse looked back at the four men standing behind him, then turned to the crowd with a pleased expression. "The war, for these four individuals, is over now, but our enemies should mark well what they have accomplished. Not for the sheer audacity of planning, or the brilliance of tactics—though each has exhibited those traits. They should study these men to understand that a people nurtured in freedom and given the ability to do what they choose, are a people that will do anything—no matter how humiliating or personally painful—to ensure that their way of life will endure for eternity!"

54

ComStar First Circuit Compound
Hilton Head Island, North America, Terra
1 December 3029

Primus Myndo Waterly looked down from her exaulted position to where her former peers stood at their crystalline podia. Her golden silk robe flashed with highlights slightly darker than her hair and felt very good against her skin. *Almost as good as having won election to the Primacy.*

She smiled benignly. "I wish to thank all of you for your support. These will be trying times for ComStar, but we shall see to it that the Word of Blake will be fulfilled. Our unanimity in this cause is vital."

Her dark-eyed glance recognized Villius Tejh, granting him permission to speak only moments before he would have usurped that right. *You still smart at losing, don't you, Precentor Sian? You would have won had I not reminded everyone that you failed to discover or inform us that Justin Xiang was really a Davion agent. You laid the blame for that on poor Julian Tiepolo as he lay dying. You avoided the repercussions, but it still hurts you. I'll have to put you out of your misery, like some wounded animal.*

Precentor Sian met her stare evenly. "Primus, I would like to know what you are planning to do with the Federated Suns? Justin Allard, during his debriefing, will have undoubtedly informed the Prince that the Death Commandos who hit the NAIS were not from Liao. The attack you urged upon us could cause serious problems."

Myndo raised one eyebrow. "Could it? I was unaware that we had informed Prince Davion that we attacked the NAIS. Indeed, as the

316

attack failed in its objective and, in fact, gave the Prince a political boost because of his personal involvement in dealing with it, I should think he would thank us for having staged it. Though we might have used a different organization to mask the assault had we been *aware* of Xiang's true nature, we did not leave ourselves open to discovery."

Myndo preempted his desire to follow up with a defense against her attack. "I have, in fact, begun a dialog with the Prince of the Federated Suns. We have reached an agreement, in principle, to lift the Interdiction."

Ulthan Everson, the golden-haired Precentor from Tharkad, leaned forward. "How now? You were the one who pressed so fervently *for* the Interdiction. The Federated Suns has all but snapped up the Capellan Confederation, but the Interdiction has slowed the pace of war considerably. Why are you going to lift the Interdiction now?"

Myndo folded her hands into the sleeves of her robe. "It's rather plain, isn't it? The Prince, after perhaps one more wave of attacks, will no longer pursue the war. The Free Worlds League is moving to snap up worlds if Liao shifts its forces to fight Davion's invaders, but the Prince would never dream of letting Janos Marik steal worlds away from him for so little cost. Further, if he leaves part of the Confederation alive, it will force Marik to maintain troops on that border to face any Liao threat. These are fewer troops for Davion to worry about on his border with the Free Worlds League.

"Lastly, Princess Melissa is pregnant. Hanse Davion will move to solidify his holdings so that his child will have a stable realm to govern. The Capellan Confederation, when the time is right, will be an excellent straw man against which to direct his people if divisions develop within the Federated Suns."

She surprised herself when she saw Precentor Tharkad nodding agreement with her arguments. Huthrin Vandel smiled and asked with his eyes to be recognized. "Precentor New Avalon?"

The black-haired man nodded. "Thank you. Perhaps, Primus, you might mention what concessions you have exacted from Hanse Davion in return for lifting the Interdiction."

Myndo kept herself from smiling. "Because the Interdiction was initiated in response to an attack by House Davion troops on one of our stations, I have demanded and won an agreement to rebuild that station and to upgrade a number of stations, all at the expense of the Federated Suns."

She allowed the assembly a second or two of murmured comments before she dropped the larger bombshell. "I also have won from the Prince the right for ComStar to station armed forces, 'Mech forces, within the precincts of our stations!"

The other Precentors looked stunned, and Villius Tejh rubbed at his chest as if this time he were succumbing to a heart attack. Myndo raised her chin high. "Yes. We will station troops on every world where we have a station. At first, we will make do with mercenaries, but slowly, over the next ten or twenty years, we will bring our own, "newly trained" troops into place at the stations. They will be there for self-protection, of course, but they will be there nonetheless. We will expand this policy from the Federated Suns into the other Successor States on a gradual basis. An attack on us in the future—real or created—will mean that an Interdiction by ComStar is far more dangerous than it has ever been in the past."

Anger gathered on Tejh's face like a thundercloud on the horizon. "Jerome Blake bade us to keep our strength hidden so that we could employ it when mankind had ripped itself apart. 'We are the savior, not the warrior; we heal, we do not destroy,' he said."

Myndo's confident smile swallowed his protest whole. "And the aggressor we will not be. We will be a presence that can step in to end the depredations of local tyrants. We can repulse raids and respond to natural disasters. We will be seen as an active agent in protecting the weak and the helpless. In this way, we will train the new generations of people to look to us for salvation even before the dark times begin."

Myndo's dark eyes narrowed. "Mark me. The technological decay Blake predicted will not occur because of Hanse Davion's farsightedness. As technology grows, so grows the power it creates. As in the past, this power will bring moral corruption and another collapse. Instead of waiting for mankind to return to flint knives and bear skins, as Blake feared we would need to do, we need only wait for man's lust for power to doom him. ComStar, in our lifetimes, will be in a position to save mankind from itself, whether it wants salvation or not."

Epilogue

Sian
Sian Commonality, Capellan Confederation (Sian Supremacy)
15 December 3029

A look of despair washed over Romano Liao's face as she entered the throne room and saw her father staring at the screen of the holovid viewer he'd ordered placed near the throne. The image's back glow etched deep lines in her father's haggard face and burned brassy hues into his newly whitened hair. His hands clutched the arms of the throne with the fierce desperation of a drowning man hanging on to a raft. Romano knew that in his battle with the yawning abyss of insanity, Maximilian Liao was losing.

Losing badly. She quickly went to her father's side to get him away from the electronic succubus that had drained him, but she made the mistake of glancing at the screen before trying to shut the machine off. The image seduced her as well.

Hanse Davion, seated behind his desk, dressed conservatively in the dark blue uniform of the Davion Heavy Guards, smiled out at the viewers. The smile seemed genuine enough, with none of the Fox's guile hiding behind those blue eyes. "And so, once again, Maximilian, I wish to thank you very much for taking such excellent care of my good friend, Justin Xiang Allard. I especially wish to express my gratitude for your having brought him to my wedding. That was an unexpected pleasure and a great boon to me. In case you were unaware, Justin has the guts of a laser rifle built into his left arm. A remarkable thing, really. He used it on the island to kill the assassin your daughter Romano had sent to kill his father. A good thing, too, or you would have been placed under an Interdiction, and heaven only knows how that would have hurt your war effort."

Mortification ran through Romano like an electric shock. Unconsciously, her hand rose to her right cheek as she recalled Justin Xiang striking her for trying to kill his father. *I should have known then that he was a traitor! Candace must have known all along and used him as her conduit to make an agreement with Hanse Davion. The St. Ives Compact...what a laugh!*

She stiffened as her father uttered a low moan. In the holovid, the Hanse Davion seated at the desk looked up as another man moved into the frame. "Did I do it well, my Prince?" he asked. The real Hanse Davion nodded beneficently and helped his double out of the chair. Seating himself, the Prince smiled coldly.

"You've wondered all along, haven't you, why I struck at you? He is the reason. Not because you tried to supplant me with him. No, that was an excellent stratagem, and one that nearly worked. For that, I salute you."

The Prince's eyes flashed like arctic storms. "I went after you because you dared, in your attempt to get me, to destroy him. You robbed him of his face, of his memories, of his life. If you could do that, if you could steal from a person all that makes him an individual— claiming it is for the good of the state—there is no telling what other inhuman acts you could justify in your mind. For that, I had to break your power, and that is what I have done."

Hanse glanced out of the frame toward where his double had gone. "We will rebuild him and try to make him whole again. We will do the same with those of your people we have liberated. But for you, and your dreams of being the First Lord of a new Star League, there is no cure. Good bye."

Anger flashed through Romano at her father's first pathetic sob.

320

She lashed out with her foot, exploding the holovid viewer's picture tube in a green flash of flame. The disk Justin had left behind shot from the machine and rolled into the shadows along the wall. Spinning about, she raised her hand to slap her father out of his weeping, but in his helplessness, he touched even her.

Her hand fell to her side. She mounted the steps to the throne itself and took her father by the elbow. She led him down the steps, then clapped her hands twice. Tsen Shang, his right arm out of the cast that had confined it while the shoulder joint replacement surgery had healed, entered the chamber. He was flanked by two Maskirovka guards.

Shang bowed to her. "How may I be of service, Madam Chancellor?"

Romano smiled at the title. "My father, as you can see, has eluded his nurses again. Please see to it that he is returned to his suite and that he does not get out again." She hesitated for a second, then nodded. "They may restrain him if they feel they must."

Shang nodded. "I will instruct them to use discretion." Leading Maximilian Liao away, Tsen Shang and his guards withdrew from the throne room.

Romano turned and stared at the smoking ruins of the holovid viewer. *So smug, so confident. You have lived up to your nickname of 'the Fox,' Hanse Davion. This I can respect.* She smiled cruelly. "Respect, but not forgive."

Romano Liao, Madam Chancellor of the Capellan Confederation, mounted the stairs to her throne. Seated there, alone in the shadowed, silent hall, she contemplated the dark and bloody future of her realm. And she smiled.

GLOSSARY

JAPANESE RANK NAMES

Throughout this book, the Kurita officers are referred to by their ancient Japanese rank names. The equivalent ranks in English are:

Warlord	General of the Army
Tai-sho	General
Sho-sho	Brigadier
Tai-sa	Colonel
Chu-sa	Lieutenant Colonel
Sho-sa	Major
Tai-i	Captain
Chu-i	Lieutenant

BATTLEMECH

BattleMechs are the most powerful war machines ever built. First developed by Terran scientists and engineers more than 500 years ago, these huge, man-shaped vehicles are faster, more mobile, better armored, and more heavily armed than any 20th-century tank. Ten to twelve meters tall, they pack enough firepower to flatten anything but another BattleMech. A small fusion reactor provides virtually unlimited power, and BattleMechs can be adapted to fight in environments ranging from sun-baked deserts to subzero arctic icefields.

COMSTAR

ComStar, the interstellar communications network, was the brainchild of Jerome Blake, one-time Minister of Communications of the Star League. After the League's fall, Blake seized Terra and reorganized what was left of the League's communications network into a private organization that sold its services to the five Successor Houses for a profit. Since that time, ComStar has developed into a powerful secret society steeped in mysticism and ritual. Initiates to the ComStar Order commit themselves to lifelong service.

JUMPSHIPS AND DROPSHIPS

Interstellar travel is accomplished via JumpShips, first developed in the 22nd century. Named for their ability to "jump" instantaneously from one point to another, a JumpShip consists of a long, thin drive core and an enormous sail. The sail collects electromagnetic energy from the nearest star, then slowly transfers it to the drive core for use in creating a space-twisting field. After making its jump, the ship must recharge its drive with solar energy before it can travel again. Safe recharge times range from six to eight days. JumpShips can travel up to 30 light-years per jump.

Jump points are locations within a star system where the system's gravity is next to nothing, the prime requisite for operation of the jump drive. Every star has two principal jump points, one at the zenith, at the star's north pole, and one at the nadir point, the star's south pole. An infinite number of other "pirate" jump points also exist, though they are seldom used.

JumpShips never land on planets, and only rarely travel to the inner parts of a star system. Interplanetary travel is carried out by DropShips, vessels that attach themselves to the JumpShip until arrival at the jump point. From here, the ship will be dropped from the mother ship.

NEW AVALON INSTITUTE OF SCIENCE (NAIS)

In 3015, Prince Hanse Davion decreed the construction of a new university on New Avalon, planetary capital of the Federated Suns. Known as the New Avalon Institute of Science (NAIS), its purpose is to recover the lost technologies and knowledge of the past. Both House Kurita and House Marik have followed with their own universities, but neither is as well-bankrolled or -staffed as the NAIS.

STAR LEAGUE

In 2571, the Star League was formed in an attempt to peacefully ally the major star systems inhabited by the Human race after it had taken to the stars. The League continued and prospered for almost 200 years, until the Succession Wars broke out in the late 28th century. The League was eventually destroyed when the ruling body known as the High Council disbanded in the midst of an internal power struggle. Each of the Council Lords then declared himself First Lord of the Star League, and within months, war had engulfed the Inner Sphere. These centuries of continuous war are now known simply as the Succession Wars, and continue to the present day. As a result, much of the technology that had brought mankind to its highest level of advancement has been destroyed, lost, or forgotten.

SUCCESSOR LORDS

Each of the five Successor States is ruled by a family descended from one of the original Council Lords of the old Star League. All five royal House Lords claim the title of First Lord, and they have been at each others' throats since the beginning of the Succession Wars in the late 28th century. Their battleground is the vast Inner Sphere, which is composed of all the star systems once occupied by the Star League member-states.